The Story of
ANDALORAX

A modern fable of black & white

WRITTEN & ILLUSTRATED BY
BARBARA LINICK

BOOKSIDE Press

BookSide Press
877-741-8091
www.booksidepress.com
orders@booksidepress.com

Each of us is lonely through his own greatness.
It could be any one of us who must act, and bring forth the light.
And just so, it could be any one of us
who must burn as the torch.

I am a hero.
You are a hero.
We are all heroes.
And there are really no heroes
At all.

For Greta and Marvin

CONTENTS

BOOK ONE

CHAPTER 1

THE CALICAB FOREST

MANDIR LAY IN PEACEFUL SLEEP beside the clear brook that ran down from the mountains and wound a narrow path through the green meadows on its way to the Sea. She dreamed beneath the wide-spreading Calicab tree she used to climb in when she was a child. This was her special place. She called the waters the Singing Stream, or Talmandir in her own tongue. Her own name, Mandir, meant "Water," and Talmandir was Singing Water, Singing Stream. And by Talmandir she slept, and Talmandir sang to her.

Ice was I,
Water am I,
Sea shall I become.
Mountains miss me,
Grasses kiss me,
I am no longer young.

The sun was warm when Mandir had set out that day, warm although early November. As she walked, she had gathered a basketful of rich Calicab fruit, some of which served as her lunch as she picnicked beneath the tree. The basket lay beside her now, fallen on its side, and the fruit was scattered on the soft grass. And Mandir lay on the grass by the waters and her hands, stained at the fingertips with the scarlet fruit, crossed her full girth. Mandir was round with a child, a child who filled her dreams and slept inside her as she slept beneath the Calicab. And the sun crossed the sky over her closed eyelids, and slowly made its way behind the Black Mountains.

She heeded not the first cooling of the air, nor the rippling voice of the water, and slept on still when the red-eyed vireo flew down from the tree and hopped and danced impatiently 'round her. "Time! Time!" it cried. And time went on, and the sun sank down, and darkness began to descend. Black squirrels hurrying home chattered and shook and ruffled her hair. A giant screech owl called out from a nearby tree. And still she slept.

The sky started lightening in the east, and the moon showed one eye over the edge of the earth. Mandir moved slightly in her sleep, her ears caught for a moment the voice of Talmandir, and it sang:

> *Heed me calling!*
> *Night is falling! You sleep beyond the sun.*
> *Water-whisper*
> *Water-sister*
> *Awake! The moon is come.*

Something struck her, something was amiss, as when the shepherd turns and gazes at his flock, suddenly aware that the bleating herd is lacking one – and Mandir's heart jumped, and she leapt to her feet, and felt herself ensnared in the trap of night. "Run, Run, Mandir!" cried her heart. "Find your way home, safe beneath its wooden roof, within its wooden walls!" And she ran, the owl screaming relentlessly, its voice drifting off as her feet carried her swiftly over the fields, towards the forest, towards her home.

She dared not look at the moon, now gliding into the bowl of the sky above her. Her body was cumbersome and awkward, and she stumbled over stones and roots. At the foot of the forest she tripped on a fallen tree and fell. Her heart pounded and she gasped for breath, and a swift pain filled her womb as the unborn child began to move. She forced herself to get up and go on, and when she was covered by the outstretched branches of the Calicab trees, she stopped to rest, and ease her heart, and gather up her strength.

As she walked, she looked around her and gradually, as her eyes became accustomed to the darkness, she could discern the thick, smooth bark reaching upward and outward, the leaves dark and thick above her. And between the leaves she could see faint glimmers of stars beginning to appear. Her breathing became less rapid. "It is rather nice, here in the darkness," she mused. "I wonder why we all stay indoors in the nighttime." She remembered her mother reading to her from the yellowed book that crackled as each page was turned:

Night hideth the color of life. Black is the blanket.
Cold is the earth. Death is the calling.
Moon maketh night. Say her Nay!

Yes, that was how it read. But the memory brought fear, and she tried to think of other things, nicer things. She wondered what Talmandir would sound like in the nighttime; she could not imagine that its song would be a song of death.

"And how pleasant it would be, if I could stand by the old tree and listen to the waters and dissolve into the shadows." And then she could hear her mother's voice again, reading to her of pale spirits that rode the night air on fell steeds, with breath of icy fire and empty sockets for eyes … "Oh yes, but that is for children, such tales, to make them fearful of the night. I am not afraid." She repeated these words out loud: "I am not afraid. I am not afraid."

And she slowly arose, supporting herself against the side of a tree, for although she could deny her fear she could no longer deny the pain within her womb. The child was fast becoming real. Mandir straightened her back, raised her head, and continued to walk the forest path. She made way slowly while, behind her, so did the brightening moon.

She wasn't far from the house, but she had to rest again. The pain was greater when she tried to sit, so she leaned against a tree. The air was growing brighter now, the trees were no longer dark masses but each one shone in the moonlight by itself. There were many leaves fallen on the forest floor and she thought, "How strange! They say the night is black, yet there is color in the darkness. For I see the rusty reds and yellows of the autumn." She had said, "I have no fear," and yet she had not looked up to see the source of light. She felt annoyed with herself. She wanted to turn and look at the moon, yet fear froze her limbs. Then suddenly she jerked her head up and faced the sky.

As she did, the wind sprang up and howled in her ears, shaking the trees, sending leaves flying through the air, parting the roof above her, uncovering her face to the sky. White light shot down in an instant and spread across her. A shiver raced through her body that made her every hair stand on end. The brilliance of the moon began to grow and strengthen; the roundness began to expand. Larger and larger it waxed, until its whiteness reached the edges of the sky. The trees around Mandir dissolved, stars faded and were lost, and her own body felt transparent and empty.

Stillness seized the air, grasping all in a sharp second, then suddenly the moon burst open, exploding in a glory that echoed with the pounding of Mandir's heart. The rich milky whiteness shattered and flew down, finding her, melting around her, seeping into her and filling her. She felt herself swelling, swelling and then radiating the pure light that flowed through her skin. Joy spread throughout her heart and leapt from her breast, and she saw the moon, calm and full, drift back into the aura of the darkening night.

Peace, sweet and gentle, overwhelmed her as she stood there, feeling herself alive as she had never known life before. It was quiet now, and she breathed evenly. But then her mind beheld fear, and she trembled.

"So small, so small am I," she thought. "So great is the night."

As peace overwhelmed her, Mandir knew what was that instant being shouted into the air by a baby's cry. It had happened. In the year of 1450, reign of King Vanamir, Lord of all Lands of the Kingdom of Pellah, Andalorax had come into the world.

The blackness of it clouded 'round Mandir's head, and she sank down to the forest floor, gave a little cry, and knew nothing more.

CHAPTER 2

A KINGLY PROCESSION

LEAVES FELL TO EARTH, AND autumn passed, and winter blew in cold and snowy. Then spring came, and with its warmth melted the frozen soil, breathing upon the softening grasses and budding trees. The sun and moon followed each other across the sky; one season followed another. So it had been and so it would be. And the sun and moon had been there with the dawning of the first growing thing, and would be there until the fading of the last.

One particular day this particular spring, there came riding through the forest path a host of fifty Knights. Their velvet mantles and silken doublets were studded and embroidered with purest gold, and they gleamed like fire in the sunlight. Upon their brows they bore the emblem of the sun, gold discs encircled by green flames. They marched in pairs, sitting proudly upon their chestnut stallions. The horses' manes were plaited and glistening, and their tails swept the earth; their saddles and bridles were fashioned of rich brown leather and suede, adorned with circlets of gold.

The procession followed a single horse and rider. This man was similarly attired, yet embellished with such a quantity of gold that his gleaming far outshone the others. His doublet was of emerald-green velvet covered with a filigree of golden threads, and he showed the crest of the sun upon his bejeweled crown. His pommel and bridle were wrought entirely of gold, and in his uplifted hand he carried a golden staff. Long and sleek, it was fitted at the top with the likeness of an eagle, an eagle with eyes of finely chiseled emeralds.

The first twenty Knights were armed with bow and arrow, strapped loosely across their chests. Their eyes pierced out from beneath their leather caps, and they noted every leaf that stirred, every mouse that scrambled in the underbrush. These twenty

Men of the Eyes guarded the man whose back was turned towards them, the First Rider, following his blaze of gold like the tail of a shooting star.

Behind these twenty rode twenty more, in like dress yet unlike armor. For they carried shield and sword, emblazoned with the crest of the radiant sun, a golden globe burning in green flames, set in a field of metal that glowed dully with a somber black. These men were of great height and girth, and a light gleamed not from their eyes, as with the first score, but rather from their mouths, for through their parted lips came the cold fire of gold. Golden teeth for Golden Warriors. From these teeth came a blade of terror that passed through the bones of anyone who chanced to see them unawares. Seldom had they need of their swords, these twenty men, and often would they smile.

This day in particular, for this day was lovely indeed. The sun was high and shone down upon them, and they blessed the light and worshipped the heat, and felt the guidance of that burning orb as their horses stepped lightly over leaf and branch. They rode onward, and saw ahead of them the backs of the twenty Men of the Eyes, sitting straight, watching all, following the First Rider, and his upraised scepter.

Behind these twenty Men of the Teeth rode ten more Knights. These men bore no armor, they bore no warning. Their horses carried on their flanks large saddlebags, the size of coffers, of a rich dark leather tied with many streaming thongs. They hung loosely and seemed a minor weight in the whole array, for they were, indeed, quite empty.

At the rear trotted a single dark gray mare, tethered to the pommel of the last Man of the Coffers. Her gait was quick and sprightly, and she did not match the even rhythm of the others. She bore a leather saddle trimmed with gold, and it was empty.

The entourage rode through the Calicab Forest, making its way to its edges, heading for the town of Milorin just beyond. The last rows of trees lay before them; through the thinning woods the twenty Men of the Eyes saw glimpses of open meadow. The First Rider halted. He raised his golden staff high above his head. The Men of the Eyes each fitted their shafts with a sleek arrow with a quickness that seemed heedless of time. A fire of gold shot forth from behind them as twenty men bared their teeth. Ten leather coffers hung motionless.

The First Rider signaled to the first pair of Eyemen, and they left their ranks to stand at either side of their leader.

"Do you see movement nigh us?" came the low whisper from the First Rider. The two bowmen strained their eyes, following his line of sight. They focused on a broad-girthed tree.

"Nay, my King," said one. "Only leaves stirring in the wind."

"Nay, my King. I see naught as well," said the other.

"Watch, watch, perchance it may move again," said the First Rider.

The three sat still as stone upon their mounts. They fixed their eyes upon the column of Calicabs fifty feet before them. Leaves quivered, and the sun sent its rays through the whole forest, filling it with patches of golden green. Suddenly a small dark shape darted out from behind the wide tree and flitted in an instant behind another.

The three did not move.

"And how shall we call this shape, my dear Haldown?" asked the King. "Say you still you see naught but the leaves?"

The First Eyeman answered, "Nay, my King, now I saw not a leaf, but the figure of a woman."

"Aye, my Lord," spoke the second. "She hath the red hair of our people, but I saw not if her eyes be green."

The King broke into loud laughter and the silence of the woods was shattered. The twenty Men of the Eyes, the twenty Golden Teeth, and the ten Men of the Coffers together turned their glance upon him, watching his chest shake with laughter, his head lifted to the sky and his long auburn red hair and braided beard blowing about his shoulders. His laughter rumbled through the body of the procession, waking them out of their stoniness, as they felt themselves beginning to quiver with the first rush of a hearty chuckle. Then, as abruptly as the King had unleashed his merriment, he stopped, sending a jolt through the Knights as they gathered themselves back into respectful silence.

"Fools!" snarled the King. "I bring you here to guard and defend me from this path in the wild, yet what purpose serve you save to shadow my laughter, even when my mirth is in mockery of your incompetence! Well, no matter. I knew of the presence of this woman from the moment we entered this gloomy wood."

The company looked at one another in wonder.

"Nay, my puppets, thy King does indeed have the eyes to outmatch all, yet even he cannot see beyond his mortal ken. This fair-complexioned lady, who does indeed have green eyes, Malthor," he said turning to the paling Second Eyeman still at his side, "hath been wending her way through this forest all this while, yet her pace matched that of our steeds – so did I purposefully design our progress–and thus was I able to watch her throughout. Until this moment, that is, when I allowed her to gain head and go on her way."

Haldown turned his eyes again to the concealing group of trees, and said, "My Lord, this seems most dangerous. Allow me to ride ahead and apprehend this secretive creature. I cannot but fear that she hath business in this foreign wood that should be brought to light. Else why kept she so hidden from us? And with what art of camouflage did she aid herself? Perhaps she is a spirit of the night that wandered too far from her lair, and, finding herself lost when the first rays of sun appeared, is now doomed to roam in pain of daylight, breathing incantations to speed the arrival of the moon –"

"Hold!" cried the King, raising again his scepter. "Enough of this prattle. You cause a very shadow to crawl over the backs of your comrades, whilst you know not of what you speak. That woman was no night spirit. She was but a woman, green-eyed, red-haired, with roses in her cheeks.

"As to her business, aye, I'll warrant it may well be of an unsavory nature! Yet her every movement betrayed her fear of us, far more fear than would be if she were in league with sorcery or night-wights. And so, enough! I entreat you, my own little boys!" – at this the King displayed a broad grin – "Repair to your positions and be at attention. For it is not yet the last step of our journey and I expect you will want to reach the safety of Milorin before nightfall."

The company immediately set itself aright – the King once more First Rider, Haldown and Malthor once more the first pair of Eyemen – and the glittering ensemble took its last steps to the fringe of the Calicab Forest, emerging upon the open path to the town of Milorin. Despite the increased wariness of the twenty Men of the Eyes, no more was seen of their forest companion.

The King and his Knights marched across the fields until they came to the great Gate of Milorin. The town lay just one mile ahead. The procession halted, and the King turned his steed slowly 'round and 'round, until he had completed a circle. Straight ahead were two parallel rows of stone pillars, ten flanking either side of the road. Fluted and twisted, they rose out of the earth like some huge overgrown plants from ancient times that had refused to die when their time was due, sealing themselves up and doomed to eternal petrifaction. They were wide yet quite shapely and graceful, as they rose to a height of ten feet. Capped with several layers of large flat discs, each bore at the summit a globe of purest gold. Indeed, each pillar seemed a long arm erupting from the earth's crust, thrusting up to the sky a blossom of stony petals bearing a shimmering fruit, a miniaturized sun.

And surrounding these two rows of pillars was neither tree nor shrub, nor any other accompaniment to the landscape. The grasses grew short in the wide field about them. Nothing could be seen save the forest behind, appearing now remote and small, and farther up ahead rose a wave of rolling hills.

"'Tis strange," mused the King, resting his chin in his palm, "that in the many long years that the line of Kings has come to Milorin each springtime, and in the fifteen years that I myself have come, not once has there been recorded a time when there was neither Guard nor Greeter at the Pillars." He sat for a moment in thought, when from behind a column came a voice.

"Times have indeed changed, my King, since last you were here."

The King and his Knights jumped to attention. The voice laughed, low and gentle. From the pillar right beside the King emerged a small, shrunken figure. An old man, whose beard hung down to his waist, bowed low. He wore a cloak of green cloth, and a little green cap rested on his gray head.

"Greetings, my King!" he smiled. "True, there be no guard at the Pillars, yet there be a Greeter. I am called Gamedon, and I am at your service."

The King leaned down to see this tiny figure, who stood now just before his horse, and had taken his cap in his sturdy hands. "Closer, Master Gamedon," said the King. "Come closer to me." Gamedon moved with the grace of one of far younger years, and stopped just beside the King's left stirrup. His face, the King could now see, was quite wrinkled and worn, yet there was a bright glint in his green eyes that had borne the mark of time with greater ease.

"Tell me, Greeter Gamedon," asked the King, "how comes it to chance that the folk of Milorin neglect to guard their Gate with properly armed men, and send as Greeter one who does not conform to regal protocol? For though I doubt not that you may have a certain charm and gentle speech, I do feel a sting of wrath at the absence of a Greeter more fitting to the coming of the King!"

Gamedon smiled, and bowed low once more, and said, "Well do I understand your anger, my Lord, yet my people meant no indignity by their behavior. You ask me why there is no Guard at the Pillars. The answer to this is long, indeed too long to tell now, but I can sum all up" – and he smiled again – "by saying that Your Majesty has just ridden through the reason."

Gamedon pointed to the Calicab Forest behind them.

"My people have become greatly fearful of that place. Their reasons for alarm will no doubt become known to you when your hosts in the town can tell you their tales at greater length. I do not doubt that you will have your fill of tales! However, there is not one of them who will venture forth, even in mid-day, to these Pillars that stand far too near the woods for their liking. And when time came due for your arrival, my people grew full of doubt. Some said that the King would come through the wood nevermore; others said that if you passed through you would be galloping at such speed that even one hundred Guards in full official array would fail to catch your eye. And all of them therefore maintained" – Gamedon smiled his broadest – "because their fear was so great, you see, that there really was no need to venture here at all."

The King watched the old man as he spoke, and pondered his words a while, sitting atop his steed whose gold diadems and studs shone in the fading sunlight, then he burst out with such a furious roar of laughter that several horses whinnied and reared, and there was an instance of chaos in the ranks.

"But this is most hilarious! Not quite what I am accustomed to, yet precisely what I should have expected. I had forgotten what a lot are the Milorin folk. Were it not necessary for me to collect what only their soil can nurture …." The King checked his laughter. "But no more on that. The ludicrousness of your people far outweighs their rudeness, my dear Gamedon … and yet, there is something that does not fit."

Gamedon bowed low and said, "Exactly, my Lord. When none will dare the forest path, how comes it that I should be here?" The King nodded. Gamedon smiled; his eyes shone like emeralds in the westering sun.

"I offer my services, such as they are, believing that an aged, shabby Greeter is better than none at all. For I have no fear. You see that I am unarmed, yet I am not without some craft, though this may be hard to believe and I must let it rest at that for the time being. Nevertheless, my King, I am here to greet you and escort you safely to the town. I feel the sun cooling upon my face, and I know that you will want to reach the end of your journey with haste."

The King looked at the old man, then turned his head towards the forest, the outline of Calicab trees merging into darkness in the paling light. He strained his eyes to catch a glimpse of any movement, but there was none. "You are right, Greeter Gamedon," he said slowly. "We must turn from these woods and this path with haste."

He sat suddenly upright, raised his scepter, and gave the command, "Ride Forth!" when Gamedon laughed loudly and said, "My King, I have said that I am not without art, yet I cannot produce a horse for myself out of the air."

"Forgive me, Gamedon," said the King. "It is customary that the Greeter accompany the King to the town. You shall ride with me. You are small, and my horse can bear us both."

Gamedon looked towards the end of the company and said, "And what of the dappled mare?"

The King shook his head. "Nay, Gamedon, she will not bear you. She has another purpose. Come up!" He reached out his arm in assistance, but Gamedon needed none. With the swiftness of a youth he leapt upon the rump of the King's stallion and chuckled, "My Lord, I am ready!"

The procession was off in an instant. It flew down the path with such speed that from a distance –from where Mandir watched – it looked like a great gust of wind, shining green and gold, and the earth groaned under its weight. Yet the great gust was made of fifty Knights, led by a King and trailed by a riderless steed, dotted by one tiny man clutching a green cap, laughing wildly in the red-streaked sky.

The road soon widened and leveled, and they came to a halt at a great town square. Long shafts of light glanced across their shoulders, just as the sun touched the rim of the western horizon. Small buildings, shuttered and silent, lay around them. Gamedon alighted and bowed low.

"I leave you now, my Lord. Goodnight and Farewell," he said.

The King shook his head.

"Nay, Gamedon. You shall dine with me at the Inn."

But the old man stood up and said, "My Lord, I beg to be excused. I have much to do before the night is upon us." The King look askance at him, then answered, "I would see more of you, old man. But, for now, you are dismissed. Surely, I shall be properly greeted here and now."

Gamedon turned and walked off and quickly disappeared into the twilight.

The King led his company to the Inn, where they all dismounted and brought their horses to the stables. The stable boys jumped to their feet upon seeing the King, muttering nervous words of greeting and bowing continually. They were soon lost in the mass of steaming flanks and swishing tails of hungry and thirsty horses.

The royal troupe entered the Inn, and a wide-eyed Innkeeper rushed out to meet them. With much fuss and flurry he accommodated them with board and bed. The King was quiet, and he endured the man's restlessness. He suddenly found he was greatly travel-weary, and directly after dinner he and his Knights went to their chambers.

Haldown and Malthor, First Pair of Eyemen, shared a room, and when they were at last alone they were quick to discuss the events of the day.

"I don't like it, Malthor," said the first. "I don't like the lady in the woods. Why could we not see her? Surely our eyes are as good as the King's. Yet he saw her from the first. And this Gamedon, why, he's a sharp little fellow, make no mistake! At the Pillars, we couldn't see him either, 'til he gave himself away."

"Aye, aye, Haldown. I follow you well," said Malthor. "Yet you know this town is on the southernmost borders of the Kingdom, and beyond it lay lands in shadow. The Black Mountains."

"'Tis a strange place to live, let alone visit every year so that the King may receive and take home his supply of what only the earth of Milorin's Calicab Forest will produce – not to mention the prize of a girl as his next bride each time, as well."

"We'll be out of here soon, so I'm not going to worry about it. Let's get to sleep! I'm so tired I think I could sleep standing up!" And they got into their beds, feeling glad to be in a warm Inn no matter where they were. They slept as did the other forty-eight Knights, the sleep of weary travelers.

CHAPTER 3

BANQUETING AND BUSINESS

BUT THE KING SAT BY the fireplace in his bedroom and stared at the blue flames, and in his mind remembered every step of the forest path and every movement of the woman he followed. After a while he began to doze, and dreamt that he had gone silently to his horse and cantered into the forest.

He saw the bright moon above him, shining through the leaves, and stood soundlessly as he saw the woman running swiftly from tree to tree in her effort to not be noticed. He dismounted, he followed her, and the darkness became heavy, and he knew he'd never catch her. He fell down upon the sweet damp earth, and dissolved away.

But the sun suddenly lit the sky, and he opened his eyes, and he was lying on the padded hearth-chair, the fire long burned out. He heard a soft knocking at his bedroom door.

"Enter!" said the King.

The doorknob turned and the large wooden door creaked open.

"Good morning, my Lord. 'Tis the hour of seven, and you asked to be awakened 'ere your hosts arrived." The King looked at the young girl who stood before him. She appeared to be no more than twelve years old, and her long green dress hung loosely from her thin shoulders.

"Well, maid," spoke the King, "rouse my men and we shall break our fast in half an hour. And send up a cleaning girl with hot water and soap." With a wave of his hand, he dismissed her.

At the set time, the King and his Knights were seated around the four long tables which met end to end and formed a square. They waited impatiently for the promised meal of steaks and bacon, eggs, bread and butter, jams and marmalades, fresh cream and strawberries, and the rare rich Calicab fruit just brought back fresh the eve before by the King's Knights.

A great silence reigned. The King seemed pensive, and his men knew his moods enough to hold back their usual mealtime jests.

The room in which they sat was completely made of Calicab wood, a rich shade of sienna, and the ceiling was quite high, rising to a peak in the center of almost twenty feet. This place was a separate wing of the Inn, with no upper stories. It abounded with windows that ran up along the entire eastern side, circled 'round in a clerestory, and continued on down the western wall. The glass had a yellowish tint to it, giving a warm glow to all within. And on this morning, as the King and his Knights sat in silence, the sun slowly began to reach its long arms out, penetrating the glass and spreading across the wood floor. Brighter and brighter it grew, bringing warmth. The light fell across the faces of the fifty-one men, causing a glow to glimmer in their green eyes and russet sparks to shimmer in their red hair. The promise of a warm spring day filled the chamber.

"Well, well, and a good morning to you, my courtly guests!" said Jack Beale, the Innkeeper, as he entered through the wide double doors. He bowed low, then lifted his head, and with a broad smile brought cheer into the hearts of the hungry Knights.

"Now for the food!" they thought.

"I trust you have all slept well, and are most eager to start off this lovely day with a hearty meal. Alice, Apris, bring in the plates and mugs!" he called through the open door behind him. "Jorind, Juris, set down the food!" He proceeded to continue giving instructions to the staff.

Ten young maids entered, carrying the breakfast fare, and set the board with care and speed. They each wore long green skirts and yellow blouses, and tied around each slender waist was a darker green apron covered all over with prints of yellow buttercups and day lilies. Their red hair was long and thick, and gathered at the nape by green ribbons, which streamed down their backs below the apron bows. The sunlight made their tresses shine like polished mahogany.

The men set to, and as their stomachs filled they became more lax and cheery. The King, too, seemed to become gayer, enjoying most of all the presence of the ten maids, calling them to him one by one and toying with their dresses. Never once did any of the ten lift up their eyes to see his face. They did their duty, to serve their masters and incur no displeasure. They knew the Innkeeper would be watching through the crack in the door.

The men ate until the table was bare, then called for more, and finished that helping as well. The ten maids brought each man a steaming towel one by one, and then left the room. The Knights wiped their beards and fingers, pushed back their wooden chairs, and arose from the table. They strode from the dining room, running their tongues over their teeth, following the King. The ten maids reentered and watched the men exit, while they stood by the empty chairs and crocks in the glow of the brightening sun. They soon were hard at work, clearing up the tables.

The royal entourage was met in the sitting-parlor by a host of five men, all bowing low at their entrance, caps in hand. The quintet repeated in unison: "Hail, King Vanamir!" The King acknowledged their greeting with a slight nod of the head, and they stood upright.

"Good day, Mayor Barth and Councilmen," said the King. "Glad indeed am I that this day has come at last, and we can get down to the business at hand." He walked over to whom he deemed to be the eldest of the five, a man with a shiny bald pate and thickening girth.

"Mayor Barth," he said, "I trust you have all in readiness for me, and that my stay here will meet with no delay." The Mayor bowed once more, not without some difficulty for his size.

"My Lord," he said grandly, "allow me to express for myself and the people of Milorin our happiness at having you as our guests once again. I trust you have had a pleasant journey, and that you found all in order for your arrival at the Inn. The townsfolk bless this day, and bless Your Lordship. We have arranged for a little celebration tomorrow at noon …."

"Spare me this slushy travelogue!" thundered the King. The Mayor trembled and shrank back. "Do not babble to me about the glorious reverence of your people. The absence of a proper herald upon my arrival at the Pillars set forth the true tone of your shabby greeting. Do not sham with me! I am the King! And henceforth, I shall know how to deal with you, in this the smallest of the small of all the lands in my realm."

The King's dark grimace was mirrored in the glint of angry gold peering through the lips of the twenty Men of the Teeth.

"But come now, Barth," he said, giving forth a slight smile, "my affairs with you are but a snippet. When I have collected what is my royal due – both in harvest of the golden leaf and of woman – I shall be on my way out of this miserable little dot on the earth and riding back to my Castle in the mountains. So let us, my dear sir, get on with it!"

Mayor Barth gathered up his strength and piped out, "Aye, my Lord. This way."

He turned and went out into the street, with the four Councilmen, King Vanamir, and the fifty Knights following behind.

They were greeted by a throng of townspeople. The sun shone warm and golden through a cloudless sky. The day was magnificent, fine for planting and waking up the soil – the rich soil that, strangely, was the only soil in the Kingdom wherein the King's much-needed Phemtas blooms would grow.

Yet for Milorin it was a holiday. The King had come, through all the perils in the Calicab Forest, riding over the lands with fearless majesty! Indeed, this was a powerful King. Perhaps his presence would drive the evils of this year from their lands … So they thought, as their foreheads touched the ground in supplication.

He strode through them, and they made a passage as he went. How his scepter shone, upraised in the morning sunlight! The gold of his garments dazzled their eyes; the stately bearing of his train filled them with awe. Forward they marched, the twenty Men of the Eyes with their heads held high. None could withstand more than a moment's meeting glance; all had to quickly look to their feet when they felt a pair of Eyes upon them.

The ten Men of the Coffers passed by in silence, bearing their empty saddlebags. And when the twenty Men of the Teeth marched through the crowd, even the bravest of the townsfolk froze where they stood, terrified, at the tiny snarl that sent a gleam of razor-sharp light across their flesh.

The group approached the threshold of a large stone building, smooth and windowless, with one tiny door fastened shut by a large beam. Two locks clamped at either end of the beam dangled in the sunlight. The building stood in the exact center of Milorin, like a large gray tomb fashioned from the minds of men long dead, heedless of the gayer wooden houses and shops that had sprung up around it. Mayor Barth reached the door, fumbling in his pockets anxiously, then produced a small golden key.

"Aahs!" and "Oohs!" were heard from the crowd. The King walked up to the door.

"Now, now, Barth!" he said. "It wouldn't do to lose the key to the House of Time, would it?" He chuckled and his teeth glimmered like white marble. Then, turning his back to the stone building, he faced the crowd. He thrust his staff high into the air. The people fell to the ground.

"People of Milorin, of the Lands of the Kingdom of Pellah! Hark the voice of your King!"

The people on the ground started raising their heads and straining their necks.

"There is no cause for trembling. Nay, not yet! May the First has come, and with it, as ever, has come your King. And as ever, he comes to collect the appropriate dues.

"The year has been good for harvest throughout my realm, and your toil for yourselves and your King was, I trust, most rewarding. I go now into the House of Time for an accounting of your labors, where Mayor Barth shall answer to me for you. So go now about your ways; tarry not in the streets. At noontime shall news of my pleasure – or displeasure, as the case may be – be brought to the general public."

Vanamir turned to his Knights.

"My men! Remain with these people; mingle at your discretion with their earthly pleasantries. But return to this very place 'ere the hour of twelve!" He motioned to Barth to open the locks and remove the beam – a feat that took four men to accomplish – and, the task finally done, the two of them disappeared into the darkness. Through the open doorway could be seen the lighting of a candle, and then the door was slammed shut.

CHAPTER 4

THE HOUSE OF TIME

INSIDE THE HOUSE OF TIME the air was still and cool, and the single candle afforded little vision. But Mayor Barth proceeded to gather about five more which he procured from a storage box, and lit them. He placed them in holders fastened to a wall, holders that were completely covered with melted wax of innumerable candles that had long since sputtered out.

Between the candles was shelf upon shelf of dusty, yellowed books, reaching from floor to ceiling, spanning the entire perimeter of the room. There was a long, thick wooden table in the center, surrounded by six high-backed wooden chairs with leather seats. The leather shone faintly with the polish of use. At the far end of the chamber, opposite the entrance door, was a narrow hallway that disappeared with a curve to the right.

"Well, now, my good Barth," spoke the King, "this room seems to have changed not a flyspeck since last I was here one year ago. Have you no recourse to ancient records of the history of your people and its harvesting of Phemtas? See here, the dust is nearly the thickness of a beard." So saying, he ran his left forefinger along the tabletop, leaving a rippled trail.

"Well, my Lord, times have been hard, even dangerous, and there's been a great deal of work to do." Barth scraped his fingernails across his palms as he spoke. "And even though many strange things have been going on of late, we have had no call to look to the words of our Fathers.

"Indeed, my Lord,' he went on, "you have touched upon a subject that I feel impelled to speak about with you. My Councilmen have told me not to trouble your Lordship with our matters, yet I feel impelled … and my wife is in absolute agreement …."

"Your wife, Mayor Barth?" Vanamir raised his bushy eyebrows. "Have I entered this gloomy chamber to listen to your domestic chatter? I do not ask of you, dear Mayor, to approach the point of business. I order you!"

"Aye, aye, my King," stuttered the Mayor. "If you will, please sit down here upon the chair that I myself just recently used in preparation of your arrival. Putting together the records, you see … but first, I must clean it." He produced a large green handkerchief, and proceeded to dust with vigor, not pausing in his speech.

"Aye, aye, sit down right here and I will bring forth the Record Book, and you may study at your leisure. I shall be seated right beside you, ready to answer any questions."

"Stop that senseless waving of your scarf, Mayor Barth!" The King was coughing. "You have risen up a storm of dust that will only settle again, this time upon me." He sat down.

"Bring me those records," he said.

Barth hastily went to the far end of the dark, little room, near the hallway that led off to the right; he stood on tiptoe and procured a thin, leather-bound volume – with much downfall of more dust. He hurried back to the table and lay the book down before the King.

The book was dark brown and quite new, and engraved on its cover were the words:

Records of Milorin
May the First
Pellah Year 1449-1450

King Vanamir opened it and went from page to page, running his hand down as he read the figures and words written thereon in thick black ink. He said not a word as he ran his finger down each page, and muttering to himself from time to time, "Aha, what is this?" and "Ah, I see!"

Mayor Barth sat at his side, most nervously wringing his handkerchief, covering himself with dust. When the King had read the last page, he slammed the book shut, and turned to the Mayor.

"Well, my dear Mayor," he said. "I see that your people are doing well, and that the crops are plentiful. There were some minor areas of disturbance –"

"Disturbance, sir?" interrupted Barth.

"Aye, Barth. Some minor areas of disturbance, particularly in late October and early November. It seems that very little work was done in the fields at that time, which is most surprising, for that is the time when storing provision for the winter calls for increased activity. The farmers brought in little store for several weeks."

"Aye, my Lord," said Barth nervously. "This is one of the things that I was speaking of earlier. It was at the end of October that many strange omens and occurrences came to pass at the borders of our town, near the Calicab Forest. You see – oh dear me, I don't know just where to begin."

"No mind, Barth," said the King. "I found that the slack in work was made up for at the end of November."

"October, yes, that was when we heard the sounds of strange birds … at least I think it was birds … and saw smoke and once, even a fire–"

"I said no mind, Barth," said the King. "You have harvested well, and I am not displeased. And as to the harvest, it is now time for me to see and test for myself what you have set aside for your King in the way of dues. Lead me to the Store Room!"

Barth nodded, biting his lip, and took his candlestick in hand. He led the way to the corridor at the far end of the room, took a right-hand turn, and stopped. The candle flickered before him, illuminating a steep stairway. The stairs ran in circular fashion downwards until they disappeared in darkness.

A cold air issued forth from the pit, and a sweet, decay-like odor instantly entered their nostrils, causing a brief rush of heat and light to flood their heads. But the King swayed dizzily. Now on tiptoe, now leaning back on his heels, he stood precariously at the lip of the deep recess, until the first blast of the odor had run its course through him, and he rapidly regained his senses.

Although the gold of his raiment glowed suddenly in the faint candlelight, the King's face was pale. But soon his color returned, and he deeply inhaled the odor from below. Gulping in the air, he filled his chest until Mayor Barth thought the King would burst open his velvet doublet.

Barth was familiar with this event, for it happened each year when the King inspected what lay in the storehouse below. Although its odor had no effect on him, he knew that the King was made stronger by it. All the gold in his robes, the gold buttons thereon, and the gold circle in his crown burst forth with a blinding light of gold.

Still, he asked, "Are you alright, my King?"

"Aye, aye, Barth," came the slow answer. King Vanamir's voice was soft and weak at first then rose to its usual loud pitch. "Proceed, man. On with our purpose!" He gripped the curved wooden railing, and cautiously began the descent. Barth followed.

The spiral stairway threaded a steep channel, and the two men inched farther downwards by degrees. The rush of odorous air steadily grew still and became damp and almost stifling to Barth, but the King was now clearly rejoicing in it. At the last stair, Barth held his candle out before him. The burning wick sent out a faint, flickering light, but they had no need of that light because the glow of all the King's gold lit up the scene.

They were in a small, round cavern carved of roughly-hewn rock. The crumbling roof was braced here and there with mossy wood beams, and was just high enough for the King to stand upright. Thick layers of gray cobwebs stretched over everything. All that showed of recent use of the pit was a row of voluminous barrels.

Made of firm, curved wood planks and belted with hoops of shining metal, the chest-high casks bore no trace of mold or mildew. It was from these barrels that the odor emanated. King Vanamir fixed his eyes upon them. He did not glance upon the cobwebs, or upon the decaying structure of the cavern. He had been here before. Fifteen times had he made this underground journey, and fifteen times had he turned his eyes to the row of barrels.

He walked toward them. The pungent scent of decay that had assailed him at the top of the stairway returned with a mighty strength, grown in power somehow, and this scent rushed to the back of the King's skull. He stumbled, sinking to his knees, and he covered his face with his hands.

And then slowly, without the slightest movement, King Vanamir began to make a faint humming sound. A single note swelled and vibrated within his broad chest, and soon the entire room was filled with the clear ringing. Then the note gave way to other notes, and woven into the soft chant were these words:

Breath of Fire,
King's Desire,
Phemtas! Phemtas!

> *Meadow-weed,*
> *The King hath need,*
> *Phemtas! Phemtas!*

King Vanamir raised his head, lifted his arms high above him, and his voice grew louder.

> *Mountain King*
> *To thee doth sing!*
> *Thy power strong*
> *Follows my song.*
> *Fading Sun-King leaves his Hold*
> *For Phemtas! Mightier than Gold!*

He raised himself to his feet. In the suffused light, he seemed to have grown in stature. The strength of his bloodline waxed full in his limbs. On his helm, the gold sun-disc blazed forth like a torch.

Barth, crouched in a corner, was trembling amidst the cobwebs. The odor in the room had abated and grown mellow, falling more gently on the senses. Barth tried to catch his breath. He stared at the huge figure of the King, wondering what magic powers were in this plant that seemed to give the King strength. "Surely it must be magic," he thought.

King Vanamir stood silent for a while, then the glow of his helm faded and died out. He turned around to Barth. The sight of the shrunken figure half-buried in the mass of stringy cobwebs shattered his somber thoughts. He laughed.

"Mayor Barth!" he cried betwixt roars of mirth. "Mayor Mouse! Come out! There is naught to fear! Must I always remind you that these matters here deal not with you but only with your King? Come, come, Mayor Mole! Ha, ha! Mayor Spider! Ha, ha! Oh, but my dear Mayor, you are a sight!"

Vanamir went to him, still laughing, and helping him to rise, while the Mayor struggled to disentangle himself and get up.

"Aye, aye, my King," he moaned. "You may laugh! Yet have some pity on a poor man who can never quite seem to fully prepare himself –"

"Nay, my dear Barth," interrupted the King. "Think not that you have displeased me. For what purpose think you that I bring you here, save to check my own heavy thoughts? Come along now. It is over. You have done as ever, and your King is pleased.

"This store of Phemtas harvested for me is far better than I have ever known," he continued. "This very afternoon, it will fill the empty saddlebags that travel with my ten Men of the Coffers. You have cause yourself for mirth, Barth, for your payment of dues is nearly done." Barth had brushed off all the cobwebs and taken hold of his candlestick, and the two men carefully ascended the narrow stairway.

They emerged from the spiral tunnel and followed the little hallway to the Room of Records. King Vanamir sat down at the table, and Barth still trembled at his side. They waited some time in silence. Then the town bells rang twelve times, and Barth walked along the walls, putting out the candles. He went then to the small wooden door to the square, slid back the bolt, and was about to open it when the King whispered: "Barth!"

The little man jumped and turned around.

"Barth," came the coarse voice. "You have pleased me in the matter of Phemtas, but do not be hasty to forget: there is the second share of payment which we have yet to settle. I expect you in my quarters at the Inn when the bells toll three. On with you now. Open the door! Let me see the sun!"

CHAPTER 5

KING VANAMIR'S EMBASSAGE

THE SUN HAD BEEN STRONG that afternoon and had filled the King's chambers at the Inn with its warmth. There was no need of a fire upon his return from the House of Time, yet the King sat before the hearth. He stared at the cold gray ashes as if to his eyes they were ablaze. On the mantelpiece lay his golden helm and golden girdle, and in the corner of the room stood his scepter. Atop it, the eagle carving on the pommel bore eyes of emeralds which smoldered like green coals.

King Vanamir's thoughts traveled back. There was no order to his thinking; it was a mélange of the sounds of fifty-one horses clip-clopping behind him, of the odor of the weeds seeping through the barrels, of the brightness of the sun glancing in through the window and resting across his lap. And throughout his daydreams flitted the woman of the forest. Glimpses of her waist-long shining hair shot through his mind; of her thin green dress and the slender calves beneath it; of her viridian eyes, turning back upon him, frightened.

Yet there was a sound, a less agreeable pervader of his thoughts, and he strove to bury it. But it kept, insistently, coming back. Clearer it grew.

It was a man's voice.

"So therefore, you must forgive me, my King," it ran on. "Forgive my lateness. The girl was nowhere to be found, and once found she refused to give herself up, and I was required to use some force –"

"What? What is this?" thought the King. "Have they found her? Have they brought her to me?"

"Where is she?" he cried out.

The monotonous voice stopped.

King Vanamir snapped his mind back into the room, back to the cold hearth, back to the sunlight on his knees. He turned his head around. A man sat there, head cocked to one side, eyes staring wide and blinking.

Beside him, hiding herself in the man's bulk, stood a young girl. Slender but rather tall and robust, she was wrapped in a dark green woolen cloak that hung nearly to the floor. Her hood was pulled over her eyes, and indeed fell so far down over her face that the King could barely discern her pointed chin. At her side was a small bundle of cloth, knotted at the top into a handle.

Slowly, and with much effort, King Vanamir began to pull his mind back up to the surface, reeling and hauling as the fisherman will slowly bring his net up from the deep.

Bells rang out: One! Two! Three! Four! The sunlight moved across his knees and slanted across his leather boots. The man behind him came into focus. He recognized Mayor Barth.

"And the girl … who is she?" he thought.

Ah, now he remembered.

"You are late, Barth," he said.

The voice began again. "Aye, my King," it droned. The tedious intonation was now familiar. "I was just explaining to you, you really must forgive me. It was the girl. She refused to come. I had to enlist two of your men –"

"Never mind," said the King, holding up his hand. "She is here."

He looked at the young woman. "Come here, maid. Aye, that's it. Now pull away your hood, show your face." A smooth, pale arm emerged from the folds of the cloak and a strong but clean hand brushed back the hood. A small heart-shaped face was revealed, with full red lips and cheeks, smooth high forehead, and large green eyes. Her russet hair was combed back and clasped behind her neck, around which was tied a long, flowing scarf. She wore thin, gold wire earrings.

"She is beautiful, is she not, my Lord?" asked Barth quickly. "Is your Lordship pleased with her?"

"Aye, aye, Barth," came the answer. "Beautiful. Tell me, maid, what is your name?"

The girl opened her lips a bit and whispered, "Reseda, my Lord."

"And tell me now, why were you reluctant to come to your King?"

The girl turned her eyes to the floor, pursing her lips together, and tears began to roll down her cheeks. They fell in large drops onto her cloak.

"Forgive me, sire," she faltered. "Forgive me, but I do not want to leave my mother and father, my sisters and brother, my little dog … please forgive me. I know it is an honor to be chosen for the King. They say your Castle is made of purest gold, with tall spires reaching to the sky. And that there are gardens filled with rare flowers and sweet-smelling herbs, and that I will have gowns of satin and velvet, embroidered with golden threads and polished gems … and slippers of silk …."

The young girl stopped crying for a moment, and her face was lit up as she stood amidst the world of her visions. But then a furrow went across her brow, and she cast her eyes upon the King, and fell to weeping again.

"Reseda," said the King, leaning toward her. "Tell me, what is your age?"

"Eighteen, my Lord."

"And you do not wish to leave your home?" asked Vanamir. His hand reached out and touched the edge of her cloak.

"Nay, my Lord," came the reply.

"And you are happy here? Speak! What is it that you do to while away your time?"

Reseda stopped weeping, her breath came in quick gasps, and she said, "My father is a farmer, and has ten cows, which I feed and milk and care for. I do house-cleaning, and cooking, along with my three sisters and my mother. I also sew and mend. In the spring and summer I am at work in the garden, and in the wintertime … this past winter I made cloaks for all my family. I made this cloak." She ran her fingers down along her sides. Her hand accidentally touched the King's, and she pulled it away.

"Have you no desire for living in a Castle of purest gold, and for the wearing of fine dresses?" asked the King.

"Aye, sir," she answered. "Aye, I do. Yet I would pine in my heart for my family were I far away and never to return."

"Then, maid, stay you shall."

The King withdrew his hand from her cloak and raised himself to his feet.

"The maid is to be released. Let her go back to her cows and her kitchen, Barth."

The Mayor stammered, "But my Lord! She is what you have always been pleased to bring away with you. You have said yourself that she is beautiful. I doubt that there is a girl more suited to your requirements. Perhaps you should think again —"

"Silence!" shouted King Vanamir. "You seem to forget who is King, Barth. Send her away; I'll not have her. But you, my friend, stay here with me. There is a matter I would settle with you instantly!"

The girl burst into fresh weeping, and fell to her knees at the feet of the King.

"My Lord, oh my gracious King!" she cried. "You are indeed the kindest of Kings! Thank you for your pity, and forgive me, my Lord, for fearing you and thinking you cruel to take me away. For I see now that you are of a good and gentle nature."

"Get thee gone, maid!" shouted Vanamir. "I do not wish to hear any more weeping and blubbering!"

Barth ushered Reseda to the door, and closed it behind her.

"My King," he stammered, "I don't understand. Have I displeased you?" He whispered to himself, "Think, think, you fool! Perhaps Lilium, daughter of the road mender … or Alyssum? Nay, she is grown fat –"

King Vanamir was laughing. He walked over to the window and looked down upon the street. He watched Reseda go running from the doorway beneath him, hurrying through the groups of people clustered about, still in their holiday finery. She ran past the Bell Tower, past the blacksmith's shop, past the stonemason's, causing everyone to look up and start chattering wildly.

"That's Reseda, isn't it?"

"Why, isn't she to go with the King?"

"Perhaps she forgot something at home."

"Oh, my, think you that she displeased him?"

They all fell to talking, and some went hurrying home with the news. "She displeased him! Oh, whatever shall we do?"

The King looked down, watching, noting their growing fear, and laughed all the more. But just then his eye caught something, a figure sitting on the pedestal beside the stairway to the Bell Tower. This solitary figure, this little man, was laughing too. He was laughing very quietly, sitting there all by himself, and no one seemed to notice him. His head was turned sideways as he watched the girl go running down the streets. He followed her with his eyes until she turned a corner and disappeared behind the buildings. Then he turned back around and put his green cap on his head. The King saw his long wavy beard and bright green eyes, and he whispered, "Gamedon!" just as the little fellow rose to his feet, crossed the crowd of people who seemed not to notice him, and he slipped off down a quiet lane, and was gone.

The King stood thus at the window for some minutes, then wheeled 'round.

"Barth!" He addressed the man standing by the door and mumbling to himself. "Barth, I have in mind another."

"Aye, Sire," said Barth. "It will take some quick thinking, yet I believe I know of two or three –"

"Nay, man! The girl I will bring back with me this year is known to me already."

The Mayor tilted his head, blinking, and blurted out, "My Lord? Known to you?"

The King spoke calmly, unraveling his words as though he were suddenly clearing his mind.

"Yesterday … can it be but one short day ago? … My men and I set out with the sunrise on our journey hither. The ride was most uneventful, as we stopped neither to tarry nor revel by the roadside. As the sun rose and passed the noon, I steadily grew quite bored. Indeed, it was as if a cloud were descending upon me, and my thoughts were dimmed. The path grew vague; I noticed neither stream nor stone and I let my horse carry me along. By the time we entered the Calicab Forest bordering Milorin, I had fallen into a trance-like state, and my mind wandered as if in a dream."

King Vanamir's hands were now raised, and he slowly swayed them back and forth in the air about his head. "The air grew cool about me, and I felt the shadows of the trees upon my body." Vanamir returned his hands to his sides.

"It was then that I first saw her."

"In your dream, Sire?" interrupted Barth.

"Nay, nay, Barth," continued the King. His voice was lethargic, forming words that seemed to come from far away. "My eye caught the flash of green, and of pale white skin. The cloud that lay heavily over me wavered and thinned, and by degrees my senses returned to me. I became aware of my horse beneath me, of the scepter in my left hand, of the sound of my men following behind. And then I saw it again, that quick little bolt of green and white, darting from one tree to the next. I saw then that it was a woman.

"My first impulse was to rouse my men and take her captive. I deemed the maid to be a wood-wight; else, why would she be alone in the forest, seeking to escape my sight? But I checked my tongue, for I noticed that I felt no fear from the creature. My curiosity was stirred.

"Sure enough, she appeared once more, and then again, flitting from tree to tree as does the cat when hunting its prey ... nay, as does the mouse when stalked by the cat! For this woman meant to elude my eyes – she feared me, yet she was in such great hurry to be through the wood that she dared not waste a moment by stopping to let us pass blindly by. And as for her being a wood-wight, then why, if that she was, kept she to the path? She could have performed some magic and disappeared!"

The King paused, turning over in his mind the words he just spoke, and he laughed faintly. "Aye, she surely is no wood-wight. She kept to the path until it ran out of the forest, and then she left it, making her way over uncharted ground."

Barth, noting that the King was in a gentle mood, ventured a remark. "And so you followed her, and you caught her, and now she is yours!" He was carried away by the tale, as a child is by a bedroom story.

King Vanamir turned to him; he had forgotten the man's presence.

"Nay, Barth. I let her go on her way, and I proceeded onward to the Pillars. The lack of fealty of your people quickly turned my thoughts elsewhere. I would have ridden to your very doorstep, Barth, and in great rage had your insolent head, had that Gamedon fellow not been there to show me the comedy of it all. I deemed it unworthy of me to waste my energy upon it."

Barth looked at the King and seemed puzzled by his words. "Gamedon, my Lord?" he queried. "Gamedon? At the Pillars?"

"Aye, Barth. A rather ridiculous sort of old fellow, short of height and long of beard. Why come now, man! Recollect the Greeter you sent me!" The King sat down and faced Barth, who stood yet by the door. The Mayor seemed very perplexed.

"I sent no Greeter, my Lord," said Barth. "This ... Gamedon, of whom you speak, if I be correct in my guess, is a man whom my people banished from Milorin nearly forty years ago. There is no other with the same name, in my reckoning. A singular name, 'Gamedon,' aye my lord, belonging to a man I'm not likely to forget. He must be the same man. And yet how –"

"So you sent not even a Greeter to your King?" snapped Vanamir, his voice cold and sharp.

"Nay, my Lord," answered Barth, his head low. "I must explain to you somewhat of the minds of my people. Greatly fearful things have fallen upon us of late, and much of the dark times we attribute to the old Calicab Forest and whatever it hides within its ancient trees. It all started happening in the autumn, at the end of

October, when Yedro the Sibyl came from her hut, running and shrieking as though taken by a fit. I was there and I saw her, her mouth foamy, her eyes wide as a cow's, and she ran to and fro, tearing at her hair –"

Barth stopped his tale. The Kind had suddenly burst into a roar of laughter.

"So your fortuneteller was foaming at the mouth?" he managed to say between convulsions. "Her eyes wide as a cow's? Oh, Barth, indeed I should really bring you back with me to keep me amused."

"Take me on a perilous journey, Sire, and bring me to your faraway Castle? You might just as well banish me to the dark and lonely Black Mountains!" Barth shook in his shoes. "Oh, I pray you, Sire, do not make me go!"

King Vanamir was laughing with such abandon that tears glistened in his eyes. "Fear not, Barth," he pealed. "My interest in Milorin lies not in its fat old men!" The King's round of mirth abated, and silence fell upon the room. The sun had left the windows and the air had grown colder.

The King spoke: "Your tale somewhat interests me, Barth, and I would hear it in full. But later, I pray you. I was speaking of the maid in the wood. Know you who she is?

Barth shook his head. "Nay, my Lord. I know of none who travel through the forest nowadays, save on a major errand such as yours. And to think that a lone woman would venture there, why, it is impossible!"

"And yet I say to you, Barth, that she was there." King Vanamir scowled.

"I must find her out. For she is the woman I will bring back with me to the Castle."

The King grew pensive, and stood up, pacing the room.

"I must find this woman, Barth," he said. His voice was hard. He stopped abruptly.

"Call together a gathering of all the people. I would have them before me in the Square within the hour. I should have known better than to expect anything from you."

"But, my Lord," protested the Mayor. "The sun will soon be gone, and though my people love their King, they tremble to be out-of-doors at the coming of night."

"Do not throw these words to me, Barth!" cried the King. He took one long stride and stood before Barth. His large arm reached out and grasped the smaller man by the throat. The King was tall, and broad-chested, and his legs stood thick and strong beneath his golden tunic. Barth looked but a rotund, ten-year-old boy in his shadow.

"Within the hour, Barth," commanded the King. "It matters not to me if your troupe of fools be chained to tree trunks in the heart of that cursed forest, with their bare bodies wrapped in shrouds of moonlight. If their King were to have it so, then so must it be! Do not forget my fifty Knights, Barth."

The Mayor was nearly dead with fright, the tears were pouring from his eyes and his hands were sweaty. King Vanamir glared at him, at the tiny face bobbing above his tight grip.

"Within the hour, Barth," repeated the King, releasing his hold and letting Barth tumble into a shapeless heap at his feet. "My business with them will be short. We shall all be safely cloistered by the sunset hour. Go now, and leave me some time to myself."

Barth scrambled to his feet, and was out the door in an instant. "I must think," came the murmuring voice behind him, just as he turned the latch and went fleeing down the stairs and out into the street.

CHAPTER 6

A TWILIGHT QUEST

JACK BEALE, THE INNKEEPER, AND several of his housemaids stared after Mayor Barth as he ran down the steps and out into the Square. A large crowd of townspeople, still talking endlessly about the strange flight of Reseda, stopped in mid-sentence as Barth went rushing past. He followed Reseda's path, until he came to the Bell Tower, where he went flying up the steps and disappeared inside.

"Hey, Barth!" yelled the crowd. "What's happening?" Some took off after him, calling out, "Mayor, wait! Stop!" Then suddenly they heard the bells ringing out, banging and clattering furiously, setting up a great fever in the hearts of all those who stood there. The din echoed through the hills and meadows of all Milorin.

Those who were at home heard the distant clamor, and dropped whatever they were doing, and came pouring out of the land from all directions. They swarmed over the greening fields: farmers, still carrying their spades, their hands brown with soil; women still wearing aprons, newborn babes in their arms and dust cloths in their hands; little children in great wonder at the flight of their parents, trying desperately to keep pace. Dogs, cats, chickens, and cows and horses and sheep, all barked and meowed and cackled and mooed and neighed and bleated out a chorus. Between the bells and the animals there was such a dust of alarum as had never before been heard in that land.

Some of the men who had hurried after the Mayor caught up with him at the Bell Tower, where they saw him leaping from rope to rope, pulling each with all his might and weight. They yelled to him:

"Mayor Barth!" at the tops of their voices. "Mayor Barth!"

He heard them then, and turned his head sharply around, as he clutched a rope, with his feet dangling off the ground.

"Get everybody!" he shrieked. "Get everybody and make it quick! The Square! Within the hour!" He kept on pulling the ropes, huffing and puffing, sweat raining down from his forehead and dripping into his eyes.

The men stood there, turned and looked at each other. "The Square? Now?" They murmured. "But the sun! The sun is going down!" One of them yelled up to Barth, "What of the sun, Mayor? The sun!"

Barth had pulled so fiercely on a rope that as it swung up it yanked him six feet off the ground. He lost his grip and went crashing down to the floor. He moaned, and rolled about, and managed to raise himself to his feet.

"It's the King!" He sighed, wiping the perspiration from his face with his handkerchief. "The King says we must be in the Square within the hour. He's in a fit of rage – I nearly met my death a minute ago in his room. But he says it will be short and to the point, whatever that may be. But quickly, now! Do as I say. Else I fear we are all in for it!"

At these words the men gave each other such a look of terror, fear leaping from eye to eye like a flame, that they bolted and ran out of the Tower and into the street as if all the nightmares of their imaginations had suddenly sprung to life and were clawing at their heels.

Barth stood there, his breath coming fast, his chest paining him, and watched them disappear down the stairs. He put his chubby fingers to his throat; it was bruised and burned from the King's grasp. "Oh, dear me!" he moaned. "Whatever is to become of me? Ah, alas for the day they named me Mayor!" And thus he went on, as he made his way out of the Tower and over to the Square.

Everyone he knew was assembled there, breathless and pale. There was Harley the Woodcutter, axe in hand. And, grimy with soot, Mert the Blacksmith wiped his brow with his thick forearm. Barth saw his own wife, Welda, wringing her green apron. He made his way over to her, and she threw her arms about his neck, asking him a hundred questions all at once. "What is this all about? Where have you been? Who are we waiting for?" she asked, all seemingly in one long breath. He could find nothing to say. His three little daughters stared up at him and his son, Felt, tried his best to look unafraid. Reseda was there with her mother and father and sisters and brother. Out of the corner of his eye, Barth saw Yedro, the Sibyl. Her wrinkled face was buried deep in her heavy shawl, and her gnarled fingers twisted and twirled about a small white stone.

Barth's four Councilmen made their way to his side, and asked him,

"What's up, Mayor?" "You can tell us." Barth lifted his face, scanning the crowd, and realized that all the eyes of Milorin were turned upon him. "I have no answer," he said softly. "Wait for the King. I know not what his plans are. We must look to the King." He turned his glance upon the Inn door.

For a long while the door stayed relentlessly shut. Barth strained his eyes upon the door latch in the fading sunlight. People raised their heads to the sky as though they could somehow hold fast what sun-time there remained. But the sun heeded no one, and moved steadily to the edge of the western sky. The air grew still. Not a voice was heard, not a single movement was made, and all now faced, as Barth, the wooden door before them. So intent were they upon the door that they heard not the soft stepping of many feet behind them.

Suddenly the door flew open, and King Vanamir emerged upon the threshold. There was a great clap of metal upon metal, as the fifty Knights snapped to attention at his appearance. The townspeople swerved around and gasped: they were surrounded! The Knights formed a ring about the crowd, impenetrable beyond all question. Gold glinted everywhere, and gold shined down from the helm of the huge figure in the doorway. The sunlight in the sky was dissolving into a misty blue, and the green raiment and ruddy cheeks of the crowd were mingled into a soft hazy gray. The coming of the night fell heavily upon the hearts of the townspeople, and the gold seared their eyes like the flame of an unearthly torch.

King Vanamir lifted his scepter high in the air, and his power and stature seemed to grow to gigantic size. "People of Milorin!" rang out a voice from deep within his chest. The shadowy mass before him trembled. "My business with you is short and swift, if you delay not in your response. I put my query to the women. Speak, and do not hold back the truth from your King. Which of you was it I followed through the Calicab Forest yester eve?"

Pale faces turned to one another in the crowd, and a great gasp issued from the mouths thereon. "Come now!" said the King. "It is not forbidden to be in the woods. The consequences of such an act import no punishment. Who was it?"

There was no answer from the people.

"If you do not show yourself willingly," he went on, "I shall come down amongst you and find you myself. For I know your face! Aye, and when I look upon it then will I be merciless. There may be no punishment for straying into the woods, but there is little tolerance for one who steps not forth when the King commands it!"

Still nothing from the crowd but silence.

King Vanamir laughed heartily. "So you wish to play a game with me, eh? I warn you, you shall not like the last act!" He strode down the stairs, his helm and staff blazing like a searchlight as they reflected the low, westerly sun.

"My men!" he said loudly. "Let none escape your vanguard!" The Knights moved closer together, and the people were herded by the net of their strong bodies like cattle in a barn. Vanamir stood now level with them, yet his height was one head taller than the tallest in the crowd. Golden spangles shimmered on his velvet cloak, and he swirled the silk-lined garment across his body, flinging it behind his shoulders. A vest of shining gold mail was revealed.

"I command all women to the right side!" he boomed. "Men and children all to the left." He lowered his staff to eye level, and as he began to move between the ranks the people shrank back, forming a wider cleft for his passage.

"Lift up your faces, women!" he ordered. The night was coming swiftly, yet his staff illuminated the expanse of bodies. One by one he surveyed their faces, their figures, their raiment. Several times he stopped before a woman, and his eyes squinted and glowered. With his hand, he turned one around, took off her scarf, and let loose her hair. Yet each time, he shook his head, and moved on to the next. When he had studied the last one, he pivoted abruptly around and marched back to the stairs of the Inn where he stood seeming enormous in the doorway.

"Mayor Barth!" he called out. "Step forth."

A small, round figure emerged from the group of men. "Is every woman in the town before me?" Barth looked at the group across the way, and nodded. "Aye, my Lord."

The King took in a deep breath. His eyes bulged, and he ground his teeth. "Look again, Barth!" he said, his voice in controlled rage. "Are you sure? Oh, but you shall pay dearly for an error!"

Barth did as bidden and nodded once more. "Aye, my King. All the women stand here before you. The ringing of the bells signals all to come hither immediately. I did as I was told, Sire." Barth's knees were rocking below his fat belly, which shook spasmodically.

The King's face was glowing red as the blood coursed quickly through his being. He could still feel the strength imparted to him by the Phemtas plant in the House of Time. He remained silent for a moment, then said, "People of Milorin! Heed me well! Know any of you of a woman in your town who stands not here now?"

Silence, naught but heavy silence, fell upon his ears.

"Then, know you of any woman who wandered in the woods yestereve? Or of any woman who has business there?"

And still the answer came back: silence.

"Who then, my foolish friends, was the woman dressed in green, with copper hair and emerald eyes, whom I saw yester-eve in the woods? Know ye not who comes and goes in your own lands? Must I station an army at your borders to bring order into your realm? Who was that woman?" he bellowed.

A tiny voice rose up from the crowd. "My Liege, perhaps I know the answer."

"What? Who is that? Step forth!" thundered Vanamir. An elderly man, carrying an axe, came into the light. "Speak! What is your name? You know of this woman?"

"My King," said the man, "my name is Bill Harley, and I am a tree-cutter. My business often takes me to the forest, when carpenters and the like need Calicab wood. I ain't been there since well-nigh last springtime. But the woman you've seen, why, I've seen her, too!"

People turned to one another, wide-eyed. Vanamir searched the man's face eagerly.

"Aye, aye, go on, go on!" he said quickly.

"Well, Sire, I saw her the first time some years back, and that was only for a moment. I thought she was one of those night-creatures we was told about when we was kids, and I grabbed my axe and ran for it!"

Laughter came from some in the crowd.

"Silence!" roared the King.

The man went on: "I swore I'd never go back there in my life, but business was slow, and a big order for Calicabs came in, and, well, I braced myself and went. She didn't show up that time, Sire. No, not then or for some years after. But then, early last spring. I saw her again. She was real thin, and wore a light green gown, and she didn't have no shoes on. And her hair! It was long as I'd ever seen on anyone's head before, down to the ground almost, and it was kind of wild and thick. She saw me, too, because her eyes … they were looking right back at me. We both just stood there, and I think I surprised her as much as she'd surprised me. How she stared! But then, she turned and disappeared into the woods before I had time to blink my eyes. I got out of there as fast as I could. And I ain't been there since!"

The King scowled and said, "This does me no good, Harley Tree-cutter. Saw you not where she went, nor what her business was?"

"Nay, Sire. She just popped in and then popped out, if you know what I mean." There was more giggling and muffled laughter from the crowd, but this time, the King heard it not.

"Thank you, Harley," he said, and as he spoke he reached into his cloak for his leather purse. He tossed a bright gold piece to the earth. "Go back to the men," he said. Harley cocked his head to one side, and stood motionless for a moment. Then he reached down and pocketed the gold, and slipped back into the crowd.

Vanamir pulled his glittering mantle about his shoulders, and stood wrapped in great confusion. The light from his staff cast deep shadows across his angular countenance. The deep blue of twilight filled the endless heavens, and the people drew their shawls and jackets about them to ward off the chilling air. And then a muted cackling, as of some ancient rasp-throated raven, grated against the silence.

Vanamir peered from beneath his broad brow, and he sneered.

"'Tis folly to snicker now, methinks. What unfortunate fellow seeks his doom? Speak!" A beacon of light flashed from his helm, groping through the crowd.

A small mass of shawl and mantle caught the light beam. Not an inch of flesh showed from the thick garments, but a slender staff poked through and was braced against the ground. The coarse laughter issued from within the invisible body. And then in a sweet voice it said: "Perhaps it is I whom you seek, great King?"

The King straightened himself up instantly, and strode quickly over to the figure. He grasped the shawl and yanked it back. He recoiled when he saw the bony cheeks and sagging skin of an old woman.

"Not I?" came her lamenting voice. "Ah, woe is me! My brave Prince shall never come! Ugly, wretched Yedro! You shall never have a man!" She moaned and whined piteously.

Vanamir stared at her with disgust.

"So you are Yedro, the Sibyl?"

Instantly a toothless grin spread across her face, and she leaned like a rakish youth upon her wooden cane. "Aye, Sire, you've hit upon it. Yedro. But as to 'Sibyl,' why, that's not for me to say. Maybe you can tell me."

Vanamir, nearly twice her height, leaned down and scanned her face. Bushy brows canopied her beady, yellow eyeballs and purplish lips puckered thickly about her pale toothless gums. A frail layer of skin stretched across her forehead, puffed up about her eyes, and fell in tissue-like folds around her throat. Yedro watched him as he studied her, and saw the grimace come to his face. She chuckled and blew him a kiss.

"Well, so be it!" she said. "I can see you are not partial to Sibyls. But it's just as well, for Sibyls are not partial to Kings."

King Vanamir glowered, and drew his velvet mantle about him. "Bah! I waste my time with fools!" he muttered, and turned from her, and walked away.

He heard a sudden scraping sound behind him, and swung around. The old woman was drawing a strange pattern at her feet with her staff. Then she stepped upon the markings, and scratched a circle 'round herself on the earth. Raising high her thin staff, she mumbled foreign words.

Sparks sputtered 'round her hem, then erupted from the ground in a blasting show. Yedro was completely encircled by the fiery geyser. Higher and higher spurted the zenith, sending a spray of countless tiny comets crackling through space. The flaming orange cone reached its peak, then, statue-like, hovered majestically in the celestial kingdom. For one brief moment, it was motionless, although comprised of ever-sparkling static, and then there was a great "Whoosh!" as the funnel suddenly plummeted down and was instantly swallowed up by the earth and disappeared.

Up, up, up! Every head in the crowd, King and common folk alike, had followed the mountainous rising of the fiery cone. Their bodies had shined in the great light of it. And as it suddenly crashed down, their eyes had automatically snapped back to the ground.

A chill seized their hearts at what they then saw there. Wrapped in a translucent tent of wispy blue vapor, Yedro stood just as she had when the curtain of fire had enveloped her. Yet now her skin was wax-white, and only the whites of her eyes showed beneath half-closed lids. Not a single spot of life touched her.

Then, slowly, her left hand began to move, A smooth, round stone glimmered like the fragment of a star in her palm. She pressed it against her forehead. And then she opened her lips and moaned, but the sound came not from within her. It rushed in from all directions.

"Ooohh! Ooohh!" It was like the creaking of long branches in the wind.

Suddenly King Vanamir rushed forward. He pressed his staff against his armored breast, and in a loud, clear voice, said: "Where are you, Yedro?"

She answered him, and the words came from all regions of the air.

> *Ebon-night … Infinity …*
> *I fly through space –*
> *She beckons me!*

A sad smile rose upon her face, and she began to sing the words of an old Milorin lullaby:

> *Sleeping baby*
> *At my breast,*
> *When you were born*
> *The earth was blessed.*

Vanamir cut her off. "Who beckons you, Yedro?"
The smile vanished and the old woman's face looked expressionless.

> *Ah, the Queen,*
> *The Opal Night Sphere*
> *Whispers tidings of treachery*
> *In my ear.*

> *Cool her breath*
> *Upon my cheek,*
> *Long her fingers,*
> *Dark her keep.*

The King edged closer to her, and strained his eyes to see through the cloudy screen still surrounding her. He champed his strong white teeth. "Yedro!" came his coarse murmur. "What tidings of treachery?"
The stone glowed fiercely at her brow, and a silvery screen covered her, and when she answered, her own voice came softly from between her wrinkled lips.

> *A mortal soul of might and fire*

Shall be granted his desire,
And blindly, through his own device,
Is doomed to pay a Kingly price.

A snarl leapt up in Vanamir's face, and he lunged forward, crying out "Silence!" But when his fingertips struck the curling vapors a powerful tremor quaked throughout his body. He let out a piercing scream, and yanked back his hand. It smoked and steamed, yet was icy cold. He stared at it, not believing what he saw and felt.

Meanwhile, the King's touch upon the eerie screen sent a spasm through the old woman. She sank to her knees, her eyes squeezed shut, and she said:

Flowers of the soil
Of a tiny land
Are needed for the earthly coil
Of a King's mighty hand.
Phemtas! It is called
To work its magic
But the ending
Will be tragic.

Then suddenly she snapped open her eyes, and stared directly at the King. With a quick gust of wind, the foggy curtain was swept away.

Vanamir drew his velvet cape about him, and said, "Give me that stone, old woman."

"And what stone is that, my Lord?" answered Yedro.

"Don't play the fool! Hold out your hands!"

Yedro offered up her bony fingers. The right one held her thin staff; the left one was empty. Vanamir looked at her, then said, "You are mad, old crow. Be gone!"

Then, turning towards the crowd, he waved his hand brusquely. "All of you – be gone!" As if a spell were broken, the people jumped to attention, and turned and fled. The ring of Knights fell back and the Town Square was soon emptied of the folk of Milorin.

The King walked up to the doorway of the Inn, and then turned around. His men stood loosely banded around the pediment of the steps, awaiting his orders.

Twilight had faded; black night now came swiftly. Vanamir thought of the gloomy night ahead, of further plans to ferret out the woman of the forest.

Just then he noticed that one small figure was still standing in the barren circle where the crowd had been. As the King's glance fell upon it, the figure nodded his head in greeting, taking off his green cap and bowing low. A voice came out of him, with a tiny laugh that hung upon the tail of each word, as he said:

"So you seek the woman in the woods, my Lord? Then I shall take you to her."

The King stared out in the growing darkness.

"So we meet again, Gamedon," he said.

CHAPTER 7

A HEARTHSIDE ARRANGEMENT

THE DAY FINALLY GAVE WAY to the night. The deep blue sky was filled with the luminous light of infinite stars. Gamedon stared from the window in the King's chamber, the glitter in the heavens glowing in his green eyes.

"My people," he said, his eyes still fixed, "my people call the stars 'Fires of Evil,' and they believe that the black fist of night, rising over the land's edge, opens wide and flings the burning globes at the setting sun. Implements of the night's malevolence! That is what those distant diamonds are! And each one of them houses the soul of a fiendish wight, a nocturnal demon, who roams the earth from dusk to dawn – in the guise of a human." He turned 'round to face the King, who sat in his hearth-chair, staring at the newly kindled fire.

"And the moon," Gamedon continued, "she is the true wife of night, fed and fattened with the blood of these cold spirits. As she waxes, so does her evil power. Ah, but she must be happiest at her roundest!" Gamedon returned his gaze to the window. "But we have no moon tonight, my Lord. She is in the new."

"Gamedon," said Vanamir, "what you say is not true for your small town alone. The ideas hold true for all the lands in my Kingdom. And as I judge them to be ultimately, indisputably precise, all the lands over the earth most probably would mirror us. Indeed, until this very moment, I have never had cause to believe that there were those who thought otherwise." The King lifted his head, and Gamedon turned from the window, and their eyes met.

"I would hear a tale of you, Gamedon," spoke Vanamir. "I would know who you are, and who the woman of the forest is, and I would know it now. But pluck not too lustily at the string of heresy, old man, for my humor is not of a carefree mood this night. Speak to the more weighty matters." The King leaned back in his chair, and waited for Gamedon to proceed.

The old man removed his green cap, and his large ears stuck out from either side of his beard. "The telling of the first history unfolds the second, my Lord," he said. "May I be seated?"

The King nodded aye, and Gamedon drew a small chair over to the window. He faced the night, and began. "I am most willing to strum lightly over my own tale, Sire. Suffice it for the moment to say this: Milorin is my birthplace, my home. And I know this town as does no other, for I was of a curious mind and had access to all the town's annals. Every book in the House of Time came before my eyes. I read of the first settlement here, of the passing of generations, of the strengthening of customs and superstitions … ah, but the subject now becomes tender, my King. Quickly then! I found no proofs for their idolatries and systems, formed my own convictions, and openly stated my mind. The result was banishment.

"My wife took ill one day and suddenly she died. Our sole child, a fifteen-year-old daughter, we named Mandir – a word which means, in the ancient tongue, 'water.' Mandir chose to go with me. Yet when we reached the borders of Milorin, she begged me not to wander far. It was easy for me to grant her request, for when we reached the Calicab Forest we found the land there so pleasant that we wanted to roam no farther. The region was little known to the town, so we built a little hut, and spent our lives quietly.

"Mandir grew into a beautiful, red-haired, green-eyed young woman, and her heart was so at peace in the forest that I felt happiness for the first time at my exile. She spends every day there, whether rain or sun upon her face. And it was she, my King, who hurried through the woods before you as you made your way along the forest path."

The King turned 'round as Gamedon said these last words, and his eyes shone in the firelight. "You know my purpose, Gamedon," he said. "Yet why tell you willingly where I may find her?" Gamedon smiled, and said, "Aye, my Lord. You have your purpose: to take Mandir back to your Castle in the Gold Mountains. Yet, I, too, have mine. I would only ask of you two requests: first, that you let me go with her to your Castle, and second, that you take her child as well."

"What?" cried Vanamir, astonished. "She has a child?"

"Aye, my King," replied Gamedon softly. "She has a daughter, who is but six months old."

"And who is the father?"

"I know not," answered Gamedon. "She will tell no one."

"Is it some brat of some featherbrain from Milorin?" Vanamir asked angrily.

"I know not, my Lord. Mandir knows of the town, for it was never my wish that she be ignorant of her own ancestry. She was taught by her mother, my now-dead wife, the beliefs of Milorin, as I told you. I myself have other, more over-reaching thoughts about the world in which we live … but I did not force my thoughts upon Mandir." Gamedon paused. "Yet as to the father" … Gamedon shrugged his shoulders.

The King raised himself to his feet and scowled. "I will take with me no child, and I will take with me no old man. I will take with me this woman, this Mandir, and none else."

Gamedon opened wide his eyes, and curled up the corners of his mouth. "Then, my Lord," he said lightly, "you shall take with you none at all."

The red blood rose to Vanamir's face, and he clenched his fists. "You dare to command your King?" he said fiercely. "Know you not that I can have you ground to fine dust by my fifty Knights for your insolence? Or that I can leave you to the sentencing of your own people? You! An exile who was declared blasphemous yet defied his wrongdoing by remaining secretly within the land!"

"Well do I know the array of consequences that stand before me," answered the old man. "And yet, my Lord, you forget one thing."

"And pray, dotard," mocked the King, "what may that be?"

Gamedon looked straight into the eyes of Vanamir and said, "You forget, my Lord, that only I know where Mandir can be found. And without me, you shall never have her."

Vanamir snickered. "Now it is my turn to laugh, Gamedon, for you let it slip that she lives at the edge of the Calicab Forest. I can force my Knights to do my bidding in the darkest of nights, and I shall have her within the hour."

"My daughter, my King," continued Gamedon calmly, "awaits me in a secret place far from the woods. If I do not return to her quite soon, she will leave the town of Milorin far behind her and never return. She is an expert woods-woman, as you yourself have noted, and you will never find her trail."

King Vanamir's smirk fell at once into a scowl, and he sank down into his chair. He sat for a few minutes, watching the embers of the fire glow with heat. Then he turned to Gamedon, and said: "It shall be as you request, Gamedon. Happily, it comes to my mind that you have much knowledge and can do me service that no other can. We leave at sunrise."

Gamedon arose, bowed, went to the door and said, "Good night my Lord. I shall await you at the Pillars in the morning," and went out.

CHAPTER 8

A KNIFE AT DAWN

BLACK AND MOONLESS FELL THE night, and it wove a space through time. During that space, the Knights slept deeply, the people of Milorin took off their holiday clothes, hung them up and put them away, and passed the night under the warm cover of their wooden homes.

Many of the men stayed up late, talking together in their parlors, conjecturing about the King's odd behavior before the Inn and of what else happened there.

"His madness grew as twilight descended," said one.

"Aye, 'twas the workings of the night upon him," said another. "We were lucky we were set free before the black night swept in."

"It would have swallowed us all," said a third.

And in another household, two brothers recalled another scene.

"And what of Yedro the Sibyl? What did she mean by 'the magic will be tragic?'" asked one brother.

"She was talking about Phemtas, that stinking weed that grows only in our soil," answered the other.

"Aye, what need can he have of it? Maybe for him it is magic?"

The other brother laughed, and said, "Such magic! It is so ugly a plant, with nary a flower that I've ever seen when we harvest it."

"Treachery! Don't forget Yedro said there was treachery!" Both brothers were silent, then one asked the other, "What exactly is treachery?"

"I think it is when someone is disloyal or betrays his friend," answered the other.

Meanwhile, the fire burned quietly in the King's bedchamber. Across the windows, heavy curtains had been pulled shut. Vanamir, Seventeenth King of Pellah, roamed the realm of sleep and oblivion. In his dreams he wore a heavy mask as he labored to cross the endless seas on a crewless ship. Torment gnawed at his breast; he was powerless to remove the facial disguise, and he sweated on his sheets as he strained to remember his real features.

One by one, the stars began to dim and then disappear, as the first streaks of the morning sun shot up over the eastern hills. The earth swung into that red-gold region, and the night chill blew off the land. The birds began to whistle and dance. Eyes opened up, sleepy brown eyes in the trees, on the moss, peeping out of burrowed soil. And the sleepy green eyes of the folk of Milorin opened, and saw the sun come in through the windows. It was morning, May the Second, and the cycle of the sun had come to its allotted time above Milorin.

The sun came not into the chamber of the King, for the curtains barred entrance. He slept, while all else in the household rose, and washed, and dressed, and thought of food. There was much lightness of heart among the fifty Knights this cheery dawn. May the First had passed. The road homeward loomed up in their minds.

Today they would be on it.

They sat at table as on the previous day, waiting for their King. But he made no appearance. Haldown and Malthor conferred, then decided to send a maid to see how it went with the King. A girl was fetched, and she bowed politely, and went off to do as bidden. In several minutes she returned.

"My Lord sleeps," she said. "I could not rouse him." Haldown and Malthor looked at one another, and spoke softly behind open palms. Then Haldown arose, and left the room.

He went to his King's chambers and knocked lightly on the bedroom door. Hearing no response, Haldown entered. Darkness greeted his eyes, and he opened one of the curtains. "Stupid little maid," he muttered. "This was her job."

Still, the King moved not.

"My Lord," spoke Haldown softly. "'Tis well past our appointed rising-time." Vanamir made no response. "My Lord," said the Knight, somewhat louder. "'Tis the hour of departure." And he thought, "He's got his own valet at home in the Castle; I suppose that's me today."

Not a flutter of an eyelash did King Vanamir make.

Haldown grew uneasy, and his heartbeats sped. He threw open all the heavy curtains and approached the large figure that lay motionless beneath the heavy, dark-green quilts.

"My Lord," Haldown said abruptly, laying his hand on the sleeping man's shoulder. "My Lord! My King! Rise, Sire, rise!" Haldown's body trembled at the silence of the King, and terror leapt into his breast. He grabbed now the other shoulder and shook with all his might.

"My King," he cried. "King Vanamir! Rise up! Rise up!"

The sunlight burst into the room and spread across the bed, lighting up the two men as the forest fire does the dry leaves that skip unwittingly into its path. And suddenly the King opened his eyes, and his lips parted, and he felt the mad grip of two strong hands bearing down upon him. Up, up flew his right arm, and his hand reached down beneath his pillow, and still the madman shook and yelled. Vanamir pulled out his hand, and in it shone a fiery gold blade fashioned with serpents that seemed to writhe and spit from his fist.

Haldown suddenly felt the body beneath him grow tense, and from the corner of his eye he saw the emeralds in the eyes of the serpent-blade, and saw it jump and bare its fangs. But he felt not the cold bite of its teeth upon his neck, nor the sudden hot rush of his blood spurting out, nor heard he the sudden wail of his life as it burst out of his body and flew up into the air and, in an instant, was gone.

The arms that held the King ceased their shaking, and they stiffened, and then collapsed. The body of the King's attacker fell upon him. Vanamir thrust forward and heaved the man upon the floor. Golden sunlight danced upon the emerald snake eyes that lay so still now above the steady streaming of red blood. Vanamir groaned, and sat up on his bed, still half covered by his quilts, and rubbed his cheeks, and then his eyes, and looked over the edge of the bed.

"What fiend was this?" he said aloud. He pushed the limp body over onto its back, and from the depths of the pit of sleep his mind snapped to the surface, for he beheld the face of Haldown, red with blood. King Vanamir let out a cry that sent a chill through the hearts of all at the Inn. He tore at his long red hair and moaned.

"Ah, Haldown! Haldown! What fit was upon you to wrestle with me thus? What have you brought upon yourself? Ah, Haldown, Haldown!"

After the Knights learned of Haldown's fate, they took no breakfast and went to saddle up their horses. There, in front of the Inn, they awaited their King's orders.

Silence reigned.

The departure from Milorin was somber. The King, as ever, led the procession, while behind him rode the forty-nine Knights, heads slightly lowered. There was no mirth, no jesting amidst the ranks. Behind the Ten Men of the Coffers, their leather bags now full and heavy with Phemtas, rode the unburdened horse of Haldown. The dark brown steed was restless, and fought the bit. His eyes rolled madly, and he strove ever to look behind him. His martingale harness prevented that. The scent of death pierced his flaring nostrils.

They had laid Haldown in a small wagon, and covered him with black drapes. The wooden wheels creaked as they rolled along the pebbled road. Two grey palfreys from the stables of the nearest farm were bought by Vanamir for some bits of gold, gold that lay now in that farmer's calloused palm to the delight of his wife and children. The palfreys were harnessed and pulled the bier, following the anxious, riderless stallion. Haldown's leather boots were upside-down in the stirrups.

They rode out of Milorin, past the sparse groups of people who were going about their daily chores, past the bowing Mayor and his four deputies, past the stores that ran along the road and ended as it curved sharply into the countryside. At the turn-off, the King raised high his scepter and halted. All stopped in unison behind him. He turned his horse around, and a cloud of dust blew up, and he faced the few people that still stood gazing after him.

"People of Milorin!" he cried out. "I am come to the part in my travels where I must head home. Be assured that I shall ever cherish in my heart the tears that were shed at my leaving." He turned his head and scanned the stony faces in the street. Gold glittered upon his body, and upon his brow the sun-disc seemed to boil. And then he burst out in a loud rumble of laughter, lifting his head high to the sun. Russet hair blew about his cheeks.

"Ha, ha! Until my Knights – with or without their King – return!" he called, and swiftly did an about-face. He marched off, and the forty-nine Knights, Haldown's frightened steed, the two gray purchased palfreys and the little wooden wagon bearing the body, and the one dappled mare all moved on behind him.

Jack Beale stood at the door to his Inn, and his friend Tom stood beside him. "Now, what do you make of all that?" asked Tom, staring down the road. The Innkeeper shook his head, and answered, "There was murder in my Inn this morning, the first time we have had blood spilled in our town. I don't like it one bit, Tom. Nay, 'tis not good, to my way of thinking."

Mayor Barth stood with his four councilmen, and they all fell to talking.

"Is our King a madman?" asked one deputy.

"Nay, not a madman," Barth shook his head in reply. "He walks as one half asleep, so to speak. I myself have seen him falling in and out of some kind of dreams. His own Knight tried to wake him from one and got himself killed. I tell you, I'm glad they're gone."

"Why does he come around here anyway? Just for one occasional woman to take as his wife in his ongoing hopes of a male heir," said one.

"And to fill his bags with that smelly weed," grumbled another.

"I don't know," said Barth. "But if that's all he asks of us, why, I'm happy. Imagine if he wanted men instead! And if he wants some of that useless Phemtas in the bargain, why, that's okay with me as well."

They all stood there for a minute or two, and watched the dust of the departure settle back upon the path. Then they turned around and headed back for their office. But at the Square, Barth left the group.

"If anyone comes looking for me," he said, "I'll be in the House of Time. I've got some unfinished business there." He walked towards the windowless gray building.

"Gamedon, Gamedon," he muttered. "There must be something about him in one of those old books."

CHAPTER 9

THE MAID OF THE WOODS

GAMEDON SAT AT THE PILLARS, and next to him sat his young daughter, Mandir. She held in her arms a sleeping babe completely covered in a green wool blanket. They sat and watched the sun rise over the horizon, and climb slowly into the sky.

"The King is late," said Gamedon.

A little more time passed and Gamedon turned his head to stare at the road to Milorin. "Sits fear beside you, Mandir?" he asked.

Mandir lifted her face to him, and her eyes were green as the deep, dark sea. "Nay, father," she replied. "Nay, fear has naught to do with me. Fear points a finger at my child. And of the moment when the King shall see her, of only this do I know fear."

Gamedon turned to her and smiled. "Aye, Mandir," he said. "You speak rightly. Yet we are lost if we do not show her to him here. If he is repelled, he may well come to violence. And better for that to come here, where we have some hope of escape should we require it. We have little craft once we are beyond the ken of our homeland, where the swift running of one in pursuit can only be met with high stone walls and far more than just fifty Knights."

Mandir breathed deeply, raising her head to follow the row of Pillars about her. "If I must go, then so must my baby." Her voice was soft and steady. "I would never abandon her in the woods."

Gamedon spoke gently. "Mandir, my dearest daughter, do not forget to follow your heart. I know the sadness of leaving one's home. Yet I know, as you, that a time has come for us to step into a new realm. That you are delivered of such a child, that you chanced into the forest at the same moment as the King, and that he calls upon you now to go with him – all these things are not without purpose."

Mandir nodded.

"Aye, father, I feel it is so. Yet to what purpose do we deliver ourselves?" Gamedon knelt and bent his head to the ground. "To this question, Mandir, I have many suspicions. Yet they are all so vague. I am without clear answer."

After this, they said nothing else, and soon the dust of a great riding could be seen gathering on the land's edge. The earth moaned lightly beneath the weight, and the glint of gold emerged from the dust-cloud.

"They bear some new burden," said Gamedon.

As they came nearer, Mandir said, "One of them is dead, father."

The host approached the Pillars, and when the King's horse reached the first pair of tall monuments, it stopped. All stopped behind it. The King raised his staff at his side and commanded his horse to walk slowly forward. Down the entire length of columns he marched, and, reaching the end, turned around and looked back.

"Gamedon!" he shouted. "Gamedon, show yourself!"

"I am right over here, my Lord," came the old man's voice. Vanamir looked to his left and saw, sitting between two Pillars, the old man, plus a woman clad all in green. His heart leapt up. He trotted over to her.

He had no need of asking, for he knew in an instant that this was the woman who filled his mind ever since he rode through the Calicab Forest. Her long auburn hair lay about her as a cloak, and her eyes shot forth in a green flame. The air about her fell sweet and cool upon the King's face.

"Rise!" he said.

The woman rose with ease to her feet. She held the small bundle close to her breast. Gamedon rose with her.

"Speak!" said Vanamir.

Mandir felt her heart pounding against her child, and felt the baby wakening, moving its tiny arms.

"Speak!" repeated the King. "Know you whither you shall journey this day?"

Mandir's voice blew cool and steady into the air. "Aye, my Lord. I know that I journey with you, yet I know not what lies at the end of the road."

"At the end of all roads in our Kingdom lies naught but the Gold Mountains and my Castle Pellah thereon." He turned to Gamedon. "Yet I have but one horse to spare." The tiny old man removed his green cap, and bowed slightly.

"My Lord," he said with a smile, "I myself see two."

"A dead Knight's horse cannot be ridden ever again, except by one of his own lineage," said Vanamir. "I have but one horse."

Gamedon said, "And is one of your Knights dead, my Lord? Is that his body lying shrouded in the wagon?"

Vanamir answered, "Aye, Gamedon, 'tis the body of Haldown, First Eyeman to the King. And none shall ride his horse."

"Shall I believe, then, that you have cheated on our bargain, my Lord?" queried Gamedon. He felt his muscles tensing. "Or shall my daughter and her babe and I ride one steed?"

Vanamir laughed scornfully. "I toy with the vision of scattering your bones all about this ancient place. Yet I will not be out-maneuvered by your trust in my word. You are to come with us, old man, but you shall not ride the dappled mare. Did I not tell you yesterday that she will not bear you? You shall ride in the wagon along-side the bier, pulled by the two palfreys. The woman shall ride the mare, with the child." He pulled out his sword instantly and brought its point to the edge of the baby's blanket. Andalorax stepped back. The King laughed and circled 'round her.

"I doubt the babe weighs overmuch," he said, laughing.

In her arms, her child had awakened and had begun to cry, softly at first and then more strongly. King Vanamir raised his scepter, and signaled to his men to approach.

"Time moves swiftly this day, and we must be gone at once," he said. "Malthor, bring me the horse." Malthor went to the end of the company and took the reins of the little mottled gray mare in his hands, and rode forth to his King.

"Mount up, make haste! Gamedon, get to the wagon!" commanded Vanamir, keeping his eyes on the woman. A broad grin spread across his face, and his large white teeth gleamed, and he said, "'Tis homeward, now, man! Homeward with the forest's prize!"

Just then, Mandir rushed forward and stood before the King. Without saying a word, she threw the green blanket off her child and stretched out her arms. She held out her child, naked, before him. He turned abruptly towards her, and his eyes flashed, for behold! The child bore a thick crown of snow-white hair upon her head and her eyes shone forth black as the darkest night. She cried at the top of her small voice, and writhed madly in her mother's firm hands.

"What monster is this?" roared the King. All the Knights drew back and their horses beneath them began to sweat at the fear that swept up into the air around them. "This freak, this creature – is your own child? Speak! I command you!"

"Aye, this is my own babe, grown in my womb and fed at my breast! She is as beautiful and healthy a child as ever there was, but has not the coloring of the rest of the Kingdom. Aye, her hair is white and her eyes be black. Yet, what say you now to me, my Lord?" Vanamir glowered and his whole body filled with feverish energy.

"What say I now, maid?" he thundered. "I say you have begat a nightmare, a macabre phantom from the pit of hideous dreams. I will obliterate this thing from the earth!" He unsheathed his long dagger from his girdle, and the green serpent's eyes flashed. Forward he rushed while Mandir began to run.

Suddenly Gamedon threw himself in the path of Vanamir's charging stallion. "Vanamir!" he cried. "Is there not already blood on your hands this day?"

The King's horse reared before Gamedon, and the King fought to keep in the saddle. Yet he halted, and knitted his brows, and ground his teeth, and his breath came hard and quick.

"You shall know my revenge upon your reason one day, dotard!" he growled. "Wrap the babe and get to horse," he cried. "My mind is bent homeward, and I shall not surrender your daughter, my prize!" He turned sharply and rode to the head of the procession, which was immediately brought to order behind its leader.

Gamedon bent to the ground, picked up the green blanket, and handed it to Mandir. He helped her to mount the grey mare, and then seated himself beside the shrouded coffin.

Just as they were to set off, Vanamir turned his head around and yelled back to them, past the Nineteen Men of the Eyes, past the Twenty Men of the Teeth, past the Ten Men of the Coffers, past Mandir and her babe, and past the riderless steed and the wagon bier with Haldown and Gamedon.

"Your monster!" he cried out. "What is its name?"

Mandir cupped her right hand around her lips and called out:

"Andalorax!"

The King knew the ancient meaning of that combination of letters: "Night Black, Moon White." What it meant, he had no way of knowing. He decided on the spot to peruse the written histories of former Kings, and wise-men, wizards and sibyls in the Castle's vast Library, and the King's mind returned to the task at hand ....

"Onward!" he cried, and the Pillars were left in a cloud of dust.

BOOK TWO

CHAPTER 10

THE MANY-COLORED GIRL

ANDALORAX WALKED LIGHTLY OVER THE gold tiles that paved the outer ring of the Castle. Her sandals tapped the even rhythm of her even gait, and the wind blew gently through her long, white hair. How she wished her hair were red and her eyes were green, as all the people of the Kingdom of Pellah. Then she would be accepted!

On, on she walked, ever spiraling the Castle's girth, as around and around she went, gradually descending. Ever to her left were the heavy stones, encrusted with gold and ancient markings, which formed this, the central turret of her home. And ever to her right was the waist-high wall that offered protection to those who strode the outer ring from any precipitous fall to the lands and waters below.

The sun had risen barely a quarter of an hour, when she had left her small room that fitted snugly up in the cool, western flank of the fortress. How good it felt to have the heat of the yellow sun upon her heart-shaped face as she rounded each bend into the eastern pastures of the air!

It took her nearly one-half hour to attain the earthbound regions of the mountain-hold, and with each minute she sensed all the life of spring breathing around her. The sweet smell of the air rising from the blossoming trees, the lighthearted singing of wakening birds, the warmth of four-footed creatures playing and working upon the solid earth … she moved closer and closer, as the stone walls rose heavenwards above her head. Inside the walls life stirred as well, but that was all too distant from her thoughts, and fell steadily away from her with each step. Somewhere in there was the King, she mused, and she laughed as she pondered what his mood would be today.

"And somewhere behind stone is my mother, Mandir," she said aloud, and fell in shadowed loneliness for her. But then she reached the lowest golden ring, and the massive metal gate stood just before her, guarded by four men-at-arms. Gold-studded helms and scabbards glittered in the playful sunlight.

The guards turned their attention towards her approach, and she raised her hand in greeting.

"Good morn-" Andalorax was cut short by a quick whistling sound from above, and a swift blow struck her on her left cheek. She fell, stunned, and felt the warm yellow pavement along the length of her body. A trickle of blood coursed down over her ear and dropped onto her shoulder.

She looked up, to see a head dart inside an open window. The four men-at-arms moved not, but stood quietly watching. At her side lay the well-aimed missile, a piece of broken rock.

"Who is at the window?" she cried. "Show yourself, if you be not a coward!"

Voices tittered through the empty opening, and she rose to her feet.

"You may laugh, but the wind bears my message: you are, all of you, nothing but cowards!"

A child's round face popped through the window and jeered at her, and the mouth opened and sang out:

Andalorax! Andalorax!
With ugly hair as pale as wax!
Na! Na! Na! A silly freak!
Growing uglier every week!

A chorus of laughter rang behind the window, and several more faces peered down at her. They all took up the tune, bleating and bellowing, and pushing each other to get a closer look at the girl who stood not ten feet below them.

Quickly, Andalorax stooped and grasped the stone. It bore the mark of her blood. The singing faces pulled swiftly away as the rock hurtled through the air and into the open window. A cry flew up from inside, and angry voices yelled "Monster! Devil! You'll pay for this!" But none dared show their face. The voices broke off, and disappeared into the depths of the Castle.

Andalorax stood there for a minute, expecting a crowd of girls and boys to come running down into the golden ring, and she tensed, ready for a fight. But none came, and her heart grew quiet, and the trembling of her body ceased. She turned and walked to the gate. Her anger quickened as she faced the cold eyes of the four guards, and her eyes flashed.

"Open the gate," she said, her pride forcing a monotone. They heaved aside the heavy metal bolts and pushed open the doors. Andalorax strode through them. But her anger had risen in her again, and she felt the cruel sting of the guards' silence. She turned 'round and cried back at them: "You could have helped me! It's you who are ugly! I hate you! I hate you!" And she rushed away into the forest. The gates heaved to behind her.

She ran for a while, until her slender legs grew somewhat weary. Then she sank down upon the mossy ground and wept, and her tears mingled with the dried blood upon her face. With some leaves, she wiped the stains away. But ever came new sobbing from her breast, and new tears from her eyes, until at last her pain was spent. She sat there, her uneven breathing being all that lingered of her outburst.

A flood of green filled her vision, the yellow-green of springtime's youth. The leaves that roofed above her were still unfolding, so that, majestically blue beyond her, the sky reared into space. The earth was damp beneath her, and she rose to her feet lest her cloak be soiled. Her cheek smarted, and she searched the ground for healing herbs, but found naught but red mushrooms and uncoiling ferns. So she walked further on, and the gentle spirit of the tall trees soothed her, and made her want to laugh and run about.

But she was lonely for a playmate, and she closed her eyes, raising her face to the sky, breathing deeply. Andalorax, white-haired child, standing in a sea of growing green, reached down past the loneliness of her heart and entered the land of color that swarmed anxiously within her mind. Streams of crimson and gold, of purple and sapphire, of burnt umber and henna swirled through her inner eye. She formed patterns, and painted, and beneath her closed eyes, her rosy lips parted and she smiled.

The workings of her mind slowly took to form, and she saw within her that the colors whirled around and around one central point. The rainbow-glow formed a nest of flickering heat and light. Greater and greater grew the point, until it filled the whole space of her thoughts, and seemed to have swallowed up all the madly flowing colors. And suddenly Andalorax shot open her eyes.

Standing before her was a girl whose eyes shone back at her. A gentle smile played upon her lips, and two dimples perched upon her cheeks. Her gown and hair merged together in a wondrous fashion that could not be called by any one color. They shimmered white, then silvery blue, then fiery scarlet, and no one color stayed longer than an instant upon its surface. And as Andalorax stared at this magnificent girl, she saw that not only her robe and gown and hair were of ever-changing hue, but her eyes as well.

Andalorax felt the great beauty of this being, and there was no room inside her heart for fear, and she said:

"Marvelous girl! Who are you?"

The girl laughed and as she did her hair flashed saffron, and her gown shone like a cherry, and her eyes were soft lavender.

"Why, Andalorax, don't you know me?" came the ringing voice from her red lips. Her laughter rippled in the forest air.

"Nay, I know you not," answered Andalorax, shaking her head. "Where do you come from? Why should I know you?"

The Many-Colored Girl shook her long hair, and it danced azure blue, and she answered, "I come from where you called me, Andalorax. And as to why you should know, why, if you cannot guess, then this shall be our game today! I will sing the riddles, and you must sing the answers. Then you shall surely come to know all that you wish. But let us now walk awhile! I want to see springtime with my own eyes!" She reached out and took Andalorax by the hand, and they moved along quietly through the trees.

They passed groves of old and shaggy oak, and fields of young saplings, and crossed a narrow stream that was cool and clear. Andalorax had to remove her sandals before she crossed, and she noticed that the girl wore no shoes, and that her bare feet were as smooth and frail as those of a newborn child. Yet if the stones and twigs underfoot hurt her, she never showed any sign.

They came to a meadow of tall grasses, and the girl withdrew her hand, and ran off, dancing and leaping about with great joy. Then she sank down upon the soft earth. Andalorax came up to her, and lay down beside her, and said:

"Please ask me the riddles now, for I really must know who you are!"

The Many-Colored Girl laughed again, and sat up, and smoothed her gown. It shone amber, then dark purple, and indeed changed from this color to that with such fickleness that Andalorax could not look upon it for too long, for it made her head spin.

The girl looked at Andalorax and her eyes were lemon-yellow, and she said: "Very well, here's the first:

> *Night-black, Moon-white,*
> *It came a-crying in the night.*

"There now, that one's easy. What is it?"

Andalorax still lay upon the grass, but now she sat up beside the girl, and pondered her riddle for several minutes.

"Oh, I give up!" she said. "I don't know what it is. You'll have to tell me more."

When Andalorax said this, the strange girl turned to her in amazement. But she said nothing to that matter, and continued with another riddle.

> *It makes its home in gold and stone,*
> *But wood and water are its bone.*

"Now, that ought to help you, Andalorax," she said.

Andalorax stared at the girl, whose hair fluttered topaz in the warm breeze, and again she thought over the riddle, and again she shook her own mass of white hair.

"Nay, I cannot guess at this," she said sadly. "'Gold and stone' remind me of the Castle, but 'wood and water' don't remind me of anything at all."

The many-hued girl rose to her feet, and gazed out across the field to where the sun was reaching the treetops on the horizon. She turned to Andalorax and said: "Why, Andalorax, I don't think we can play this game too well, because you don't seem to know the answers to anything."

Andalorax stood up and faced the girl, and stared at her purple eyes. "I don't think that's very fair of you to say," she retorted. "You ask me two riddles that seem simple enough to you, but if you'd ask me better riddles, that were simple enough to me, why, then I'd have a lot of things to say."

The strange girl started to laugh, and she leaped up in the air with her mirth, and did somersaults and hand-springs, and came running back to Andalorax, putting her hands on her shoulders and saying, "Andalorax, my friend, let us not quarrel! I do not have much art in riddle-making, I'll admit to that, but I shall assay one more. Be patient for I must think on it for a minute!" She was silent for some time, and then she smiled, and sang her riddle out.

Fifteen winters has it seen,
But not through eyes of favored green.

She thought for another second, then hastily added:

I could tell with one quick peek,
It has a wound upon its cheek!

"Nay, I shouldn't have put that in. It gives it all away," sighed the girl.

She turned her ochre eyes upon Andalorax, and watched the white eyebrows knit together. Suddenly Andalorax opened wide her eyes, and jumped up and said: "Why, that's me! I had forgotten about my cheek, but it's me, it's me!"

The Many-Colored Girl clapped her hands in joy, and laughter sprinkled in the air like the dust of countless powdered jewels.

"You see, Andalorax," she cried out. "We did it! Now you know the answer to your questions."

"What do you mean?" asked the white-haired girl, suddenly shaken from her pride in solving the riddle. "I still don't know who you are, and why I should know you. Nor, for that matter, do I know the answers to the first two riddles." She was becoming annoyed with the whole game.

The Many-Colored Girl flashed blood-red eyes, and her hair foamed about her in a purple glow, and she stomped her foot.

"I can't play this game with you!" she said petulantly. "You don't even know who you are!"

"Oh, yes I do. I know who I am well enough. It's you I don't know!"

"If you knew who you were, Andalorax," came the girl's reply, "you'd know who I am. And what's more, you'd know who it was in the riddles."

"I don't want to play at riddles with you anymore!" cried Andalorax. "I wish you would just go away!"

The girl vanished. Andalorax blinked her eyes; there was no trace of the Many-Colored Girl anywhere. "Where are you?" she cried. "Where are you?"

But there was no answer. The girl was nowhere to be seen. Andalorax thought she was being made fun of and waited for the girl to come back. But soon she got tired of waiting.

"And anyway," she said to herself, "I wanted her to go and now I'm rid of her and her tiresome riddles." So she turned around and headed back for the forest and the Castle, as the sun began to sink in the west.

CHAPTER 11

DOORS, LOCKS, AND A KEY

ANDALORAX REACHED THE SAFETY OF the Castle just as night was beginning to settle upon the lands. As soon as she passed the gates, she realized she hadn't eaten all day and became intensely hungry. She headed straight for the pantry on the lower level. On the way, she passed only a few serving-women, for all the lords and ladies and Knights had already partaken of the day and its occupations, and had retired to their own quarters for the coming night.

She threaded her way along the least-used passageways, as she generally did. The gold-tiled floor led her from one vaulted chamber to another. Thick wax candles perched along the walls, casting long shadows over the tapestries and portraits that had hung silently through the ages. The air grew cool as evening fell, and the moisture rose up from the massive stones, letting forth a sweet, musty odor. Andalorax breathed it in deeply; she liked this part of the citadel.

After several minutes she came upon a closed wooden door, and without hesitating she pushed down on the lever. The door swung open. A flood of yellow light poured forth through the doorway, and Andalorax strode inside the room. The place was full of cooks, of cleaning women, of pot-scrubbing and the piling up and putting away of bowls, mugs, and pitchers. There was a great din of talking, laughing, singing, whistling, all of which was accompanied by much gesticulating, head-nodding, belly-shaking, grimacing, and the like.

But the women's hands were forever busy with kitchen work. They paid little attention to the slight, white-haired girl. Her sudden entrance and her raiding of the pantry was a common event. They knew, for they oversaw the meals of the Castle, that she was rarely – if ever – sitting down to board with the other children.

So she helped herself to cheese and bread, and to fruit and dried meat, and swallowed it all down with goat's milk. A cherry tart added the last sweet taste. And still no one said anything to her, or indeed even nodded to her, or seemed to notice her in any way at all. She just sat there on the wooden stool, and the life in the kitchen bustled on at its own pace.

All of a sudden she became aware of someone calling her name. Softly, she heard "Andalorax." She turned quickly and saw an old bearded figure seated not too far behind her.

"Why, grandfather!" she cried. "How you startled me."

The old man smiled, and a pattern of wrinkles crisscrossed his face. His bright green eyes shone like a bird's; the yellow light in the room suffused him with a muted glow. The hubbub in the room still hummed on.

"I've been waiting for you, Andalorax," came his soft voice. "Have you finished your meal?"

"Aye, grandfather," replied Andalorax. "I'm so happy to see you!" She got up off her stool and gave him a great hug and a kiss. He stroked her silky hair, then put his fingers to her cheek.

"What wound is this?" he asked. How his fingers cooled the soreness!

"Oh, it's nothing, sir," said the child. "But I have so much else to tell you, and the story of my wound is but a trifle in comparison. The most marvelous thing happened to me today, and it was so wondrous, that … ah, I fear now it was all but a dream." She sighed, and went back over to her seat. "Aye, perhaps it was naught but a dream."

Gamedon laughed, and said, "Andalorax, to have a marvelous dream is certainly worth the telling of it, and it makes me glad to know you would tell it to me. But this must wait until later."

"What is it, grandfather?"

"As I said, I have been waiting for you, and now I must take you to the King." He rose, straightened up his back, but still his full height was no taller than his granddaughter's, who was tall for her age but not fully grown at fifteen.

"The King?" asked the girl, her eyes opening wide. "Why must I go before the King? I have done nothing wrong. Why does he wish to see me?"

"Fear not, Andalorax, for I shall be with you."

"Aye, sir," she said. "But you are with the King all the time, and for you, 'tis a simple matter to see him but one more time. But for me! Oh, grandfather, I am afraid!"

"Nonsense, Andalorax," said Gamedon. "It will all be over in a little while. The King does not deal solely in black matters, you know."

They wound their way through innumerable passageways and corridors, down and up dark, curved stairways, and Gamedon ever led the way to the King's quarters with familiarity. Lighted candles showed the way along the corridor.

Andalorax had not been this way; her acquaintance with the King had been limited to public appearances in the banquet halls, or in the open courts, or whenever he rode away with his private company of Knights to the cheers and banner-waving of the entire household. So she followed closely at Gamedon's heels.

Around and around, climbing and descending, they circuited the innards of the Castle as the fly confronted with the network of the spider's art. Neither smell not sight could aid Andalorax when she sought for her position in the latitude and longitude of rock, for they passed no windows.

They came to a smooth wooden door, with the carved shape of an eagle protruding from its center. Gamedon placed his palm flat against the grain just below the eagle's jutting talons, and rubbed across the door, circling the bird. As Gamedon repeated this motion three times, Andalorax studied the bird. It seemed to her that, although it was made of wood, its eyes were shining with two pinpoints of green light.

The door slid smoothly back on its hinges. The old man entered quickly, and Andalorax hastened behind him. Once they were through the portal, the door slid silently shut of its own accord.

The chamber breathed golden light. The vaulted stonework was inlaid and adorned with gold, and the fluted columns that rose evenly along the walls were rippled and embossed with the dully shining metal. Rich, wine-red tapestries spanned between the pillars, depicting scenes of the glories of the reign of the House of Pellah. Braided tassels of woven gold threads trailed down along their borders, and the lowest tipped the gold-tiled floor. How that floor shimmered and blazed beneath the worn leather sandals on their feet! It bore the bright polish of time and use, and seemed made of golden glass.

Along the right wall were huge casks, and these too were pegged and studded with gold. A peculiar odor reached out from them as Andalorax set her eyes upon them. Suddenly, she felt threatened, and drew back. Her breath came in a long, hissing rush into her chest. Her scalp crawled. She wanted to turn and flee.

Gamedon sensed her movement, and clasped her hands in his. "Nay, Andalorax," he said gently. "Fear not. We are in the King's quarters; there is no danger here." Andalorax listened to his words, and looked across at his old, winkled face, and for the first time in her fifteen years she disbelieved his words. Confusion spread through her mind, and she thought: "Why does he not feel the danger?" She wanted to cry.

At that moment a door at the farthest end of the room flew open. A figure ablaze with dazzling light shone before her. Great heat spread all around it, and it seemed to Andalorax that the sun was rising man-shape over a foggy sea. The splendorous figure raised its arms, and its eyes shot forth green beacons. Her mind flashed to the eagle swelling from the wooden door.

"Andalorax!" How oddly it pronounced her name ….

"Andalorax!" came the deep voice from within the fiery figure. And then a great laughter burst out of it. The sound splintered and crackled in her ears.

"The laughter is like to the King's," she thought. "Is this the King?"

The figure advanced, looming brighter and bulkier with every stride it took. It came to within two long paces of the girl, then stopped. All about it, Andalorax could discern the nimbus of heat-distorted air; the tapestries and vaultings rippled and swayed rhythmically through its translucence. Left, right, left … her eyes automatically followed the even tempo, while her heartbeat synchronized: *lupDUP! lupDUP!* She felt the blood coursing through her, the rhythm accelerated, and her head seemed ready to explode into flames.

Then everything ceased. The heat and light were drawn out of the chamber as though a flue had suddenly been opened. Only a sullen yellow haze remained. And where the center of this conflagration had been, stood a tall man. His beard and hair were thick, the color of ripe persimmon. The emerald cloak that draped in thick folds from his shoulders reached down to the floor, trailing off behind him. It was clasped at the throat with a gold sun-disc that glowed in its depths with the memory of heat.

And he shall bear the token of molten gold,
And we shall crown him King!

The words of the Book of First Kings registered on Andalorax's mind, and at once she knew who it was before her.

She also became aware of all the details of his body and dress, and noted that earlier, when he appeared wrapped in flame, she could discern none of these things. And how quickly her mind had snapped from a world swarming with strange visions and sensations to that of focused clarity. She remembered what the Many-Colored Girl had said that day: "You don't even know who you are!"

Andalorax suddenly became terrified. "Everything is silent now," she thought. The King said nothing; Gamedon said nothing. She stood there and waited. "Grandfather!" her mind cried. "Please help me!"

And then: "Good evening, my King!" The words shattered the heavy air, and Andalorax, taking a deep breath, heard her own voice repeating Gamedon's.

"Good evening, my King!"

The King looked upon Andalorax. "Her voice bespeaks her ignorance," he thought. "She means nothing to me."

"And greetings to you, Gamedon," he said aloud. "It has taken you overlong to answer my summons. Still, you are here. Follow me." He waved his hand, and turned about.

At the end of the room was a small raised platform mounted by a carved wooden chair. King Vanamir seated himself upon it, motioning Gamedon and Andalorax towards two smaller chairs opposite it.

"And yet," he thought, "I wished to use the Fire upon her ...."

Vanamir studied the girl's face, the large black eyes of childhood shining high above her cheekbones; the tiny pointed chin; the full lips now drawn tight against the teeth. The billowing frame of white hair flashed across his eyes.

"I'll dip her mane in a bucket of paint," he mused, "and not be troubled by that cursed whiteness!"

"Do you paint, child?"

The question shocked Andalorax. Gamedon looked up at the King. "I mean, child," the King went on, "what do you do for play? Do you paint, do you study the letters, do you 'broider with golden needles? Your grandfather here has you always in his mind. I feel it even now, Gamedon!" he snapped, looking hard upon the old man. He gazed back towards Andalorax, his eyes staring into the air above her, "She's always here," he thought, "yet I truly know her not. But now," his eyes swooped down upon her, "now, I will know her."

"I do as the other children, my Lord," came her even voice. She heard the knockings of fear against her breast, but heeded them not, being suddenly cradled in fatigue. "I play out-of-doors, I make friends with the wild creatures beyond the gates, I work in the garden that I have planted—"

"You do nothing like to the other children!" thundered the King. And he thought, "Does she think to fool me?"

"What of kitchen work?" he said. "What of weaving and stitching? A garden, indeed. Gamedon, how have you plotted in this child's education? Speak up, man! You stink of treachery!"

Gamedon looked directly at the King. "And how treachery, my Lord? The child is spat upon in her every attempt to work with the household. Surely you know that, Sire. I have not the cruelty to force her to play the victim."

"I was too rash," thought Vanamir.

Gamedon spoke again. "You said treachery, my Lord. What is there in this child's life that summons your thoughts towards treachery?"

"Aha!" thought Vanamir. "He thinks to test my knowledge! I'll not show this man my mind."

"A subject may do many things," he answered, "to draw off the power of his master. I merely wish you to know that I omit no one from the range of my suspicions in attempting to usurp my power." He stroked his long red beard and twirled his mustache.

"But you, child, I have great pity for your obvious plight. It is not my wish that you endure greater hardships by my hand. I'll meddle not in what happiness you can grasp in this world."

There was silence for several minutes. Gamedon looked strongly at the King. "Another thing I would know, Andalorax." The King pronounced each syllable of her name: An-da-lor-ax.

"Know you aught of swimming?"

The little girl's eyes lit up. "Aye, my Lord! I love to swim. I often go down to the one of the lakes in the forest when the sun is strong, and swim all day long. I—"

She stopped abruptly. The King had swiftly risen from his chair, and his chest heaved mightily beneath his cloak. Two green coals glowered down at her between his eyelids and he gnashed his teeth. "So she swims, does she?" he growled. "The little water-rat! This I'll not allow, Gamedon. Take to the water just once more, and you seal your own doom. Bah. I wish no longer to waste my time playing Papa! Get thee gone; my eyes weary of you."

"Then we shall bid you good night, my Lord," said the old man. "Come, Andalorax."

Turning to the old man, Vanamir said, "You are to bring the child as far as the public chambers. From there she should know her way back to her own domain. Then you are to return here, Gamedon. I expect you back in a quarter-hour. There are matters I would discuss with you. Make haste now! Be gone!"

Andalorax rose, made a quick curtsy, and then said, "I hope I have done nothing to offend my King. You say you have pity for me; it is a kindness from you that I shall not forget."

Vanamir looked at her face, at the irises which flowered black within her eyes. "Nay, she's not the one, you fool!" he thought. "She's but a freak. And yet, the words read, '*and when it comes, it shall tread the path of the pariah.*'"

"Good night, An-da-lor-ax," he murmured, sinking back down into his cushioned chair. The old man went to the wooden door, pressing his palm upon its center where the eagle jutted out on the other side. It opened, and the two disappeared down the dark corridor, and the door closed behind them.

A quarter-hour passed. Gamedon returned to the King's chambers.

"I will speak plainly, Gamedon," said King Vanamir. "There was a purpose to my seeing your grandchild this night."

"Aye, my Lord," said the old man seated before him. "Well do I know you play not with your time."

"I went to my bed chamber this mid-day, and sought some rest from much weariness of the morning's business. I fell asleep, and had a dream that lays heavily upon me even now.

"I was walking along the cliffs that border my land with the sea, and the air was hot and still. There was not a single cloud in the vast blue sky, and no sea-birds called, no fishes leaped upon the waters below.

"Then, suddenly, a great black storm cloud arose from the east, billowing and swelling at the far edge of the sea. The wind swept up, and blew loudly about me, and I fought to keep my feet upon the earth. Within an instant, the black cloud filled the entire space of sky, and lightning shot down with a thunderous clap. All the grasses about me caught fire. The sea boiled and fumed; a torrent of spray from the huge waves crashing on the rocks smashed upon my body. My cloak was ripped from me, and I watched as it was swept up and disappeared into the thick clouds. All the golden symbols of the sun snapped from my leather tunic, and my helm blew off my brow. These, too, were sucked up into the sky.

"Then I heard a great rumbling from the sea, and I looked down, and saw a furious churning of foam. Suddenly a vast white shape began to bubble up from the deep waters, and burst out upon the surface. I strained my eyes – the precipice was nearly fifty feet high – and behold! A sleek white horse leapt from the waves, and stood on the sandy beach. It shook its ivory head, and green seaweed flew from its long white mane, and it stretched its lanky legs as though newly born to the earth's crust.

"It ran to the foot of the cliffs, just below me, and I watched as it made its way up the steep slopes. Sea foam crashed behind it, threatening to pull it back into the deeps. But the beast had colossal strength and kept climbing! Terror surged through me, and I tried desperately to stop it from reaching the top. I hurled rocks down, but they all missed their mark. I became desperate for a hiding place, yet there was nothing around me but burning grass.

"Then, its head and straining neck rose up over the cliff's edge, then followed by its strong chest, and then there it stood. Its limbs were trembling, and its eyes darted back and forth, head lifted high into the wind. It was looking for something, smelling – it was trying to find ME! I lay rigid upon the ground. The grasses burned, yet I felt them not. The great horse seemed to catch a scent on the wind, then took off with such amazing speed that it was instantly gone.

"I was sweating profusely, and felt the weakness of my near-naked state. I rose to my feet and wanted to return to my Castle. But I had no sense of direction. I found myself following the path of the white horse, I know not why."

King Vanamir, who had been leaning forward during his telling of his dream, sunk back into the cushions of his throne.

"Ah, Gamedon!" he sighed. "Even now the sweat breaks out upon my brow, and my limbs ache with the battling 'gainst the great winds! But I put it to you, Gamedon, who are well-versed in the magic working of dreams: See you not why I, immediately upon waking, saw Andalorax in my mind? This dream is a great trouble to me, therefore I cannot pass it by."

The old man began to speak but the King quickly raised his hand to silence him. "The dream came to me in my own bed chamber, upon my bed carved by hands endowed with magical powers – no dream that I may have there can be a deception! Nay, no matter how strongly I may wish otherwise, the dream was real!"

As the King narrated his dream, Gamedon's mind filled with thoughts that were so great in number and so vast in sequence that he could barely contain himself. He knotted his hands together, then rubbed them against his thighs, breathing heavily. When the King had finished, he remained silent for some time, then summoned forth his energy and said:

"My King, your dream is a great trouble to my own mind. Well do I know that the bed upon which you lay burdens us now with the fact that the dream is no idle nightmare." And he thought to himself, "Aye, I catch myself. 'Twas indeed a mare of the night!"

He continued. "And you wake to face my granddaughter, because she too is a white-haired creature."

Vanamir shook his head. "Nay, Gamedon. Not merely because she is white of hair. Come now, man, don't lead me to believe you know nothing of the ancient prophesies!"

"What prophesies I know of, my Lord, are ones spoken by those of my own birth-lands. I know naught of prophesies of the greater Kingdom."

Vanamir said nothing. He pulled his lips tightly against his teeth, and stared ahead at the stone floor and the tapestries thereon. Then he heaved a heavy sigh, and rose from his dais.

"I cannot unravel to you this night the legends which cluster about my throne," he said. "My energy wanes even as I stand before you now, and I try myself sorely by denying sleep. Yet I would leave you something with which you may unravel for yourself, and perhaps give me your wisdom and advice as to this matter."

He went over to the wall, pressing his thick finger against a tiny chip of golden tile. The tile moved gently from its place and he took it in his palm. There was a darkness where the tile had been, and into this darkness King Vanamir inserted his thumb and index finger. He slid them back out again. A frail gold key shone faintly between his fingers.

"This key, Gamedon," he said, holding the object at eye-level and gazing upon it, "is the key to a small room which adjoins the passageway at the left of the Eagle Door. If you search the seams and cracks in the stone walls, you will find the shape of a low doorway, and ultimately, the keyhole."

The King turned towards Gamedon and looked at his lengthy, gray beard, and the little green eyes shining from within wrinkle upon wrinkle, and he suddenly doubted his own sanity.

"Why do I seek advice from an old man?" he thought, and clutched the key to his breast.

Gamedon watched the eyes of his King, eyes that he had watched for fifteen long years. He placed his words carefully.

"If you would doubt my knowledge now, my Lord, I beg you to remember that you have always doubted! Yet I have never failed to give you of myself, of the powers for which I have worked so long and hard. I have seen the evil heart hidden by many a deceptive smile, and in such ways have I proved a valuable Minister. I have threaded with you the windings of many other dreams, and searched out their meanings. And if there is aught that I must know if I am to advise my King, I would beg to know it without delay. You speak of prophesies," he continued. "Ah, my Lord, the words of the prophets must be marked, and we must all struggle to fulfill our parts. Allow me to fulfill mine!"

The King smiled bitterly. "You know me well, old man, and know even better the words that woo me. So be it then! Here is the key. Find the hidden chamber, and within you will find the words of … nay, find what you will. I am too weary to speak further. I would see you when you are done. Good night."

King Vanamir strode from the room and pulled behind him a thick velvet curtain, disappearing into his bed chamber.

As Gamedon exited, the key now in his hand, he mused, "This key is so tiny. I wonder what great mysteries it will unveil for me."

CHAPTER 12

YESTERDAY, TODAY, AND TOMORROW

THE FOLLOWING DAY BLEW IN cool and cloudy, sunrise felt only as a white haze spreading across the sky. The Castle's morning bell tolled from the topmost regions of the mountain-hold. Life blinked open within the stone walls, reverberating the heralding of the day. The working-women started on their chores, lighting hearths, pulling back heavy curtains to let in the morning. And morning crept in, somewhat lazily this day, revealing the vast inner network of this, their home, the Pellah Castle.

The Knights and their ladies emerged from their sleeping quarters, filling the corridors and rooms with the echoes of heavy boots and fine silken slippers upon tiled floors. The kitchen women carried out their duties: cooking, feeding, and clearing the board. And the Knights, attired as befitted their various ranks, set out to take up the call of the day. Some went to relieve the night wardens; others were posted as sentries along all the levels of the Castle. Still others went to attend to the King; these were his private assembly of men. They were formed of three groups: the Twenty Eye-Men, the Twenty Men of the Teeth, and the Ten Men of the Coffers.

Soon, the rooms were filled solely with women. Not the common chore women, but the Knights' wives. Dressed in silken gowns and satin shoes, hair coiled and coiffed and twined with golden threads about their beautiful faces, they moved about with grace and leisure. Golden bracelets circled their slender wrists and sparkling gems from the Gold Mountains adorned their smooth fingers, as they sat down to embroidery with golden threads and needles. Some were studying illuminated manuscripts, while poems, arranging flowers, and occupations. others were reading novels and performing other mostly domestic occupations.

And in a separate, smaller turret on the northern flank of the Castle, the King's wives moved about in their own fashion. They kept to their domain, and mingled not with the world of the court. They rose with the bell's tolling; they dressed and prepared their meals; they set their quarters in order for the day. And there they remained, while the sun made its way overhead. Forever, the rustling of a satin gown, the humming of an ancient lullaby, the soft laughter and the muffled weeping could be heard stealing from an open window and drifting up into the skies.

And on this day, this cool, misty day, Andalorax stood at the very foot of this smaller turret, looking up, scanning the stones, listening, straining her ears. And suddenly, she smiled and laughed aloud: she'd heard it! It was so distinct! Although her life had given her neither time nor place for learning it, she knew in her heart the sound of her own mother's voice.

Mandir was laughing this morning, and how it sent light into the heart of her daughter, Andalorax.

But Mandir knew this not.

Andalorax turned from the turret, and headed for the forest.

Ah, but today would be a lovely day! She would go back to the trees; she would look for her many-colored friend. Her meeting with the King had almost caused her to forget the marvelous girl.

"But that was yesterday," she mused. "Today I shall forget that horrid King!"

As she walked, she passed a company of Knights on their way to the mines. They looked quickly from her, pressing the sun-discs embroidered upon their tunics as they crossed her path. This day they did not make her feel ashamed.

"Let them go down underground, and watch over the laboring there," she thought. "I'll not think on their hatred for me. I'll find my friend." She walked on, and was soon plunged into the forest, her heart beating quickly with anticipation.

Gamedon fitted the slender gold key into the keyhole, and the stone door heaved aside. A cloying odor rushed out; he had to leave the door open for several minutes before attempting to enter. As the vapors filtered out, he heard rats scurrying about inside. One, two, three minutes elapsed – and then he stepped over the threshold.

He found himself encompassed in a tiny space filled with all manner of lexica: folios, manuscripts, notebooks, archives, diaries, atlases. The candle flickered in his hand as he ran his finger from shelf to shelf. He put it down.

Slowly, the character of each book altered as the time they were written progressed. There were unbound parcels wrapped in heavy cords, followed by crudely bound leather ones. Then carved leather jackets appeared, in increasing length and width. Handsomely inlaid works appeared with thin, deckle-edged papers, the use of gold tooling becoming more frequent.

Gamedon reached up, and carefully slid a yellowed packet from a shelf. A light flurry of dust drifted down. He went over to an old, wooden block table in the center of the chamber, stood his candle upon it, and gently untied the wrapping cords. Edges of paper broke off beneath his fingers.

Borgan Pellah: My Dyarie

The words were set down in a large, sprawling hand. And added beneath them, more carefully spaced:

Pellah Yeares 1-7

Gamedon sat on the wooden chair, and turned the page.

> *My shyppe's Captyne, Ordau, handed me the Spye-glass,*
> *and lo! Before me was the Lande, the sweet fyrme Yrthe!*
> *My breste hyved, and I grypped Ordau's forearme.*
> *Pyce at laste! The Mercyfulle Sunne opens Lyfe to us*
> *yette agyn! To-morrow we shall lower sayle, and tuch*
> *shore. I spende my last nyte in thys lekyne hulke …*

Gamedon's head grew light and dizzy, and he gripped the edge of the table. The thought struck him like a flash of light: every recorded gesture, word, occurrence in the history of the Kingdom of Pellah stood silently in its allotted space along these four walls. The forward movement of time suddenly shifted and fell away from him, and the long corridor of the past stood endless before his mind. Vague silhouettes, formless ghosts, flitted in and out: visions of those long dead, who left behind for all to see the words of their minds and hearts.

"For me to see!" thought Gamedon, and the knowledge of the present time locked up with the appearance of the past and, having merged, they formed a clear vantage of the future. The nape hairs crawled along his scalp. The moment crystallized triangular in the room, and he felt himself standing along every spot of its perimeter. When he placed himself in this instant, he looked across and saw himself standing in the past, the leaves of yellowed parchment blowing past him as the leaves in autumn winds. And when he touched along the side that was the past, he perceived his body to be in the future. He was filled with the secrets, the words of despair and joy, and the consciousness of evolving life.

The candle dripped; a pool of melted wax widened and swelled. Outside, the full moon rose unseen.

Gamedon raised his head. His eyes roamed the centuries of words. Stacks of parchment, cloth, and leather – he stopped. The film of dust which lay over the books was missing on one row of volumes. Those volumes shone faintly with dull gold. "It seems that someone has been reading them," he thought, and knew that only one who held the tiny key could be that person. Vanamir! He got up and went over to them.

There were five books, neatly bound and tooled. He took down the first book. It was heavy. The leather was dark and smooth, and the gold lettering pressed deeply on its surface.

King Mundarak: Dreames
Pellah Yeares 257-321

Gamedon slid down the second book.

King Mundarak: Magycke and Sorcyrye
Pellah Yeares 260-321

The two books weighed much; Gamedon went and placed them on the table. Then he took down the third and fourth.

King Mundarak: Herbes and Medycynes
Pellah Yeares 260-321

King Mundarak: Legyndes
Pellah Yeares 275-321

These two volumes Gamedon also placed on the table. He went back over to the shelf, standing before the fifth book. Suddenly, he felt as if the book were almost waiting for him to touch it. It shimmered as if in a golden haze. He reached up and clasped it in his palm.

King Mundarak: Prophysyes
Pellah Yeares 275-321

Below the inscription, filling up most of the bottom half of the cover, a gold symbol had been stamped. It was the sign of the sun, ablaze with fiery rays, and it bore in its center an eye. Gamedon felt that eye looking back at him through the dust of many years, and he felt himself balanced once more on the trimorph of time. He knew at once that King Vanamir ("My present King," he thought), had read this book. Gamedon's hand went to his beard, and he stroked it, and he saw his shadow cast across the wall before him. It fluttered in the candlelight, dancing like some huge phantom in a sea of words. Gamedon laughed, and the sound of his voice made him laugh more.

"Aye, 'tis me!" he said aloud. "'Tis Gamedon and his shadow." His laughter steadied him. He went over to the table, placed the fifth volume before him upon it, and opened the cover.

The paper was yellow yet still supple. The first page bore the same symbol as the cover, an eye within a sun, and beneath it were the words:

Whosoever followeth myn Eye
Wyth hys lyfe's Bloode
Shalle sygnyfye.

Gamedon turned the page. The following sheet was splattered with patches of red-brown smears. Some of the dried blood had flaked off, and settled into the compressed binding.

Gamedon needed no time for thought. He unclasped the sun-disc from his breast and drew the sharp edge of a sunray along his left wrist. The blood swelled, and Gamedon raised his arm over the page. Two red drops fell upon the yellowed surface. He watched, waiting for the blood to dry, but to his surprise the drops dried the instant they touched the paper. He pressed his handkerchief to his small wound, and turned the page.

In dark, red-brown ink, in a long flowing hand, were the words:

> *From the grayve though callest me back-*
> *Speke the nayme of MUNDARAK!*
> *Vysyones shall I showe to thee*
> *Of pre-ordayned Eternytye.*

There was a still in the chamber that fell so swiftly, that Gamedon's heart quickened. He drew in his breath, and whispered:

"Mundarak!"

The candle flickered and sputtered; a raw wind blew into the room, swirling, massing over his head. A piercing chill ran through his bones. He heard breathing … long, drawn-out rasps of breath that carried with them a long, piteous wail. Gamedon looked about him. He saw no one.

And then a voice, reaching up from far, far away, called out:

"Aiee! Aiee! Who calls me from my rest?"

"Who speaks?" cried Gamedon. How his blood raced! A great moaning filled the air.

"Aahh! Oohh! Who calls King Mundarak from his peace?"

"Gamedon calls thee, King Mundarak!"

Grim laughter thundered in Gamedon's ears.

"Hah! Hah! Gamedon! I have seen thee, Gamedon! Hah! I can smell thy blood!"

Gamedon fought the fear that loomed up in his mind. He sought a foothold on sanity. The words of the opened book lay before him. He said:

> *From the grave I call you back!*
> *I speak the name of MUNDARAK!*
> *Visions shall you show to me*
> *Of preordained Eternity.*

The laughter roared on, then faded into silence. A sound of steady breathing hovered above Gamedon's head. And then it wailed mournfully.

"Aiee! Time! Shall it never know of death? Shall it never let me sleep?"

"You have the eyes to see, King Mundarak," whispered Gamedon. "Time shall never know of death."

A low hissing sound scratched the air.

"Why dost thou call me, old man?" came the voice, low and strong.

"To see what you have seen, Mundarak," answered Gamedon. "To mark the course of the Prophesies."

"Thou claimest the wisdom to follow my course?" came the now angry voice. "Thou seeketh to find thy place in Time?"

"You claim to have seen me, Mundarak," said Gamedon, and he looked down upon his body, his faded cloak and weathered boots, and thought: "Do I claim this power? An old man …."

"Look upon me, friend!" he cried. "I seek to find the Future, and the Future of our King Vanamir. I seek to find the Present and unravel the meaning of his dreams! I seek to claim the wisdom of the Past in your eyes and mine!"

The air grew warm and still, and the steady breathing returned.

"Thou shalt know of fear, Gamedon. Thou shalt know of death! Aahh! The memories fall down upon me. The burden of the Prophet never ceases."

"And the burden of one who follows the pointing finger – shall I know of that burden, King Mundarak?"

The voice moaned. "Aye, old man. Thou shalt know."

Gamedon closed his eyes, and took a deep breath.

"So be it," he said.

"So be it," returned the voice. "Turn towards my words, Gamedon. I shall project before thee all my visions as they appear. Only … I would warn thee! My powers cannot determine when a vision shall occur. 'Tis for thee to be the Marker of Time."

With great effort, Gamedon lifted his arm to the paper, bent his head to the writing, and turned the page.

CHAPTER 13

GAMEDON'S BURDEN

ANDALORAX GREW TIRED OF WAITING. She fidgeted, and rearranged her dress, studying her fingernails. Every now and then, she would call out for her many-colored friend. Not knowing her name, she cried, "Hello!" and "Where are you?" And "Andalorax looks for you!" But each time she did, even if she strained her ears, she heard not a whisper of response.

Ah, she was learning of impatience! She began to pout, and stomp the earth, and she cried out at last, "Show yourself, coward!" But nothing happened. Only the sun kept crossing the sky and, with growing heat, had begun to pierce through the hazy clouds. Patches of light shot down upon the forest floor, then faded away, then reappeared. And Andalorax soon became weary, and lay herself upon the warming grass and leaves, looking up at the treetops through half-closed eyelids. Soon she closed her eyes completely, and was deep in sleep.

She dreamed, and in her dreaming felt herself arise from her body upon the ground. She flew up and up into the sky, ever looking downwards at her sleeping form. Smaller and smaller that form grew, until it was just a tiny speck in a world of endless specks. There was the speck that was Andalorax; there was the speck that was the Castle; there were the specks that were the mountaintops; there was the liquid flowing of specks that was the vast sea. But nowhere was her many-colored friend ….

Wait! A shimmer of amethyst – no, topaz – traveled towards her sleeping form. It must be her! Andalorax swooped down to earth as fast as she could, and slipped back into her body, just in time to hear a tinkling voice breathe into her ear:

Call and call – I cannot come!
Of paths to me there is but One!

But you are slow! So here's a clue:
The Silent Lake knows what to do.

Quickly Andalorax jumped up and looked around, but the Many-Colored Girl was nowhere to be seen. "Was I dreaming?" she wondered. "'The Silent Lake' – what could that mean?" She felt so stupid. She thought and thought, but all she could guess was that the girl was speaking of the lake at the edge of the forest. She was annoyed that the girl had said that she was slow, and really wasn't quite sure whether or not she wanted to find this girl anymore. Still, she walked to the stream that ran through the forest, and began to follow it to reach the lake.

After an hour, Andalorax saw the trees thinning out, and she passed out of the forest.

Smooth as polished glass, the lake lay dark and obsidian blue before her. Down to the water's edge she went, and gazed upon the calm surface. Little long-legged water bugs skated over it, making the tiniest of ripples that quickly dissolved. The air was cool and sweet.

Suddenly, Andalorax recalled that she had been here before. Once, when just a baby at the Castle, her mother Mandir had carried her down to these waters. The vision of her mother's face, the scent of her hair, passed before Andalorax for a fleeting moment and was gone. "I like this place," she thought, and sat down upon a rock.

She wasn't exactly sure how long she had been sitting there, when she realized she hadn't heard a single sound during that whole time. The realization made her start, and she remembered: "The Silent Lake! Then this is the right place," she thought. But her white brows knitted together. "Now what am I supposed to do?" She tried to work it out logically: "If it is silent, then it cannot tell me what to do. So it must either show me, give me a scent, or I must touch or taste it."

She went over to the water's edge. The land sloped off sharply into it, making it abruptly deep. She crouched down, and dipped her hand. How cold the water was! She put her fingers to her tongue; they tasted sweet. She leaned her head down, and looked.

There was her own face, framed in its mass of white hair. Suddenly, ripples appeared, concentric rings expanding and blurring the image. Then it cleared, and the face of the Many-Colored Girl stared back at her. She was laughing! Then the girl opened her lips and said in sing-song:

Say the word that ends the game!
Tell me now: what is my name?

The answer came to Andalorax in a flash, and she sang back:

Girl of ever-changing hue,
"Water" is the name for you!

The face in the water scowled, and the hair blazed magenta. She said:

This game has now become a task!
Gamedon is the one to ask.

The face dissolved into ripples; Andalorax once again was peering down at herself. Jumping to her feet, she felt anger. This game had indeed become a task – she was so weary of it!

"I'll not ask my grandfather anything!" she called out. "You are so so disagreeable! I don't care if I never see you again!" She turned from the lake and headed back to the forest. The day was ending; she had to turn towards home if she was to arrive before sunset.

Later, after her dinner, Andalorax followed the inner ring of stairs that spiraled up through the innards of the Castle. They branched off continually into narrow passageways, leading to different regions inhabited by the Castle-folk. As she rose, step by step, her mind half-consciously noted what lay on each of those landings. She did this habitually, more out of necessity than idleness. Too often had she been surprised with sudden outbursts of mimicry and insult, with fear and hate. When she was a very little child and Gamedon had discovered this, he drew a plan for her of the Castle's anatomy, and Andalorax had sealed that plan into her memory.

"The King's quarters," her mind said, as she approached a landing carved of speckled granite guarded by two Knights-at-Arms. "The Halls of Harps," "The Halls of Children," her mind reeled off effortlessly. "The Halls of Elders" … she stopped.

The tunnel branched off to her left, curving out of sight. "Grandfather's quarters," she said to herself, and repeated aloud: "'Gamedon is the one to ask.'" She stood there, hesitating, then shook her head and continued up the stairs.

"Nay," she thought. "It grows late; the last bell has tolled and the Castle sleeps." But still, the words came back to her: "Gamedon is the one to ask." She glanced back. From this higher viewpoint she could follow the curve and see the carved doorway. "I'll just walk past his rooms," she thought, "and see if he sleeps."

The doorway to the Hall of Elders opened easily. She peeked her head into the space beyond; all was utterly silent. "The old courtiers and councilmen are in bed," she decided. The latch made a little "click!" as she closed the door behind her.

On tiptoe, she walked past a low green door, and a tall red one; past a doorway draped with a gauzy white cloth, past a yellow one that was an exact sphere. She followed the hallway until she came to a dark, sienna-toned doorway, framed with elaborate carvings of plants, vines, flowers and fruit. The door itself was carved by nature: the grain of the tree from which it was cut rippled along its surface. Knots and boles stuck out. Yet, time had worked upon it, for it was smooth to the touch.

In its center was a large golden knob, and Andalorax wrapped her hand around it, at the same time pressing her palm directly beneath it. There was no sound as the door slid wide open.

The small chamber was unlit, but the light shining in from the corridor faintly revealed a sitting chair by a cold hearth, books scattered everywhere, row upon row of bottles, jars ....

"Ssshh!" The door closed behind her. Darkness was complete, and she blinked her eyes.

"Grandfather!" she whispered. No answer came. She noticed a slit of light along the right-hand wall, indicating the seam of another doorway.

"So he is awake!" she thought, and smiled. In six steps, she had crossed the room.

"Grandfather," she repeated. Still no answer. Her hand fumbled for the latch and pressed it. The door creaked open.

Andalorax cried out at what she saw. The window shutters banged against the wall, and a fierce night wind tore past her at the canopied bed. Lantern-light leaped and flickered madly. Shadows flashed across the ceiling.

A figure lay sprawled upon the bed, arms thrown across its face.

"Gamedon!" Andalorax rushed to the bedside. "Grandfather!" Terror and panic filled her cry.

Slowly, the arms of the figure moved away, and the old, wrinkled face was uncovered. The eyes were forced open, and they fought to focus. Two green irises stared out at Andalorax. The old man threw his arms back across them, hiding.

"Aaahh!" he moaned. His chest rose and fell, as he breathed through his open mouth.

Andalorax ran to the open window and slammed it shut. The draped canopy fluttered and then hung limp. The light steadied.

"Aaahh!" wailed the figure on the bed. And then suddenly it struggled to sit up, turning sharply towards Andalorax. How the green eyes burned within the pale face! How they clashed with the blackness of her own! She began to tremble uncontrollably.

"Grandfather!" she called. "Are you ill? Has something happened? Oh, please don't stare at me so!" Tears rushed into her eyes, and she stumbled over to the bed, and sank to her knees, burying her face in her cloak.

The old man raised his hand, passing it across his eyes. "Andalorax ...." His voice was slow, so weary. "Andalorax, granddaughter, as if my own child ...." A great spasm shook his body and he floundered in the bed-folds like a ship lost in a tempest.

Andalorax raised her head.

"What happened, Grandfather? Your clothes are ripped and stained have you been outside ... in the night wind?" She whispered this, and her mind raced fresh with fear. "Has he been besieged by the stars? The open window! What perilous night spirits have filled the room?" She looked wildly about her, saw the disarray of scattered clothing, fallen books, broken glass ....

And suddenly, in the corner of her eye, she saw the Many-Colored Girl! She was smiling. Her eyes danced crystal blue, her hair rose in a frothy, purplish halo, and without opening her lips a song passed from her mind into that of Andalorax, and then she said:

Quickly! Take not overlong!
Sing the music of my song!

And Andalorax, still kneeling, stared ahead, and the words fell from her lips:

I call you, Gamedon, from the Pit,
Back to the bed whereon you sit.
The night is black, the moon is white!
Let terror vanish from your sight!

Gamedon's mind focused in his head, and he turned towards his granddaughter. His thoughts came clearly now, and he remembered where he was ("I am in my bedchamber," his mind repeated slowly), and where he had been ("I was in the … the Library!"). And he heard once more the words of his grandchild's song: "The night is black, the moon is white," and a stream of words faced him.

And there shalle comme a vaste Whytenesse,
And yn yts wayke the Eye of Blackness
Shall brynge the Storme.

"She knows who she is!" The thought flashed in his head. He reached out his hand, caressing the soft hair of her head, and thought: "But who is she? Who is this strange child, white of hair, black of eyes, like the moon and the night? What destiny has taken seed within her breast? Would that she does not have to face this alone …."

"Grandfather, are you better now?" Andalorax looked up at him.

"Aye, child," he answered, and he smiled and thought, "Nay, she shall not be alone in this!" Then he sank back on the bed, and passed into deep weariness, and fell asleep.

CHAPTER 14

GOLD IN THE ANTEROOM!

GAMEDON WALKED ALONG THE HALLS of the Elders and opened the door to his rooms and proceeded further to enter into his Laboratory. He turned and bolted the latch, then took off his old cloak. From his shirt he withdrew a small parcel, wrapped in crisp brown paper and tied with a thin cord. He lay it on his work desk.

Sunlight shone in through the open windows. It fell across the sitting-chair and the thick green hearth-rug. Gamedon went over to the windows, leaned out, then pulled them shut and drew the curtains. He lit a candle and placed it in the glass lantern, picked up the package, and, unbolting the door now, returned to his bedroom.

The disarray of last night's events after being in the Hall of Time had been brought into order. This morning, he had replaced the torn bed canopy, picked up the books and papers from the floor, smoothed the velvet quilt across clean sheets. He went over to the open windows there, and shut and draped them as well. Then he walked to the dresser, placing there the parcel and lantern, and stood for some minutes before the dressing mirror.

He watched his hands as they moved to the back of his neck, and his fingers untied a golden thread. Several odd-shaped keys dangled from the thread. Gamedon took one of frail solid gold between his fingers and slipped it off the thread. He retied the thread and placed it back over his head and under his cloak.

Turning from his reflection, he reached behind the mirror, and touched a tiny keyhole. The little key fitted snugly in the opening, and there was a sharp "click!" as he turned it in the lock.

Seams appeared along the stone wall. At the pressure of Gamedon's palm, a group of stone blocks moved back. He passed through the opening, parcel and lantern in hand.

The room he entered was filled with plants and herbs, giving off a thickly sweet aroma. Gamedon breathed deeply, and smiled. Large, recessed windows let in the bright sunlight. Bottles, jars, containers of all shapes and sizes sat on layers of shelves along one entire wall. At another wall stood a standing work-table, long and fairly wide. It was cluttered with more bottles and tubes, yet these were mostly filled with different colored liquids. There were heating lamps and bits of curved glass, metal tongs and clamps, basins and pitchers, piles of rags, and numerous other tools and equipment.

Gamedon cleared a space, set down the parcel and lantern, and began untying the cord. The gleam of a small chunk of solid gold was unveiled, shooting forth with such fierceness that an image came to Gamedon's mind, an image of an animal from the wilds which, kept for years in a windowless cage, is suddenly exposed to the light. He picked up the gold in his hand, lightly tossing it. It was the size of his little finger.

"Aye, ever playing the power game!" he said. "But you have no power over me." He laughed. "Gold, gold! You're beautiful. Pure and malleable … and necessary now. Shall we see what you can do for me?"

He tossed the shining metal chunk back upon the wrapping paper. Then he took the other keys from his neck. They jingled as he undid the knot in the golden thread. The key he slid off gleamed darkly. It was quite small and slender, with a looped handle.

Through the one open window, the sun burst out from behind a cloud and filled the room with hot light. On the wrapping paper, the chunk of raw gold bathed in the sudden glow. The little key in Gamedon's hand gleamed harshly, and instantly became white-hot, searing into his skin. He jerked back his arm. The key clattered to the stone floor.

Sweat broke out upon the old man's brow. He glanced furtively around the room, went over to the wide windows and peered outside. The treetops swayed in the breeze, stretching out to the horizon like a leafy sea. Gamedon's eye swept across the distance, and the blood rushed to his head, and he felt dizzy. Quickly, he swung his body around and faced the room once more. The sunlight had mellowed, and cool shadows played in and out among the bottles and plants and books.

Gamedon felt the tension in his body, and began breathing deeply and slowly. When he felt relaxed, he walked over to his work-desk and began assembling some tools and apparatus. He lit an oil lamp and placed it beneath a raised hotplate.

From a stack of various metal dishes he took a small one, and placed the gold nugget upon it, and placed the dish on the hotplate. For the next few minutes he was busily searching for and dusting off a set of thin pliable files. He lay these neatly across the tabletop, alongside a pair of metal tongs, a small broad-headed hammer, and a thick iron slab.

Then he picked up the key from the floor, as it had completely cooled off, and he lay it beside the slab. All the heat had gone out of it, and it was cool to the touch. Taking the necklace of keys in hand once again, he stooped beneath the desk and slid a small chest to the center of the room. He unlocked it with one of the keys, and lifted the lid with a "creak!"

The casket was snugly packed with leather folders, huge and tiny books, silk-wrapped bundles, some twisted pieces of dark brown wood lying here and there like nuts in a cake. Gamedon withdrew a leather case, and a hand-sized notebook bound in some bark-like material. Everything in the chest smelled old: old and musky and sweet.

But when Gamedon snapped the lid shut, the aroma quickly vanished, except for the gentle reminder arising from the case and notebook.

Gamedon opened the leather case he'd found in the casket, and ten shiny instruments lay inside, nestled in a bed of green velvet. There was a slender compass delicately balanced, some narrow capsules, a sharp-pointed tweezers, a round miniature magnifying-glass, a few sheets of metal punched with holes of rectangular, oval, square, and triangular and various other shapes. There was also a tapered tube, so slender at one end that it ended in a little wiry point exactly like the tail of a bee or the mouth of a hummingbird.

Gamedon lifted this tube out of the case, and put the case aside. He went to the work-desk, found a bottle filled with purplish liquid, and pulled out the stopper. The thick end of the tube he unscrewed, and it came off, and, using a funnel, he poured the liquid into the tube. Then he reassembled the object, shook it out very gently, and a bead of the purple liquid swelled out of the fine end. He plugged the bottle back up.

He took the small notebook in his hand. Turning past page after page of writing so fine and uniform that it was nearly impossible to distinguish one word or thought from the other but for the occasional diagrams and side-notes, the old man stopped when he reached a fresh sheet of blank paper. He took the metal tube in his left hand, and placed its point to the page, and began to write:

May the Twenty-Sixth, Year 1465. Castle Pellah.
My Laboratory. Notes on the copying of a key.

Gamedon closed his eyes for a minute, his eyelids twitching at first then lying still. Then he opened them, and went back to writing.

The gold heats. I shall temper it and carve out a key.
No time for molds. Also, the King must not find a mark
of mine upon his golden key ... Note: Pulse quickening,
skin tingling. Aye, I'm afraid! I plunge into the torrential
river and ride with the currents of choice, chance, and chaos ....

Gamedon laughed softly, and the sound of his laughter made him grin. His eyes sparkled like the shimmering sea. He looked towards the one open, large window, at the blue sky framed by his collection of plants. Something new, new and odd, shone in the corner of his eye. He moved his head.

"Is that a blossom I see?" he asked aloud, walking over to the greenery. "A blossom on the Phemtas plant?" He peered down, brushing aside a mass of hanging leaves and ivies, and lifted out a small pot.

The stem and leaves of the plant were pale and sickly, its edges tinged with brown. Yet, rising from its center was a bright yellow flower, its five wide petals partly open to reveal a cluster of fluffy orange pollen-caps.

"Aye, 'tis a Phemtas blossom," he mumbled. "A thing I have never seen. The dying plant puts forth her last flower, eh?"

He carried it back to the work table, and placed it at his right side, near the instruments and the melting gold.

"Ah, the gold!" he said, quickly turning to his left where the hotplate stood. He poked at the softening nugget with tongs, and turned down the flame, and went back to his notebook.

> *NOTE: The Herb of the Pellah Throne, Phemtas,*
> *blossomed for the first time before my eyes.*
> *Specimen is approximately six years old; was a very*
> *rare find in these parts of the Kingdom. Information*
> *is what I need! It is what I do not know that causes*
> *me such grief. Andalorax is chosen; this much is clear.*
>
> *But chosen for what?*
> *The key has already led me one step higher … nay,*
> *it was just the first step! Beginnings are such hard times …*
> *I want to read those books Andalorax must—*

A shadow moved across the page. Gamedon jerked his head up, letting out a quick "Oh!" The yellow flower had risen on its stem, and was curving out, reaching across the table. Gamedon watched with raised eyebrows. It glided slowly in front of him, past him, and stopped just before the hotplate. The five petals were larger now, and they glistened and shone with a hazy glow, fanning out and out like cold fingers extended before a warming fire. Gamedon did not move, but watched for some time in complete fascination.

He proceeded to write:

> *Here is a thing which I cannot understand. The flower*
> *reaches for the fire – or is it for the gold? Aha! The*
> *Herb of Kings, Flower of the Golden World, Royal Due*
> *of the land of Milorin – Ah, new secrets unfold to me*
> *in my hours of despair.*

Aloud, he said, "Let that be a lesson to you, old fool!" He laughed, yet tears stained his cheeks. "Do I make one golden key, only to find yet another? And another key to what? Aye, Gamedon, aye, you do! And you, little Phemtas flower, go on worshipping your gold. Don't mind me! Have your drink! Aye, there's plenty more, there's a mountain of it beneath this earth!"

He touched one of the yellow petals, and the flower instantly recoiled and folded up. "Aha!" said Gamedon. "It shrinks from my hand! I must make a note of that."

CHAPTER 15

MOON MUTATIONS

THE SUN BURNED HOT AND golden-white in the western sky, occasional clouds floating across it and making shadows that rolled slowly over the earth.

Gamedon walked through the forest that flanked the eastern borders of the Castle. He sniffed at the clean air.

He approached a cluster of small trees that ringed one enormous, spreading oak. At the base of it, he lay down his walking stick, and sat upon a thick protruding root. Straightening his posture, he lifted his head, and waited. From the distance he heard the muffled clanging of bells: "One! Two! Three!" The leaves rustled over his head.

"Three hours past noon," he said to himself. "Perhaps she missed my note?"

The sound of laughter rang above him. Gamedon looked up to see Andalorax perched upon a branch, her legs dangling.

"Andalorax!" he said. "I didn't see you!" And he thought: "And yet, she was right before me!"

"Aye, Grandfather!" laughed the girl, scrambling out of the tree and landing on her feet before him. "I was hiding from you."

And Gamedon thought: "Can she render herself invisible? What powers are growing within her?"

"Andalorax," he asked. "How do you do this thing, cause me not to see you when you are right there?"

"Why, Gamedon," she said. "That is something I have learned from you! I've watched you … blend in with things … melt into the background. It used to frighten me, when you'd suddenly appear out of nowhere. But then I worked at it, and discovered that all I had to do was tell my body to be absolutely, perfectly quiet."

Gamedon burst into laughter, and thought: "She's right! I must keep my mind clear, else I will start thinking that everything she does is a sign of her powers ...."

"Are you feeling stronger today, Grandfather?" asked Andalorax.

Gamedon turned to her. "And yet," he thought, "she has powers growing in her right this moment!"

"Aye, child. Last night's turmoil has passed."

"I am glad that you wanted to see me," she said, her eyes lighting up. "There are things I would ask of you. Do you remember, I had told you of a dream I had?"

"A dream?" he asked, trying to think back. "Ah, I remember. When I met you in the kitchen." And he mused in his mind: "How long ago that seems, yet it is but two days."

"Aye, in the kitchen," she said. "It troubles me, for I feel, although it must certainly be only a dream, that it was real."

"I would that you tell it to me, Andalorax. Yet, there are things that I would ask of you, and the day grows short."

"Then I'll tell it quickly!" she said, and sat down on the fallen oak leaves beside him. She unfolded the whole tale to Gamedon: Of the Many-Colored Girl, the riddles, the search for the strange girl's name, her sudden disappearance, and their second encounter at the Silent Lake. She stood up, moved her hands about in the air, and played the parts of both herself and the strange girl while she spoke.

Gamedon sat quietly on the tree root, watching, seemingly half-interested. But in his head his mind was noting everything. It raced along to ferret out possible connections to his own experience yester-eve in the Library with King Mundarak. He felt a burden, and that burden grew and grew as Andalorax spoke.

"Somehow," he thought, "it becomes more complex ... it all starts to fall into place. Somehow, she is a link." A mixed feeling of horror and elation spread within him.

When Andalorax narrated the final encounter with the girl, when she had seen her in Gamedon's bedchamber and had been given the words to speak to him, his eyebrows shot up, then knit together, and he repeated her words:

"Gamedon is the one to ask, eh?" And inwardly he wondered: "And how shall I give my answer? How can I tell her my suspicions ... that she is more than an 'accident' of nature ... how can I cut out her ignorance and inflict no pain?"

"Tell me, Grandfather," she said, "Who is this strange girl?"

"Does she ask of her friend," he thought, "or of herself? Does she know she asks of both? That they are one and the same?"

He answered, "You cannot guess?"

"Ah, Gamedon," she pouted. "Will you also think me stupid? I wish I knew – she said you would tell me. Don't you know?" She looked up at him despondently. "Ah, maybe you don't. How I am growing tired of this mystery!"

"Let us see, my child. How did the first riddle go?" Gamedon looked up at the sky and said:

Night-black, Moon-white

He thought: "Nay, she knows nothing, nothing at all. And how could she know, when she has never been told of the moments of her birth?"

"Aye, Grandfather," returned Andalorax. "That's how it went. Yet I cannot see how she could be either black or white, when she changed into so many colors."

Gamedon went on:

It came a-crying in the night.

A memory arose before his eyes: of him searching the woods in the nighttime, finding Mandir lying against a tree, her newborn baby crying at her breast, the full moon sailing through the sky ….

"Andalorax," he said softly. "Andalorax, the Many-Colored Girl …" and the thought raged through his mind: "Tell her quickly! Out with it!"

"The Many-Colored Girl is YOU!"

"Me?" She leapt to her feet. "Why, Gamedon, what are you saying? I am not as splendid as she! She is every beautiful color! I am only white-haired, black-eyed –" Suddenly her mind focused: "Night-black, moon white." She turned the words over in her thoughts.

"Your name, Andalorax, in the ancient tongue, means precisely that: Night-black, moon-white."

"My name?" she murmured. "Yet how can she be me, or I be her, when I am but one person? I don't understand, Gamedon!" She burst into tears.

Gamedon stroked her long tresses, and thought: "Let her weep. Let her know the ease of tears. She is but a child."

After a while, Gamedon said gently, "Andalorax, if you would understand this, and all daydreams, night-dreams, thoughts and fantasies that come to you, you must always keep in mind who you are, what your life has been up to that point."

"You mean, that I am a freak?" she said.

"Aye, I know well that many would use that term," said Gamedon, searching her face for fresh tears, but they didn't come. "You must not forget that you are a child who has known loneliness. Does it seem so astonishing to you that you would create a playmate, a friend?"

"Nay, Gamedon," she answered. "I … I think I understand now. It was a dream." She wiped her tear-streaked face.

He thought, "Don't stop here. The road does not end here."

"What I want to know," he went on, "is why your creation looked as she did. It would seem that you would have designed her to look like you, yet she was all but black and white."

Andalorax nodded her head. "I, too, Gamedon, don't know why. It just seemed to … to happen that way."

Gamedon turned his question over in his mind, then shook his head. "If you did not seek to create her thus, then why?" Suddenly he jerked his head around and their eyes met.

"It happened of its own accord."

The words fell softly from his lips, and echoed in the pause of silence. "As if this part of you … as if it has a will of its own. As if it were a … a power."

The memory of his own quest rose before him.

"Old man, you wished to see Andalorax," he thought, "through the eyes of one who has seen the Prophesies. Now you look, but can you see? Is this a true sign that there be powers sleeping – nay, awakening! – within her?"

"Andalorax, I …." He stared at her, trying to verbalize his thoughts. "There are things … that I must tell you."

"Where do I start?" he asked himself.

"There are things … I should have told you sooner. About your birth. The night you were born … under the full moon!"

"The night?" Andalorax looked back at him, trying to think clearly. "I was born in the night? Under the full moon?" A shudder ran through her as visions came: a blackness so vast, so infinite; the stars burning white, flickering like ageless eyes through space; and riding through the utter blackness, the moon – round, full, white. A powerful Queen, terrifying in her absolute supremacy. Yet somehow, it seemed to Andalorax, somehow she was also gentle and comforting.

Andalorax looked up towards the sun, and thought: "Even as I watch you, you slip away from me, and the moon rises at my back." A strange wave of distance, of separation passed through her, and the sounds of the forest drifted from her ears. She felt as if she were no longer seated there, in the point of space she had always occupied. In some way, she had shifted to another point, to many points. And she could see from every point of view.

She saw her grandfather, sitting on the tree root, and saw the weight of confusion on his face. "Gamedon," she said, putting her hand upon his brown, wrinkled cheeks. "You fear that you bring me pain. There is pain, somewhere. I cannot locate it exactly. Yet I feel happy! Mystification is far more grievous than the truth. All that you would tell me, I would know. All about being born, all about the moon. You will tell me, won't you? Indeed, it makes me feel better. Sort of … special. The other children, they are of the sun. But I, I am of the moon!"

"There is far more to tell than the story of your birth, Andalorax." Gamedon took her hand between his palms. And he thought: "There is far more that I must learn as well."

Gamedon told her the story of her birth, outdoors in the Calicab Forest, under a full moon. He told her of finding his daughter Mandir leaning against a wide-spreading tree, smiling and feeding her white-haired babe. He knew then for certain that his longtime supposition was true: there was nothing evil in the nighttime, for look what it had brought to Mandir and to him. True, the child was different, but he was instantly in love with her. No matter the color of her hair and eyes.

Gamedon paused and sighed deeply. Their eyes met.

"We must know of time, Gamedon," said Andalorax. And they sat there awhile without speaking, listening to the chirping birds and the wind in the leaves, watching as the westering sun sent long shafts of light through the trees. Andalorax closed her eyes, and whispered to herself: "Do you listen, Many-Colored Girl? I know who you are! You're me!"

And a voice laughed softly within her, and sang:

White-haired girl, your words are true
But now, I wonder, who are you?

"You lie!" The voice thundered down from the golden throne and crashed upon the polished floor. "You lie, else you are an utter fool! I tell you, old man, I'll not cradle your sting against my breast. Look up at me, snake, when I speak to you!"

Gamedon raised his head and met the King's blazing stare. All the gold in the room flamed in the hot wrath. Gamedon said: "I have done as requested—"

"As ORDERED!" yelled the King.

"Aye, I have done as ordered, Sire," continued Gamedon, fighting the tension knotting inside him. "I have read the Prophesies. Perhaps there were other books I overlooked—"

"Nay, nay," interrupted Vanamir, waving his hand abruptly before him. "You have read the book of Mundarak; there is none else."

Gamedon went on. "Perhaps I am not endowed with the power to see beyond what visions I was shown. You must remember that I am not a King."

Vanamir snickered. "You humble yourself overmuch, and underestimate my acquaintance with flattery. Yet it is so, you are not a King. Perhaps you made your exit from that room knowing no more than when you entered. But your former counsels to me have shown no lack of perception."

"I have never dealt in prophesies, my Lord," said Gamedon. "I have never dealt in aught save my own mind."

The King stood up, and strode down from his throne. His richly embroidered cloak swirled in bright green folds about him. Golden rings adorned with precious gems mined from the Gold Mountains adjacent to his Castle flashed on all his ten fingers. Gamedon held his back straight against the chair, concentrating on his breathing. A little gold key pressed against his heart. The King was at his side, and he leaned over and hissed these words into Gamedon's ear:

Harke! There be a growynge Fuyrie in the Sowthe, and
Blacke Trumpettes calleth oute 'Sevyntyne.' The Sea
boyleth and swelleth. A gyante whyte-crestyd wayve
poureth downe upon the Eagyl. Alas! The Days of Doome!

The King straightened himself up.

"Do you recall those words, Gamedon?" he asked.

"Aye, my Lord," answered Gamedon. An odd thought crossed his mind: "He does not know the ancient tongue in the Prophesies of Mundarak. His speech falters with the accent."

"Well do I know Mundarak's words," returned the King. "I want to know what you think of them. This I am most curious to hear."

Gamedon said: "My Lord, my first thought was to the number 'seventeen,' knowing that you are the seventeenth King of Pellah."

"Ah, so here you would not deny me my suspicions!" cried Vanamir. "What else?"

"Yet I also turned my thoughts to the words, 'Day of Doom.' I concluded that, rather than referring to you, the Day of Doom would fall on the seventeenth day of either a month or year."

Vanamir's eyes squinted, and he stroked his beard. "This may be so. Mundarak sees the destruction of the reign. According to you, it may not necessarily fall upon me, but upon some other future King on the appointed seventeenth day."

Gamedon nodded. "Precisely, my Lord."

Vanamir smashed his fist down upon the table before him.

"Do you take me for an idiot?" he roared, pacing back and forth. "There are many other allusions to me, and to my being the last King in the Pellah reign. Why do you persist in twisting the words of Mundarak's Prophesies?"

"Indeed, my King," answered Gamedon. "There were other signs that brought you to my mind. Yet they could all, if one kept an open mind, be interpreted in other fashions. Just as the one you quoted."

And inwardly he said: "I must hold firm. I must try and believe what I am saying."

"And, Gamedon," said Vanamir, walking back to his throne and seating himself, "what of '*The Sea boyleth and swelleth.*'?" The same cracked grin formed around his words.

"Here I was reminded of your dream, my Lord," said Gamedon. "The sea raged in it as it does in the prophesy. This was a great point of unrest for me, for it seemed clear that you dreamed of that very Day of Doom, and saw yourself in it."

"Why, Gamedon, how nice of you!" snickered the King. "This is precisely my point."

Gamedon looked at him, watched how the cheeks trembled as he spoke. "He grows fat," he fancied.

"And yet," said Gamedon.

"Ah, indeed, of course!" mimicked the King: "'And yet'?"

"The words of Mundarak do not stop at this. He also wrote:

Alas! The Daye of Doome! Yet none shall see it
rysynge fromme the Sea, for the eyes turneth Sowthe.

"In your dream you saw the sea. Mundarak says that none shall see the wave of doom. I believe you trouble yourself for naught, my King. Your dream was of other matters."

King Vanamir scowled, yet said nothing. Gamedon searched the regent's face, hoping to find there signs that the meeting would soon end. He was tired of putting on this show for Vanamir.

Yet, Vanamir spoke again.

"And what do you think these 'other matters' to be?" he asked.

"I think, Sire," replied Gamedon, "That you fear as you have not yet produced a son and heir."

Suddenly he saw Mandir's face in his mind, his daughter who had birthed Andalorax under the light of the full moon and still lived in the faraway turret with the King's other wives. He wondered if she was thinking of him this very moment ....

"This is not my fault!" cried out Vanamir, clenching his fists. "For years now, since I became King, the women have progressively failed me. All they bring into this world is girls, and more girls! And after they have singly given me their pretty, pink daughters, they go stale on me. Their wombs simply cannot bear another fruit." He pouted.

"My wives last but one season in the royal bed. I must go and plant another tree, to put it metaphorically, old man."

Gamedon and Vanamir sat in silence for a moment. Each man simultaneously had the vision of the Turret of the Wives in his mind. Gamedon wondered why he didn't see a moment such as this in Mundarak's visions.

"But he did see Mandir's daughter, Andalorax," he thought, "and that was largest of all his prophetic images."

"Aye, I fear for my reign!" continued Vanamir. "I have yet to see a son, a strong-chested lad who can grasp the scepter … not a mewling, scrawny female …."

Suddenly Vanamir stopped. His eyes darted towards Gamedon, who was quietly listening and watching.

"I speak that which it is beyond wisdom to reveal. Forget what I have said, old man," said the King. "What was it we were … ah, the dream … other matters … a son. Ha! That is no great worry! One day I shall have a son, as did all Kings before me. Nay, Gamedon. I believe you know what lies upon my mind. I told it to you after relating the dream. What is it, then? I'll tell you: it is your granddaughter, Andalorax."

Gamedon pulled air into his chest.

"Here it is," he thought, and said, "Andalorax."

His response sucked the air out of the room.

"Aye, Andalorax," continued the King. "For what is the white sea-horse that searched for me, sniffed for my blood, but that white-haired girl? And what is she, but the '*whyte-crestyd wayve*'?"

Gamedon struggled for an answer. "My King, I –"

Vanamir cut him off with a sharp wave of his hand. "No more, Gamedon. I do not wish to be counselled out of this belief … Gamedon, I have toyed with the idea of killing her."

The old man's face paled. He didn't move a muscle.

Vanamir saw this, and a grim smile flickered on his face. "Yet I am not so powerless that I cannot out-devise my would-be undoing. I am King Vanamir, after all!" He tapped his chest, and went on.

"Yes, she is to live, yet she is to be kept forever in the chains of ignorance and isolation. After all, Gamedon, what is she but a freak of nature, a mistake? And a girl at that! Her growing shall be in body only. Her freedoms of movement are henceforth to be severely restricted, and watched."

Gamedon sat in silence still.

"Do you hear me, old man?"

Gamedon, staring blankly at the King, said "Aye, aye, my Lord. I hear you."

The King ran his fingers through his beard, his green eyes sparkling as he devised his plans. "Aye, gardening is fine. She may continue in that. Swimming is forbidden.

Embroidering – why, I shall put her to work in the Spinner's Workshops! Nay, she would have too much communication with the rest of our Kingdom. In women's circles there is so much chatter and gossip! Nay! None shall speak with her.

"I must also not forget that her appearance is on my side in this! Ah, poor creature. None will be her friend. None, save the King.

"She shall come to me often, that she may pour out her heart to my commiserate ears. I shall be there to study the passage of her growing, and I shall prune and snip accordingly."

King Vanamir leaned forward and peered down at the old man. "I am afraid, Gamedon," he said slowly, "that your connections with her shall henceforth be almost completely severed." Vanamir put his face against the old man's ear.

"Why, Gamedon," he whispered, "what ails you?"

The King watched flashes of pain cross Gamedon's face. The old man's eyes were half-closed, his breath came heavily yet he struggled to regulate it. His hands lay limp across his knees.

"Gamedon!" snapped Vanamir. "Answer me!"

The old man slowly lifted his head, opened his eyes somewhat, and the green flicker of his eyes focused on the King. His stare was so fixed, so sharp, that Vanamir felt himself unwittingly responding.

They glared at one another: Gamedon, small and wizened; King Vanamir, bristling in the kindling golden light. Hatred filled Gamedon's body, and he felt himself swelling and growing with it.

But a thought rushed through his mind, words he had spoken to his daughter fifteen years earlier when she was taken from Milorin to be the latest wife of the King. The words were ringing clear:

"Hate is a bitter ally, too easily made, impossible to get rid of. Hate will avail naught. Pity this King!"

He turned his gaze away, and Vanamir unlocked his own, leaning back on his carved throne. And Gamedon thought, "Aye, pity this King, who thinks to stem the tide of Fate with his two hands. How hard shall he fall! How deep shall he sink!"

Vanamir regained his composure. "I can forgive your little play, old man," he said, fingering his rings. "She is your granddaughter, and the daughter of one of my wives. You doubtless feel great sorrow for her miserable state. I, too, must admit that I feel sorry for her whenever I think of her wretched, unalterable appearance.

"But come now, man, cheer up! I shall not be cruel with her. And I have no intension of dismissing you from your counsels with her in other matters."

"Well now, it is determined. I shall attend to the details myself, so you can rest assured she will not … ah, she will not find you responsible. Your hands are clean."

"Aye, my Lord," Gamedon repeated softly. "My hands are clean."

"Exactly, Gamedon!" laughed the King. He rose from his throne, and drew his cloak about him. Gold spangles shimmered on the rich cloth. "Well, then, I believe there is naught else I would speak of with you. My dream falls away from me, and I am content with my plan. You may go now, Gamedon."

Gamedon slowly raised himself to his feet from the small bench before the throne. His legs ached.

"I believe you have forgotten something, my King."

He reached into his cloak and took something from an inner pocket.

"The key to your Library."

He held the tiny golden key in his palm, and it shone fully in the chamber.

King Vanamir stepped down and grabbed it with his thick hand.

"Aye, the key!" he laughed. "I would not have this key long in another's hand. Also, I intend to return to my Library and learn more about the dangers foreshadowed by that white-haired child." He put the key atop his nearby nightstand.

"Thank you, Gamedon."

Gamedon nodded slightly, and said, "Aye, my Lord. Good night." He turned and opened the door.

The new gold key, a precious copy of the King's original, pressed against his breast, and he thought:

"So begins the deception," as the door closed silently behind him.

CHAPTER 16

LOYALTIES AND DECEPTIONS

GAMEDON'S HAND SHOOK NOT AS he held aloft his lantern, despite the sudden darkness he found himself within when he shut the Eagle door behind him.

"The King would have me do a great many things of which I do not approve," he thought. His brow became furrowed. But soon he could see well, as his eyes became accustomed to the lanterns and candles snugly posted along the walls within the circular staircase that snaked through this, the central turret of Castle Pellah.

He lifted his wrinkled old head and sniffed the cool, damp air of the stones on the floor, the walls, the ceiling. He reached one hand out and ran it across the rich, dark woodwork of lumber from the Calicab Forest outside Milorin. The timbers, the doorways, and the rafters along the ceilings adorned the otherwise somber stairway.

Presently he came upon the door to his own quarters, and entered a large room. This was his living area. He went from place to place, lighting several oil lamps, and some thick, scented candles that he himself made for his pleasure in his Laboratory behind the doorway – now closed and locked for the night – at the other end.

He walked over to a niche in the large room. It held books from floor to ceiling and along three walls, which formed his Library. In the middle of it was a leather-tooled reading table aside a leather reading chair. The bergamot-scented candle thereon, he lit. He sat down in the chair with a sigh, and put his feet on the nearby embroidered footstool. He looked at the books around him, which gave him immense peace all at once, and he sighed again, and closed his eyes.

"Priorities," he said aloud. "I must itemize my list." He raised his right index finger into the air, keeping his eyes closed as he thought out loud.

"Andalorax. Number one," he stated. "Always." Then, holding his finger aloft for a minute, he swiftly raised a second finger and said: "Mandir. Number two." His third finger then flew to another point in the air and he said: "The People of our Kingdom of Pellah. Number three."

Then he dropped his hand back in his lap and opened his eyes. He looked down at his long-worn wool pants and vest, his checkered jacket with the velvet collar, his well-worn but heavy leather sandals. He realized he was quite warm, and he hadn't changed his outfit since he'd woken up that morning and made a copy of a golden key… all day long, in fact, until late in the evening after he returned to the King his little original golden key.

"I'm tired."

With those words, he lay back in the ample leather chair, closed his eyes once more and gave another sigh, and fell into an immediate, deep sleep.

The very next day, Gamedon wasted no time from the moment he opened his eyes to the sputtering candlelight in his little Library. He reached over and unlaced his sandals, putting on maroon leather slippers from under his chair that were shining with wear. Standing up, he threw off his jacket and vest, revealing his thick, striped suspenders.

"Andalorax," said the old man out loud to himself, "you are not prepared properly yet, not for this perilous journey, my dear grandchild …." He stopped for a moment. He imagined her, with her flowing white locks and coal-black irises – they called her "freak!" – and he knew how unprepared she truly was. She knew nothing of what the ancient King Mundarak had shown him, pointing to the Day of Doom for the current King, and showing that she had a part to play in that day – a major part whose significance she would only be able to grasp when that day will have, overnight, just passed.

"Nay, Gamedon," he continued, as he began to sort through his clothing and personal items, placing them one by one in a large leather backpack. "She does not know enough, and that's your fault! She knows nothing of the secrets of King Vanamir, and of his vile plotting to keep her as impotent as possible. Disempowered and just a little girl of fifteen years …." His voice trailed off as he imagined all the things he could have told her. The meaning of her birth under the full moon and out-of-doors. The wondering of who was her father …. For that matter, who indeed was her own mother Mandir, and why is she over in that Turret of the Wives with a series of other queens?

What, too, of her powers to make herself invisible to others, to meld into the background like a chameleon?

"Aye, old fool. She said she learned that from me," he mused aloud, scratching his beard as he packed. "I certainly never taught her how to do that, so she must have picked it up by watching me and learning. And yet she know nothing! You should have told her all this much sooner but it's too late now ...."

Leaving his half-filled backpack open, with bits of clothing strewn about it, Gamedon went and unlocked the door to his Laboratory. The key to it hung from his neck on the golden chain, which had been forged of purest gold which came down from the Golden Mountains that made up stronghold of Castle Pellah. From that chain dangled a total of seven keys, to various hiding spots of both his and of the King's, for Gamedon was an able Minister and Vanamir had great faith and trust in him.

Slipping the chain over his head, he held one of the hanging gold keys and pushed it into the door's keyhole. Doing so, he entered the very room in which he had, just this morning, forged the key to the King's Library.

"And there it lies, pressed against my heart," he mused. "I thought to have access to the continued words of King Mundarak, and learn more of his prophesies. Yet now, it is of no use, for we must flee!"

The sound of that simple word made his skin crawl.

"Yes, old man," he stopped as he went on to speak out loud, "you must get that girl and flee, under cover of darkness and in the light of the stars and moon, before which all the King's guards stand terrified. And you must achieve this whether she be ready or not."

He knew that Andalorax and he shared no such notions of fear of the night. The entire Kingdom thought otherwise. But Gamedon and Andalorax were equally at home with the night as with the day. Still, however, she knew not of her moonlit birth, only what he had told her just that same day.

"One day very soon," he said to himself, "when we are not running anymore, I shall tell her the details." He paused.

"We shall follow the Golden River," he announced, "of which I know as far as the Golden Woods. Once safe in those woods, we shall be free. Not even the King's brave Twenty Men of the Eyes venture there, and surely never at dark! And most certainly not the King himself!"

Gamedon laughed, but he knew he had to hurry in the Laboratory, and take only the most precious objects with him – wondering if he would ever return to this place again. He suddenly imagined for one second that Andalorax might one day come here .... But he shook his head at the thought and continued packing for their escape. Still, however, he touched another fragile key – the one to the King's Library that hung from the chain under his shirt.

"My scissors and knives," Gamedon whispered to himself, going through his huge assortment of stuff. "A long rope made by the King's workmen, my medicine kit, my chain mail vest ...."

He turned to the Phemtas plant and there in all its golden glory was that flower, the herb of King Vanamir, still shining so brightly after finding its way to gold.

"Just this morning, old man! Just this morning ...."

CHAPTER 17

ESCAPE

"BUT GRANDFATHER, WHY MUST WE leave? And why tonight?" Andalorax sat up on her bed and looked up at Gamedon, who was pacing back and forth in front of her.

"You must trust me, Andalorax. My dear, my only grandchild, of course you must have complete faith that I am doing this to protect you."

"Protect me? From what? From whom?"

Gamedon sat down beside her on the bed and turned her head so that she and he were staring into each other's eyes. His irises, emerald green; hers, coal black.

"From the King. From Lord Vanamir, my child."

"But, what happened?" she asked. "Did I displease him yesterday when he summoned me to his quarters? Besides, what do I take with me – I have so many things all about me! Protect me? Oh, I am terrified! "And she threw her pale arms around him and began to cry.

"Nay, Andalorax. Be not afraid." He stood up, pulling her up out of bed. "We have very little time if we are to leave at sunset."

"Sunset?" cried out the girl.

"Ssh! Quiet now! Aye, aye, my child. I will help you. Now, bring me your largest carrying bag – no, bring all your bags out so I may decide which is best for a long, quick flight from the Castle and towards the shadows of the Golden Woods."

"The Golden Woods!" she cried, once more wrapping her arms about him. They stood there, the fifteen-year-old girl – as tall as the old man – and Gamedon, who quietly began going through her closets while she brought out three carrying bags.

Gamedon chose two, and immediately began to roll up what he had taken out of his granddaughter's armoires and dressers: two deeply hooded capes (a third was kept out for her use that night), two pairs of walking trousers, a pair of sturdy leather walking boots (the second pair he kept, again, for that night), socks, woolen undergarments, a black woolen cap, and gloves and other items, "for being on the run, my dear Andalorax," he said to the girl, still in tears.

"Now, now, you must pull yourself together and do as I say. Also, please try to understand. We must escape tonight. That is my final word on the matter. I will tell you why once we are safely in the Golden Woods."

She shuddered visibly.

"You know very well," he went on, stopping his work to hold her gently for a moment, "that we shall be able to make our way across the plains and fields and reach the forests. We're a couple of 'naturalists,' we are, dear child! Now, get together the following." And then he rattled off a list of about ten items, each one of which she retrieved and he placed snugly in her bag, which, like his, was more of a backpack with its double straps.

As they worked, the sun made its way through the open windows in Andalorax's room. A slight breeze blew the white lace curtains there, curtains made by her mother, Mandir.

"And what of my mother?" she said to Gamedon, as she handed him her binoculars. "Are we taking her with us? Will I meet her again at last? I only get to see her on my birthday, you know, Grandfather."

"Nay, Mandir shall have to stay. She is not involved in this quest we are on."

"Quest? Why do you call it a Quest? What are we seeking?"

Gamedon didn't know how to answer her. "How do I say," he wondered, "you are predestined to figure in the history of the Kingdom of Pellah? Your coming has been foretold!" He looked into her face and remembered King Mundarak's prophesies, and sighed.

"But what do I know about the future and what role she will play during her lifetime?"

So he answered her, "A Quest that we are already on, dear child. From the moment of your birth."

"My birth? What of my birth?"

He looked her straight in the eye and blurted out the truth for the second time: "As I told you, you were born under the full moon, Andalorax. Yes, in the nighttime. Under the stars. That is the meaning of your name in the ancient tongue: 'Night-

Black, Moon-White.'"

"You mean, being born like that is why I have white hair and black eyes?"

"Very possibly, my child," Gamedon said as he kept looking into her coal-colored irises.

Andalorax looked back at him, then up at the sky. Soon it would be twilight, and the Castle's windows all be shut to the outside.

"And is that why I'm not afraid of the dark, and the moonlight, and the stars? Because of my birth?"

"I'm quite certain, but I cannot say beyond every doubt, my dear."

"Then why are you, Grandfather, not afraid either? You have the red hair and green eyes of the people of Pellah. Yet I know you do not share their beliefs."

Gamedon turned and looked into the horizon, which was only as far as the open window in Andalorax's bedchamber. Again, he wondered how to tell her.

"There's only one way," he reasoned. "Out with it, old fool!

And so he said, boldly, "I will tell you the truth, child. I am not afraid because there is no reason to be afraid. The night isn't inhabited by evil. It is a made-up myth … designed, most likely, by the ancient Kings of Pellah. To keep their subjects – people all over the Kingdom – in line, obedient, and easily made afraid. To be their superiors and not have their reign threatened. To stay in power!"

Gamedon raised his fist. Andalorax stared at him, and when he made such a movement with his arm, she saw a bright gleam in his eyes that shone out like a beacon.

"Grandfather," she said, trembling with alarm, "why do you say this? Isn't it against the Pellah laws and beliefs?"

"Aye, Andalorax. It is. And that is the reason for my banishment years ago before you were born."

Gamedon, seemingly to snap out of a trance, sharply added, "Now, back to work and the game at hand, dear child. We leave at sunset when we shall not be bothered and discovered. Things would not go well with us if we are.

"And please remember above all to use your ability to blend into the background, as you have learned from watching me."

Andalorax sighed, and went back to her packing.

"Of course, grandfather. I do it practically all the time anyway!"

And so it went that these two small creatures, wrapped in their floor-length hooded capes, made their way along the steps of the Castle's innermost ring. Carrying two sacks each and a walking-stick that Andalorax felt was her lucky charm – "or perhaps even magic!"— and wearing their backpacks, they felt their way along the inner wall as they wound their way down, down … down to where they were at last on the ground floor. Gamedon could smell the earth.

Bypassing guards who stood at attention all along the hallways, Gamedon and Andalorax sidled their way along the walls unseen. When they reached the bridge across the moat, they were relieved to see that it was down. Soon they were able to cautiously make their way along the side of the wooden structure.

At first it seemed that none of the guards saw them as they made their final steps out of the Castle, but a loud uproar put that thought to an end. Thundering across the parapet of the Castle walls was the sound of horses pounding athwart the cobblestones. Gamedon was sure he could smell the snorting breath of the huge, four-legged beasts and the crashing of their armored body plates against each other.

Gamedon saw them heading quickly for the moat bridge and knew in an instant – because he was so familiar with the mind and meaning of the King – exactly who was coming for them: Vanamir's own special guards! Sure enough, after hearing the great clamor and pounding of hooves, the old man saw that he was not mistaken. The Twenty Men of the Eyes coursed freely along the pavement, followed by the Twenty Men of the Teeth.

"Close the bridge!" cried out the first Eyeman, the huge and maleficent Malthor. "Prisoners are escaping! Close the bridge and secure the moat!" His terrible yell rang out and was carried swiftly to the ears of the moat guards who were lined up along the bridge palisades.

Malthor, still in hot pursuit of the two escapees, pulled his bow and fitted its shaft with an arrow. His nineteen followers did precisely the same, all in unison. They came charging, arrows at the ready, towards the moat guards. Following directly behind, the Twenty Men of the Teeth bared their lips and shone their golden tines to the dark night air. How they glistened with their frightful smiles!

"Andalorax," whispered Gamedon in a tiny voice, "you must work your hardest this very moment to render yourself invisible! You must blend into the wooden passage and we must continue to cross the bridge!"

"Yes, Grandfather," came her timid voice. "We are almost across. I am doing as you ask."

Gamedon was pleased to note that, as he darted his eyes behind him, he himself could hardly pick up a vision of his granddaughter. Perhaps they would succeed ….

The two of them pressed more firmly against the timbers and their cloaks and knapsacks were wrapped closely against their small bodies as they fled onwards. They advanced as urgently as possible, brushing against the wooden structure like feathers touching a sleeping giant who did not awaken – at least not yet!

"Keep moving!" said Gamedon. "We must run for our lives to cross the waters while the bridge is up, and reach the lands of Pellah and the safety of the open fields! Night is here and I do not know if the Knights shall cross as we do. Hurry, girl!"

They made not a sound as their stealthy movements took them to the end of the bridge. But Gamedon could hear the sounds of the bridge gears going into action, and the heavy metal chains being rolled up to raise it and close off their sole means of escape from the Castle.

Suddenly the clamor of the Knights ceased at their approach to the link across the moat. "So they would not be crossing after all," thought Gamedon. "Perhaps we shall make it safely across!"

As they reached the end of the bridge, it began to lift vertically – but not before the two travelers leapt across and landed hard upon the grasses of the fields. It was indeed a miracle that they were unseen by the able and aggressive Knights.

"Aha!" said Gamedon in hushed tones. "They are afraid of the blackness of the night, and the presence of the stars in the heavens."

They still had to maintain their secret ability of hiding when actually being in plain sight, however, and up they jumped to scramble across the fields straight ahead.

Meanwhile, behind them, to their utter delight, the bridge went up, up, up until it was flush against the Castle wall. That effectively closed the large gateway and they knew then that they would no longer be followed. The bridge was the sole means of crossing the moat. Their hearts raced as they maintained their speed and carefully placed their footsteps along the grasses.

"Where are we going, Grandfather?"

"We will go south, out of the Kingdom of Pellah where the King has no power over us. We shall follow the Golden River where it spills alongside the nearby fields," said the wizened old man. "We shall pass to the other side of the river, and on our journey past all the small towns in the Kingdom, we shall stay out of sight from every human being lest the King send his men in the daytime in their continued search of us."

"I cannot run much farther, Grandfather," said Andalorax. "Surely we can stop and rest somewhere now."

"We can continue until we reach the Calicab Forest." And he remembered the township of Milorin, where Andalorax was born that fateful night so long ago ….

"What shall we find there?"

"That, my dear child, is for us to discover!"

BOOK THREE

CHAPTER 18

BACK TO MILORIN

"WHAT WAS THAT? I SAW something move, over there, in the jasmine bushes," said the chubby man in suspenders and a green jacket. He had rolled his chair around and was looking out the window of the small building that was Milorin's Town Hall, while he talked with his six councilmen.

"Mayor Barth," said one of them, "please turn around and continue our discussion! This is a most important matter!"

The Mayor, who continued staring out the window, and in fact had rolled his chair even closer to it, said, "just a minute, Tom Eader! I tell you, something is quietly lurking about in the bushes and trees outside of our building." He had rolled all the way up to the window glass. "See! There it goes again!" He twirled his bushy mustache and pointed his finger at an outside shrub.

All six councilmen left their posts around the conference desk and hurried over to Mayor Barth. His Mayor's badge, tightly pinned to his checked woolen shirt, glinted in the late afternoon sunlight. They followed his outstretched hand to where he was indicating something existed.

"I see nothing," said Tom Eader, as ample in belly as the mayor.

"I don't see anything neither," said another, Charlie Pickford. He coughed. "But this may be tied in with what the townsfolk are saying is happening in the nighttime. Precisely what I am thinking! Let us consider this new development!"

Mayor Barth said, "Tom, and you, Charlie Pickford," now indicating with that same finger the two men who had just spoken up, "are both correct! The entire town is talking about it. Someone or something – or maybe some animal – is stalking our homes and farmlands, and they must be found out."

"Aye," chirped in Tom Eader. "They must not be allowed to frighten us, whomever or whatever they are. We can only hope that they are not wicked spirits."

"Maybe they are night animals that have strayed from their herd," said Charlie Pickford, patting his round stomach and snapping his suspenders. "Let us not get so excited!"

The Mayor rolled his chair back to his place at the head of the conference table. The other men followed suit and resumed their original places. Some tapped their piles of paper together on the desk; one had a glass of water. They all turned their eyes on their Mayor, who was fingering his golden star pin with the word "Mayor" inscribed thereon.

"Now then!" he cleared his throat with an "Ahem!" and continued, leaning forward on his hands.

"We must accept that something is going on in the distant shrubbery and perhaps is somehow tied in with what Harley the Woodcutter says is happening in the Calicab Forest," he stated most emphatically. He picked up his little gavel and banged it once upon the table. He raised his voice: "Sneakery and sabotage! Who knows what is going on in our little village? Gentlemen, I have said this before: this is precisely what happened fifteen years ago in Milorin – when King Vanamir came for his dues, and, just as we had been thinking there was something lurking in the Calicab Forest – that little old man and his daughter popped out of the woods!"

"I don't recall that time, Barth," said Tom Eader. "I was not on the Council then; I was only twelve years old!" Everyone laughed heartily.

Barth folded his hands together and leaned forward on the desk and said, "We all know the King comes here whenever his supply of Phemtas is low. He's been here many times since I've been Mayor, and that's about twenty years." He pushed himself back and sat bolt upright.

"Well, about fifteen years ago, mighty strange goings-on were being reported by our citizens – in those very woods at the edge of our township. It turned out to be that an old man, who had been banished from Milorin, had been living there for that same amount of years. With his wife and daughter, mind you!" Mayor Barth snapped his wide suspenders. "No one had the slightest idea they were there. We all suspected that, of course, any movements we perceived were simply night creatures. Instead, it turned out to be that old fellow named Gamedon and his daughter … I've forgotten her name. It was a very odd name, one that sounded, uh, significant, as far as names go, that is."

"But tell us about when King Vanamir was here fifteen years ago, which would make it in Pellah Year 1450, since this is year 1465," said Eader.

"I'm coming to that!" said Barth "Those fifteen years ago, we had great suspicions that there were dreadful things happening in the forest, and we were right in our fears. There were reports of campfires that suddenly went out … of strange whistling sounds that didn't seem to come from any bird or other animal. We judged it to be the wood spirits communicating. Now, perhaps, the same thing is happening!"

Mayor Barth again picked up his gavel and banged it on the desk, and said, "We must secure our borders, men! We must send out scouts to discover just what is happening in Milorin."

There was a short silence, and then with another "Ahem!" he said to his Councilmen, "I authorize the expenditure for these necessary services."

Tom Eader spoke up. "The problem is, Mayor Barth, we don't have any scouts who will go as far as the Calicab Forest. They are afraid of the magical spirits that live there!"

"We shall see to it that some of our men get their nerves together to achieve such bravery!" Mayor Barth let out a hearty laugh. "Which one of you is it that has connections with the men who know our lands?"

"That would be me," came forth a small voice from a small and skinny man. "Jasper Jingle. At your service, fellow Councilmen. I shall handle this matter at once. Allow me to round up our knowledgeable landsmen and make appointments for them to do their work!"

"Won't they be afraid?" asked Mayor Barth. "How can you be so sure they will accept your assignments? It will take going into the woods … it may even take some nighttime operations, eh, old Jingle?"

"You said you will pay," answered Jasper Jingle. "I will make certain that there is a large hole in your coffers so that will pay them well!" They all laughed.

Then, of a sudden, Charlie Pickford jumped up and pointed towards the same window. "I see it! The leaves in the bushes moved. Something really is out there!"

Going over to the glass window, he opened it wide. The checkerboard, lime-colored curtains made by Mayor Barth's wife, Welda, fluttered in the soft breeze.

"I say, Mayor Barth, you were correct! Something moved and it doesn't want us to see it!" He popped his head out and searched all around. The sky was a bright blue, and the sun was nearing the western horizon, while some wispy clouds crossed its golden glow. Below him, the green lawn spread out like a carpet, and rose bushes and jasmine shrubs dotted it with color and scent.

"I'm going outside to see if I can discover anything," said Tom Eader, who, immediately upon arising from his chair, launched himself towards the front door.

The others followed. Mayor Barth went to his desk, pulled out a drawer, and retrieved the small pocketknife he'd had since childhood. Putting it in his jacket pocket, he, too, followed Tom Eader into the fresh air of Milorin.

They all congregated on the front porch, some leaning on the balustrade, while they faced the Town Square. They all shook hands, and Jasper Jingle said he'd let them know at the next meeting what he found out about scouts, and then they all went their separate ways.

Mayor Barth was the only one of this contingent who remained, so he walked back into his office and shut the front door behind him.

"Hmm," he said out loud. "Wonder what is up? What I saw before through the window seemed like a person. Hmm … Let's see what the scouts learn." And with that, he promptly sat back in his office chair, put his feet up on the desk, and pretty soon was snoring into his shirt.

Outside, just beneath the open window, a small creature rested against the wall. He was quite invisible, he made sure, to human eyes. He had the ability, as did Andalorax, to "blend in with his surroundings."

"Like a chameleon," he and Andalorax had agreed, when utilizing this art.

Hence, when that man from Milorin stuck his head outside the window just above him, Gamedon was doubly glad of the power he possessed.

He was listening to Mayor Barth and the six Councilmen. Now he waited for Barth to leave so he could achieve his goal this evening: to obtain the golden key to Milorin's House of Time.

While Mayor Barth slept, Gamedon thought back … back to a time fifteen years ago in Pellah Year 1450, when Andalorax was newly born and Vanamir came to Milorin for another bride and had taken Mandir. He recalled that – from right out there in the Town Square – the King had gone into the House of Time, and he had checked to see that the harvest of Phemtas was up to his specifications and desires.

But he now wondered: why did the King need this herb so much? What does it do for him? What had the King looked at all those many years ago? What were the "dues" that the King had spoken of to Mayor Barth that the people of Milorin had to pay? He knew that they meant the giving to the King of a great harvest of Phemtas plants. But why did the King have need of this plant?

"How foolish of me never to have wondered about this plant prior to now!" he thought, not daring to make a sound. "The King, since these fifteen years that I was his private counsel before our escape a few months ago, has been to Milorin many more times to collect the Phemtas plant. Yet I have never accompanied him; he wished it so. I now wonder why? What was the secret?"

He heard Barth's deep snoring coming from the open window. He remembered how, just a few months ago, the one plant he had in his Laboratory in the Castle … how the little blossom was so attracted to the gold he was melting in his little metal plate on the burner … what need had the King of such a plant? Why did this plant go straight towards the gold as if the gold were its sunshine, or its food, perhaps?

The only solution was for Gamedon to get the key and enter the House of Time and find out for himself. Surely, there were records of the Phemtas plant. Surely there were records of the earlier Kings who may have come here for the plant ….

Gamedon also recalled when, as a young man, the House of Time was open for inspection to anyone who showed an interest in its contents. Hardly anyone did so, but Gamedon was fascinated with history and, particularly, in the history of the people of the entire Kingdom of Pellah.

So he went there often. He knew now that there would be records of goings-on that had anything to do with the plant. In his youth, going through those records, Gamedon had never given a thought to Phemtas. Quite possibly, he thought back then, there would also be some explanation of why the people were so afraid of the night and worshipped the sun. He recalled, as well, how over the years of reading those records, he came to the conclusion that it was all balderdash and hocus-pocus! He proved that by testing himself in the nighttime, going out into the fresh night air, looking up at the stars … and nothing evil ever came to him.

This was the reason he was judged by the Council of Milorin to be a conspirator with the evil night spirits. They must have protected him, the Council protested, when he committed his acts of treason by venturing out at night.

The result was his banishment. He and his pregnant wife Floribunda, the plump, smiling woman he so dearly loved and adored, were driven in a cart to the edge of the Calicab Forest and left there to their own devices. They worked hard, and they survived. Floribunda birthed their daughter Mandir and brought her up in this forest.

Yes, Gamedon remembered it all, while crouching against the wall beneath the window of the building.

As he waited for Mayor Barth to awaken and leave him to his task, Gamedon remembered, too, before he was banished, that he was a celebrated, much-adored citizen! He was known for his wit and wisdom. But that was before he proclaimed his beliefs.

Yet all those days and years of study in the House of Time never gave any hint as to what exactly the King desired – nay, needed, perhaps? – from the Phemtas plant.

Living in the Calicab Forest, he began to feel more emboldened in his powers to render himself invisible, or be "chameleon-like." After all, they had never been spotted in all these months on the run and in hiding. He and Andalorax had safely made their escape from the King's Castle and the Gold Mountains, had followed the strong-flowing Golden River Road through towns … never exposing themselves, sleeping out-of-doors on dried leaves or in haystacks … feasting on seeds and berries and nuts.

A hawk screeched from the nearby woods, and Mayor Barth shook his head and said "Huh? What was that?" He saw from the still-open window that the sun had made its way to a low point on the horizon.

"Time to go home," he said. He closed the window, dusted off his hands, and went to his desk. There he picked up his briefcase which he proceeded to stuff with some papers, and went to the front door. He took a knitted scarf from a peg on the doorway, wrapped it around his neck, went outside and locked the door. He went out into the street and started to walk home.

CHAPTER 19

PHEMTAS!

AT THE OTHER SIDE OF the building, Gamedon heard every step, every breath the Mayor made, so finely tuned were his rather large ears.

Still, Gamedon waited for the cover of night, when he could attempt to steal the golden key to the House of Time without real concern that someone might see him. This was, after all, the Town Square, with its streets of merchants and tradesmen; people such as they would surely be safely locked-up in their homes when the sun had set. Gamedon could make his move then ....

Finally, he reached up and felt the window sill. Good luck! The window was unlocked! Gamedon proceeded to go through all the drawers in the Mayor's desk until, lo and behold, he found a small golden key in a little wooden box easily labeled, fortunately, so simply, "House of Time." This little box, he put in his pocket, went back out the window, and headed out of town.

He made his way across the lawn, gliding along unseen from thereon all the way until he came to the edge of the Calicab Forest. There, he followed a narrow path, erasing his every step with a fallen branch from a Calicab tree. It was a long walk, but he wasn't tired.

Eventually, he stopped at a small tent with walls fashioned with large tree fronds and with large-spreading Calicab leaves for a roof. There was a small fire burning inside, its smoke escaping through reed pipes to the out-of-doors, and its golden light shining out through the doorway. At first he didn't see her ....

She saw him, however. As easily as they both could make themselves invisible, so, too, could they both see each other during these episodes. It made them comrades in a greater sense, and gave Andalorax a feeling of maturity, like a grown-up girl.

"Grandfather," she said, from where she sat as she sewed a button on his shirt with her single sharp needle. "Is that you?"

"Of course, my dear, 'tis I! Whom else would it be?"

They both laughed, but kept their voices low. It had become a habit. Another "habit" was their ongoing use of their powers to make themselves unseen, invisible.

"Even now, approaching the little tent, I saw the flame before I saw her," Gamedon thought. He found this fascinating, and the two of them acknowledged and shared this gift.

Gamedon proceeded to put his walking stick in its proper place, and did the same with his cloak and scarf.

"Keep that fire as low as you dare, child," he said, coming over to her and holding his hands up against the flames. "We've been here at the edge of the Calicab Forest for months now, and so far have seen no one from the village here – not one person save that woodcutter! But that doesn't mean someone hasn't seen us." Then he walked over to a low stool and sat himself down next to his grandchild.

"Grandfather, we've traveled so far, and never before have we stayed this long a time in one place. How much longer shall we stay in the Calicab Forest on the outskirts of Milorin?"

"Presently, we shall find out," he said, taking out his pipe and preparing a smoke.

"Don't get me wrong," she said, as she stitched. "I like it here in this wood. Perhaps because I was born here? Perhaps because my dear, departed grandmother and my faraway mother spent years here? Do you think so, Grandfather?"

"Aye, my dear. That could be two reasons. However," he said, puffing away on his pipe, "it is a quite simply just a very pleasant place, I find. We three – Floribunda, our daughter Mandir, and myself – lived here and there in the forest itself when your mother was just a child, and all through her growing-up years.

"In the beginning, you will recall," he said, as the two of them settled into their own special rhythm, "when my dear wife was alive ... your grandmother ... when we had to live in these woods because of my being exiled from Milorin. Well, dear girl, I never believed in their notions about night being evil and day being good. Plain and simple!"

"Grandfather," she replied with a laugh, "I remember nothing of those times. I was just an infant!"

"Ah yes, Andalorax. It is true, my dear one. Now, tell me, how was your day?"

"You mean you're not going to tell me tonight again that story of the day the King took us all away fifteen years ago? I know it by heart, dearest Gamedon!"

They both looked at each other for a moment, then both burst into laughter.

"Then how long shall we remain in this lovely forest, Grandfather?" she asked. "And where shall we go from here?"

He would be honest with her, he had decided, and continue to tell her all he could about herself, from her birth here in this very Calicab Forest to where they sat now, having returned to it.

"Andalorax," he said, reaching into his vest pocket and retrieving the little box. "I have this small item here, which I lifted this sunset-time from the Mayor's office." So saying, he opened the box, took out the key, and held it aloft.

"It is the key to the House of Time," he pronounced.

"The House of Time?"

"Yes, each town in the Kingdom keeps its records and histories. This is the key to the one here in Milorin. I intend to find out why it is that King Vanamir requires this plant, Phemtas, to be harvested from the Calicab Forest – the herb will only grow in the Calicab Forest, I should note. I already know he comes here to collect it when his supply runs low but what does he do with it? I have never been sure. Nor have I considered why."

Gamedon shook his head and muttered, "And what a fool I have been all these years to never have thought of it. Why should I have, however? It never seemed important. Now I want to know, and that it why we came here to Milorin, at the edge of the Kingdom, at the edge of this vast forest.

"How long we shall stay here in this hiding place," he went on, puffing his pipe, "I cannot say. It depends largely upon what I find out. If it has something to do with the people of the Pellah Kingdom, I must return to the Castle and help them. For surely, this Phemtas plant can only mean something grave or devious is going on with the King. Else why would he keep it such a secret?"

Andalorax stopped her sewing and folded up the shirt, and put away the one needle she took with her when they left the Castle so hastily.

"Where else is there to go, Grandfather?"

"Through the woods lie the Black Mountains. There, a strange creature lives who dominates the mountain range, so have I heard."

"But, Grandfather! The Black Mountains … it sounds so frightening. Almost ominous! Let's not go there!"

"Then we can simply wander through this forest until we learn what is at its eastern or western borders, rather than head south to the Black Mountains," said Gamedon, as he got up and crossed over to the fire. "I think what we should do is follow the Golden River as it wends its way through the woods.

"But come, let us eat dinner and put out this fire. I don't like the idea of it, my dear girl, and I have told you so. Who knows who is out there looking for us, their noses to the ground, searching. Surely the King would not allow us to escape without a chase! He might even send his Knights one day. We are blessed that none have come after us yet. We must take no chance!" So saying, he stomped out the little flame, leaving them standing in the quiet woods. An owl hooted.

"Grandfather, let us eat some fruits and berries and nuts from our little food sack and you can tell me some more stories about my mother, and my birth, and the day King Vanamir took us all with him to Castle Pellah."

"You could hear that over and over, and never tire," said Gamedon.

"I tease you but I love to hear these stories. Come, let us feast!"

Came the time when Gamedon let himself into the cube-shaped House of Time. It had an ominous look because there were very few windows. He chose a dark, moonless night. The little key easily slipped the lock open, and the huge wooden door opened slowly, revealing a vast, musty room. Gamedon spied spider webs everywhere over what he saw, where he had spent those years in his youth investigating the history recorded in these books. Before him was the huge, high-ceilinged room of old, whose walls were lined with an assortment of various sizes of time-worn, yellowed books. There was a long wooden table with six, high-backed chairs covered with leather seats.

He was quickly struck by a strong, pungent odor that seemed to permeate the entire room. Gamedon quickly looked about him, searching for its source, but found nothing. He dismissed it.

He placed his small candlestick on the table, then proceeded to light the candles that were ensconced along the walls. The room slowly lit up. Gamedon could imagine the decades … indeed, the centuries … of time that were recorded herein.

All the writings of the people of Milorin since it was registered in Pellah Year 240.

As he reviewed them, he came upon what he thought would be most helpful: the records of Pellah Year 1450, when King Vanamir was here to collect his supply of Phemtas – the year he himself revealed Andalorax to the King, and went onwards to the Castle where he, Mandir and Andalorax lived those past fifteen years.

"What was Vanamir reviewing these records for? Simply to see the harvest?" Gamedon had his doubts. He was beginning to suspect some secret link between the Kings of Pellah and the Phemtas plant – something that no one outside of the Reign of Kings knew anything about. Not a single person outside of the Reign of Kings, not even his deepest counselor, Gamedon himself!

Gamedon studied the records, but found nothing strange. He noticed the lack of activity that happened when Andalorax was born in early November of that same year, the year the three of them went to Castle Pellah; he saw also the subsequent fortitude of the villagers to make up for that loss, with hard work for sure, in December.

"Why?" Gamedon scratched his cap. "What is so important about these particular books? What clue am I missing?"

He got up and looked at the other books and records. He went to the first books ever written in Milorin, from the days when it became a new, official township of Pellah. Running his finger along, creating a trail along the way as the dust of time was wiped clean, he read:

Records of Milorin
Pellah Year 240

Blowing off some dust that made him cough, he wiped it with his green handkerchief and took it over to the table. He couldn't believe what he saw before him: A manuscript from Pellah Year 240 – that was more than twelve hundred years ago! He had to be careful with the pages, which were in remarkably good condition. Probably, Gamedon reckoned, because they were never exposed to the sunlight or fresh air.

He turned over the first page. Inside, on the second page, he read:

May the First, 240

*Wonder of Wonders, I dare to take Penne and Inke to this
clean page and write down the Firste Words in the Records
of what is now, officially, the Towne of Milorin. And I am its
Firste Mayor. I, Huntley P. Thrasher, III, whose Familie has
lived here since Pellah Year 25, when pilgrims from the
newly-forged Kingdom of Pellah, and its Grande Castle,
came to settle here by the Calicab Forest. That is 215 years ago!
And I have this Grand Privilege!*

*Let it be now Noted that the Grande Purpose in beginning
this Firste Particular Series of Record Books is to keep
watch over the King's royal dues: the mighty Phemtas Plante.
We are told that the Phemtas Plante, which all the Pellah
Kings from Year 1 adore so much, is grown only here,
where our town rests at the Edge of the Calicab Forest.
Therefore, we are Promised to give the King a goodly supply
of the Plante whenever He requests it.*

His finger was poised over the beautifully scripted handwriting of Mayor Huntley
P. Thrasher III, and he thought back: "Why do I know so little of this plant? All I
know is what I saw just a few months ago in my Laboratory in the Palace, the day
I melted the gold to make that key … how the Phemtas blossom stretched its way
towards that gold. Like a plant reaching for the sun! Hmmm … Does the plant love
gold as other plants love the sun? But what is its attachment to the Kings of Pellah?
Why do they *need* it?"

Gamedon stopped his train of thought and said aloud the word, "Need!" He
jumped up and down in a little jig, and laughed heartily. "That's it! This little
Phemtas plant is not just *desired* by the Kings, it is *needed* by the Kings!" But he
stopped his merry little dance and, discouraged, said aloud, "Needed for what?" He
scratched his little olive-green cap. "Aye, for what? That's now the bigger question."

"I want to know more of this Phemtas plant," he decided, and went back to the
wall of yellowed books to search for anything else that might help him. He read
aloud as he ran his finger again down the row of books and manuscripts:

Mayor Huntley P. Thrasher, III Pellah Year 240, Recipes
Mayor Huntley P. Thrasher, III Pellah Year 240, Poems and Sonnets

Finally, his finger landed upon this:

Mayor Huntley P. Thrasher, III, Pellah Year 242, Phemtas

"How lucky to come across this!" said Gamedon, but then he wondered why this Mayor of old would be so interested himself in this plant. Gamedon sat down and began to read:

> *Let it be here Recorded that I, Huntley P. Thrasher III,*
> *shalle this very day record my search for the Powers*
> *of the Phemtas Plante. What Powers does it have*
> *over our King — or of all Pellah Kings? Every time I*
> *come into this House of Time, I am assailed by*
> *the odor of barrels of it that we have at the ready*
> *for the King. They are kept in this colde stone*
> *house for preservation — here, where the Leaves*
> *and Flowers wille last for decades and never wither.*
> *Such a strange plant! And that odor is overwhelming!*

> *Laste yeare, of my own accord, I brought a Phemtas*
> *Plante I found at the edge of the Calicab Forest, where*
> *it grows abundant and wilde, into my house. My wife*
> *did not approve, as it has a very potent scent and is*
> *so ugly and pale. All this yeare, it has not grown, nor*
> *does it seem to need water. It simply exists. I know it*
> *to be so because I have seen and smelled barrels of it*
> *where we store it right here in this House of Time — 'tis*
> *our dues to the King! We began this in 240, just two years*
> *ago, when Milorin was granted official Township status.*
> *Also when I became Mayor, I might add.*

This yeare, however, I thought to test it. I ate a leaf.
Nothing happened. I ate its root. Again, nothing
happened. I dried it out and smoked it in my pipe,
with, once more, no results that I could tell of.
I fried it, added it to soups, all to no avail.

So my conclusion thus far is that I see nothing
special about the Phemtas Plante. Still, I wille
continue my search. My curiosity has the beste
of me! There must be some reason why the
Kings of Pellah all need Phemtas!

Quite suddenly, Gamedon felt himself to be spinning. Everything was whirling about him — the yellowed books, the wooden chairs — and he was so dizzy that, in fact, he had to take off his pointed cap and fan himself.

"That odor of the Phemtas plant is overbearing!" He needn't have sniffed hard until he could catch its scent it again. He saw a stream of air, wispy like a cloud, starting to come towards him from around the corner. It seemed to be carrying that odor, beckoning him as the wisps came up a staircase at the end of the room, and wrapped around him.

That cloying, pungent odor took shape and led him down a winding staircase at the end of the hall. The scent increased with every step down. Eventually, he stopped and found himself in a small, round cavern barely high enough for him, short as he was, to stand upright. The smell in the room was so strong that it made Gamedon dizzy enough that he reeled forcefully backwards against the stone walls. The walls and ceiling were braced by wooden beams and he clutched at them with his hands.

Alongside the farthest edge of the room was a large group of barrels, hooped with steel and numbered with, what seemed to be, dates. They were all stamped with the date. "PY 1463" read one. "Pellah Year 1464" read yet another. Then he saw closest to him, "PY 1465."

"That is this year, right now!" he said aloud.

"This is the Storage Room for Phemtas! The very same room that Mayor Thrasher referred to all those centuries ago, here in the House of Time!" he cried out. He could barely breathe, even though he held his handkerchief against his nose and mouth. He stared at the many wooden barrels and said, "Why does the King – nay, perhaps all the Kings of Pellah – need you, strange plant? No one else has any use for you, and you sit here in your barrels, waiting for the King to require you and take you back to the Castle."

So saying, he followed the bounty of casks until he counted thirty of them, all dated back various years, including this year's crop. "Hmmm … thirty casks of various years. Perhaps they saved the best of each year's crop!"

He took out his pocket knife and approached the barrel of this year's harvest. He managed to remove nails that held the iron hoops together, loosening somewhat the tension of the contents. Gamedon could then reach inside and remove the top. Plunging his strong fingers inside the barrel, he grabbed a hold of a patch of what he thought would be Phemtas … and he then managed to pull some of it through the opening.

"'Tis Phemtas alright!" he spoke to the room. He beheld the leaves of what was once a waxy, pale-green, long-stemmed plant now dried and cured to last indefinitely. Each leaf was about six inches long, and they were in abundance on the stem.

Sitting down on the floor, one hand holding his handkerchief to his face, the other holding a Phemtas plant, Gamedon marveled in silence for a long moment, then said: "Oh mighty Phemtas! Tell me of your secret with the Kings of Pellah! Why do they need you so?"

To his surprise, the plant began to flesh out, its leaves plumping up and turning a sparkling emerald green. A small bud at the end of its stem began to blossom and Gamedon beheld what he had once before seen in his Laboratory: a Phemtas flower!

This happening so rapidly, he was quite astounded and he immediately dropped the plant on the ground. There, it withered up and became brown and dried up once again.

"Aha, pretty plant, pretty flower! You sprout and bloom at my touch but recoil at the cold stone." He reached down and picked up the leafy bundle, which now, once again, quickly became lush and alive.

"Now, why is that?" he asked aloud.

Reaching into the barrel for more Phemtas, he took all he could manage to stuff in his pockets. He also wrapped some into a neat bundle which he stuffed into his cape. Then he tightened up the barrel as best he could, and, using the same narrow, winding staircase, made his way back into the Room of Records.

He retrieved the manuscript labeled:

Mayor Huntley P. Thrasher, III, Pellah Year 242, Phemtas

He folded it up carefully, and stowed it, too, under his jacket. Then he went and returned the books he had removed.

"I bet you will be helpful to me, little book," he said, as he made his way out of the House of Time, back into the Mayor's office where he returned the little gold key, and at last was on the path home. He patted his pocket.

"Now to learn what Mayor Thrasher III figured out about you centuries ago, dear Phemtas!"

CHAPTER 20

KNIGHTS ON THE MOVE

IT WAS MID-DAY ON A Thursday afternoon, just a few days later, when the slender, hawk-nosed Jasper Jingle came bursting into the Town Hall and called out: "Mayor Barth! Mayor Barth! Where are you? There's someone coming, and coming at a nice clip!"

The stout Mayor was busily polishing his belt buckle, and looked up at the willowy figure who had suddenly appeared before him.

"What is it, you say, Jingle?"

"A scout just reported to me. You know, the scouts we hired to find out about the goings-on near – and maybe in! – the Calicab Forest? It's our first report since they took on the job two days ago." Jasper Jingle put his hands on the desk across from Mayor Barth.

"What is the report then, Jingle?"

"A scout just this hour saw a group of twenty horses, ridden by the King's Knights, he figures – that's because they're all covered with gold and wear gold badges on their green cloaks. He said they were riding along the Golden River Road heading for Milorin. He said they are within an hour's march of here! What shall we do, Mayor Barth?" His hands wringing together in supplication, Jasper Jingle had also begun to tremble.

Barth immediately became quite confused as to what he should do, but knew of only one remedy for this situation. So he ran out into the Town Square and rang the large and heavy bell just as loudly as he could.

People came from everywhere to see about the noise. They surfaced in doorways of shops, in windows where workmen were busy, and appeared from around corners.

"What is it, Barth?"

"Why ring the bell, Barth?"

"Barth, speak up! You're the Mayor around here!"

The Mayor, who was panting and now trying to catch his breath by inhaling enormous gulps of air, raised his hand and cried out, "Just a minute! Just a minute, folks!"

Eventually, Mayor Barth stood up and said, "The King's Knights are on their way and will be here within fifteen minutes! We know not what their intentions are but we must continue to be loyal and humble servants to King Vanamir! Quickly, everyone in the center of town! Near the statue of our blessed King Rathbone who reigned when Milorin became a town in Pellah Year 240. Remember, we are servants to our King. Quickly now, I say!"

The entire community hurried to and fro and managed somehow to form a circle around the statue. Everyone was staring towards the main road, straining their eyes and necks looking for some sign of the Knights' appearance. Then tall Harley the Woodcutter, who never missed seeing anything before anyone else, craned his long neck and said, "There! I see them! Coming down the road just as plain as day. Heading straight for us!"

Other people began to chime in; they, too, saw the dust from galloping hooves, and the glint of gold from the Knights' armor and shields.

The trembling group of people stood motionless as they watched the cavalcade of twenty giant chestnut stallions, their manes streaming in the bright, glistening sunlight, swiftly make its way up the main path to the Town Square. When they reached Mayor Barth, who stood – with all the bravery he could muster – in front of the assembly, they stopped. Their horses reared and snorted, and finally settled down.

One among these twenty men rode his horse – covered as it was with golden raiment and a golden bridle, the leather saddle having a golden pommel – up to the Mayor and, with a swift move of his hand, he removed his leather headgear with a flourish. An enormous plume of feathers sprouted from the top of it. He bent his head slightly in friendship.

A round, pure gold sun disk was pinned at the throat of his green velvet cloak, and when the Knight sat back upright, it shone greatly in the afternoon light. He had a bright orange-red beard, braided down his chest. His all-seeing eyes glittered like emeralds. His hands were gloved in finest suede with handsome whip-stitching and leather fringes. He said:

"Greetings, people of Milorin. We come from the Castle of Pellah, at the wish of our great King Vanamir." He raised his hat majestically. "Do not trouble yourselves overmuch for our sudden, unannounced arrival. We are on official business so gather 'round." The people did as told.

"We must seek out and find one old renegade called 'Gamedon.' He's a heretic, actually, and we must capture him!"

The Knight dismounted, and proceeded to march back and forth in front of the increasingly-growing crowd. "Know any of you folk about this man and a young girl, a very … strange girl. His granddaughter, so they tell me." He coughed. "She has white hair. An otherwise pretty and normal girl. Except for her long white hair. Oh, and yes, her black eyes!"

Everyone looked at each other. They shook their heads left and right. No. No one had seen the fabled citizen of Milorin who was banished about twenty years prior. And a girl with white hair and black eyes? Absolutely not.

The Knight laughed heartily. How silly these people were compared to him and the many other inhabitants of the Castle Pellah! His sparkling eyes shone out like a bright beacon, for he was, after all, one of the Twenty Men of the Eyes. And he was their leader, put there for his superior ability to see what others couldn't, not matter how acute their vision be. He tested best of the Eye Men for a reason! His name was Malthor, and he had been here before. It was his fellow Knight, Haldown, who was murdered by the King when he was mistaken for an assassin. That was fifteen years ago, remembered Malthor, who had now risen to the top of the ranks.

He continued his business.

"I'm certain that had any of you seen this man, you would have immediately told the rest of the townsfolk, correct?"

They all in one chorus cried out, "Aye!"

Again he laughed. "Has any of you gone in the Calicab Forest lately?"

Again, they shook their heads.

"Nay."

Malthor's smile quickly turned sour and his eyes shone like piercing blades. "You will go into that forest, in a group if you like to keep your frightened selves from falling apart, and you will search for any signs of human activity in there. Ha! Ha! I said human activity, not magical activity! I don't mean the other kind of activity, 'something magical from the woods!' We are searching for an old man and a young girl. Real people, folk of Milorin! Remember this as you make your way in the forest!

"And you shall go into that forest, mind you! It is the King's direct order to me, to make you search that woods. Vanamir is familiar with that Calicab Forest. He says it is safe! No matter what stories your mothers told you, not matter how you fear it might have magic properties ….

"I've been told they know how to live in the woods; apparently, the old man lived here in these very woods when the King found him and brought him back to the Castle, yes, fifteen years ago! I told you, the King knows those woods and says to fear them not.

"Yes, I'm sure they are hiding there, for we have been to every village along the Golden River Road and all the towns along its tributaries, and this, Milorin, on the southernmost border of our Kingdom, is the very last. He must be here! He and his granddaughter, and I remember now her odd name – it's Andalorax! And we must find them! YOU must find them!"

With trembling voice, Mayor Barth spouted out the words that broke the silence of the crowd. "Oh glorious Knight! We have already sent scouts into the woods – or at least to the edge of the woods – because we have been noticing some activity there …."

"What?" thundered Malthor. "You have detected life in the forest? Life that may be human?"

"Aye, sir. We are attending to that this very moment, with our spies and searchers penetrating the woods …."

Malthor laughed loudly. "You say you are scouring the woods, yet you admit to not having penetrated the edge of that self-same forest! Do not lie to me, Mayor!"

Barth was taken aback. "Well, we shall venture into the woods this very afternoon, this I can promise you!"

Malthor the Knight ceased his pacing, and remounted his horse with a clattering of his spurs and the rustling of his cloak and the smoothing of his leather pants. The big-chested steed was impatient and stomped the ground. Malthor had to wrestle with him a bit. When the horse finally calmed down, Malthor said to Mayor Barth, who was standing, mouth agape:

"We shall all require bed and board, and we shall stay as long as it takes to find these two escapees! Twenty Knights we are, mind you. Take me to your Innkeeper! But make haste to scour the Calicab Forest immediately." Then he raised his voice and cried out to the people, "Yes! Even though it will shortly be sunset, we still have some daylight." Turning back to Barth, he said, "Now, to the Inn!"

CHAPTER 21

RECORDS FROM THE PAST

JUST ABOUT ONE WEEK EARLIER, as soon as the new dawn awoke him, Gamedon had sat down in a sunny spot, leaned against a stout Calicab, and began to read the diary of Mayor Huntley P. Thrasher, III, written more than twelve hundred years ago, in Pellah Year 242. It was wrapped in thick yet supple brown leather, tied with a slender, strong leather strap. The pages, made of pressed bark of the Spotted Elm Tree, were yellowed but neither crumbled nor rolled up. The package wasn't very large, but Gamedon sensed it held some powerful bit of knowledge for him regarding Phemtas and its connection with the Kings of Pellah.

After all, he said to himself, almost with a chuckle, it was titled, "Phemtas!"

The elaborate, scripted handwriting was extraordinary, thought Gamedon, as he stared out at this man's words written so long ago. Words of a man long dead.

"Wonder what made him curious about Phemtas, as am I?" He was determined to find the answer and hoped he'd find it here, in this slender notebook. The outside of it read:

Mayor Huntley P. Thrasher, III, Pellah Year 242, Phemtas

Gamedon applied his recent knowledge in the King's Library to this diary, where he got to meet King Mundarak and see his prophesies. He surmised:

"Although not written in the Old Tongue of the Pellah reign," he mused, "as did Mundarak at the beginning of it all when his ship landed here, the language has similarities. The 'I' isn't always a 'y'; the oddest words aren't capitalized, such as 'sun.' But the spelling is somehow different. Yet, it was far easier to understand than Mundarak's prophesies, all written and spoken in the Ancient Tongue of their forefathers."

Gamedon guessed, as he read the opening words to the manuscript, that the writer used a feather quill and crushed berries for ink, although the letters were, in some passages, it seemed to Gamedon, the color of dried blood! Gamedon once again recalled that fateful night when, to be allowed into Mundarak's Prophesies, he had to drop his own blood on a page in the book. It looked just like this ink ....

Ye Gods of the World, Protect Me as I am about to
embark upon a voyage of which I know of no way to Begin.
Begin at the Beginning, then, oh Thrasher old man!

In Pellah Year 240, our township of Milorin became an official part of the Kingdom of Pellah. We exceeded all their Rules of Order for achieving such an honor: we appointed a Mayor (in this case, myself), created a Towne Square, held regular meetings with our Councilmen, kept records of our agriculture and of women's work including stitchery and knitting and tapestry-making. We kept all our recipes, including those for annual, festive occasions. We kept records of weddings, births and deaths; we studied certain favorite passions such as astronomy, music, and secret medicines!

We also studied plantes and hyrbes. But we never studied Phemtas! Phemtas is a plante that grows only in this Calicab Forest, and for some reason unknown to us, is desired by the King in such quantities that he must never run out of his supply! Sometimes a group of special Knights comes through and raids our secret stash in the House of Time, stuffing their leather, gold-studded coffers which hang from their horses' saddles, with Phemtas. They turn straight around and rush back to their Castle in the Gold Mountains.

I, however, know there is some special power that this plante possesses that the Kings know about, perhaps only the Kings, for some unknown reason. Why do I know about a special power? Because I have experienced it. No, not I personally! Yet I have seen its effects on our King, when last he came in 240 to declare us an official city-state. Just two years ago.

Shall I tell it here and now? Yes! Else I will never do it!

We had just built the House of Time, which, being new and therefore empty of any records of Time itself, but hopefully would in the future have centuries more of literature, and manuscripts such as this one, and record books such as the newly-created Record of Phemtas, created by our glorious King Rathbone.

We built a long, circular tunnel, exactly as King Rathbone described with architectural details, with plenty of room to store at least thirty King-sized barrels of Phemtas. Just the King and I went to see the records that year of 240, in that stone-hold, the House of Time. As he reviewed our records for the year's harvest, I remember the pungent odor emanating from downstairs in that Phemtas storage room. My eyes started to burn, my nose began to itch – yet King Rathbone seemed to feel it not, but instead he began to hum a little tune, over and over. No words; just sounds. Very quietly, to himself, it seemed. To whom else, then, I wondered?!

When we made our way down there, following that spiral staircase, the King fell to his knees and brought a small book out from under his cloak. He began to utter the strangest words—words which I can now read because his small book is here in my possession, as I have borrowed it from the Library at the House of Time.

Just two years ago, my Lord our King Rathbone uttered these exact words:

"Oh! Phemtas Root!
When our first kinsmen landed here 240 years ago,
From evil seed, you pierced the soil
And made Black Magic plantes for Pellah's Kings –
Kings who need you to vouchsafe their power – But
pay a heavy price! They cannot live without you,
little flower! We Kings of Pellah! We must keep
our Lineage!

Gamedon slapped the little book shut, raising up a flurry of over twelve-centuries-old dust from the mayor's journal. With more care, he lay it down upon his lap, as he realized that the morning had passed swiftly and the sun was already well up into the sky. Where was Andalorax, then? He wondered about this, and rose from his spot on the tree root.

He found his granddaughter cleaning their little living abode, which consisted of large plant fronds for a carpet, and soft mimosa branches with their puffy red flowers as their mattresses. They couldn't put down anything permanent; they were on the run. Had it already been four months, wondered Gamedon, as he greeted Andalorax. Aye, four months! No sign of the King sending any men to follow them, something which caused Gamedon some worry. Granted, when they traveled it was at night, being unafraid of the night as their other kinsmen were. And yet, perhaps he wasn't quick-witted enough to notice that they were, indeed, being searched for.

"What is that journal you carry, Grandfather?" she asked as she shook the earth off their carpet of leaves. "Is it what you wanted to get from the Mayor yester-eve?"

"Aye, dear child. And it is already enlightening me as to why the Kings might have need of Phemtas. Somehow, it is linked up with their power to rule the Kingdom of Pellah and all its people."

He recalled what he had just read in the First Milorin Mayor's diary. Part of it was an ode to the Phemtas root itself: "*When our first kinsmen landed here 240 years ago, From evil seed, you pierced the soil, And made Black Magic plantes for Pellah's Kings*" – that read as if the plant was created just for the Kings and no one else. Was that its sole purpose for existing? And how did the first King come to find this out, and then continue it on down the line?"

We Kings of Pellah! We must keep our Lineage!

"Aye, they must keep their lineage," muttered Gamedon. "And so on 'down the line.' But wait! King Vanamir fails to conceive a male heir! That is why he is continually in pursuit of a new wife! For once his wife bears a child – and it invariably is a female child – she can bear no more!"

"But this could not be the fate of previous kings, or there would be no successor to the throne," mused his granddaughter.

"So it went with my poor Mandir," he said aloud.

"Mandir, Grandfather?" Andalorax must have heard his mumblings. "What about my mother? Remember, we are to have no secrets between each other! Not a one! You have told me about my birth, and knowing about that event has changed my life! Now, pray tell, what else is there to say to me now?"

"Nothing, Andalorax. Truly. You know, of course, that I refer to her now because that is precisely why she was taken away and brought to King Vanamir, to beget him a son. But she couldn't even give him another girl. She had you, my dear Andalorax, and that was that."

"How many wives has he had since then?"

"Fifteen more. One every year. All mothers to daughters then no more child-bearing. No male heirs, as of yet."

"And they all live isolated in the Turret of the Wives in the Castle?" Andalorax pouted her pretty, pale face. Her dark eyes began to shed tears. "I wish so dearly that we could be together."

"That is not how our King rules the Kingdom of Pellah. We have no choice. No one else seems to mind because these new wives all come from some other town where they know no-one. They who live in the great Castle know nothing of the suffering a family must go through to lose their daughter to their King! And the poor daughter, doomed to a life in the Wives' Turret forever!"

"And what about the girl children of the King?"

"They, too, live in the Wives' Turret." Gamedon shook his head.

"But, right now, I'm just thinking about Phemtas, and why the Kings need it. Why does Vanamir thrive in its presence? I didn't realize until now, after fifteen years – how blind I was! – that perhaps our good King Vanamir needs Phemtas in the belief that it will somehow bring him a son … when he uses it.

He continued, "I've seen him use it, Andalorax. In his chambers, there is a hidden room wherein he keeps his Phemtas treasure trove. He performs a ritual … Hmmm… I wonder if the writer of this diary" (he thumped his jacket pocket) "experienced anything similar with his King? I must make a note …."

Gamedon studied that little book until he knew it almost by heart. As they lived silently and as invisibly as possible in their little rudimentary quarters, little did they know what was about to befall them.

After about a week, he and Andalorax were standing under the shade of a Calicab, discussing the revelations Gamedon was making as to the link between Phemtas and the Kings of Pellah, when suddenly Andalorax grabbed him by the arm and pulled him down to the ground. They immediately both did their "game" of blending in with their surroundings – like the camouflage of the wild duck when she is being stalked by the hunter and his dogs.

They both also knew instinctively to be completely silent. Then Gamedon, too, heard and felt what Andalorax had: there was someone coming their way, coming most urgently along the Golden River Road towards Milorin.

The sound of many horses' hooves thundering down the road told them it was the King's Knights. Whether or not they were coming for them or for some other reason – such as gathering a fresh supply of Phemtas – it didn't matter because they could not be discovered. Whatever their reason for coming to Milorin, Gamedon knew they weren't far away from the Calicab Forest at the edge of the town. Although the two of them were hidden deep within the forest's boughs and branches, they had to act immediately.

They had no chance to try and rub out any sign of their presence there, any footprints, and stray piece of clothing … their rucksacks – filled with all their gear, from cooking utensils to the spyglass – were suspended from a tree branch way above their heads, to be hidden in just such a necessary moment.

So they lay, splayed out upon the earth and grass and fallen leaves, and slowed down their breathing, and waited.

Eventually the sound of the horses began to fade away as they approached the town and passed Gamedon and Andalorax. Within a moment of realizing they were safe from being found out, they jumped up and gathered their gear and made for deeper areas of the dense woods. As they hurried along their way, they made every effort to be silent and unseen, but they knew it was danger that lurked not far from their backs.

And so that day was a turning point for both groups: the Knights came to Milorin and set down the law to the townsfolk. Little did they know what was happening simultaneously in the forest. Gamedon and Andalorax were running for their lives while plans were put in motion to follow the Knights' commands.

And that night, while the Knights slept comfortably in Jack Beale's Inn, Gamedon and Andalorax were resting, sleeping intermittently, sheltered by their ample, hooded cloaks, beneath the cover of a wide-spread ancient Calicab tree.

Two days passed and Jasper Jingle's scouts, working in pairs, were out and about at the edge of the woods.

"We've got to enter the forest," said one to the other. Frankie Monroe and Timmy Goode summoned their courage and plunged into the woods.

"We've crossed the line now, Timmy," said Frankie. "Good thing we have the daylight with us for hours now, so we can escape if we are confronted with any evil creatures that we might stumble upon."

"Don't be ridiculous!" said Timmy. "They will know we're coming long before we spot them, and that, my friend, is a fact! So let's keep moving while we have the courage because if they've spread a net, it will be wide and we'll be trapped for sure."

Deeper into the forest they walked, until one of them spotted something dark upon the ground: it was the place which Gamedon and Andalorax had abandoned just two days prior, when the Knights came to town.

The two scouts got on their hands and knees and felt the ground, when one of them gave out a little yell.

"Ouch!" he cried. "It's a Calicab nut. You know how hard they can be until they open up and bear fruit!"

"Quiet, there!" came the prompt, hushed retort. "It won't do for the King's Knights to hear that we scared away our quarry, now, would it?"

Both remained still and silent for some minutes, then one of the two men said, "Wait! What's this?" and he stooped down to the earth, whereupon he rubbed his thumb and forefinger together and said, "Charcoal!" He rubbed more fingers in the dirt and said, "Someone's made a fire here, Timmy. Look!"

His partner got down on his knees and had a look, and came to the same conclusion as Frankie. They stared at each other, all a-fluster, and jumped up at the same time, knocking each other on the forehead in the attempt.

"Ouch!" said both.

"What do we do now, Frankie?" asked Timmy.

"We have a look-see for evidence of people being in this here wood," said Frankie. "That's our instructions from old Jingle. Then we ride home and bring our news to a man named Malthor, First Eyeman and Captain of the King's Knights."

"We did it! We did it!" They both jumped up and down and clapped their hands.

So they shuffled and pushed aside leaves and bushes, and searched for a sign of a path or anything else, and they stopped, looked at each other, and silently agreed without another word that the charcoal was all they had as evidence that something was afoot in the Calicab Forest, and they scrambled as fast as their legs would take them out of the woods and onto safe, green-grassed territory.

As they exited the woods, both men exhaled sighs of relief that they had been in the dreaded Calicab Forest and lived to tell about it! Now, however, they had to face those twenty terrifying Knights.

The two scouts ran quickly out of the forest to safety, and rushed to the Inn. There, standing on the porch with his arms folded, was the First Knight, Malthor. He had already spotted them! After all, he was the First Eyeman!

"Tell me, now," he said in his deep baritone voice, "and make no wasted blabber about it! What did you find? Surely it was in the Calicab Forest, for you were running so fast even a jack-rabbit couldn't have caught you." Herein, he laughed robustly.

"We – we found where there had been a fire, Captain Malthor! Someone – someone made a fire out there in the forest, not far from the edge where it begins." Timmy Goode's sweat was now dripping down his face. He was still out of breath.

The scouts showed their bits of charcoal, some of which had smudged off their fingers and was residing on their cheeks and noses.

"Approach! Instantly!" said Malthor, holding out his hands. The two scouts showed them their bits of blackened wood. The Knight grabbed the hand of one, the dirtiest one, and said, "Aha! Here we have what we are searching for. This is proof that the two escapees are in the Calicab Forest! No evil spirits have need of fire!" Abruptly he disappeared inside the Inn but within a few minutes returned followed by the group of nineteen more swarthy Knights.

"We must make haste now, men, for we are on the chase! To horse!"

The Knights ordered their steeds from the stables and, when the beasts were saddled and ready, the twenty men rode off down the Golden River Road until it veered north. There, they left the path and headed south for the woods, as the sun was still high in the sky.

Meanwhile, Gamedon and Andalorax were on the move themselves, also heading south. The actual density of the forest and the thicket of lower, young seedlings forced them to keep to a slower pace than they would have liked, yet they continued to plow ahead. Little did they know that the Knights were now in the woods themselves. But knowledge of that wouldn't have mattered, for they went as swiftly as their feet would carry them. Their knapsacks added to their burden, keeping their pace slow but still steady.

For both the two of them — sturdy slippers on their feet — and the Knights — wearing thigh-high leather boots with cuffs — at that very same moment, the sunshine was warming their long paths ahead.

CHAPTER 22

THE SEARCH IS ON

"HURRY, ANDALORAX! WE MUST MAKE haste!" said Gamedon. They were scurrying deep into the Calicab Forest now, running for their lives, or so they felt. While not a young man any longer, Gamedon was still spry and fleet-footed. Andalorax was thin and light of weight, and her laced-up suede shoes allowed her to move quickly. Surely the King would not forgive them for escaping and ruining his sinister plans to keep Andalorax a prisoner for the rest of her life. That he was terrified of her and what she might do to his reign and indeed, his very life, Gamedon knew from that last meeting in the King's quarters.

Gamedon also had been in the private Library of King Vanamir, and therein learned that King Mundarak's prophesies of the King's dreams were very real indeed: Andalorax had a definite role to play in his future as the reigning monarch of the Lands of Pellah. He knew that in King Vanamir's recollection of his particular dream, wherein she – in the guise of the "sleek white horse" that "leapt from the waves" and rose from the sea and challenged his might – was most exceedingly real. It resided uppermost in Gamedon's mind.

Yes! It was Andalorax who was the uncompromising white wave that reached up to the King and brought him tumbling down the cliff into the sea. She was the white mare – she with her white locks and colossal strength! It was Andalorax and none other, as shown by her mystical physical appearance and auspicious birth under the full moon.

Gamedon knew there were no things to fear in the night simply because it was dark. But he also knew there were mythological beings in the world, and he knew somewhat of magic in his own small way.

Andalorax herself was unlike to anyone ever known in the Kingdom of Pellah.

Yet Gamedon knew not what role she was destined to play. He felt deep-rooted fears for his gentle granddaughter and knew she would not have a simple, pleasant life. No. She was fated to do something.

But what?

"Grandfather, I am weary. Can we please rest here for a while, under this craggy old Calicab? See! It has dropped many leaves for us to lie upon and catch our breath."

"Aye, dear child. Let us rest," answered Gamedon.

They unburdened themselves of their knapsacks and walking sticks, and, not even bothering to remove their cloaks, they lay down upon the fertile soil and foliage of the forest. Their faces were upturned to the high, midday sun, which filtered through the boughs of the mighty Calicabs. The two weary travelers were speckled all over with the mottled design of the greenery.

Immediately, they fell into a deep sleep.

The woods were full of activity: squirrels gamboled from limb to limb in the vastness of the trees, making their clucking noises as they went along. Red cardinals and yellow-headed blackbirds sang their cheerful tunes, as did the blue jays and warbling vireos. Every now and then, the sound of a Calicab nut could be heard falling to the soft earth. The lively concert went on for hours.

All was right in the forest.

The sun continued to make its way across the sky, and still Gamedon and Andalorax slept on. They heard not the rustling and the hooting of the great horned owl as he awoke from his den in a tree bole. They felt not the coolness of the air as it crept in and lay its dampness upon the green mosses and brown twigs.

They heard not the clip-clopping of stallions of the King's Knights, who were fast upon their heels.

A wise old crow flew down and settled itself upon Gamedon's rucksack.

"Caw! Caw!" it cried out. Awakening from a dream, Gamedon finally heard the scratchy noise of the bird's throaty call. Instantly, he felt the rumbling of the earth beneath him and knew that they were about to be captured.

"Awaken!" he whispered in his granddaughter's ear. "They are upon us!"

Quickly, they gathered their belongings and stealthily wove in and out of the tree trunks and overhanging branches. They were ever-mindful of their power to become practically invisible and hoped it would help them to elude their would-be captors.

But, although the woods were almost completely dark now, still the Knights kept coming. Gamedon wondered why the Knights were not afraid of the night and the stars, and the full moon rising in the east. Perhaps, he thought, they have learned to overcome their trepidations, in the name of their King. Perhaps, he thought, their King had threatened them with oblivion should they not overcome the fear of the night.

Suddenly, the horses came to a halt. Gamedon could hear much noise and rustling arising from the following pack. He could finally make out their voices.

"Hush, child," whispered Gamedon. "I am going to attempt to see what is going on and learn just how near they are to us." Putting his index finger to his lips with a "Sshh!" he threw aside his cloak, took off his checkered jacket, and proceeded to climb up the ancient Calicab that had been their protector all that afternoon. He used the branches to gain a foothold with every nimble step. Andalorax dared not breathe even a small sigh as she watched him disappearing into the foliage above her. Soon, he was completely out of her sight.

Finally their noisy hubbub reached the old man's long pointed ears. He could even make out the steam arising from the nostrils of the steeds.

"We shall camp here by this lake, men," said their leader, Malthor. "Let us be quick about our business!" He gave orders for the cavaliers to administer to their overheated horses, to water them and fill their own canteens, and to spread out their velvet cloaks for sleeping.

And then they did what helped Gamedon to understand why they were not afraid of being out in the nighttime: they didn't lie on their cloaks! Instead they lay on the soft ground made of fallen Calicab leaves and covered themselves with their cloaks, burying their heads in the hoods. They couldn't see out! So it stood to reason – which gave Gamedon a chuckle – that if the Knights couldn't see what was about, then they wouldn't see them! Gamedon couldn't help but grin!

Within fifteen minutes, they were settled. Gamedon watched as they enveloped themselves in their cloaks, resembling a sea of embroidered velvet. He retreated from his perch and scrambled back down to where Andalorax stood waiting.

"They are making camp for the night," he told her. "They are hiding in their cloaks and will not venture out anymore this night. We are safe to travel freely, until sunup. We must take advantage of this and continue to flee."

Picking up their knapsacks, they used their magic walking sticks which directed them to their destination, and they immediately resumed their narrow path in the woods. But as they went on and the night hours ticked by, the foliage about them became thick and the trees seemed to be closer and closer together, so that it was difficult to forge their way through. They sometimes tripped over roots and the stumps of dead trees and their mantles were continually being caught on brambles.

"Alas, Andalorax," said Gamedon, holding up his hand and coming to a halt. "We are at an impasse and I know not where to go."

They were standing between row upon row of very primeval Calicabs, and Gamedon sensed they were in the very heart of the forest. Strangely enough, though, there were pebbles and small stones beginning to appear on the ground. Soon, the small stones turned into rocks, and shale, and the ground seemed to be rising as if they were climbing a hill.

"We can no longer forge our way through this dense shrubbery and we are stumbling over these rocks," he said. "I must stop and figure out the lay of this land. Give me time to think, my dear one."

The night was blanketing them, despite the bright moon sailing above. Moonbeams peeked through the thick foliage and cast long rays of white light into the damp forest as the moonlight was reflected upon the moist air.

"It's like being inside a crystal," thought Andalorax. She was tired. But fortunately with no fear of the nighttime and the moon and the stars, she also felt glorious. A thought came to her that being born in the light of the full moon was perhaps causing her to blossom.

While Gamedon sat on the ground trying to assess their next move, into the stillness came a rustling in the trees that was foreign to them. Was something in the thicket and the densely packed Calicabs? Gamedon faced Andalorax and put his fingers to his lips, indicating complete silence.

After a while, they realized that the sound was an ongoing chorus of life rather than one or two little mice scrambling in the bush. With his finger, the old man pointed straight ahead and indicated that they should advance. This they did, for almost an hour, and they realized the sound kept getting louder and more insistent in its nonstop pattern.

Ahead was a small opening in the trees, and here they found the source: a small rivulet was rushing past them! They approached the banks of the small stream with wonder. Was this a branch of the Golden River that trailed all the way through the

Kingdom from north to south, wending its way through the woods? Gamedon knew of no other water source than that of the mighty Golden River.

"It must be so," he thought. They bent down and put their hands in the water, finding it cool and fresh and sweet. It was flowing downstream at a constant pace.

Gamedon withdrew his compass from his pocket.

"This water flows southwest, Andalorax. Let us follow this winding river," he said. "Perhaps it will lead us out of the tangled and tortuous woods."

He did not have the courage to tell her what he feared by discovering this clue: if they continued southwest, they would eventually reach the Black Mountains.

"A dreadful destiny may await us there," he thought to himself. "I know naught about these peaks except that they are thought to be ruled by magic and sorcery." Rumor had it, back in Milorin, that the Black Mountains were barren of life, and would provide little sustenance for food. But he said nothing to his granddaughter, who now was of a much more cheerful frame of mind since they found the Golden River.

"Tell me if there are any legends about the Golden River, Grandfather. Or of the Black Mountains."

"I only know the tales told me by the gentle folk back in the days when I was a simple citizen of Milorin. No one I know has ever traveled there, and, if they have, they never returned to tell a tale of what they found."

Southwest it was; he decided to continue their course, and he put his compass back in his pocket with a little pat, and they went on their way.

They walked gingerly along the rocky banks, which were riddled with pebbles and hampered their speed. But the sound was glorious to their ears! It was a refreshing reminder that life still existed here in nature, and for some reason brought down their heartbeats to a steadier rate. They poked their walking sticks into the damp earth as they traversed the water's edge, and Gamedon began to whistle, ever so softly.

"Mandir – your mother – has an auspicious name, you know, my dearest child, and it is here that I am reminded of her sweet countenance and gentle disposition. In the ancient tongue, 'mandir' means water, and we find ourselves happily comforted by that very element in this difficult time."

Andalorax replied, "Yes, Grandfather. I know the source of my mother's name. Just as I have recently learned from you that my name also has an auspicious meaning."

"Night-black, moon-white," he hummed. "All these elements bring us sustenance and strength! Let us be of good cheer for these gifts from nature."

The small, narrow branch of the Golden River soon became stronger and flowed more rapidly downstream. Its sound was loud enough that they could barely hear their own footsteps as they clumped their way along the rocky bank.

Gamedon, with his keen vision, saw something far ahead at the edge of the river bank. As they approached, he saw that it was a small wooden boat, handily equipped with two oars. Upon examination, he saw that it was carved out of a Calicab, for it bore the mottled markings of the trunks and branches and extraordinary root system of the large and ancient trees that surrounded them.

"Come, Andalorax," said Gamedon, "we must take advantage of this good luck and leave the rocky path." But secretly he wondered what strange creature had placed that boat there, so conveniently. Without any further thought or speech, the two quickly stowed their knapsacks and walking sticks in the center of the little vessel. Andalorax got in and seated herself in front at the prow, facing the course of the river, while Gamedon, from the shoreline, gave the boat a heave. It caught the current, and he jumped in at the rear, handily grabbing the oars and managing the small craft with ease.

Off they sped, downriver. The waters were flowing southwest, and Gamedon wondered where they would take them. Now they were under control of that inimitable natural source: flowing water. They swiftly passed rows of Calicabs on both sides, but soon the trees began to thin out and small hills made their appearance. These hills grew in size as they sped along, and rose in stature to become small mountains.

Gamedon said, "Granddaughter, I recognize not where we are, but we are certainly leaving these woods and entering a territory of which I have no knowledge." But he knew – and feared – that they were heading towards the Black Mountains.

The very idea of those unknown, mythological mountains caused a chill to crawl up his spine and made the hairs on his head stand up. Happily, his feathered felt hat stayed tightly bound to his head. The waters were still navigable as the boat took the two passengers deeper into the darkness caused by the shadows of the mountains. As it was still nighttime, and the bright moon passed in and out of dim clouds, the gloomy panorama widened and appeared quite vast in size. The trees slowly disappeared and were replaced by craggy black peaks.

"Grandfather," cried out Andalorax, "where are we?"

"My dear girl," he said in studied tones, with the tune of the rushing waters somewhat muffling his words, "we are now in the Black Mountains."

CHAPTER 23

CAPTURED!

MALTHOR AND HIS KNIGHTS SHED their protective cloaks and greeted the sunrise. Once again they were on the trail of Gamedon and his "white-haired granddaughter." They made their royal procession through the Calicab Forest, dressed in their golden-threaded finery. They had no idea that what they sought was now far beyond their reach – for Gamedon and Andalorax had been swiftly and surely taken far, far away by the little boat.

The two of them were, indeed, at the foothills of the dreaded and unknown Black Mountains.

The Golden River wound its way steadily along when they felt the first warmth of the sun on their faces. While the Twenty Men of the Eyes simultaneously awoke and continued their search, the waters carved their way through hard rock and stone.

Presently, the ebb tide seemed to slow somewhat and brought the little wooden craft to a halt at a particularly narrow strait. Gamedon seized the opportunity to maneuver their vessel with his oars so that he could in one fleeting moment jump out and touch land. Andalorax stepped lightly upon the rocky soil, dampening her shoes and the edge of her cloak. They removed their belongings from the boat, which was wedged between some boulders, and sat down on a large rock beside them.

All was still and quiet except for the sound of the waters. Despite the expanding sunlight that outlined the craggy mountains surrounding them, there was no other sound. Not one singing bird, not one falling leaf, not one fragile butterfly entered the darkened terrain. The air was cold and moist; there was a slight breeze, and the shallow rippling river exposed its pebbles … but that was all the life that Gamedon and Andalorax could feel or see about them.

Finally Andalorax asked again, "Where are we, Grandfather?"

And Gamedon answered simply, "In the Black Mountains."

"What shall we do now?"

"My dearest child, now we must consider our position and decide upon our next move." He withdrew his trusty compass and proclaimed that they were definitely southwest of Milorin – indeed, of all the lands of the Kingdom of Pellah. And here, in this uncharted territory, they sat in silence. Presently, the sun made its way past the mountaintops and shone rays of bright light into the dark valley. They could see now that they were surrounded by rock. Not one tree was left on the banks of the river, which had once seemed so mighty but was now drained to a thin stream. Perhaps, thought Gamedon, they had ended up taking a smaller tributary ….

Gamedon arose and said, "We must continue on our way, Andalorax. Our journey is not over by any means. Here, let me put your backpack upon your shoulders once again, and here, too, is your dependable walking stick." This he did, and hefted his own knapsack upon his back as well. Thus outfitted once again, they began to make their way along the riverbank. Their little boat was no longer of any use for them, and they walked forward, leaving it behind being lapped against the beach by little ripples.

Presently they came upon a flat area, on which the sun was shining somewhat more brightly than elsewhere. They stood there, leaning on their walking sticks, braced against the unknown territory that rose high up all around them. Gamedon leaned down and picked up a few stones. They were as black as coal and smooth to the touch, probably worn down by many years of water rushing across their surface. With his keen sight, he spotted an opening in the nearest hillock and immediately they headed for it.

They had to lower their heads to pass through, and they found themselves in a darkened passageway. Within another twenty feet, the corridor opened into a spacious cave.

"Let us rest now, dear girl," said Gamedon brightly, for he intended to cheer up his granddaughter who surely must be frightened by this lifeless landscape. Rock, rock, and more rock was all their eyes could see. Not even the brightest rays of the sun found their mark in here. They strained their eyes but it was almost impossible to see anything. Gamedon put down his knapsack, and opened a pocket, found a matchbook and a candle, set the lit candle upon a small boulder, and presently their eyes could see in the darkness of the cave.

Its roof seemed interminably high, but the black rock walls were quite visible, reaching about ten feet away from them on all sides. However, it clearly showed them that they were at a dead end. By the light of the single taper, they slumped down to the black earth beneath their feet. Silently, they partook of some of their bread and cheese, and drank water from their canteens. The air moved not, and the candle never flickered. An hour went past, and Gamedon announced, "We will sleep here tonight and continue on our way in the morning."

As they went to pick up their knapsacks, Andalorax saw something white on the black earth. She bent down and found a cluster of little plants that appeared to be some kind of mushrooms. At least something similar to mushrooms, she thought, for what other plant could grow here in the damp darkness without sunlight? She plucked one, and held it in her palm. It withered to her touch within a few seconds and dried up into a small twig. "Oh!" she cried out, for it tickled her when it curled up, and she dropped it to the ground.

At the sound of her cry, Gamedon went over to her and she showed him her discovery. He, too, plucked one and again, once in his hand, it dried up into a tiny sliver. But Gamedon held onto it and brought it to the candlelight. When the plant was in the light, it instantly turned white again, fleshing out and resuming its initial appearance.

"Interesting," he thought. "And somewhat familiar ...." The plant instantly evoked the moment when he was in his Laboratory at the Castle Pellah, and saw the pale white Phemtas plant reaching for the bright, molten gold he was using to make his golden key to the King's Library.

"But it is strange," his mind told him, "for this is unlike the Phemtas plant I am familiar with. It is more like a small toadstool mushroom, whereas my little plant had a long stem and flowered when it found the gold. Perhaps it is a variety of the plant that I have never seen, until now. Or vice versa."

He dropped it on the ground, and no more was said about it.

Then they laid out their cloaks upon the black rocky floor scattered with black soil, and made pillows from their scarves, and presently fell fast asleep.

They were awakened to find that their tiny candle had flickered out and the cavern was completely dark. Gamedon felt for yet another taper and lit that one. Now they could see the same dismal surroundings into which they had fallen earlier. They knew not whether it was night or day, and headed for the gateway to the outside.

All of a sudden, they realized that a single large boulder had rolled – or been rolled – in front of the passageway and their exit was blocked! Gamedon pushed against the huge rock but had no power to move it even one inch. They were trapped! Yet there was free-flowing air coming from outside, somehow, for the candle flickered in a slight breeze along edges of the boulder. Aha! Here was some light after all. Then it must be daytime still, thought Gamedon.

Then they saw it: an enormous, menacing shadow passed by them outside of the cave. They could see the darkness as it moved across the boulder's perimeter. Something or someone was out there ... something large enough to cast its shadow across the enormous breadth of the boulder. "Something probably large enough to have placed it there, as well," thought Gamedon.

"I am so terrified, Grandfather!" whispered Andalorax, as she tightened her belt and hoisted up her leggings from where they had become creased during their repose. "What is that enormous shadow that just passed outside?"

"I know not, dear child," came the answer.

They waited a few more minutes, then saw the shadow again. And then they heard the coarse sound of some kind of animal, something they had never heard before. A deep, scratchy vocal sound like a stone scraping another stone. It was outside! Perhaps it came from the creature that patrolled the entranceway to the cave.

"Who hides in the lair of my mighty Sovereign?" came a husky voice. The words were clear but the sound was peppered with hoarseness.

Gamedon and Andalorax, startled by the sudden question in their own language, looked quickly at each other.

"Two wanderers from the Kingdom of Pellah," called out Gamedon.

"And what do you seek here?" croaked the voice.

"We are seeking shelter from the Knights of King Vanamir, Lord of all the lands we know."

Silence reigned. Then the voice recommenced its questioning:

"Why do you seek refuge here in the Black Mountains?" it asked. The sound resonated its way through the cracks in the boulder and filled the cavern with an ominous echo.

"We came here with a boat down the Golden River," said Gamedon.

"It brought us to this cave."

More silence.

Gamedon pulled himself up to his full height – and, short as he was, it emboldened him – and he continued to speak.

"And who are you?" he asked. "All I see is your shadow and this boulder, which you have presumably propped up to forfeit our exit."

"No questions!" thundered the voice. "Only answers! What are your names? Who follows your party of two helpless humans?"

"We are Gamedon and Andalorax, a small meek fellow with a small meek girl-child. Except for those who might be chasing after us, we come alone, oh Great One," retorted Gamedon, trying to sound big and strong while withholding any tinge of fear or anger.

"Well do I know of thee," responded the throaty voice. "I have been expecting your arrival. Now that I know you are who I think you are, I shall set you free!"

And with that, the voice cried out words that can only be described as some sort of magical incantation that sounded like:

Madjibay-mitsbee Galorth!

Immediately after the words were spoken, the large boulder began to creak and moan and make crunching noises, and inch its way out of the opening to the cave. Eventually, it had completely rolled aside.

Gamedon and Andalorax drew back in sheer terror, for what remained in the doorway took away the breath of the humble duo: it was the two, four-toed feet of a bird of clearly enormous proportions. The feet were bright yellow. The feathers on the legs, however, were black. Its feathers were so black that they seemed to almost glisten like the black rocks wet from the Golden River's waters, and they were so huge that only his strong, pointed feet and talons were visible.

"Why, he must be … twelve feet high!" calculated Gamedon. Never had he known any animal, let alone a paltry bird, to be so vast in size.

"Come forth!" roared the bird. "Now!"

At such a command, they had little choice but to stoop once more through the passageway into the outdoors. They raised their heads slowly and could see that it was, indeed, another dawn rising above the mountain peaks, as they took in the vastness of the bird that stood before them.

Indeed, his plumage was almost all black, except for red and white stripes crossing his wings and a big red spot on his large chest. His beak was red, his feet a lovely bright canary yellow. His feathers were long and shiny, almost as glossy as an oil slick. They were opalescent, with rainbow colors in the blackness. His breast was wide and protruding; his neck was long and thick.

Of a sudden, he lifted its wings and spread them out so quickly and widely that Gamedon could feel the wind rushing beneath them. Then he folded in his wings and lowered his head to meet the two wanderers face-to-face.

Lo and behold! He had but one eye, and that big, oval-shaped eye was as scarlet red as his thick beak and chest and wing markings, and the pinhole in its center was as black as pitch.

"I am Siddles, the One-Eyed, Evil-Eyed Guardian of the Black Mountains! Bow down and behold my glory! Bow down, I say!"

Gamedon and Andalorax bent their heads as low as their chins would allow, and they folded themselves at the waist.

"Greetings, oh Siddles!" they both said in unison. Andalorax grabbed hold of Gamedon's hand.

Once again the bird flapped his enormous wings, creating great gusts of wind that knocked Gamedon and Andalorax, still wearing their knapsacks and now also holding their magic walking sticks, to the rocky ground. Siddles raised his bony head to the sky, which was filtered with the sunlight's shooting rays, and cried out more mystical words:

Yanook jambu Siddles osage wazow!

Then he coughed, and decreed, "You are my prisoners, ye little folk of the Pellah Kingdom." And with a mighty swoop of one of his muscled feet and thick talons, he picked up Gamedon and Andalorax with all their gear and, the duo nestled in his claw, he pushed himself off the ground and flew up into the sun-streaked afternoon sky.

CHAPTER 24

SIDDLES AND THE BLACK MOUNTAINS

SIDDLES ROSE HIGHER AND HIGHER into the sky, and flew on for what seemed like hours, rising way above the craggy peaks of the Black Mountains. Gamedon and Andalorax watched in tremendous fear and awe as the landscape sped beneath them. The great bird's wings flapped steadily on into the morning, and soon, into the rising sun in the east. They were headed west southwest.

Then he began to fly lower and lower, creating a generous vista of the horizon and its high, ragged black edges. But the rising sun sparked a blaze in the east, of ruby and orange and pink striated clouds reflecting the prisms of the dew in the air. Such a spectacular view, and such a wondrous voyage in the talons of a bird, Gamedon never anticipated he would experience in his lifetime!

As the bird reached the lower terraces of the air currents, his captives saw that he was fast approaching a peak which rose to a magnificent height, higher than all the others around. It was the highest peak in the vast mountain range, albeit they all were beyond the scope of the old man and the young girl held fast in the talons of their captor.

Instantly, at the same time, they both saw that the mountain Siddles was headed for was a volcano, and he was going to fly right down into it!

As they switched into a rapid descent, and entered the cone of the volcano, the sky suddenly became quite dark and the air had a chill, for the sun was now gone. The bottom of the pit was fast approaching as the terrified prisoners closed their eyes and screamed.

But then they glided downwards, going 'round and 'round more and more slowly, and Andalorax opened her eyes and saw below a large area where the rock of the volcano was flat and polished. Now, that flat area was zooming up into her vision!

And with a great "Swish!" of his tail, and a great flapping of his mighty wings, Siddles reached out one enormous foot as he hit the ground with a big "Thud!" Then he opened his other claw and out rolled Gamedon and Andalorax.

They were on black rock, flat like shale, and shiny like black pearls.

"We must be at the bottom of the volcano," said Gamedon, brushing off his trousers.

"Aye, Grandfather!" replied Andalorax, shaking out her long, white hair and bending her head back. "Look! Look up!" She reached her arm up into the air and pointed at a distant blue hole, which was all they could see of the sky from inside this enormous but clearly extinct volcano. They both stood there in awe of their surroundings. Everything was black rock. It was all illuminated by bright globes of light that simply floated in the air.

Gamedon wondered: "Where is their fuel?"

Andalorax whispered back, "Magic?"

With a wink, he answered, "Who can say?"

Tall pedestals of stone ran down the left and right sides of a pathway leading straight to a large, open-air cave. In the distance somewhere at the end of this small trail, fountains and small waterfalls made a distinctly pleasant sound, but that is all they could see from here where the pathway ended.

Atop each pedestal was a flaming ball of tremendously bright light, which illuminated this otherwise-dark volcano pit. There were also smaller, daintier globes of light that floated next to them but were of equal strength and brightness. The pillars were taller than Gamedon but only reached the wingtip of Siddles, he was so tall!

"Follow me, Gamedon and Andalorax," said the giant bird. He put his enormous bright yellow foot out and proceeded to walk down the stone pathway.

As they walked along, they noticed a small rivulet on their left side. The globes illuminated what the weak sunshine could hardly show: the beauty of the water as it flowed downstream, even this small stream. Andalorax could hear it sing out as it went by.

Hear me sing a Water-whisper
To my magic Water-sister:
All is Black and All is White

> *Together they create the light.*
> *Half is White and Half is Black*
> *Together they bring wholeness back!*

What? Was she hearing things? The water was singing to her?

Suddenly, she recalled the Silent Lake! And the Many-Colored Girl! That silent lake had spoken to her, and she thought nothing of it then. She thought about the Many-Colored Girl, which surprised her because she rarely thought of her, as her life was continuously so eventful and demanding. Now she had to deal with who knew what at the end of this path, accompanied by a gigantic bird with spectacular, iridescent plumage.

"Grandfather, do you hear the water singing?"

"No, I don't. Do you? Your mother could talk with the water. Remember, her name 'Mandir' means 'water' in the ancient tongue of Pellah."

"Aye, I do hear the water," she continued, as they made their way behind the giant bird.

All the while, Siddles attempted to quiet them, but they could not curtail their sense of relief at being back on the ground and being able to think this out together! What, indeed, was this enormous talking bird?

Siddles brought them to an abrupt halt at the end of the footpath, and they found themselves at the very wide-open entrance to a cave. The opening was at least sixty feet long and fifteen feet high, for, as far as Gamedon could tell, it would probably accommodate the estimated twelve-foot-high Siddles without him having to bend down and crane his long and thick neck.

"You will both now pay attention me," rasped out Siddles, as he strutted along the floor. Then he lifted his big bony head, and cried out:

Haspir madji-bay Siddles Mitsbee Zandorfska!

Siddles proceeded to fluff up his feathers and fold in his big wings, as all of a sudden his size diminished to about six feet.

Then he said, "Prisoners! You are now in the domain of my great master, Zivat-Or! He reigns over these mountains as he has for over two centuries. Yes, that's correct. I said over two centuries, and I am his devoted advisor and friend."

"What do you mean, we are your prisoners?" asked Andalorax.

"You shall see, you shall see." He hissed out his "esses" and shook his bony head that wobbled on his long neck when he spoke. How his plumage shone from the illumination of the globes. The crimson and white stripes, the red beak, the yellow feet! Andalorax admired the bird so much!

She found her breath after a few moments, and asked, "Who is this aged creature, this Zivat-Or?"

"He is the grand and glorious Man of Rock!"

"I have never heard of him. Centuries old, you say?"

"Yes," answered Siddles. "Two and one-half centuries, in fact!"

"How can it be that a man is so old? Is there any sorcery involved?"

"You may call it sorcery if you like, yet it is also his forceful will and the will of nature that allow him to continue on in this world for such a space of time, because of his Great Purpose!"

"And what might that Great Purpose be, pray tell?"

Siddles bowed his big head, and tapped with his crimson beak the rocky terrain upon which they all stood, then turned his one piercing, red eye towards Andalorax and spewed his hoarse voice into the growing evening light, "This (he hissed out the letter "sssssssss" like a serpent), I cannot reveal to you, little female human, for it is a key to his powerfully long lifespan and is a secret. Do not try to know more, I advise you. I have already said enough, as I am his devoted servant and protector."

Suddenly, in the center of the darkened cave, many globes lit up and circled around a raised platform, whereon sat a man. He was glowing in the light. All around his throne, the circular lights glowed and spun around, seemingly with the wind. They made a buzzing sound now, getting louder and louder, as they circled around the man upon the throne.

Andalorax turned her attention to the dais right before them, and the man seated thereon. What was that moving about around him? He was seated upon a strange, moving, living thing, like a creature from a nightmare … it was white and fleshy looking, with tendrils and flowers just as if it were a plant.

It was a plant! She immediately realized this and so did Gamedon. This man was seated upon a writhing, living, substantive plant! Andalorax then took in the rest of him: He was of red beard and hair, streaked with gray, both long and braided down his chest. He wore an enormous, gold crown that sparkled with the colors of many stones. His raiment was a golden chain mail vest that shone in the dimming sunlight of the faraway volcanic outlet to the sky, and had golden scales in the plating. On his hands were black leather gloves whose wide cuffs were embroidered, too, with gold.

Then she looked deeper into his face: Why, he was an old man! Wrinkles surrounded his eyes and lips, his cheeks sagged and his eyes looked dark and sunken.

"How can this be, Gamedon," she asked in a whisper, "that a King is so old?"

"SILENCE!" shouted the man on the throne. "You will not speak in front of the King unless given permission!" As he spoke in his loud, deep voice, he leaned forward to get a better look at Andalorax and Gamedon.

"SIDDLES!!" he shouted. "Come here!"

The great bird leaned his head down to the level of the man's face – which was about five feet higher than Gamedon and Andalorax due to his raised dais – and said, "Aye, My King. I am here, Sire."

"Siddles, what prize have you brought to your King?"

"Two strangers I found at the very edge of the mountain range to the north. They came here by boat down the Golden River. If you remember, you had a premonition of some activity in the northern boundary, and sent me there. This is what I found, Sire."

"And you came straight here?"

"Aye, my King," replied Siddles.

"Now you must go and make some form of accommodation for our guests!" He laughed, throwing back his head, and his red- and silver-colored hair flew wildly about him.

"Accommodation here in the Black Mountains is not luxurious, is it, my dear Siddles? What can you create for them, oh Siddles? Be sure not to treat them better than you treat your sovereign!" He reached out his long and bony fingers, and said, "Don't use your magic to give them anything that is gold, mind you!"

"Aye, my Lord. With your permission, I shall take my leave and obey your command."

"Leave then!"

The enormous bird bowed his head down so low that his red beak touched the ground. He tapped it several times. Then he turned around and, flapping his wide wings, he flew off into the darkness of nightfall.

The man turned his piercing green eyes towards the two and stared at them with a menacing grin. Then he twisted the grin into a smile and said:

"Greetings!"

His voice was very loud and echoed in the great chamber. The only other sound was the soft waterfall at the back of the cave. It was then that Gamedon noticed that there was no one else in the large space. The man leaned forward and asked, "And who may you be?"

"We are your humble guests," said Gamedon. "We were brought here by Siddles the Great Bird."

"Ah, yes! My gifted slave, Siddles! However, who do you think I may be?" He patted himself on the chest as he spoke. All the while, the white, fleshy plant writhed and moved about him, as if caressing him.

"I don't know, sir. Who may you be?"

"I," he bellowed out, "am Zivat-Or, Sole Ruler and King of these Black Mountains! Bow down!" ordered the deep voice from the tall, ancient-looking man.

Gamedon and Andalorax obeyed, bending as low as possible before this strange creature. Everything was happening so quickly now, after that terrifying flight in the talons of Siddles, that they obeyed without hesitation. The peaceful little stroll on the way to meeting this frightening man no longer gave the two any comfort. Who was this new "King?" And what was that strange plant upon which he was sitting – or appeared to be sitting?

"Perhaps," thought Gamedon, ever pondering the why of things, "perhaps he is seated on a throne and the plant lives in a pot by his side. Perhaps the plant comes from roots elsewhere," as the fading sunlight continued in the darkening cave. The plant had long vines that were crawling about as Gamedon and Andalorax watched, the actual living arms and branches and pale, yellow-orange flowers of a plant!

However, despite the fact that he was seated and the light was fading as the sun escaped, the globes lit up his face in great detail. Gamedon knew this was a tall man, an elderly man yet somehow still in prime health and condition, and that he resembled his own King Vanamir, being about the same height, at six feet four inches much taller than the average five-and-a-half foot tall Pellah citizen.

Suddenly, the man puffed up his chest.

"Did you hear me?! I am King Zivat-Or!" he spoke loudly. "I am familiar with your kind, for I, too, am human. My history is long and arduous and not relevant at the moment. What is most relevant is who are you two and what are you doing in my Black Mountains?"

A shirt made of gold covered his chest and shone blindingly in the paling light. He was not sitting on a throne – his throne was made of the plant, and that's what he was sitting on! The plant mysteriously carried him through the air and brought him to Gamedon and Andalorax, face-to-face. He was floating on the writhing plant as if it were a puffy cloud. Instead, it was a pale, damp-looking, fibrous plant making continuous undulations. It had several extraordinary flowers blooming, which looked waxy and had long pistils piercing out, like little swords, and displaying colorful, sticky stamens.

Too, at that moment, Andalorax flared open her nostrils and sniffed deeply because the air smelled quite strongly of some opulent flower that could have appeared in her dreams.

The man was definitely tall in stature, but now that Gamedon and Andalorax could see as they adjusted to the illumination of the globes that drifted around in space, some actually going underneath Zivat-Or and his plant throne, they noticed with greater detail the thing that enveloped him … it made the man seem almost twice his normal size. His legs, his torso, up to his waist, were wrapped in the vines of the plant. And these vines kept growing and reaching around and intertwining with one another. The sound it made in so doing was a kind of "buzz" that accompanied Zivat-Or like music in the background. It also went with the sound of the waterfall behind him.

Zivat-Or reached out a long arm and pointed to them both. "Well, let me have it! What do you want here? Speak and speak now!"

His outstretched arm had a vine wrapped around it but the King didn't seem to care. His golden blouse covered his entire torso and arms, and waved fluidly in the air with his movements and the malleability of the golden vest.

Gamedon spoke: "Oh, mighty King Zivat-Or, we come from the Kingdom of Pellah, from the town of Milorin within. We were traveling from that small town, going through the Calicab Forest, when we stumbled upon your territory."

"But you are omitting the fact that you two are running away from something!" responded the King, "Else you would not be so deep into the forest to begin with. Do not omit anything! At once, speak up or there shall be trouble!"

Andalorax, in her soft young voice, told Zivat-Or that they were renegades, hiding from the King's Knights. This fact seemed to perk up the King and his eyes opened wide. "They, too, are green, as are the citizens of Pellah!" noticed Andalorax.

"And why are you running from your King?"

"My grandfather is long-banished from Milorin; I was born there, as you see me now: white of hair, black of eyes. I am and have always been an outcast due to that 'disfigurement.' I lived in Castle Pellah for fifteen years, since my infancy. But my King, Vanamir, decided that my destiny was to be a prisoner in the Castle."

Zivat-Or seemed very interested, leaning forward, watching Andalorax intently.

"And why would he do such a thing?"

"Because he believed that I am destined to be part of his downfall."

"How did he come to such conclusions?"

"From dreams. From prophesies. Anything he sees that is black and white brings me to his mind and I am worrisome for him and for myself, to say little else."

They were all silent for a moment. What else could she say that would make him see their plight, and perhaps help them on their journey?

Zivat-Or sat up and said to Andalorax: "Why is it that you look as you do? You are different from any other woman that I have seen. Are you a sorceress?"

"No, Sire. I am a simple maid of the woods who was born in strange circumstances that seem to have affected the way I appear."

"What circumstances?"

"I was born outdoors, at night under the full moon, your Lord."

"There!" she announced to herself. "I said it."

Then King Zivat-Or sat back and sighed, and whispered very softly, now leaning forward towards the pair:

"Come closer, you two!" He stuck out his long, knobby index finger and beckoned them to approach him. They both moved up as closely as they could without touching the vines of the writhing plant. It was too alarming an idea to touch it!

"You, old man," he said, quietly, "you know of banishment? Well, so do I." Gamedon and Andalorax exchanged quick glances of surprise. "I want to know your story of exactly and precisely why you were banished! Tell me now, for I have a notion that I know why!"

Gamedon cleared his throat and spoke up.

"I do not believe in the myth that the night is evil and we must worship only the sun. I had supporters. But I was made to leave the town and go live elsewhere. I chose the Calicab Forest."

"Aha!" Zivat-Or slammed his fist into his other palm, and threw back his head and laughed wildly! "You do not believe in the ways of the Kingdom of Pellah?" asked Zivat-Or, craning his neck forward and staring at them.

"No, my King," said Andalorax and Gamedon simultaneously. At those words, they reached out and held each other's hands.

"And for this you were banished?"

"This is true, almighty Zivat-Or."

The King again threw his head backwards and laughed most horrifically. The globes about him began to hum and buzz and encircle him with their energetic moves around, across, under and above the throne that was made of a plant and its occupant thereon, who, it seemed, would never stop laughing.

But suddenly, he did stop, and propelled himself and the plant close to the two, and said in a gruff manner: "I, too, know of banishment! Old man, you and I, another old man, have something in common."

CHAPTER 25

ZIVAT-OR'S STORY

"MANY, MANY YEARS AGO – MORE than you could possibly imagine – I, too, lived in the Pellah Kingdom. I was and still am a true King from the line of the Kings of Pellah. The Kings all put forth, from the beginning, the notion that the night was bad and the day was good. It became almost mythological or spiritual.

"I studied this theory and came to the decision that it simply wasn't true! Why did the Kings push this on their people? I calculated the reasons why: To control them, to keep them indoors at night, to spur production on farms and the countryside life. To rule over a gentle, peaceful land with this fear!

"When I put forth my own ideas, the councilmen rallied against me, and the people went against me as well. I was dethroned by my own son, the next King of Pellah upon my surcease. But he overthrew me and put himself on the throne.

"For this I was banished for life from the entire Kingdom and forced to live here in the Black Mountains, which at that time was just an undeveloped, unpopulated chain of high hills with rugged cliffs and valleys.

"But you, old man, you were given a choice of where you wanted to live! You lived in a forest! How lovely! I was not given that privilege."

Zivat-Or stared at Gamedon with hatred in his eyes, and then pointed his finger in Gamedon's direction, and raised his voice and said:

"No! No privilege for me! It was to here that I was tossed out and exiled!" He was waving his arms and the plant was flailing about, hissing almost at the madness in the air. "Here, where the mountain peaks are jagged and insurmountably high, and create a ring around the base of this volcanic valley.

"Also, around this very volcano in which I reside, the soil is covered with volcanic dust from an explosion many countless years ago from this very volcano. Where the only living plant is this pale weed you see about me!"

Then he did a strange thing. While Andalorax and Gamedon stood silently, still holding hands, listening to this story, Zivat-Or grabbed hold of one of the writhing vines and held it in his hand. He stroked it as if it were a pet. The plant stopped moving about and just lay there, resting on his palm.

The King put his hand to his chest and pulled out from under his shirt a long golden chain from which hung a large cube-shaped object.

Gold! It was a chunk of purest gold; Gamedon could see that right away. As he and Andalorax watched, the plant in his other hand began to move, and to rise, and to lean towards the golden object.

Phemtas! The plant with which the man found himself intertwined was Phemtas!

Gamedon knew this at once. He knew it could be no other plant and he recognized it now beyond a doubt. Just like the first one in his Laboratory in the Castle Pellah, which actually bloomed for the gold, reaching out for it, lusting for it. "And now," thought Gamedon, "here it is, encircling a King who is dressed in gold; perhaps the plant lives for the gold!"

He recalled also what Mayor Thrasher, the first Milorin Mayor, wrote in Pellah Year 242: "The pale plant needs neither sun nor water." And here the plant was, without benefit of sun – and perhaps without water.

And, too, Gamedon recalled, there was the dried Phemtas he had seen in King Vanamir's private closet. They looked like ivory-white parched corn husks, laid out and tightly bound together in bunches. He recognized this plant from those withered dried leaves and flowers.

Gamedon's head was spinning with questions about the plant: Why was this old man so interwoven by Phemtas here in this big volcanic cavern? How could the plant transport him away from the dais without showing any root system? Did the plant subsist off of the King? Or perhaps it was the other way around …?

King Zivat-Or continued to speak, as he fingered the gold on the chain: "Yes, I was banished. My family and some of my friends came with me to this horrible place. But it wasn't always so horrible! No! My banished band of supporters of my philosophy and I made something of a life here. The land that is behind you, not around this volcano, was once green, forested, and had fruit-bearing plants and trees. My companions and I built diminutive homes here, and we subsisted for many years.

"But time has taken them all from me, alas, as they are all now long dead. And this plant has taken over all the valley, with its inherent evil and wickedness!"

"How can a plant take over an entire valley, Sire?" asked Andalorax.

"Its evil is so great that all the innocent and pure natural life – the animals, the greenery, the lakes, a small forest, and large fields for farming, whereon we made our homes – was overtaken and destroyed. Beyond that, the why of it, I cannot explain. I do not know. But it happened!"

Gamedon's large pointed ears were standing out and his hair was on edge as he listened to these words of Zivat-Or.

And Andalorax then asked, "Why is it, my King, that you alone remain? How can it be that you have lived so many years – two centuries, you say?"

"AHA!" shouted the King, as he pointed his long index finger towards her. "Almost two and a half!" He laughed in a voice that sounded like a sneeze. "That is a question that I cannot truly answer, for I know not why. I simply know 'How.' The 'How' is Phemtas.

"This pale weed that you see encircling me has been at the forefront of my existence here. I became familiar with its properties somewhat, but the second-most important property is, of course, its love of gold! You can see this for yourself, my dear young lady. See how it twists about me? It's because I am wearing a shirt of purest gold! And I am holding a piece of gold in my palm!" So saying he put his hand out and sure enough he was holding in his hand the chunk of gold the size of a carnation that hung from his long chain, and a couple of vines began to crawl along his arm heading towards his open palm.

"I have had this shirt since the first day I arrived here many years ago – more than I will reveal! It was made for me before my journey here, by a seamstress friend of mine back at the Castle. It actually is a shirt of gold mail. She made it to protect me, for I was indeed a soldier going away to war. And as gold is common up in the Castle – as you know – that was her choice of metal for the shirt."

Silence. Then he added, "She is long dead, as is everyone else."

Andalorax looked deeply into the face of this strange man, wondering how it was that he could still be alive if all of them were long dead. Was there some magic or witchcraft or sorcery or actually even some natural force that caused this man's condition, wrapped up in the cloud of a plant the color of wax ....

So – as she watched a plant coil around his finger then unfold itself– she spoke out, "Oh, King Zivat-Or!" as she bowed to him out of politeness and respect for a King – "If, as you said before, love of gold is this plant's second-most important property, what, then, pray tell, is its most important?"

"What's that? You dare to ask me such a personal question? Don't you know I'm the King of all you survey and could do away with you in a moment?" Zivat-Or growled out his words." Then he smiled wickedly, showing long, yellowed teeth.

"But I applaud your bravery, young girl! Tell me again, what is your name?"

"Andalorax."

"Well, Andalorax, I shall answer you. I shall answer you because it is so extraordinarily rare that anyone has come to my Mountain abode that I want to learn more about you and what's going on in the Kingdom of Pellah.

"Therefore, Andalorax, the most important attribute of this plant, before its love of gold, is many things combined. It is not an object; it is, rather, a quality. It includes enchantment … persuasion … prepossession! I am bewitched by its magic.

"Because of these 'alluring' qualities, I have learned to need it. Without ingesting it, I would not be here today. It has overwhelmed me to the point where we are one and the same, the plant and I."

"Ingesting it?"

"I dry it and smoke it in my pipe. See it over there, on the table? I will go over there and fetch it for you."

They looked and, sure enough, there was a desk sprinkled all over with gold dust, in a corner of the cave. Zivat-Or was carried along by the Phemtas plant to which he was harnessed, followed by several of the golden globes. Atop the desk were various boxes and a few bottles, but the largest object was a tall pipe made of wood and glass.

Zivat-Or floated on his throne of Phemtas over to the gold-spattered table where he parked himself, and proceeded to fill his pipe. He began to cut some dried leaves, which were very long and yellowed, with a large scissors. He didn't pay attention to Gamedon and Andalorax, which gave them an opportunity to speak with one another at last.

"Andalorax, listen to me, quickly now! Something extraordinary is happening here right now in this cave in the Black Mountains," he whispered in a low hush. "At this very moment, we are facing not only a former King of Pellah – Yes! But also the true King of the Black Mountains – who is using his plant to continue to receive its gifts."

And, at this one moment in time, King Zivat-Or was busily filling his tall pipe at the top with dried Phemtas, and taking a light from a candle he lit up his pipe and began to smoke it. The odor reached them immediately. Gamedon recognized it, for it was the same scent he was assailed by in the House of Time in Milorin. Also probably from when he was with King Vanamir, and he didn't know what the odor was caused by.

Now he knew.

Phemtas!

Now the King was enthusiastically twirling a vine around his fingers, then watching it unfold and move elsewhere in the network that surrounded this man from waist to feet.

"The plant upon which he sits is Phemtas!" Gamedon spoke very firmly, as they were now out of hearing range from Zivat-Or. "You know, my dear, I know a lot about Phemtas and I am trying to understand what the connection is between this plant and the Kings of Pellah, and I have never known of a common man – one not born to the royal bloodline – being affected by the plant.

"This news to my thinking cap helps me to connect the dots: Therefore, Phemtas is needed by the Kings to not only maintain their reign and stay in power, but also to live longer through its magic. Look at the power it has given this man, to live so many years – two and one-half centuries! It is potent indeed!

"Aye, yes, certainly now," he continued, "We know the Kings not only needed it, they were addicted to it, and imbibed of it throughout their reign …. That is why they collect the Royal Dues from Milorin! Do you realize this, dear girl?!"

Andalorax and Gamedon turned and faced each other. They knew it was a significant moment.

"And, Grandfather," said Andalorax, looking into his green eyes as he looked into her dark ones, "this Zivat-Or has become strangely bonded with the plant. He wears a gold shirt which keeps the plant around him all day and night. It lives because of the gold! It rewards him with long life and power … Gamedon, I'll bet that the plant once was quite small, when Zivat-Or first became beguiled by its abilities to bring long life and power …."

CHAPTER 26

MALTHOR AND THE KING

MALTHOR RAISED HIS LANCE AND the other Knights of King Vanamir followed his example. They were all too weary to do anything else, having marched through the Calicab Forest – and slept there in the night! – for three days now. And here was another night coming soon, for them to endure.

"Men!" he called out, "We have searched the forest as much as I, as First Knight for our valiant King, deem realistically possible. We also are very low on provisions. Let tonight, therefore, be our last night on this search, and let us return tomorrow to the Castle Pellah.

"We should take another day or two to exit these woods, and then a week to ride north along the Golden River, on the Golden River Road, heading home. On the way home, as we travel once more on our own soil, we can refresh our food and drink for the rest of the journey. What say ye now, Knights?"

"Aye!" came the chorus of Knights. They all started chatting and laughing but Malthor cried out, "Hold still, gentlemen! We must again bed down for the night now, and prepare so that at first light we can leave these woods behind us."

This was followed by another chorus of cheering men showing their gleaming white teeth – men who had slept under the ever-sturdy Calicab trees, with their long, waving branches. The soldiers felt that those branches offered some protection from the white orbits in the sky, that circle 'round the single Guiding Star, the North Star. They all studied astronomy during their training as Knights and, despite fear of them, they knew stars and constellations familiar to their sky. They could all navigate by the stars.

Morning found the Knights on the path out of the forest. By noon they were at the very edge where the town of Milorin began, and the lands of the Kingdom would be there to greet them at last! It felt like months – no, years – since they'd touched their own soil.

By sunset they were in Milorin, at Jack Beale's Inn, looking forward to sleeping in beds for the first time in four days and nights.

In the dining room Malthor met up with the ten Knights of the Coffers, who guarded the supply of the King's herb, Phemtas, in their large leather saddlebags. The chief Knights of the Coffers, Pengor and Isidro, assured Malthor that they were completely ready for tomorrow's departure back to the Castle.

Malthor was pleased. Ah! Now he could ride with assurance that they had done their best to find the old man and his granddaughter – although they had failed. But Malthor felt great confidence that his King would understand their circumstances. They had roamed large portions of the forest, and never picked up a trail. Also, it was difficult to sleep outside at night, with who knew what roaming out there in the woods while they slept. Malevolent spirits ... witches ... wicked fairies ... the legends went on and on.

In the gold-studded coffers with leather fringe that swayed when the horse moved, was more of the Royal Dues for King Vanamir.

"At bringing back the strong-smelling weed, at least, our King shall be pleased," Malthor told his men, to which they all broke out in a hearty laugh.

"Now," he continued, "go to sleep in your feather beds instead of being wrapped in your cloaks and dream of your wives and the ladies of court with whom you will soon be reunited. Off you go now!"

Milorin being the southernmost town in the Kingdom, the royal entourage had to cover the entire territory from south to north, where their Castle lay at the feet of the Gold Mountains, in order to return. The voyage was calculated to be about a week, as it was traditionally, coming from this far south, and when going by horseback versus by donkey cart or on foot. The road home would require that they follow the well-traveled Golden River Road, which followed the Golden River. The River wound its way south from the Gold Mountains, all the way to Milorin, and then out to sea. It branched off as it made its way south, and roads were made that branched off alongside them. Towns were born this way and filled the countryside all over the Kingdom.

So the Knights made their way north along the Golden River Road, passing by those towns which were directly alongside the path. There were more towns in the

Kingdom that lay alongside the river branches. But they were staying to the main road as they made their way north; they would stop at inns that were directly along the main river. They were on a mission now: to get home as fast as possible. No sidestepping other villages to glimpse their fair maidens at markets, or imbibe in wines and fattening food feasts.

On this main road, the Knights passed the little and medium-sized towns of Longden-on-Golden, Bunting, Kingstown, Riverwalk, Stroud and Sheepville. They also passed Pellah's inhabitants along the dusty path, carrying goods in wagons and carts hauled by donkeys and horses. They met up with the occasional wanderer, and some individuals galloping by at breakneck speed on an urgent mission.

Eventually, they found themselves back at Castle Pellah. Malthor, upon his return, dismissed the other Knights and instructed the stable boys to care for their horses, and to deliver the Phemtas plants to the King's quarters. Then he made his way most urgently to King Vanamir.

He found the King upon his throne, speaking with a few of his counselors. Upon announcement of Malthor's arrival, he dismissed them all with a wave of his hand. They immediately left the vaulted quarters, and there was the sound of their heels clacking away and becoming distant upon the stone floor, and suddenly, all was silent.

"Show him in!" shouted Vanamir to the sentry.

Malthor entered, still in full riding gear: embroidered green velvet hooded cape with suede collar, a white shirt over a vest of golden mail, knee-high leather boots with gold buckles, and a plumed helmet– which he now doffed and flourished as he dropped to his knees.

"My King! 'Tis I, Malthor, First Knight of the Eyemen at your service!"

"Aye, Malthor! Rise! Rise up, now! What is your report? Get on with it, man!"

Malthor rose and gave the King a detailed story of his mission to find the "old man" and "his granddaughter" – which was all Malthor and his Knights knew about their quarry. It had begun almost a month ago, when the Knights left the Gold Mountains on their quest.

The King listened in silence, interrupting every now and then to ask a question.

And he watched Malthor's every expression and movement as he narrated his tale.

Silence.

Malthor bowed low once more and said, "That, Your Majesty, is what happened."

"Malthor," said Vanamir in a low voice, "come closer, man. That's it. Closer now! Yes, right up to my face. Look at it and tell me what you see. Would you do that for me please, Malthor?"

"Aye, my Lord," said the Knight, standing so close to the King he could almost touch his bejeweled leather boots as he sat on his raised throne.

"Well, then, what see you?"

"I see my King upon his throne of gold."

Vanamir laughed, such a voluminous laugh that Malthor could feel his breath upon his cheeks.

"Then you do not see a fool? Of course not!" thundered the King. He reached out and leaned over to tap the Knight on his embroidered cloak and say: "What kind of wild tale have you prattled on about here before my very royal being? How dare you insult me with excuses for why you failed to capture those two scoundrels? You would actually have me believe that you stayed outdoors in the forest for four or five nights?" Then he sat back and continued his laughter, which far outweighed his thunder, in Malthor's perception.

"You have failed; that's all I really need to know," said Vanamir. "They are still on the loose!" He paused and thought, "Why should I explain to this imbecile why this is so important! I alone understand the magic those two escapees are capable of … Aye, in yet more dreams, in many forms, Gamedon and Andalorax come to me for my demise! I should have locked her away when I had the chance! But they got away that very night!"

It took a moment for him to regain his composure. Then he said: "But you have also brought back vital information about these two: That they can render themselves practically invisible, exactly as I was beginning to think when they made their escape! By some form of magic or act of nature, they practice that art.

"Also, they live in the Calicab Forest – managing to stay out of sight of my Twenty Eyemen in the bargain – which means they live in both the day and the night, out in the open, under the stars and the moon! This tells me they have no fear of the darkness! That, plus no fear of what everyone else will think of them. They are traitors to the throne!"

With that, he banged his golden scepter on the ground and abruptly stood up and dismounted his throne.

"I needed you when you were gone. It is almost one month. I require that you be here. You are my Twenty Eyemen and I need you for my protection. I dare not leave the Palace grounds without you – you know that, Malthor!" He pointed his long, strong finger at Malthor, then began to pace the floor.

"I shall not send any more Knights after these two, who are named Gamedon and Andalorax, if you care to know. No … now I shall send scouts. Real traveling men who are not afraid to stay in that Calicab Forest after sunset for more than five nights. They shall scour the woods until they find them!"

Malthor bowed again and the feather atop his helmet touched the ground. "As you wish, my King," he said.

"Of course it shall be as I wish!" said Vanamir, who stopped pacing and looked Malthor in the face. "I shall make plans for this with my counsellors. Now, be gone, for you must be desirous of your own quarters. Be gone!"

The very next day, in the Castle's War Room, found the King seated around his grand round table, made of beautiful slices of walnut with ebony inlay butterflies. He was arranging with his councilmen for scouts to be sent on a mission to find and capture and bring back to the King those traitors known as Gamedon and Andalorax.

Two brave-hearted soldiers stepped forward and offered to do it – for the King was paying many gold sovereigns as an enticement to volunteers. They had no wives to worry about at home, they said, and were quite eager to see the world.

The plan was for them to return directly to the Calicab Forest, to ride south along the Golden River Road until they got to Milorin, make their presence known to the town's Mayor Barth, and then just the two of them would enter the forest. They were to stay together at all cost and not be separated or lost. That sat well with the young volunteers.

They were outfitted royally with leather trousers and vests, and with heavy velvet cloaks embroidered with the King's royal crest. They didn't wear the traditional helmet with a few tall resplendent feathers, choosing instead to wear a plain green wool cap. Leather saddlebags held changes of clothing and ample food and water for the ride to the next village.

Within twenty-four hours of their council meeting, the plan came to fruition, as the two young men, Chester and Goshen, having said farewells to their sobbing parents and friends, were outfitted for the voyage. Standing at the stables, they were met with King Vanamir, who arrived in a grand flourish with his Twenty Men of the Eyes, Malthor riding at his side.

"Young men," he said, "Remember that this is a true mission you embark upon. You must find these two people – I described them well enough to you yester-eve in my chambers. They have some sort of magic or witchery in their blood! The old man is named Gamedon, and his granddaughter is called Andalorax."

He pointed at both of them very sternly.

"Be careful – not only of them but of the woods. Be brave, and be wise. Chester!" he said, pointing to the taller of the two who was wearing a green checkered cap. "Remember what I said to you when you questioned me last night: It is unwise to doubt their art of making themselves invisible! They can be right next to you and you won't notice them!"

"Aye," agreed Malthor. "Keep your eyes open even in your sleep, if you take my meaning, Chester."

King Vanamir and Malthor, First Eyeman, sat atop their steeds at the ceremonial dropping of the bridge over the moat to send these boys on their way. Many people were lined up along the parapets and calling out through open windows to wish them good luck.

"'Tis a very cheerful picture," said Malthor, as Chester and Goshen trotted off, with the sun at their right, for they headed south.

"Aye, Malthor, that is so," answered King Vanamir. "But I wonder if we shall ever see those boys again."

"Don't think that way, Sire."

"I tell you truly. I can say that there is more beyond the Calicab Forest than you know," said Vanamir. "What will they find when they reach that part of the woods, I wonder?"

"Aye, Sire. I know naught of the forest's end and lands that lie south of it."

"There lie the Black Mountains at the forest's edge .... They say there is a valley surrounded by high peaks, and that some monster lives there in a volcano," spoke the King.

Both sat quietly on their mounts for a moment, then Malthor turned to Vanamir and said, "Let us hope the two boys can come back and tell us all about it."

BOOK FOUR

CHAPTER 27

SIDDLES FLIES FAR

THE BLUE SKY WAS A pinhole of light at first, when Siddles swept up into the early morning air, holding Andalorax in his right claw. But she, accustomed somewhat to being held by this giant bird, now kept her eyes open and saw, as they soared swiftly up towards the entrance to the volcano, that the blue pinhole had become their exit point. And it was expanding by the second as they rose upwards.

"Wake up, Andalorax," Siddles had said to her that same morning. "Time for you to discover these Black Mountains." So she said a short fare-thee-well to Gamedon, who was getting ready to leave their tent and visit Zivat-Or to discuss the olden days of Pellah, and their shared banishment.

Siddles had created for Andalorax and Gamedon a replica of what they imagined in their minds for him: an environment which they could call "home," wherein they could sleep, change their clothes, wash, eat, and perform other daily functions.

"What happens is this," he told Gamedon and Andalorax when they had finished meeting with Zivat-Or that afternoon. "You imagine in your mind what your ideal home or refuge would look like. If you do that, and fill it with all the details such as soap and food and a bed, I can make it real."

They had stared back and forth at one another, and then Gamedon asked, "How can such a thing happen, Siddles?"

"I was created way south of here, on a deserted island. During a cataclysmic event there, the skies opened up with rain and lightning and thunder. There was a volcanic eruption that spewed forth colossal plumes of smoke and lava. There was magic in the skies and on the earth that night; some even spoke of seeing comets. Somehow, when the dust had settled, I was standing there. Fully grown, as I am now. Able to use magic spells that I somehow knew and was never taught. Who could have taught me? There is only one Siddles!"

So, Gamedon and Andalorax had spoken together and taken out pencil and paper from their belongings, and sat on a black rock and drawn up a list for Siddles of what their ideal dream home would be like. When they presented it to him, he looked it over and said, "Thank you for being so detailed! I shall work on your home in the volcano right now."

What they delivered to the great bird, with drawings and notations all over many scraps of paper, was a replica of their home in the Calicab Forest, just before they were made to flee from the King's Knights. That was their vision of supreme happiness. Their makeshift tent, their little campfire, their walls made from the large graceful leaves of the Calicab tree – all that was presented to Siddles as their perfect abode. And that is exactly what the great bird provided for them.

Now Siddles and Andalorax were soaring up and out of the mouth of the volcano, and into the wide-open expanse of the Black Mountains. Here, the blue sky was vivid and warm with the heat of the rising sun. Siddles caught a great air current and began to soar higher and higher, ever-circling, and leaving the huge volcanic cone behind as he made his way towards the vast mountain range.

Andalorax noticed that there were patches all over the landscape of what seemed to be fields of something white. As they skimmed along the tips of the highest mountain peaks, she saw that these large white spaces were everywhere in these Black Mountains, not just on one solitary crag or terrace. She felt, as well, that there was animal life here in these mountains, for she sensed she could hear them speaking to one another. What they were saying, of course, she did not know and, furthermore, had no time to consider.

As they cruised along, the wind whistling in her ears, Andalorax called out, "Where are we going?"

Surprisingly, Siddles heard her, for he turned his neck around and called back, "You shall see. We are going for a landing pretty soon now!"

Siddles began to circle downwards, in a gentle spiral, until they were near one of those white fields. He landed smoothly and out rolled Andalorax onto the black rocky ground.

"Here we are," said the great bird, "in the heart of the Black Mountains, where the life that once was here no longer exists, except in rare pockets and in the volcano."

"Why did you bring me here?"

"I shall show you," said Siddles, and he began to walk towards the white field just ahead of them. As they approached, Andalorax saw that the whiteness was comprised of some sort of plant that was growing there. It seemed to be spread out all across the entire surface of the field, and it seemed to her to be mostly a fleshy, thick-leafed vine. But when they came to the edge of the whiteness, Andalorax immediately knew what the white plant was: Phemtas!

She turned and raised her head and cried out to Siddles, "I know what you are showing me! The evil weed that has taken over King Zivat-Or has also taken over these mountains."

"Yet it happened in the reverse order," he replied. "First, the plant overtook the Black Mountains and then, afterwards, when it had a stronghold on the landscape, it began to work on Zivat-Or. Of course, he had brought with him a few sizable objects of pure gold, which made the plant extremely pleased. You might even say it was happy!"

Then the bird did something Andalorax never expected: he laughed! It was a loud "Ha ha!" which echoed in the mountains and valleys. And then he continued to amaze Andalorax as he knelt down, folded up his legs, and nestled his large chest atop the black earth.

They were now, once again, face-to-face. Andalorax found herself staring into his one ovoid eye, large and red with a black pinhole in the center. "I wonder what he thinks when he looks into my black eyes," she immediately thought.

Siddles began what became a quick tale:

"When Zivat-Or was banished from the Kingdom of Pellah, and sent to live in these Black Mountains, he came with a small band of followers who agreed with his ideas about the night being not an evil thing, not a frightening thing. They brought their families and built several buildings and homes. There were trees in these mountains then, about two-hundred and fifty years ago. Yes, and grass and flowers and even some livestock.

"But all that changed once the Phemtas plant gained access to their hearts and minds. The insidious plant came seemingly from nowhere. One day, it was suddenly there, sprouting up into the air. It began to cover the green valleys with its insidious vines and shrubs, swallowing up any other plant life or vegetation of any kind.

"Eventually, when the last of the followers died off, Zivat-Or was a lost man on an empty throne. He continually wore and still wears his shirt of golden mail, which you have seen just yester-eve. The plant lives for gold and has taken him over! True, it has endowed him with its power to give long life, but what kind of a life is this where he has no freedom and no happiness? I say, Zivat-Or is indeed at the end of his rope! I can only hope that Gamedon will agree to stay here with him when you leave."

"What?" she cried out. "When I leave? Am I leaving? And Gamedon might stay behind? What news is this, oh Siddles?" And she began to weep, for the sadness of the story as well as for the shock to her own heart about being separated from her beloved grandfather.

They had never been separated for one single day of her life.

"Forgive me, Siddles," she said after she regained her composure. "It is a long time since I have cried." She instantly recalled being hit with a stone from the Castle Pellah, by the children who taunted her about her different coloring. She had cried then. "But that's when I met the Many-Colored Girl," she said to herself, then thought, "and I wonder what has happened to her …." But she quickly brought herself upright and back into the current situation.

"Yes, you are leaving the Black Mountains, Andalorax," announced the giant bird in a nonchalant manner. He was still adjusting his plumage as he was perched upon the smooth black earth. "You should not be in these surroundings when you are meant to do greater things."

"What greater things?"

"I do not know the answer to that question, dear girl," said Siddles. "I only know what Gamedon has told me, and it is you who must move on because you are young and have a role to play in Pellah history."

Andalorax sucked in her breath at hearing this. The concept was not new to her by any means. She knew all about the prophesies and the dreams of King Vanamir, but most of all, she knew all about herself, her coloring in her hair and eyes which was different from every person in the Kingdom, even Gamedon and her mother, Mandir. She felt that she was meant to do something important. That feeling was growing stronger every day.

"Tell me more about this Phemtas and what it is doing to the Black Mountains," she said, moving forward in her thinking.

"All that you have surveyed during our flight this morning, the lack of any foliage except Phemtas, the large swaths of the plant overtaking the hills and valleys, slowly, insidiously, is the answer to your question. You saw those white patches, Andalorax. Eventually, these mountains will be covered completely with the plant. Eventually, I expect, the volcano will also be devoured by this plant."

"Siddles," said Andalorax, sitting down next to him, "why can't you use your magic to destroy all this?"

"I can create," he answered, "but I cannot destroy." Again, the great bird laughed, which was an astonishing sound …. "It's as if he's whistling into a deep well," thought Andalorax.

"What is funny?" she asked.

"Your question! To answer, let me tell you a story, a quick tale. You wanted to know where I come from. About one hundred and fifty years ago, I was a young bird, and often took long flights from my nest. One day I flew over this same mountain range, coming from the south on a stormy day. The skies opened up, pouring rain very suddenly, so I landed here. At the storm's end, I ventured into the volcano, and there, I met Zivat-Or."

Siddles raised one enormous wing and waved it across the landscape.

"To make all this go away, yes, I thought perhaps I could. I had never tried to destroy anything before. I was a young bird then. Yes, Siddles was young once! I could change the course of history and save Zivat-Or! Destroy the plant! Of course! I thought of that immediately when I became aware of Zivat-Or's addiction and the power of Phemtas!

"But, it was not to be. I tried to think of spells, which always came to me without thinking. It is in my nature to create. But I cannot destroy, plain and simple."

They both rested there quietly for a while, contemplating all that they had just discussed.

"I am to leave," thought Andalorax, then she asked, "Where am I to go? And how shall I get there?"

Siddles stared at her with his one red eye, and she felt as if he were looking right through her.

"I shall take you away," he answered. "Where we shall go is still a matter for us to decide."

"Who is 'us'?"

"Zivat-Or, Gamedon and myself."

"Don't I have any say in the matter?"

"Of course!" answered Siddles. "I shall tell you right now what the alternatives are, and there are only two.

"First, there is the Calicab Forest, which you know so well having lived there for fifteen years and just recently again for several months with Gamedon. You could probably survive well there, providing you avoid the King's Knights. But you will be living in constant fear of being found, which would very likely happen one day.

"Secondly, and last, is the Secret Island of the Galinda-Hussadi, to the south and across the Sea of Iolanthe. That is my choice. I have flown over that island several times, and when I was young I circled it quite often. There is a delicious air current that always rises over an island, and I can soar and fly to my heart's content. I believe there is ample choice for landing sites as well, if I recollect correctly."

Andalorax asked, "Who lives there?"

"That, I do not know. But I have seen people there over the years. I believe it to be a busy place. Very active. Other than that, I have no idea. It is a great chance to take."

"Siddles, as you have traveled far over the years, what else is there surrounding these mountains? Do I have any other choice? Who knows what the people are like on the Secret Island? And what is the 'Galinda-Hussadi?'"

Siddles adjusted his plumage, and said, "So many questions! To the west of the Black Mountains, there is a vast desert. To the north, is the Kingdom of Pellah; to the east, the Calicab Forest. To the south, the route to the Island of the Galinda-Hussadi. No, my dear girl. You have to accept this, and quickly, as I intend to take you away tomorrow."

"So soon? Why?"

"The sooner the better. This is an evil place, Andalorax. This Phemtas is sinister and crafty. And it knows how to destroy! I am not a match for it. It is potent! You must go away from it. Remember, I do not have the power to destroy or I would destroy it!

"Yes, we leave tomorrow. Now, let us be on our way back to the volcano and you can say your farewell to Gamedon."

"He truly will stay here?"

"Yes, Andalorax. He wishes it to be so. Gamedon and Zivat-Or have become friends, in a strange way. They share something: both were banished from the Kingdom – Zivat-Or by his son, the next King of Pellah, and all the Ministers and citizens.

"But, I also suspect Gamedon wishes you to go forward and meet your fate, and he is an older man, far wiser than you. You are a young woman and must accept your responsibility to fulfill your destiny."

They both remained silent again, staring at each other with the power of these new developments spinning in the air.

"Come," said Siddles, rising from his nestled position in the iridescent black earth. "Let us away back to the volcano."

And leave they did most immediately.

CHAPTER 28

ACROSS THE SEA

THE NEXT DAY FOUND SIDDLES once more awakening Andalorax, and telling her they were to fly away. With many tears, she said her farewell to Gamedon, hoping that someday they would be united again.

"Grandfather, I have seen you every day of my life, and now all this will change! I shall be lost without you!"

But Gamedon knew she had to leave and follow her destiny, whatever it was.

"Staying here, my dear girl, is not in your future. You must away to the Secret Island, and find a way to survive there. You are taking your precious knapsack full of all necessities and your magic walking stick with you, so you have all the tools you need. Now be off! Destiny must come into play!"

Once again, after goodbyes to Gamedon and Zivat-Or, Siddles had Andalorax in his right claw, and they were zooming up out of the volcano and into the bright blue sky. Siddles veered southeast and caught an air current and off they went.

Siddles had told Andalorax on the eve of their departure what to expect during their three-hour voyage. They met inside the tent Siddles had created for them. Gamedon took a back seat and listened carefully.

"First, once we leave the Black Mountains," said the great bird, "we'll reach the Ravenal Forest. We'll cruise over that in about one hour, then we reach the Cliffs at the Sea of Iolanthe. Once over the Cliffs, we'll be over the Sea of Iolanthe itself. From there, we continue until we reach the Secret Island."

"Sounds like we'll have much to gaze upon as we ride the winds, dearest Siddles.

But, because I love trees so much, tell me: what is the Ravenal Forest?"

"Home to the beautiful Ravenal trees. They are quite tall, with very dark green needles like pine trees – no, more like fir trees. Soft needles! They say that wood elves and faeries live in the forest."

"Wood elves and faeries!" She was astonished. "Tell me about them, Siddles."

"I've been in that forest once in my youth. I flew in on a moonless night and landed with great care that no one should see me. I shrank my size and so was able to wander about with ease. I saw the elves, funny little men and women who are about three feet tall, and live in wooden houses all made from Ravenal trees. They are also said to be very friendly, living in communities throughout the forest, keeping in constant touch with the aid of the faeries. I never met any of them, keeping away because they would never understand who I am. I merely landed, and walked about, then left. But these tales reach me even in the Black Mountains."

"And the Cliffs and the Sea of Iolanthe?"

"The Ravenal Forest comes to an abrupt end with the Cliffs," he answered. "They are very steep, Andalorax. Huge waves crash into the rocks there, and the Cliffs themselves are said to be constantly crumbling into the sea."

And now that they were flying over those Cliffs, Andalorax stared down in wonder at the white foamy waves that rode in with the tides and crashed against the Cliffs which were indeed steep.

Suddenly she remembered Gamedon telling her of King Vanamir's prophetic dream wherein a white horse was clambering up a cliff, trying to reach the King, who was caught in a windstorm and terrified of the horse.

"That white horse symbolizes me," thought Andalorax, as they glided along on the air currents. "I truly am meant to be part of his downfall!"

That thought entered her head and from that moment on, it never left.

Gamedon, of course, knew this all along.

Soon, they left the tormented frothy cliffs behind and were soaring over the Sea of Iolanthe. Andalorax knew nothing about this body of water, except for what Siddles had told her yesterday:

"These waters run very deep," he had said with serious intent. "You can tell it by the darkness of the blue. There are currents running from north to south; I can tell by the movement of the fish and the debris from florae and vegetation along the shores. Look! I'll wager these are pretty strong currents, too."

"How far does the Sea of Iolanthe go?" Andalorax had sat on her small bed that evening, while Siddles, who had reduced his size to accommodate the height and width of the tent, had burrowed his way into the earth and perched there.

"That, I do not know," he answered. "I have flown as far as I dared when just a fledgling. I have soared over the Secret Island several times, and there seems to be plenty of greenery and lakes and rivers. There are plenty of people, too!"

"What kind of people?" Andalorax began to imagine wood elves and faeries, but mostly just regular people such as herself. She knew of nothing else!

"I have never flown so low, not daring to show myself, being such a queer looking sort!"

Andalorax had laughed at this, saying, "You're a queer looking sort? Look at me!" Again, Siddles gave forth with his deep-throated laugh, which echoed through the little tent in which they sat, discussing their voyage, just last night. Gamedon had listened but had not said a word.

"Siddles," Andalorax had said, "do you realize there is only one of each of us? One Siddles, one Andalorax."

"Don't go huffing and puffing about that now," chimed in Gamedon. "There's only one Gamedon as well!" They all laughed.

But now, Andalorax was leaving behind the new world she had discovered in the Black Mountains and heading for yet another unknown place – the Secret Island – where a people lived called the "Galinda-Hussadi."

"I wonder what they are like," she mused, while watching the dark waters below and the puffy white clouds above them as the air whizzed past her bare face. "Do they look like me? What language do they speak?" She had asked Siddles so many questions about them last night, but all he could say was that he had never seen them but found the island to be cultivated and there were homes and other small buildings.

After a while, the sky became cloudless and the sea looked to be a lighter color blue. Then she saw it, the Secret Island! It was as round as the full moon, surrounded by waves crashing into beaches and cliffs along the perimeter of the island.

She saw, too, the large black and white and gray seabirds and orange-beaked terns that squawked in the air as they flew, then dove for fish in the deep sea below. She sensed they were speaking to one another, but, again, knew not what they were saying.

"Perhaps one of them is speaking to me?" she thought. Oh, how she wished she knew!

"Prepare for descent," Siddles abruptly called out.

Siddles, of whom she had grown quite fond, had a wide wingspan which created a kind of warm chamber wherein Andalorax felt quite safe and peaceful. "He's so much larger than these small and puny seabirds," thought Andalorax. "He is more of a vulture-type with that enormous bony head and beak, perhaps a Wood Stork …."

They began to circle slowly, ever so gently descending towards the land mass. As they came closer to the earth, Andalorax could see a few forests, and lakes, and a wide river that branched off every which way, snaking along across the fields and forests until the tributaries reached the open sea.

"Ah, you beautiful island!" she cried out. "I love you!"

Siddles called out into the wind, "Hold tight!"

There was no time for reflection. Quickly, as they zoomed towards the earth, Andalorax could see that Siddles was heading for a large field in which to land. His speed thankfully was significantly diminished when all of a sudden he hit the ground, gently but with much wing-flapping and some wobbliness due to only being able to use one foot, as Andalorax was tightly enclosed within the other.

Out she spilled – her backpack tightly strapped in place with her magic walking stick protruding out – from his open claw, and rolled over onto a field of wheat, tall and brown and fuzzy at the tops where it was sprouting. She stood up and surveyed the field. Ah, but it smelled delicious! She took several deep breaths, while Siddles stretched out and rearranged his wide wings, folding them into his broad chest. He was magnificent at his full height of twelve feet! Andalorax looked up at the sun and knew it was nearly mid-day and they had left the Black Mountains just three short hours ago. Her stomach growled.

Siddles looked deeply into her eyes, his one red eye studying her face. "She is tired, but she is young," he thought. "She will get over this. She will adapt here and live among the people." And he said to her, "Now, for your destination!"

Andalorax laughed. "You mean my *destiny*, don't you?"

"I mean both!" And he croaked out his own laugh, which again intrigued and delighted her.

They proceeded to push their way through the tall wheat and carve out a narrow path in the direction of the nearest town that Siddles had spied from the air. But their full destiny would take longer to uncover than this simple route.

Presently, Andalorax held up her right hand and yelled "Stop!" Siddles halted by her side.

"I feel the earth moving beneath my feet," she told him. "Someone is coming … nay, two are coming! Quickly now, for they are almost upon us! Lie down!" They both pressed their bodies against the wheat stalks which broke under their weight, as they flattened out and listened. Then they could hear the approaching sound of two people talking.

"I tell you, I saw the great bird land right about here," came a deep voice.

Andalorax and Siddles shared a quick smiling glance: they spoke the same language!

"And I say, it was farther south," said another, higher voice. The voice of a woman! Oh, they were in luck! Fear fell away from them all of a sudden, and it was at that moment that they realized how truly afraid they actually were. Again, they shared a knowing glance.

Siddles stood up and said out loud, "Here I am! Here! Over here!" Now he could see the two people who were talking: it was a man and a woman of the same size and shape and build as Andalorax and Gamedon and the rest of the people of the Kingdom of Pellah.

Andalorax could see, when she stood up as well, that both people were also dressed in similar attire to what they wore, although slightly more colorful: He was clad in brown checked trousers with red suspenders, a loose-fitting yellow flannel shirt and had a small red scarf tied around his neck. He had on ochre-colored leather shoes laced up his ankles, as did the woman beside him. They were very sturdy shoes.

She, too, was in pants, not a skirt as Andalorax was accustomed to seeing on girls and women, although she, herself, was wearing pants. The young woman's were a deep red color, and she, too, wore suspenders but they were of pink and white stripes. Her white blouse was loose at the arms but tight at the cuffs and open at the throat, where Andalorax could see a bright crystal necklace catch the strong midday sun. Her thick blonde hair was done up in many curls with multi-colored ribbons pinned to her head.

"Hello! We are friends!" called out Andalorax.

"I hope they are friendly," she thought, but there wasn't one more second to think for the two people rushed out of the wheat and fell headlong into Siddles and went plummeting down to the ground. There they sat, both rubbing their heads, and looking up at Andalorax and Siddles.

What a sight for these people! Andalorax, with her long white hair and coal-black eyes, with her well-worn hooded cape about her, her knapsack on her back and walking stick in hand. Siddles, a huge, twelve-foot-tall iridescent black-and-red feathered bird with a thick, bright red beak and yellow feet, looked ominous.

"We have never seen the likes of you," said the woman. "Who are you both and where do you come from?"

"My name is Andalorax, and I come from the Kingdom of Pellah. This is Siddles, from the Black Mountains." She curtsied low and Siddles tapped his red beak onto the ground, in his fashion of greeting.

"And who are you?" she asked them both, looking from one to the other and back again.

"I am Tag," answered the young man in his bass voice, "and she," he said, taking her hand and pulling her forward towards him, "is my wife Skye." He shook his dark black hair, which was down to his shoulders, and he smiled widely.

"This may sound odd to ask," said Siddles, "but are we on the Secret Island? Surrounded by the Sea of Iolanthe?"

"Aye, that would be true," said Skye, freeing her hand from Tag's and taking that of Andalorax in friendship. After sharing their right hands, Skye put her left one upon the clasped ones, and Andalorax did the same, following the woman's ritual.

"And we two are of the Galinda-Hussadi, also just called the 'Hussadis.' We Hussadis occupy most of this island, which Outsiders know as the Secret Island but we have, for centuries, called it Budgerigar Island, so named for the birds that inhabit it. They are everywhere!"

As if to illustrate what Skye was saying, up from the northern horizon in the sky rose a dark, wavering cloud, moving very quickly, until it became clear that it was a flock of wild birds. They were squawking and screeching in unison, as they flew overhead in bright green streaks and continued on their way.

"Awk! Awk!"

Andalorax, with her keen sight, could distinguish the bright green shimmering feathers and the yellow face of the fist-sized, parrot-like bird.

As they passed overhead, Skye lifted up her blonde head and called out a perfect imitation of the budgerigar's sound. Andalorax stood stock still in disbelief at what she was feeling: she was understanding what Skye was saying to the birds. She was saying, "Welcome and fly in peace!" And the budgerigars were all crying out many different words to her and all the people and life below: "Hello! We are flying to our nests! Fare-thee-well!" It was a great shock to her system. How could this be possible? How could she be understanding their language?

All her life, she knew, she had sensed what animals were thinking, but understanding how they spoke, knowing what they said ….

Siddles, on the other hand, was just quite simply amazed at hearing Skye talk to the budgerigars as they flew overhead, for he, although also being a bird, could never be able to replicate any sound from his fellow birds. And he had met others over his long years. He had even met Wood Storks, which resembled the singular type of bird he was. Unfortunately, they did not all speak the same language as he did.

The young woman's warbling and screeching echoed across the wheat field and followed along with the passing parrots. Soon the flock was out of sight and sound.

"You can made a sound like the budgerigar?" Siddles asked her, intensely curious.

"It is more than making a sound like one. I can speak their language. I just sang with them as they flew on their way to their nesting trees along the beach."

Siddles was stunned. "You mean, they heard and understood you?"

"Aye," answered Skye, in a nonchalant fashion.

"Perhaps," thought Andalorax, "here it is an everyday occurrence …."

"What other languages do you speak, Skye?" he asked.

"I speak the languages of all the animals here on the island. I have the Gift. Tag here, he doesn't have the Gift. Either you're born with it or not. I got lucky, I suppose."

"You mean to say, you converse with all the animals on this island?"

"Aye, I do. And so do the many others who have the Gift."

"And what types of animals do you have here on Budgerigar Island?"

"That is asking a lot, my new friend!" answered the smiling young woman, still holding Andalorax's hand. "Let's see: We have dogs, horses, cows, pigs, goats, llamas, kangaroos, elephants, tigers and lions … oh! And of course, a multitude of varieties of birds. From hummingbirds to ostriches. Not only budgerigars here! No! I should say not! We have a parade of animals!"

"And you have the Gift to speak the language of all these animals?"

"Aye, that I do. And so do many others, including the Great Overseer."

"Who is the Great Overseer?"

"Why, she is the elected top official in our government!"

"Your government?" asked Andalorax. "What is that, a 'government'?"

Skye let go of her hand, and took a deep breath.

"Andalorax, you are a newcomer to this place, and I suppose it is all new to you. I don't know if I'm the correct person to ask about these impressive matters."

"Who would be, then?"

"Why, the Great Overseer herself, of course!"

"Do you mean to say, that this Great Overseer would have time to see me and Siddles?"

Skye chuckled softly. "Of course! You have arrived from the sky, fallen out of the clouds, here to our island, and we will wish to make you welcome, I am certain." Again, she took and stroked the hand of Andalorax, then let it go.

"Let us be on our way, then," said Andalorax. "Don't you agree, Siddles?" She turned to her twelve-foot-high companion, and said, "Perhaps it would be best for you to shrink yourself, so you could look everyone in the eye!"

Siddles proceeded to chant the magical incantation that reduced his size to about six feet tall.

Haspir madji-bay Siddles Mitsbee Zandorfska!

Within one second – Whoosh! – He was face-to-face with the trio. Tag and Skye both dropped their jaws at this phenomenon, but Tag said, "We are familiar with magic here on Budgerigar Island, but this is new to me! How do you do it? What is your gift?"

"My gift to change size is one of many of my gifts. I will tell you of them presently, Tag, when we are together in a more protected environment. Shall we go to visit your Great Overseer?"

CHAPTER 29

SKYE & TAG AND THE TRIBUNES

SKYE AND TAG WENT IN the lead, holding hands, while Andalorax and Siddles followed just behind.

"Who are these Hussadis, Siddles?"

"I was afraid you would ask me that. I know little. I am learning as much now as I ever knew, in fact, so we know as much as each other does." He cleared his throat, which was always raspy and he continually hissed his "esses."

"The Galinda-Hussadi," so he began, "or the Hussadis, have lived on this island for at least as long as I have been alive, practically, as I was quite young when I discovered it, as I have already told you. And that is a long time ago! I did not let them catch sight of me, not knowing if they were aggressive or hostile or friendly, as we now find them to be, for which I am very grateful!"

"How many years ago was that, Siddles?"

"You force me to tell you my age, Andalorax."

"Only if you wish," she replied softly, and added with her sweet smile, "but I am very curious to know!"

"I will be two hundred and eighty-nine years old this spring, which is roughly in one month."

What first astounded Andalorax was not his age, but the fact that it would soon be spring. Time seemed to be out of kilter in her life for months now. Of course! Springtime!

Then she realized what Siddles had revealed to her and she turned her head and looked straight at him as they walked along in the wheat field. He looked back at her.

"Yes, I am an old bird," he said. "I do not know how long I am supposed to live because there has never been another bird such as I known to the rest of the earth. Neither people nor animals that I have ever met have known of or seen anything such as me. Some people liken me to a bird called the Wood Stork; others say I'm a Sandhill Crane. Then they say I'm a black vulture. But those don't have long handsome tails such as I do. Besides, I'm splattered with red! Oh well, Andalorax; in the end, all I am is a freak of nature!"

"There is no such thing," Andalorax replied. "Every creature is unique, if there are many of its type or not. Each bird is one-of-a-kind! One male crimson cardinal is unique to his mate – you know, they mate for life – even though there may be billions of crimson cardinals in the skies!"

"I am, then, unique unto myself," he said. "No other creature such as me."

"And the same goes for me," she answered.

Once again, they shared a little glance and both broke out into laughter, she, giggling heartily and he, with his throaty gurgle.

"So, who knows, therefore," he said, "how old is old for Siddles? All I can say is, my bones and tendons ache and my feathers need more oil! My skin feels old, Andalorax, so I must be old."

Suddenly, Tag held up his hand and said, "Stop!" There ahead of them was a group of people, all dressed in clean, crisp colorful outfits. Andalorax looked at them from top to bottom, while the people just stood there, looking back at her and Siddles.

Most of the people wore clothing similar to Tag and Skye, with long pants, suspenders, and shirts, and leather laced-up shoes; some wore felt or wool hats with green budgerigar feathers sticking out. Andalorax was again surprised to see that the women also wore trousers.

Andalorax looked at all their faces. They were all gaping at her and Siddles, but she expected that. At the same time, they were smiling.

One of the people, wearing glasses, came up to the pair and said, "Greetings!" The way he strutted forward made him appear to be the leader of the small group. He held out his hand; Andalorax took it. His grip was firm yet his hands were smooth. He put his other hand atop their handclasp and, remembering what Skye had done, she in turn put her other hand atop his. Then they both let go.

"You have come from the skies," he said. "Yet from where did you set out?"

Siddles leaned forward and, in his customary greeting, tapped his red beak against the ground. Then he said, "We come from the Black Mountains, and have flown across the Sea of Iolanthe."

"Ah!" said the man. "We have heard of the Black Mountains, but none of us has ever been there."

"Who is 'us?'" asked Siddles.

"The Galinda-Hussadi, of course," answered the man. "The 'Animal People.'"

"The 'Animal People?' Is that the meaning of Galinda-Hussadi?"

"That is correct," answered the man. "That is in our old tongue. Our language has since evolved over time, as have we."

"Forgive me," interrupted Siddles, "but we have not introduced ourselves by name," which he promptly did. Andalorax, in her customary demure fashion, gave a little curtsy.

"And I am Clyde Brenner, a Tribune in the Order of the Law. Several of these people with me are also Tribunes of the law. But come now. Let us proceed forward and bring you before all the citizens of Bhatura and our Great Overseer. We will explain our government to you at that time."

"Bhatura?" asked Andalorax. "What is that?"

"Our capital city, where the heads of our government work."

Once again, Andalorax and Siddles were escorted along their way.

"I hope they do tell us about their 'government,'" Siddles whispered to Andalorax as they walked.

"Whatever that is," she replied.

They eventually came up to a cobbled street, and saw many people staring out the windows of their small, wooden houses. Some of the homes were carved into hillsides, and most had round windows. Many people, though, remained in the streets and waved at the strange pair, who waved back.

"Greetings!"

They all cried out, one at a time, over and over, like a musical clock.

"Greetings!"

Andalorax and Siddles responded by saying "Hello! Hello!" and she waved her hand a little as they proceeded forward. Siddles nodded his large bony head.

"It's a little like an echo," laughed Andalorax, which made Siddles chuckle as only he could do.

The people began to come out of their homes, and soon a crowd had gathered, with all their eyes on Andalorax and Siddles. They lined up the street that the pair was walking along. That path widened, and soon they came to the foot of a very high hill. At the very top, very far away and looking pretty small, was a round, white-stone circular dome. There were numerous broad steps leading up to it, steps that seemed to reach unto the sky, there were so many.

Clyde Brenner, the main Tribune, walked beside Andalorax and Siddles and Tag and Skye, with his group following apace just behind them. It took quite a while, perhaps half an hour, for all of them to climb these stairs. As they walked, the five of them spoke together.

"We elect a new Great Overseer every five years," explained Tag, beginning to huff and puff with the ascent, "and he or she appoints his Cabinet of specialized professionals to be tribunes. That changes every five years, unless of course, the Great Overseer is re-elected."

"And that is what you mean by 'government?'" asked Andalorax.

"Yes," said Tag. "We live by the rule of law that is decided by all the people of the Galinda-Hussadi, for the good of all."

"You mean, you vote on who becomes your Great Overseer?" Andalorax was confused. "In the Kingdom of Pellah, where I am from," she explained, "the Kings are all born into the role. The first-born son becomes the next King, and so forth down the line for centuries."

"How amusing!" laughed Skye. "I cannot imagine a world where the ruler must always be a man, and you are stuck with him even if he turns out to be a monster!"

Andalorax looked down at her feet as they continued up the steps, rising higher and higher.

"It's true. That is our way."

"Well," said Tag, stepping up to Skye and taking her hand once again, "here we choose who we want to be our Great Overseer by obeying the will of the people. That's an election!"

"Yes," she replied. "I know about elections. The schoolchildren in the Castle where I lived all voted for their class presidents, treasurers and such. But in the Kingdom of Pellah, it's more or less a game and not applicable when it comes to the top ruler and his associates."

"Well, here it is so, my friend. Come now," he continued with his walking, "and follow me."

At last they came to the very top and the front door of the dome. There, Tag and Skye stopped. Clyde Brenner and his group of Tribunes waited quietly.

"We are at the very heart of the city," said Tag, opening wide his arms. "It is called Bhatura." He turned towards Andalorax and Siddles. "Here in this building is where our government is carried out. I myself have just recently been here to be presented to the Great Overseer." He laughed. "You see, I was randomly selected by her for the mission to discover what the tale was of the Great Red-Beaked, Yellow-Footed Black Bird, and I'm mighty glad!"

Andalorax smiled at him, trying to imagine King Vanamir being so easily accessible to anyone. And a woman! She then turned around to see the wide expanse of the island. They certainly were high up, here in this city of Bhatura, having reached the top of what seemed to be the tallest hill around. Several other hillocks and small mountains were scattered across the landscape, along with lakes and forests. This was the only building that was shaped as a dome, and was pure white.

"Some sort of official building," thought Andalorax, and she remembered the official Town Hall building in Milorin, a simple square and light-brown stone edifice with a few scattered windows – what a different type of architecture!

What intrigued her most however was the shoreline, which she could see from the great height, where there were many boats tied up, or out at sea. This was something brand new to her and she wanted to know more.

"What must it be like to live near the water's edge?" she wondered. Even though she was at a high viewpoint, she found herself standing on tiptoe as she scanned the island.

"This building is like a shining edifice compared to the rest of the wooded and lake-filled countryside," she said to Siddles.

"Yes, it is different from all the countryside around us," interrupted Tag, who, like Andalorax, was deeply inhaling the fresh air blowing in their faces.

But now she wanted to focus on where they were going, to meet the Great Overseer of the Galinda-Hussadi.

"I'm surprised," she said to Siddles as they stood there, with the west wind whipping up about them, "that we have instant access to their highest ranking person, the Great Overseer."

"And she is a woman!" inserted Siddles.

"This fact is not lost on me." Andalorax stared out into space. "I have never heard of a ruler being a female!"

Standing up there on top of the hill, feeling the strong breeze in her face, she couldn't help but sigh as she saw the new and exciting landscape. And she couldn't stop thinking about the fact that their mightiest ruler was a woman.

They all turned at once and faced the dome-shaped white building before them. They looked up and leaned their heads back as their eyes rose to see the top of it. It was pretty high up, about six stories, and the place was filled with openings and windows everywhere.

On the front of the stone structure was carved in large letters:

"GOVERNMENT OFFICES OF BHATURA"

And below it, in smaller letters, it read:

"ON BEHALF OF ALL THE GALINDA-HUSSADI"

Tag pressed a button to the side of the lettering, and a hidden door slid open, as if on rails, but Andalorax could see none. She looked up as she passed beneath the arched doorway; it was very high up, this doorway! It was about eight feet high and six feet wide. "Each landing, then," she said to Siddles, "must be twelve feet tall," to which he nodded yes in agreement. Were he to be his greatest height, his big bony head would probably brush the lintel.

Tag released his hand from Skye's and lifted up his arms and said, "Look at the great expanse of our government! Look what we have achieved! It has taken many years, I can assure you, to build this property."

"We have worked hard to complete this wondrous edifice and to carry out the work of the people!" echoed Clyde Brenner.

"It is, indeed, a wondrous thing of great awe and beauty," said Andalorax. "So pristine, so pure, so simple."

"And so huge," added Siddles. Being now his reduced size, he felt even more diminished by the breadth of the place.

They all passed through the opening, and the Tribunes stopped once they were inside.

"We shall wait here," said Clyde Brenner. "We shall meet you in this Grand

Lobby when you return. Be off, now!" The Tribunes walked over to one corner and sat down on some chairs. They began to talk amongst themselves.

After they had passed through the entrance, behind them the thick door had easily and noiselessly slid back into closed position. Inside, all was also white, and the air was cool and refreshing, "not stale and contaminated by lack of sunshine as so many large buildings are," thought Andalorax, as she remembered Gamedon's recounting of the King's hidden Library he had seen in the Castle and the one in Milorin. Huge open windows let in all the outdoors. Andalorax could see practically the same view as when she was outside.

Ahead of them was a circular staircase, and Tag put his foot on the first step and the stairs began to move forward and he began to rise.

"Come along, now," he said to Andalorax and Siddles. "You've got to get on the Gizzet once it has started to move!" He grabbed hold of Andalorax's hand, and pulled her onto the staircase. It was moving quite slowly, which was fortunate for Siddles who, with his clawed feet, was not easily able to get aboard. Skye and Tag together jumped on last.

The Gizzet snaked its way up along the inside walls of the dome-shaped building, so that passengers could actually touch them. Slowly winding around from floor to floor, it passed by layer to layer of large rooms. Andalorax saw that there, in those rooms, life was happening right there before her very eyes, a life she had never imagined.

"What are these people doing?" she asked Tag. "Who are they? Are they the Galinda-Hussadis like you and Skye?"

Tag laughed and said, "They must all be Galinda-Hussadis – just simplify it to 'Hussadis' – for those are the only people on this island."

"I did not realize that."

Tag suddenly pushed his hand hard against the wall which made the Gizzet come to a sudden halt. "See how easily it stops?" he asked. Then he pressed hard against the wall again and they continued the slow ascent.

Tag recalled her question and answered: "And as for what the people are doing, they are here to discuss life."

"In these rooms?"

"People gather to talk about things that are of interest to them. For example, there is a group of people who study herbs, and they are provided a place to learn, and plant and grow them. They meet here regularly."

"Another group is the occasional citizen who has brought a personal problem before one of the councils. They come here to discuss the situation. That's why we say that we live by the rule of law. When the council listens to a complaint of one citizen, they are doing their jobs," continued Tag. "They all are elected officials who work on behalf of the rest of the people on the island. They do all that and so much more that is needed to live a full and happy life. That is our goal here on the island. We live by the rule of law!"

"So that's what they are doing, these Hussadis." She pointed towards the people in the rooms as they slowly ascended on the circular staircase.

The Gizzet stopped circling the interior walls at that moment, on the ground floor, which was the last level inside the white dome.

Tag and Skye helped them to depart from the Gizzet and then took them to the inside edge of the staircase, which paralleled the somewhat magical moving staircase. Andalorax and Siddles both gasped at the vista that stood before them: They were inside a nautilus! An enormous nautilus whose walls and framework comprised the Gizzet, the charmed staircase, and whose interior core was rooms of stone with enormous windows. They looked down the three stories and it took their breath away. Andalorax felt dizzy and had to pull herself back and away from the edge of the dome.

She looked around and could see people coming and going, and working, through the large glass windows and wide open spaces without any glass whatsoever, just open to the fresh air. There weren't many people, but there were enough for Andalorax to realize she was watching a world that was totally unfamiliar to her: people working together! People who had voted, one by one, for their Great Overseer!

They went down the corridor to a door that slid open at the touch of a button.

A young man looked up from a desk, and peered over his thick spectacles.

"May I help you?" he asked. Then he realized that there was a human-sized bird standing before him, as well as a young, wild-looking woman dressed in a well-worn cape and hefting a backpack. A young woman with white hair and coal dark eyes.

Tag stepped forward and announced, "This is the bird that landed here yesterday, the one I was sent to scout out."

"But he was so much larger, surely …."

"He was then but now he isn't, my friend. Please inform the Great Overseer that we have arrived. The bird and his companion, a young woman." Tag motioned to the pair, then looked back at the young man. "She will want to see us immediately, my dear man."

The man knocked on a large door, a voice behind it told him to "enter!" and the door slid open and then closed behind him.

Within five minutes, Andalorax, Siddles, Tag and Skye were standing before the Great Overseer.

CHAPTER 30

THE GREAT OVERSEER

THEY WERE IN A MEDIUM-SIZED room and around them were several men and women, all dressed in the same attire as the country folk who had greeted them earlier: corduroy or cotton pants, loose shirts, suspenders, and leather shoes tied up past the ankles or to their knees like leggings. They were all standing beside a woman, dressed in a long white robe, and seated upon a large chair in front of a large writing desk. The desk was scattered with books, piles of paper, folders and manuscripts of different sizes and colors, bottles of colored ink, small tubs of sealing wax, odd gadgets and other knick-knacks – the use of which Andalorax could not imagine.

The woman arose and walked around her desk. She wore a wide silver bracelet and long, draped silver earrings shining with clear crystals that tinkled slightly when she moved her head. A large silver necklace studded with a sky-blue stone was around her neck. She held out her hand to Andalorax, who took it. The Great Overseer placed her second hand atop their clasped palms.

"I am Grace Waggoner," she said in a gentle voice. "I am the Great Overseer of the Galinda-Hussadi here on Budgerigar Island, and I officially welcome you and your companion to our small home." She then held out her hand to Siddles, who responded with his traditional nodding of his head and tapping the ground in respect and greeting. She sensed his friendliness, however, and reached out and smoothed his beautiful iridescent black feathers.

They were all instantly friends.

"Oh Great and Wonderful Grace Waggoner," began Andalorax, to which the Great Overseer interrupted by saying, "Grace, call me Grace. And everyone refers to the Great Overseer as the 'G.O.'"

"Very well then. Grace, I am Andalorax from the Kingdom of Pellah, and this is

Siddles the One-Eyed from the Black Mountains. Your world is so different from the one I know, back in the Kingdom. We do not have what you call a 'government' and we do not vote for our Kings. Our Kings are always the firstborn sons of the current King. This has stood true for over one thousand two-hundred and fifty years, since the Kingdom was first settled."

Grace Waggoner smiled and then laughed, and her whole face lit up. Her blue eyes sparkled, and her cheeks became rosier, and her long brown hair spread down across her shoulders.

"I know of your system of Kingdoms," she answered. "We here do not practice it. We have been on this island for over one thousand years and have learned great things about how best to live.

"Here, therefore, we have the rule of law, which says that every person on this island is equal to the other, including me and my Tribunes. We live in peace and harmony, and share some splendid notions about how we, the Galinda-Hussadi, the 'Animal Folk,' should live."

"What are these notions?"

She raised her hand and motioned to the center of the room.

"Let me guide you to a chair, and you, Siddles, can easily perch yourself on that comfortable rug over there in the corner I think … yes, that's right and good. Now, Andalorax, these notions are part of who we are as a people. We have a list of beliefs.

"First, we live in peace and harmony, as I said. That is our first tenet.

"Secondly, we hold all Nature as our one God, and we live here at peace with Nature and all its living creatures. Hence, we are all vegetarians and eat no meat, nor do we hunt. We do farm and raise chickens and eat eggs, and make cheese and drink milk from cows and goats.

"Hidden in that second tenet is the reality of the Gift, which people are either born with or not."

The room was silent.

"We have heard of it, Grace," interrupted Andalorax. Siddles nodded in accord. "What does it mean, to have the 'Gift?'" she asked.

"Those with the Gift can communicate with all the animals on Budgerigar Island. Gifted people and animals talk back and forth with one another. It is not something you can work for and achieve, but is, rather, a Gift at birth. We know not why it happens."

Grace continued explaining the beliefs – the laws – of the Galinda-Hussadi, whom Andalorax was now referring to as the 'Hussadis.'

"Thirdly," she went on, "we share the art of Totemism. Yes, in our society each person is assigned some living creature or natural phenomenon – an animal, an insect, a star, a body of water – that represents his or her inner soul. I, for example, was given the totem of the dog. When I was born, my mother looked up at the sky and saw a cloud in the form of a large dog. Hence, she pronounced my totem. Many other people have this totem; there are plenty of dogs to go around and the totem can, therefore, be used more than once."

Andalorax had never heard of this way of living and was greatly intrigued. Deep inside her mind was the possibility that she had the Gift, but had never used it or been made aware of it. Yet sometimes she understood animals when they spoke! She had heard the flock of budgerigars flying overhead just earlier that morning when they were atop the white domed building.

She also asked herself, "What is my totem? If I am a natural phenomenon, which I should like, what would I be?"

Her answer was immediate: the Moon!

Andalorax sighed, and sat back in her comfortable chair, and looked at the men and women standing around her. She counted six of them.

"Who are all you people?" she asked.

One of them stepped forward. "We are the special Tribunes assigned to the Great Overseer. You have a Tribune with you in your company; raise your hand, Tag!" and Tag did so. "He is not assigned to the Great Overseer – er, uh, I mean the G.O. We six make sure her laws and decisions are carried out across the land. We have other Tribunes and Ministers in every district who report to us, and we report back here to our chief, Grace Waggoner."

He coughed and said, "I am Barry Bingham, Andalorax." He held out his hand and she took it. As Grace Waggoner had done, he placed his second hand atop their two, and Andalorax finished off the four-handed shake, forming a tighter bond.

"I am one of the special Tribunes," he said, "and my specialty is agriculture and farming." They looked into each other's eyes and they were instantly friends.

Andalorax stood tall – taller than almost everyone in the room including some of the men – and faced the entire group, and raising her voice to be heard in the general hubbub, said, "I thank you – and so does my companion, Siddles the One-

Eyed – for your warm welcome to Budgerigar Island."

At this, the six Tribunes applauded and yelled out "Hurrah!" and "Yay!" and smiled towards each other.

"We come from a faraway land," she began, "and it is our great hope, Siddles' and mine, that you will accept me as your guest and future resident. I hope to settle down here on your island, if that is appropriate for you."

Grace Waggoner smiled broadly and said, "It is our grand pleasure to have you here as our guest and, ultimately, resident, Andalorax. We shall make you welcome and help you to find a home that you will find suitable for yourself."

She turned to Siddles, seated on a blanket in the corner. "But what about you, Siddles the One-Eyed?" she asked him.

"I shall be returning home to the Black Mountains, where my master awaits me," he said quietly. "As soon as I know that my charge is well situated here, I shall be taking my leave of Budgerigar Island."

"Well," said Grace Waggoner, "you shall have no cause to worry, dearest Siddles, and can plan on your return to your homeland within a day or two. Or longer. It is up to you. You, too, are welcome here."

Siddles bowed and tapped his thick crimson beak on the ground, in his own method of giving respect and saying thanks.

"I personally am not Gifted," said Grace Waggoner, "but I know what this bird is saying with his beak-tapping gesture, that he is grateful for our welcome and understands the profundity of our invitation."

"Aye, Grace," responded Siddles, "you read me correctly!"

"Now that we understand one another somewhat better," said Grace, "let me proceed to show you around the building. You, my Tribunes, may return to your duties." She stepped over to her doorway, pushed a button, and the door slid open. When the five of them – Grace, Andalorax, Siddles, Tag and Skye – stepped out of the doorway, they were once more in the interior of the great nautilus-shaped building.

The Gizzet, the moving circular staircase, was standing quietly in attendance. Grace walked towards the center of the stairwell, facing the core of the building. She was tall, and her long white robe touched the ground. She was wearing soft tan leather boots, laced up her calves. Andalorax could see clear across to the other side of the building's interior, where the Gizzet – when moving – swept its way up, up, up as it snaked around, and then back down again to the ground floor.

"See how there are doorways along the length of the winding Gizzet?" Grace asked them. "They lead to either the workroom of some Tribune or a meeting room for the Galinda-Hussadi to discuss anything related to the rule of law." She swept her arm widely across the expanse inside the building, and to Andalorax the place seemed, while she knew it was busy behind the doors, quite serene. The light streamed in through numerous openings in the all-white stonework, and the interior glowed with the mid-day sunlight that streaked in.

She had the urge to call out "Echo! Echo!" to see it there would indeed be a reverberation, but she restrained herself. But Tag was not so controlled and he called out, "Echo! Echo!" and sure enough, the words bounced around within the domed interior, resonating their way back to everyone's ears.

When the place was silent at last, they all looked at each other and burst into laughter.

They walked in a row for a while until they came to the large meeting room that Clyde Brynner had referred to as the Grand Lobby, where Tribunes were who waited for their return from meeting with the Great Overseer. And now, there she was, standing before them!

"Greetings, ladies and gentlemen," she said, extending her hand, all the while fingering the blue crystal hanging from her neck with her left hand. They all shook her right hand in turn. Then she looked at Tag and Skye, and said, "It is time for you two to be released of your duties. You have performed them well, having successfully found our guests and then brought them safely to me. Go on home, now, and unburden yourselves for the night. And take tomorrow off from work as a reward!"

They said their goodbyes to Andalorax and Siddles, as well as the other Tribunes and Grace Waggoner, the Great Overseer, and, clasping each other's hands, were off into the afternoon light that spread across the steps leading down from the Great Building. Andalorax and Siddles stood there side-by-side as they watched the couple skipping down the broad steps, quickly becoming small and eventually disappearing out of sight.

"It is here that I, too, shall take your leave," said Grace Waggoner. "We shall speak much about our government in the days to come, Andalorax. But first, we must discuss what the most appropriate living quarters are for you. I have to learn something of you, your talents and desires, dear girl!

"Clyde Brenner, one of these fine Tribunes, will take you down to the town where you will stay at the friendly Four Bells Inn until we have found more permanent quarters for you, Andalorax. As for you, Siddles the One-Eyed," she turned towards the iridescent bird, "you are welcome at the Inn as well, but I believe you said you will not be seeking a residence here on the island, as our friend Andalorax has indicated she would like to have."

Siddles said, "Aye, you are correct, Grace." He turned to Andalorax.

"I will be leaving in the morning, if the winds are with me and the sun is strong," he said to her, who stood there, her backpack still strapped firmly on, her magic walking stick poking out of it, and her worn and tattered cloak skirting the ground. "I must return by crossing the Sea of Iolanthe once again, this time facing a northern headwind so unfortunately it will be more of a battle. But I won't have to hold onto any baggage as I did before!" Thus said, Siddles tossed back his bony head and laughed his peculiar, particular scratchy, deep-throated guffaw.

"You realize what this means, Siddles?" replied Andalorax. "With your departure tomorrow, I shall be utterly alone! First Gamedon, now you."

"Being alone is something we knew was in your future, Andalorax," he said to her. "Before I leave, however, I want to be assured that you will have a home and friends around you." He turned to Grace. "What sort of proposition do you make to my dear charge?"

"She will have her own home, in a lovely area with peaceful neighbors – remember, peace is our first tenet! – and plenty of furniture, and food, and supplies that will all become part of her new place of residence," answered Grace Waggoner. "As I said, we must learn of her skills and desires. Of course, she will be given tasks to do to earn her comfort, work such as farming or becoming a scribe in our city's Library …."

"A scribe?" thought Andalorax, imagining herself, plume in hand, and a scroll of blank white paper before her on the desk. Then she asked, "In the Library? Do you have a Library that goes back to when your people first inhabited this island?"

Grace Waggoner laughed heartily. "Yes, Andalorax, we have many ancient texts and tomes. Our Library is a place filled with writings of every kind there is. Novels, biographies, text books, poetry, illustrated manuscripts … you know, Andalorax. Books! All housed in one large, cool, stone building without windows to keep out the damaging sunlight. Our Library. And our Librarian, Linda Fraggle. You shall get to know of it – and her!"

"Aye," said Andalorax, and she thought, "I think I'll be getting to know many things of which I know nothing."

"Things of which you now know nothing," admitted Grace, but followed up with, "and things of which you will soon know everything! You will learn more of our tenets with time, but I see you learning things of which we currently do not even know. That is my prophesy for you, young lady."

Andalorax sucked in her breath at this proclamation, for in her heart she was feeling the same things: that her destiny clearly was to be here, on Budgerigar Island, and that she had a role to fulfill in its future somehow. Or perhaps Budgerigar Island had a role to play in her future? Whichever it was, she knew not.

"It's pretty evident that I don't know a lot of things," she said to herself. But she declared out loud, "I am willing to learn all that I can, and more!"

Siddles put his wing around her shoulders and the two of them said their farewells to Grace Waggoner, and were soon following Clyde Brenner to the Four Bells Inn.

They began their descent on the many steps that encircled the building. "Going down the steps," Siddles said to Andalorax, "isn't as difficult as climbing them."

"It is true," she replied. "What steps do I have to face now, dear Siddles, with you leaving tomorrow and me being alone here in this new land with a government and the rule of law and Tribunes and …?"

"Now, now, Andalorax," interrupted Siddles. "I can easily create for you another home such as the one I created in the Black Mountains for you and Gamedon – a home in which I presume he is still living, and eagerly awaiting my return and news of your safety and whereabouts. Perhaps then you would not feel so much like a stranger."

"I think," she said, "that your suggestion is noble and considerate, and I am grateful for your friendship and camaraderie. However, dear friend Siddles, I think it best if I learn right off from day one how to live in this new land. This means that, effective tomorrow, I will be living as they do, in a home that is well known here on the island. I shall learn their customs and ways, and yes, their government and such, of course. Don't you agree?"

"Aye, Andalorax. I do agree wholeheartedly." Siddles removed his wing from around her. "So it is all settled then," he said. "I shall be leaving in the morning."

From then on, in silence, they continued their way down the steps, following in Clyde Brenner's lead. Ahead lay several roads that branched off in different directions.

One of them would take them to the Four Bells Inn, thought Siddles. But tomorrow he would be flying away, taking a completely separate path from hers. He would be with Gamedon! He remembered the landscape of the Black Mountains, and King Zivat-Or, and the encroachment of Phemtas. He imagined the wheat field from which he would ascend tomorrow morning, and inhaled its sweet scent in his memory through the nostrils of his bright red beak.

"I wonder if and when Andalorax and I shall see each other again," he said to himself. In his heart, he knew their destinies would cross paths one day. But when, he knew not.

Andalorax, thinking exactly the same thing, also decided she knew not when, but felt that it was bound to be.

"But first," she said, "It shall be glorious, after all this wandering, to finally empty out my backpack!"

CHAPTER 31

ANDALORAX ALONE

"HERE HE COMES NOW," ZIVAT-OR called out to Gamedon, seated to his left as he rested atop and was entangled with his floating Phemtas throne. The ancient King raised his right arm and pointed towards the southeast, his long bony index finger trembling with the potency of the moment.

"I tell you, it is he! It is our Siddles! Returning from his mission with Andalorax."

Slowly but surely, the great buzzard came into Gamedon's view, which made his heart begin to race until he could hear it pounding in his ears. Zivat-Or and Gamedon watched breathlessly as, finally, Siddles came to a landing on the black rock, ruffled and then settled his feathers, shook his long bony neck, and uttered the magic incantation that reduced him to human size. Within five minutes, he had walked up towards Zivat-Or and bent over to peck his red beak upon the ground in supplication.

"My Lord," said Siddles, "I return to you with everything satisfactorily completed." Turning to Gamedon, he said, "Your granddaughter is safe with the people of the Secret Island – now known to us as Budgerigar Island."

Gamedon closed his eyes and nodded his head in understanding. He was somewhat at peace already, being alone with Zivat-Or for three days now, but this brought him great comfort. How he missed his Andalorax! A tear rolled down his cheek.

"Those people on Budgerigar are known as the Galinda-Hussadi, or plainly, the Hussadis. They are the same size and shape as both of you and your people in the Kingdom of Pellah, and they say their heritage goes back more than a millennium. They originally came from the east, across a great ocean. But none knows of where their ancestry truly lies. Shortly after colonizing, in their approximation one thousand two-hundred and fifty years ago, record-keeping began in earnest. But prior to that long-ago time, they have no hint of their forebears."

"Tell me about the girl," said Zivat-Or. "We know that she is following her destiny, some sort of secret or special fate, I know not what. But is she on track?" He turned towards Gamedon and said, "My friend here is in desperate need to know of her whereabouts and, quite frankly, dear Siddles, her state of mind!" Gamedon turned towards the ancient bird, and because Siddles had shrunken himself, the bird and Gamedon could look at each other eye-to-eye.

Siddles nodded his head. "Andalorax is being accepted by all the people there," he stated. "And the Hussadis are going to teach her their ways and beliefs and customs, and she intends to become one of them."

Gamedon lowered his head, then raised it to the blue skies that rose way far above him at the exit porthole to the volcano. "My dearest Andalorax," he whispered. "So far away, now at the next phase of fulfilling her destiny." He thought of astronomy, and the movement of the planets that he had studied back in his Laboratory in the Kingdom's Castle Pellah. He wondered how they were aligned nowadays, and what would shine upon her now, across the Sea of Iolanthe on an island named after parakeets, without anyone to guide or aide her along her path.

Gamedon burst into tears and wept into his old green handkerchief.

Zivat-Or reached out his arm and touched the old man on his back. "Tut, tut, my friend," he said. "Worry not. She is doing exactly as you have told me you wished for her. We cannot help her now; she is on her own.

"But come now, Gamedon old man! Remember what you and I have to discuss with Siddles now that he is returned. I am increasingly determined to get my revenge upon King Vanamir and all of his subjects for making me a prisoner of the Black Mountains those two hundred and fifty years ago! We shall rely upon Siddles' powers of creation."

"But we have discussed this again and again, Zivat-Or," replied Gamedon, "Vanamir is not responsible for something done centuries ago by another King!"

"Nay, I do judge him responsible, Gamedon!" He removed his large knobby hand from the old man's shoulder. "You and I, we have talked much about this these past few days! I am determined to attain revenge of some sort!" He turned towards Siddles.

"You," he said, glowering at the great bird, "you can create things! You can help me to destroy this King Vanamir and the entire Castle in which he lives! It is his fault, and the fault of those who follow him, that I am a chewed-up morsel of a man, thrown out at the front door of an entire Kingdom! A disgrace, an outcast, doomed to dry up in this dark place where I am overwhelmed with grief and sorrow for the loss of what could have been.

"Oh, had I not made myself heard when, as a young King, I aroused the wrath of my Ministers! Who cares now if the night is bad or not? Why did I make such a big nuisance about it way back then? Oh, to have kept my mouth shut!" Tears burst from Zivat-Or's eyes and he buried his head in his shoulders. The vines writhed and hissed and reared back from the salty tears.

"Zivat-Or," interrupted Siddles, "Please reconsider this way of thinking; it is useless! Nothing good can come of this!"

"You have been absent for only a few days, Siddles," said the old King, "yet in that time Gamedon and I have come to the realization that some restitution must be made to pay me back for what was my horrible doom!"

"No! No!" cried out the great bird. "This cannot be."

"It *is* already, it *is* now! It *exists*!"

"What do you mean when you talk about my powers of creation?"

"You will help me to build engines of destruction and we shall take over the King and his Knights at the Castle Pellah. I have made up my mind about this now, Siddles! Pay attention and let us tell you about our scheme!" He turned towards Gamedon, who was watching his every move. "We have to discuss our plan with Siddles now, old friend."

"Aye," answered Gamedon. "Our plan. We shall bring justice to you, King Zivat-Or." He turned towards Siddles.

"Let us waste no more time. Here is what we propose to do."

Andalorax sat on the porch of her house; her feet, dressed in soft red leather slippers, were up on the porch railing. Sitting on her favorite rocking chair, she was sipping her primrose tea and eating sweet biscuits with raspberry jam and butter, while she also managed to keep the nearby bees away by gently swatting at them. She loved bees, as they were so fruitful in their labors. She hadn't yet been stung by one, as well.

Her wooden house was two stories high, with a living room, kitchen, dining area and a bathroom all downstairs. Upstairs was one large bedroom, with wide windows on all four walls, bringing in much light during the day and many stars and the moon at night. Here on Budgerigar Island, people didn't have the same fears as those in the Kingdom of Pellah.

The house was a subdued color which Andalorax dubbed "banana yellow"; its shutters, pierced with holes the shape of hearts, were a deep orange color, with bright red framing. The living room had a fireplace that went clear through the upstairs bedroom, so Andalorax never was in want of warmth. But now it was springtime and she was enjoying watching the bees pollinating the few flowers she had planted.

In fact, Andalorax had come to love many animals and insects and other living creatures, as well as natural phenomena, since she first came to Budgerigar Island one month earlier. Siddles had left immediately, and she hadn't heard a word from him since, even though he had promised he would send her some sort of signal in a yet-to-be-determined fashion of correspondence.

She fretted about Gamedon, whom she missed greatly not only for his companionship but also for his wisdom. There were times when Andalorax could have used some of his wisdom, well did she know that. But living on Budgerigar Island – or "Budgie" Island, as they called it – had come so naturally to her that rarely did an occurrence arise where she could not make her own decision.

"Are you awake in there?" she called out.

"Yes, Andalorax," returned a soft female voice. "We're all awake and ready for breakfast whenever you are."

Poppy Buddwing was Andalorax's first friend when she came to Budgie Island. They had found themselves standing side by side in the wheat field watching as Siddles flew away, back to his home in the Black Mountains just one month ago, reflected Andalorax right now as she rocked on the porch …. She was remembering that morning right now, as she drank her tea with honey in her favorite periwinkle blue cup with the yellow daisies on it.

"Siddles," she had said to him the evening before as they walked together towards his proposed site of ascension, the wheat field, "When do you expect to be home with Zivat-Or and my dear Gamedon?"

"In three hours," he had answered, "about the same amount of time it took us to cross the Ravenal Forest and the Sea of Iolanthe."

She had continued to talk, not wanting to waste any of their last precious minutes together.

"The sky is quite blue and cloudless; in fact, I feel little breeze. Do you think that might delay your takeoff?"

Siddles laughed in his usual deep-throated fashion. "Andalorax," he replied, hissing his esses, "we settled it all last night. I am leaving today. There is a rumbling in the Black Mountains over there in the northwest ... I can sense that something is amiss. Now that I know that you are settled here – or at least, will become settled – I can leave with my mind at ease."

"Whatever could it be that is amiss?"

"I know not," he said, shaking his heavy, bony head. Then he stopped short. "Here we are. Why, look, everyone is behind us!"

Siddles and Andalorax turned to look back and there were many townspeople who had been quietly following them, noiselessly tip-toeing along in wonderment at the lovely young lady with the long white hair, and the iridescent black bird with his jagged red-and-white striping and red beak and enormous, muscular bright yellow feet, both of whom were ambling along in front of them.

The Hussadis were whispering to one another as they followed along.

"I hear she is going to live with us and become a Hussadi!" said one middle-aged man, wearing round, wire glasses and holding onto a corncob pipe and dressed in brown corduroy jeans with striped suspenders and a blue and green checkered shirt.

"Aye," answered a woman by his side. "She surely is lovely to look at, with all that long silky white hair and those deep, dark-colored eyes! I wonder why the bird doesn't want to be introduced to us before he departs. But as to her becoming a Hussadi, I wonder if that is possible. We were all born here! She's kind of a foreigner, do you know what I mean?"

"I heard that the bird is on an urgent mission to go home and cannot spare the time. Besides," said the man, looking up at the deep blue sky, "the weather is perfect for a bird, don't you think?"

"I hear he lives in the Black Mountains."

"Aye," said the man, knocking the used tobacco out of his pipe and putting the pipe in his breast pocket. "So have I heard as well. I remember learning about them mountains when I was a child in school studying geography. Never thought of them since."

"Me neither," answered the woman.

The few amount of people following Andalorax and Siddles soon became a crowd, and among the crowd was a young woman, very determined to get ahead and meet the bird before he took off. She was walking quite quickly, slipping along, almost running, like a deer, in her soft knee-high leather slippers and tan cotton pants and soft white shirt that showed off her full-figured shape.

"Wait!" she cried out, waving her hand high in the air at Andalorax and Siddles. "Wait, please! I want to talk with you! I am your friend!"

The two of them called back simultaneously, "Come on, then!" and soon she was upon them, breathless.

"Hi!" she said, holding out her right hand in friendship. Andalorax took it, and the young woman put her left hand atop it, and said, "I am Poppy Buddwing. I am so happy to meet you and your friend here," she turned towards Siddles, "because I am a bird lover and am not familiar with this type of species."

Siddles leaned forward and tapped the tip of his red beak on the ground, in his custom, and said, "I am Siddles the One-Eyed and," he continued, putting his face right in front of hers, so that she could see his one red eye with its big black pupil quite clearly, "you are very welcome to meet me and know more about me … however, to know my species, well, that is quite impossible, as there is no other bird such as I." He raised his head slightly.

"How can that be?" answered Poppy Buddwing

"I am the creation of magical forces, I believe," he replied, lifting his head even higher. But then he said, "Shall I show you something of my magical powers?"

Poppy Buddwing nodded in assent.

Siddles stood back, looked towards Andalorax and for the first time that she had ever seen, he winked his one eye at her, and said his magic enchantment, and within a matter of a few moments, was his twelve-foot size once again.

"Now I see you in all your glory," cried out Poppy Buddwing. "Ah, but you are magnificent! And magical, which you have clearly shown me and all who stand behind me." She turned around and tilted her head towards the crowd, most of which had sat down on the soft grasses of the wheat field.

"Is Siddles not a magical, marvelous bird?" she cried out to the crowd, all of whom gave a resounding "Yes!" and "Aye!" and general huzzahs.

"Does he not deserve our wonder and respect, as he prepares to fly away from us, perhaps never to return?" she called.

Again, the population swelled their voices with loud sounds of agreement.

"Let us all bow down and give grateful wishes upon this magnificent creature as he takes to the skies!"

So saying, Poppy Buddwing got on her knees, bent her head forward and touched her forehead on the ground, and placed her hands palms-down upon the soil. She remained in that position, until eventually, one by one, the entire crowd did the same.

Everyone was bowing down on their knees to Siddles!

"Wonderful people of Galinda-Hussadi on Budgerigar Island!" Siddles cried out, outstretching both wings and making himself appear even larger than he already was, at more than twice their height. "I am your humble friend, Siddles the One-Eyed. I take to the skies because I must, not because I have a choice. I am needed elsewhere, needed desperately. Do you understand?" He called out to the people in his loudest, most articulate voice, without hissing his esses too much.

There was a general cry of agreement and cheers.

"You will take care of Andalorax," he continued to cry out. "She will be making her home here among you. Promise me, or I shall wreak my magic upon you!" Thus saying, he spread his wings out as far as they would fully extend, and within whose muscular arms everyone could see the wondrous, almost fearsome sight of his red zig-zag feathering. It appeared that he was surrounded by flames which were leaping out from his body in all directions.

"We promise! We promise!" came back the calls.

Siddles touched Andalorax one last time, and took to flight in the wheat field.

Seemingly, to Andalorax, that happened in an instant, as she thought, "And now I am truly alone."

CHAPTER 32

THE GALINDA-HUSSADI & ELVIRA

YES, ANDALORAX REMEMBERED – AS SHE held her now-empty cup of periwinkle blue with the daisies on it – that sunny morning one month ago – a full moon cycle, she thought – when Siddles had taken off in the wheat field, the same field where Hussadi families on the island go for picnics with their families and friends, where wild sheep and cows and horses and goats and a host of other animals wandered freely ....

"I'm coming," Andalorax called back to Poppy Buddwing, who was in the kitchen with her other housemates: Josie Dodge, Marilyn Gaylord, Remi Singleton, and Ralph Mushrush.

"Come on or you'll be late for class!" echoed Poppy.

"Everyone will notice if you're late, Andie!"

Poppy had given Andalorax a nickname: Andie. Andalorax immediately took to it and felt as liberated as the day when Siddles left, the day when she had finally unpacked her backpack and lay down her magic walking stick. She had moved into this home that same day.

"And it won't be because of your gorgeous mane of white hair!" Everyone laughed.

"I wouldn't mind having that head of hair," echoed Josie Dodge, running her hands through her rather thin plain wispy hair which she kept short in a boyish fashion.

Andalorax instinctively put her hand up to her hair, and felt its long length plaited down her back to where she could sit upon it. She had recently become acquainted with the method of braiding and doing so in sections, adorning her hair with flowers and lovely hairpins from the other girls. Now, she was living in a place with people who didn't laugh at her hair or cringe from it – they actually liked it!

Poppy Buddwing, along with her housemates, Josie, Marilyn, Remi, and Ralph, were all in the kitchen around the round table, eating breakfast and talking freely. Andalorax went over to her usual chair, sat down, and began to serve herself some breakfast: cereal with yogurt and strawberries.

Yes, she was getting used to the Galinda-Hussadi way of living quite quickly.

Many youngsters left their family homes at the age of ten and moved into homes with four or five other children, whose ages were staggered so there was always a good balance of true youth and adolescence, with supervision of their peers. Thus, Ralph was sixteen; Poppy was fifteen; Josie, thirteen; Marilyn twelve; and Remi was ten.

They all went to school and studied what was precious to the Galinda-Hussadi as a people: magic arts and spells, totemism, animal communication, astronomy, astrology, herbs and potions, exercise, meditation and other subjects depending on the desires and gifts of the individual student.

For example, a child who had the Gift of speaking with animals – something which could not be taught but was something they could only be born with – he could want to take a class that studied animal anatomy. They also had the early training of school for all the children from the ages of five until ten, when they went into the home-sharing system.

By living in a home on their own, under the supervision of an adult in the building, they learned how to care for a house itself. As well, all children learned, as time went by, how to cook, clean, and care for their bodies and the house, the garden, their fellow housemates, their dogs and cats and barnyard animals if there were any, and so forth, depending upon the house they lived in.

But today was a special day. It was the day when Andalorax was going to meet her spiritual Guide, or so she was told by a messenger from the Great Overseer, Grace the G.O. The Guide had been appointed to her in a strange ritual involving the Elders of the Galinda-Hussadi, known as the Hodgepotters. When Andalorax asked about it, no one seemed to know anything about them – only that they existed.

This morning, the Great Overseer was coming to the house, which was named Ta Monca, meaning House of Rain in some ancient tongue. She was bringing the Guide.

"Hello, Andalorax," said Grace Waggoner, stepping lightly towards the housemates who were all gathered together at the front door smiling and waving.

She held out her hand; Andalorax took it. Grace put her other hand on top, in the symbolic handclasp with which Andalorax was now so familiar.

Next to her was another person, a woman.

"Andie," said the G.O., "meet Elvira." She took Andalorax's hand and moved it towards that of the other woman, who reached out from beneath a blue velvet cloak and took her hand.

"Hello, Elvira."

"Hello, Andalorax."

Elvira. Simply that, one word: Elvira. Elvira, about six feet tall with a big, solid frame, wore a hooded cloak that fell down to her feet, which were laced up in robin's egg blue, soft leather slippers. Beneath the coat was a floor-length deep blue velvet skirt, sequined and sparkling with long satin ribbons tied at her waist, with a cotton sky-blue blouse. Wrapped around her neck were several gossamer-like scarves that seemed to pick up a breeze and blow gently even though the air was still.

She had a long-tailed bird on her wrist – bright green and turquoise feathered, with red eyes and a red beak and red belly – who rested upon Elvira's wide and studded leather wristband. Elvira's head was bare, save for hairpins encrusted with gay, freshly picked flowers in her black and gray braided hair.

Elvira put her free hand up to her flowery wreath. "No matter what is happening," Elvira said out loud, "it seems that Elvira always wears fresh flowers!"

Andalorax was stunned! Was she reading her mind?

And why was she speaking of herself in the first person, calling herself "Elvira?"

"Yes, Andalorax," said Elvira, "I'm reading your mind. It is one of my powers. And Elvira often refers to herself as Elvira, don't you know, dear child!" She put her hands on her hips, leaned back, and laughed out loud.

"Now, come and introduce me to your family here!"

The children had all lined up according to their ages, and Elvira held out her hand to each one of them. She stopped when she came to Poppy Buddwing.

"How old are you, Poppy?"

"Fifteen last winter."

"It seems to me that I know your parents. What do your father and mother do?"

"Mother works for one of the Tribunes at the Dome, and Father is a construction engineer. He builds houses," she added.

Andalorax stood there trying to guess how old Elvira was, for she was definitely old – among the oldest people she had ever seen, except for Zivat-Or. No, perhaps she was older than even he.

When Andalorax had first met Elvira that morning, despite Elvira's commanding presence she immediately gravitated toward the bird on her wrist. She wondered if he was used for hunting, as if he were a falcon – which he was not – and was not hooded and was at rest – until the bird saw her coming, whereupon he lifted his bony head and turned it towards this strange new, white-haired creature. His nostrils sensed the presence of something totally foreign and strange and he cried out in a reflexive impulse, creating his mournful screech that pierced the ears of all around him.

"Hush now, Leeta!" said Elvira in a crisp, snappy tone. The bird was suddenly silent. Andalorax looked the bird in the eyes, and he looked back at her. And he said, "I am Leeta the Quetzal. Who are you?"

Andalorax, taken aback at this repartee, didn't know how to answer.

"Yes, it's true then," she said to herself. "I can understand the animals. But why can I not speak back to them as the others who have the Gift can do?"

"You shall learn how to speak with the animals, Andalorax," interrupted Elvira. Again, it seemed to Andalorax that Elvira had been reading her mind. "You have the Gift. But it must be nurtured. It must be tamed and made to work for you and all those in the animal kingdom." She smiled, and her grin pulled back layers of wrinkled skin that puffed out her cheeks, making her appear like a giant cherub. The rest of her frame accommodated those cheeks as, unlike most of the slender Hussadis, she was of ample build, with broad shoulders and wide hips.

"Worry not, dear girl," she said, putting her strong arm around Andalorax's shoulders. "I am here to show you the path." With Elvira's sturdy arm around her, Andalorax felt safe and protected. It was a sensational feeling! "I will show you the path of living here on this island and making a success out of your life, dear girl!"

"Here I am," she said aloud, "all alone for the first time in my life, without my mother Mandir or my grandfather Gamedon, and yet I feel as if I am with family." She leaned her head into Elvira's shoulder.

At high noon, the ceremony celebrating the joining of Andalorax and Elvira had been held under a small blue-and-white striped tent which was set up in the backyard of Andalorax's home. It had mesh sides that fluttered in a soft breeze and a little flagpole jutting out of its pointed roof, with a flag that Andalorax quickly came to recognize as that of the Galinda-Hussadi nation.

The flag had a bright, leafy-green background, with a yellow disk in the center which was surrounded by an azure blue circle – the same blue as the color of the Sea of Iolanthe – that was pierced by a red arrow. It waved softly in the morning breeze.

Yes, in her mind, Andalorax referred to the Hussadis as one nation, for that was how Elvira had spoken of them, and that was essentially how they functioned. There was no intercourse with the world beyond its shores on the Sea of Iolanthe.

And so, as the second month passed, Elvira slowly explained the island nation's history.

One day, they were sitting on the porch of Andalorax's house, she with her periwinkle blue cup filled with raspberry tea and Elvira drinking peppermint tea from a pink cup, "for my stomach," she had said.

"It is true, my dear, that we have always been an isolated place … although voyagers have come in ships from across the Sea of Iolanthe which surrounds us, throughout the decades and the centuries, but they always continued upon their way."

"Where did they come from?"

"They always said they came from countries with terribly unpronounceable names; I could never remember them. But our National Librarian, Linda Fraggle, has everything recorded in our central Library in the town of Bhatura. And why should these pirates and adventurers stay? There was very little for them to pillage here! No precious stones, no gold, nothing that could hold them. Thank goodness they always left. We feared war and occupation every time one of those tall ships landed on our shores. That terror on the part of our people is so written in our history books and ancient manuscripts kept within our Library in Bhatura.

"And this small nation, this Budgerigar Island only twenty by thirty miles approximately, has been inhabited by the Hussadis for over one thousand two-hundred and fifty years! We know nothing of the people on the lands surrounding us, except for whenever the tall ships arrived. We have no navy; our ships are for fishing and pleasure. We know not of the Kingdom of Pellah and the Black Mountains, for the Kingdom of Pellah also has no navy or ships for any use other than fishing along its coastline."

Andalorax reached out and held Elvira's shoulder, asking, "Then how comes it to be that you know of the Kingdom of Pellah when as you say the Hussadis have been isolated for more than an entire millennium?"

Elvira smiled and lifted up her head to the sky. "Whatever I know should not indicate what all others know, for I know far more than most! Plus, Andie, I, too, have the Gift," she said. "I listen to the seabirds that have flown across the Sea of Iolanthe, and they tell me these things. I hear the deep sea fish that swim far and wide across the seas and vast oceans. I have lived long enough to have learned much about our surroundings. Over one hundred years ago, I met – along with all the other Hussadis who had the Gift – with a group of Sooty Terns that flew all the way to Castle Pellah at the Gold Mountains and returned here to tell us all about it.

"Of course, everyone who witnessed that with me is now dead." She sighed. "I have lived a long, long time, Andalorax."

"Then tell me, what lies to our south? What other lands did these tall ships come from?"

"There is a great land across the Sea to our south, but I know very little of it as it apparently is too far away for any of our seabirds – even the far-flying Terns – to have made the return voyage."

Elvira then laughed heartily, and added, "Oh, dear girl, people nowadays tell what they think are tales of mountains that are made of gold but never think to follow up and find these places. And, you may ask, why is that?"

Again, Elvira smiled broadly. "Because we are happy where we are. Gold would bring us nothing that we could not find here. It has no value. And here, over the many decades, we have flourished as only a nation could that was free from war, hunger, greed, pollution … but there are times when our people have disagreements.

"That is why we Hussadis developed what we call a 'government.' And in times when there were disagreements that needed to be decided upon, that is where the government stepped in and applied its laws, laws which had been voted upon prior by us Hussadis ourselves. And if there wasn't a law, there were arbitrators in the big white dome of Bhatura who would be only too happy to assist in finding a solution and keeping the peace."

So went the beginnings of the kinship of Andalorax and Elvira, her Guide. Andalorax wondered in the beginning, "My Guide to what?" But she had since learned that Elvira was her Guide to everything and everyone on Budgie Island.

Elvira had been chosen for Andalorax's training as she transitioned into Hussadi life because of her own powers, which were substantial. Born with the Gift, Elvira also had other unique abilities.

One day, Andalorax and Elvira were preparing to walk through a small woods near her home. The earth was very dry and hot as spring had quickly turned into summer, and very little rain had fallen. As they set off down the porch stairs, Andalorax bemoaned the fact that her garden, such as it was and only two months old, was so dry.

"And shall I fix that for you, dear girl?" asked Elvira, with a hearty laugh.

"Can you do such a thing?"

"Aye, Andie. I'm feeling full of energy today so let me show you something!" With that, Elvira threw open her blue velvet cloak and lifted her arms to the blue, cloudless sky. There on the porch steps she cried out:

Articulus Mandarus Icthya!

Suddenly out of nowhere came bolts of lightning and crashing sounds of thunder that filled the air. Thunderhead clouds swelled up on the horizon and flooded the skies. A sudden downpour of rain drenched them all, and it dissipated as quickly as it came, leaving once again a clear blue sunny sky.

Andalorax's eyes opened wide at this, for it now appeared that Elvira could control the weather and whip up a storm in the middle of a summer's day.

"And now that I've brought some water to your thirsty plants, shall I also bring some life into your sad little garden?" she asked with a hearty laugh, surveying the area around Andalorax's home. It was a fenced-in area with a few plants stuck in the ground here and there, without any blooms or fruit. Several old trees were there as well, barren and gray. Elvira raised her arm and pointed at the trees, then closed her eyes. A bright light surrounded her entire body, as if she were aglow from the inside, and she raised her eyes up to the sky, and called out a strange word three times:

"*Kumo!*" she moaned deeply and loudly. "*Kumo! Kumo!*" Her long fingers were pointed directly at the trees. Then she reached in a pocket deep within her cloak, and pulled out a bag of herbs, which she sprinkled in the direction of the trees. Instantly, they caught fire like lightning bugs, then flickered out. Suddenly, the trees began to sprout branches and leaves and then oranges, apples, and persimmons burst forth into the air that were immediately ripe on the vine. Some trees bore fruit that Andalorax had never seen in picture books, and surely not in real life.

"There is no Calicab fruit here, however," she thought to herself. "Oh, that dear forest, my home for the first fifteen years of my life with my dear mother ... so far away ... and later on when I was in hiding with Gamedon ... it all comes to life in my mind ...." But then she saw Elvira begin to move towards her house and its surrounding wooden fence.

Pointing her large and long fingers at the few flowering plants in the ground around the fence, now wet from the quick downpour, Elvira pulled back her hand to her chest, then shot out her arm and pointed her fingers and cried:

Hosta Partitu Im Cimella!

The words came out of her in a deep throaty voice. Again, she repeated the incantation twice. Upon saying the magic invocation the third and final time, the leaves on the sparse plants grew larger, the plants increased in number and they began to cover the entire length of the fence. The leaves were a bright lime color, with deep olive-green veins running through each large, heart-shaped one, and the flowers were large, red crenellated blooms with spiky centers.

When the plants had completely covered the fence around Andalorax's house, Elvira commanded them to stop by lifting her arms and throwing them out towards the garden, saying:

Hosta Partitu Im Robella!

Immediately the growing ceased.

"Ah, but that can take a lot out of me," she said, walking back up the stairs to sit down on one of the chairs there. She took off her large-brimmed straw sunbonnet and fanned herself with it, the blue striped ribbon band waving in the breeze. "Whoo!" she exhaled. Andalorax stepped back up to meet her and sit beside her.

"From where does the power come, Elvira?" she asked.

"From deep within my soul, where there exists a place that harbors all these powers. I can't exactly say it's here," she put her hand on her heart, "or here," she put her hand on her head, "or even here!" She put her hand on her belly. She chuckled. "But it's got to be somewhere in this old body of mine, just as surely as your powers are living there inside of you, dear girl.

"Ha! Powers that we know not yet about, perhaps. Aside from having the Gift of being able to communicate with all animals – even though you're just learning how to answer them, at least you understand them – you have no special powers that I know of." She turned towards Andalorax and placed her large hand upon her small one, and asked, "Or do you, Andie?"

"I don't know of any special powers," she answered, "but I do feel somewhere deep inside me that I have a destiny to fulfill." She put her hand on her heart, adding, "I feel it deep within here. Yet it lives everywhere within and about me. I am meant to do something.

"You see, Elvira," she said, taking a deep breath and leaning back in her rocking chair, "I have a story to tell you. I was born in a Kingdom where I was a freak because of my white hair and black eyes. All the people in Pellah had red or golden hair and green eyes. Except for me.

"As well, the people are all afraid of the night and all its accoutrements such as the stars and the moon, and they dote upon the sun and hide away when night comes. But I! I was born outdoors in the nighttime under the light of the full moon!"

"Yes, but what does that have to do with you having a destiny to fulfill?" asked Elvira, putting her feet up on a footstool.

"It is foretold in prophesies that the Kingdom of Pellah will be brought down by some force that deals with blackness and whiteness. It was just at that very moment when the King decided that I, night-black and moon-white, was that force, and he was going to make me a prisoner for life. So immediately, my grandfather and I had to make our escape.

"We traveled south down the entire length of the Kingdom, then ended up in the Black Mountains, and now I remain here on the Island while Siddles is in the Black Mountains.

"The current King fights as well to keep his reign, as he cannot give birth to a son – only daughters – and heir."

"Ah, yes," sighed Elvira. "You have told me of your quaint method of decreeing that the next leader – your Great Overseer – er, ah, I mean King – be handed down merely because he is of that family. And it must be a man; there can be no Queen of

Pellah!" She chuckled then shook her head. "Whatever happened to government?"

Elvira planted her feet on the floor and stood up.

"Andie," she said, "let's be off. I have something to show you. It's in the nearby fir woods. Let's pack a slight refreshment, dear girl, of some goat cheese and bread and olives." This Andalorax did, wrapping it all in a checkered cloth and placing it in her handbasket.

"There is a river along the path we shall take, and we can drink from its fresh water," Elvira called out to Andalorax in the kitchen.

"Ready, Elvira!" she called out as she emerged from the kitchen. She was folding a cloth for them to sit upon when they took their repast. "Where are we going and what shall we see?"

Elvira laughed, as was her jolly custom, and said, "That is for me to know and for you to find out! See here, Andie! I'm bringing the Quetzal," said Elvira, noting her bird who sat perched upon her wrist.

They went along the forest path easily, as it was covered with the soft needles of the fir trees. Their soft sandals that laced up to their knees were perfect for these woods. Andalorax, tall and slender, was always very light on her feet. And Elvira, despite her portly figure, was still a gentle stepper.

After about one hour, as the sun was rising toward the midday point, they both began to hear the sounds of many birds. They were chirping, humming, singing, quacking, squawking, trebling, and making quite a verbal ruckus.

As Elvira and Andalorax approached a nearby opening in the woods, they found themselves standing in the middle of what had quickly become an operatic chorus.

"Ah," said Elvira. "Here in the center of this avian orchestra we can sit down and have our picnic." They spread out the cloth, sat down, and put out the meal and began to eat. The sun was still high enough that the trees did not put them in the shadows.

"Oh, but that noise is overwhelming!" called out Andalorax, for if she spoke with her natural quiet voice Elvira surely would not hear her.

"Is it noise, Andie?"

She turned towards Leeta, her Quetzal, and spoke to her in Quetzal language. Andalorax did not yet try to understand, for even though she could make out when a bird spoke, she still couldn't speak back.

"What do you say, Leeta?" asked Elvira. "What is it going on here in this little sunny glen?"

Leeta said, "It is a cacophony of birds, here in this retreat. They all live here in harmony. It is a special place meant only for birds. Isn't it wonderful?"

Andalorax stopped munching on a piece of olive loaf with raisins, when suddenly, she stopped all movement. She listened only to the birds. It was more than chirping … those birds were all talking to each other!

"I wonder, can I understand them all?" she thought. "So many years of living without knowing that I had the Gift – but do I? I understand many animals now, especially birds, and more than I was aware of before. But I don't know how to talk back to them, that's for sure!"

She tried to winnow out one conversation. She chose a group of budgerigars, feeling comfortable with that species, having already been able to understand a couple of them having a conversation some days earlier.

"See that girl over there?" said one budgie to the other. "She's new here."

"Is that so?" answered his companion. "Haven't noticed." He put his beak under his wing and scratched an itch there.

"Yes, she's new and she's different," continued the first bird. "She's got white hair! And it's very long! Stop preening yourself and have a look, Oscar my dear husband."

Sure, Andalorax understood them but didn't know how to speak their language, only understand it.

Elvira could see her charge wandering in her mind, and she said, "Andie, stop trying so hard. Maybe if you just open your mouth, the words will come out! Why not give that a try?"

Andalorax went over towards the budgerigar couple, who were perched in a tree branch at the edge of the wood, and she opened her mouth and suddenly, just like that, snap! She was speaking to them in their Budgie tongue!

"I've been listening to you," she told them, "and I am new here and yes, my white hair is long."

"Did you hear her?" said the first budgie. "She spoke to us!"

"Yes, I spoke to you, and I am as amazed as you are that I can," said Andalorax in their language, without even trying.

"Elvira!" she called out. "The Gift just came to me out of nowhere!"

She started to shake and then tears burst forth from her troubled eyes. "How can this be? And what about the rest of the birds here in this avian paradise? I must call it that, Elvira," continued Andalorax, now very worked up and still shaking, "because it is exactly that: a paradise for birds!"

All around them, as they sat on their picnic blanket in the little clearing in the woods, were birds of every different color of the rainbow. Most of them were parakeets or parrots. They each announced themselves to Andalorax as she got up and walked past them, on the branches or in nests.

"Hello!" squawked out a round-shaped compact bird, his orange beak and nose standing out against his bright green wings and breast. "I'm Leo the Lovebird! Squawk! Listen to my beautiful singing voice! Squawk! Squawk!"

"Oh, do be quiet, Leo," said a nearby bird, who turned toward Andalorax and added, "I am Susan the Snowy Owl, and I'm pleased to meet you!" Susan turned her head left and then right, as she then burrowed her face down into her white and brown striped chest.

"You are beautiful, Susan," said Andalorax.

"Why, thank you, dear child," answered the bird, in Owl tongue.

Andalorax lifted up her arms wide and said to them all, "I am Andalorax, known to you all from now on as Andie! I am and shall continue to be your neighbor, living in the nearby forest hut down this trail towards the city of Bhatura. I hope we shall all be friends," she said, turning towards all the many birds who were assembled in this feathered friends' garden.

"We are the Silver-throated Tanagers! Over here!" called out a bird with a lime-green head and green-and-black striped wings. They all were in one group of yew trees, and started chattering away in unison.

"Yes, Andie! Yes! We shall be your friends!"

Leeta the Quetzal on Elvira's wrist called out, "Crested Quetzals! Make yourselves known to us please!" Sure enough, a group of bright green red-eyed birds with long green tails and yellow beaks answered Leeta the Quetzal.

"Here we are! Over here in the Great Banyan tree!"

There, before Andalorax and Elvira and Leeta, stood an enormous tree whose roots were dangling down from the limbs, connecting the tree with the earth. The roots absorbed moisture from the air, hence watering the tree itself. It held a flock of the Crested Quetzals, who all squawked and screeched back at Elvira's Quetzal, and Andalorax understood them.

"We are here!" they said. "Here in this glorious Banyan!"

Other flocks of birds perched in this extraordinary forest full of all different varieties of trees – from fruit to palms – included the Cardinal, the Monk Parakeet, Cockatoos, Ibises and Spoonbills, pink Flamingos and many seabirds including Skimmers and Terns. They all called out welcome to Andalorax, while she sang back to each of them in their own tongues.

After a while, she could make out more specific birds: the Goldfinch with its "Swit! Wit! Wit!" call; the Yellow Warbler with his all-over yellow chest; the Common Redpoll and his trill of "Chet! Chet! Chet!" with the red cap on his forehead shining brightly. And the Blue-winged Warbler going "Buzzy! Bee-buzz!"

"I can speak with them!" cried out Andalorax, her eyes brimming with tears of happiness and celebratory joy. "It is true!"

"I think that this is how it shall be," said Elvira, patting Andalorax on her shoulder. Andalorax cried more tears, saying, "And all of us here can communicate with each other! I am definitely endowed with the Gift."

"I know, Andie, I know."

"My life is forever changed."

"I know, Andie, I know."

CHAPTER 33

PLANNING FOR WAR

"THEY SHALL PAY FOR WHAT they did to me!" cried out Zivat-Or. He was sitting upon and enthroned by the Phemtas plant which writhed and seethed and snapped at the closeness of any being or thing.

"Those monsters! That King and his Knights all banished me for my beliefs because I was a threat to their empire! They kept the people enslaved with their notions that night is bad and day is good! Yes, and they left me to rot here in the Black Mountains! Leaving me to become engulfed by this mountain weed, this Phemtas, which has taken over my life."

"But, my King," replied Gamedon, sitting on a black rock, feeling compassion for his King, who had now become his friend, "they banished me as well, yet I blame not my fate on the Kingdom of Pellah!" Meanwhile, he was thinking, "I've got to tear him away from such thoughts! It will only end in war and ruin!"

"You! Ha!" decried the Man of Rock. With every loud pitch of his voice the wax-colored plant continued to encircle his torso. "You have not suffered what I have suffered, Gamedon old man! Yes, we have become friendly, you and I, but there is a division between us that splits our friendliness down the middle. You were also banished, 'tis true, but my banishment happened over two centuries ago!

"I have seen all my followers die in those years. I have seen the weed take over these mountains and myself! I know what it is to be filled with hate, the hate which feeds this Phemtas." So saying, his arm, covered with tendrils from the plant, reached out and grabbed a hold of a particularly thick branch.

"The lure of gold, the lust for power, all have taken me over and this is the result you see today!" The gold nugget he wore around his neck seemed particularly appealing to the Phemtas vine he held onto, as it urged its tip towards it.

"Stop!" said Gamedon, facing Zivat-Or with some defiance. "Make no mistake! I, too, know banishment for my beliefs about the sun and moon and day and night, and my disbelief in the so-called evil in the nighttime. We share that horrible destiny, my King!"

"So what?" grumbled Zivat-Or. "Your banishment can hardly be called equal to mine! I was driven from the Kingdom whereas you were simply sent to the Calicab Forest. I watched all my followers and friends die while I lived on, thanks to this awful weed! Yes, I lived on in torture … until I found Siddles, that is."

The great bird was seated beside these two men, listening and saying nothing. Diminished in size to be their equal, he sat atop a black rock bench fashioned from his own powers. His red beak and bright yellow feet stood out in the darkness of the landscape, just as did his red-and-white striped feathering.

Siddles lifted up his head and stared at his master with his one red eye. He croaked, "Aye, my Lord. It was a special day when I came down from the skies and discovered you here among these black stones." Siddles laughed his deep-throated squawk and said, "You lured me here with your powers, which are surely great."

"What?" cried out Gamedon. "Tell me this story!"

Siddles' laughter became louder with every intake of breath, until it verily thundered down upon poor small Gamedon.

"I was flying, in my youth," Siddles managed to say as his laughter decreased, "across the landscapes of this world, crossing the great Gold Mountains in the Kingdom of Pellah, and all the towns therein. Then I came farther south, after I had checked out a large stretch of desert to the west and small islands to the southeast, in the Sea of Iolanthe. In fact, I soared over Budgerigar Island where Andalorax is now and has been for several months.

"The mountains were not black then; they were green and blue from foliage and lakes. It was a beautiful place those many, many years ago. I enjoyed the winds over the high, craggy peaks because I could easily soar to my heart's content. I did not land but continued on in my delightful flight. Ah, I was so young and full of life!

"Many, many years later, I returned – don't ask me why! Fate, perhaps? The mountains were totally changed. I could see from the skies – with my superb sight despite having only one eye – what was happening below as I circled. There in the dark landscape was a human, surrounded by a ring of what we now know to be Phemtas. The plant was leaping up to the gold that was in his hands.

"Then I swooped further down and saw an extraordinary thing: The man, who turned out to be Zivat-Or, was encircled by Phemtas, and he was seated upon his moveable throne. He called out and beckoned me, and I decided to touch down; it seemed harmless enough despite all the legends of black magic and evils. I landed on this very rock where we are now standing.

"Happily, we spoke the same language, because he told me his story that same evening, as I was seated right here.

"I was enthralled by his tragedy. All his followers had already died except for a few who were more than one hundred years old. I stayed on with him, feeling compassion for him in his exile.

"I helped him bury those last remaining friends. I knew of the reason for his banishment, and have stayed loyal to him all these many years. I could not believe the Kingdom of Pellah had been fooling its people with this fantasy about night and day! And now, we have Gamedon to enlighten us! He, who has also been banished for speaking the truth!"

Gamedon sat on his own stone bench, whittling away at a stick with his penknife. He looked up at his two companions and with a gleam in his eye, and said, "Then why, Zivat-Or, don't you feel proud of yourself for standing up for your beliefs? True, you have become a martyr but to whom? No one is alive who remembers the greatness you stood up for!"

"That is true," countered the King, "but I remember it," he said, beating his fist against his chest, "and that is enough for me to continue holding onto and nursing my anger and hatred for the Kingdom of Pellah!"

"And what would you have us do to help you find retribution?"

"War!" cried out Zivat-Or, pointing upwards into the night sky in the volcano. The Phemtas throne writhed around him almost as if in delight. "We must declare war upon the present King and have him pay the price of his forebears!"

"But Sire," said Siddles, "What will that accomplish? You can never regain what you have lost over these many years."

"I shall have peace in my heart if their King is dead," said Zivat-Or.

Silence filled the air. The Phemtas continued to writhe, its waxen, pale yellow color bright against the nighttime darkness.

Gamedon and Siddles were both staring at Zivat-Or, and they knew he meant exactly what he said.

"My liege," said Siddles in a calm voice, "How do you propose we achieve this? A faded King who is almost two hundred and fifty years old and addicted to a plant, will overnight assume the mantle of the King he once was and destroy King Vanamir – yes, that's his name, my liege: Vanamir! He is the one you would want dead, Zivat-Or. How can this be achieved?"

"Easily," answered the old King, fingering his gold nugget hanging from his necklace.

"How?"

"By using your powers, my friend." Zivat-Or reached his arm out and pointed at Siddles. "You shall create my army of revenge! You shall be my instrument of death to this King Vanamir!"

Siddles lowered his head and tapped his thick red beak on the ground. Lifting it and looking at Zivat-Or with his one piercing red eye, he said, "This I cannot do, not for any person or being. Not even for you, my Lord and Master. You seem to forget, I cannot destroy anything! I can only create!"

Zivat-Or laughed loudly. "I have thought of that! You can create the instruments of war that I can then, myself, use to bring down this Vanamir! You shall not be destroying anything; you shall create! It is I who shall be the destroyer!" So saying, he laughed loudly and profoundly, throwing back his head and showing the golden bauble hanging around his neck resting on his gold mail shirt entwined with Phemtas.

"What would you have me create, Master?" asked the great bird in a soft voice. "An army of foot soldiers followed by mounted cavalry on horseback, dragging cannons and artillery by use of elephants? What kinds of powers do you think I have? I am not limitless!"

Zivat-Or laughed again, tossing back his head once more. "I am delighting in your response, Siddles! You have created an interesting image in my mind, all those soldiers marching to war! But no, that's not what is needed. It is far simpler than that.

"Siddles, way back in my youth when I was a young monarch of the Pellah Kingdom, a circus came to town. I watched from the balcony of the Castle while one man, dressed in colorful raiment replete with sequins, glitter, brilliant stripes and polka dots, entered the arena of his circus tent via horse and buggy. Floating above him was an enormous hot-air balloon. It bore red and yellow stripes and was decorated with flags and ribbons that flapped in the breeze. Dangling from this balloon was a large straw basket.

"'I am going on a voyage,' he announced. 'One that will excite and thrill every one of you!' So saying, he held onto the wide leather straps which had been tightly secured to the buggy and kept the balloon afloat in the blue, cloudless sky.

"Everyone watched as, one by one, these straps were untied, and held in his strong hands.

"'Now watch closely!' he called out to the crowd. I observed with great interest as, in an instant, he clambered into the basket.

"'Farewell!' he cried out. 'My voyage begins!' and he let go of the straps.

"The balloon rose into the sky with such speed that I had to swiftly lift my chin and look up, as the man was lifted off into the blue sky and disappeared into the clouds."

Zivat-Or stopped his narrative and watched Siddles for his response. The great one-eyed buzzard asked, "And what has this to do with your plans for war against the Kingdom?"

The old, former King laughed wickedly, startling Siddles, who had never heard him laugh in such a sinister way before.

"Siddles," he announced, "you shall take me in a hot-air balloon out of these vast Black Mountains, and then due north across the great fields and plains and hills of the Kingdom of Pellah. You shall bring me to the Castle atop the Gold Mountains where – as I have learned from Gamedon – abides the King and his entire entourage of Knights.

"There, you shall deposit me with my special weapon of destruction, and I shall kill King Vanamir!

"What special weapon of destruction, Zivat-Or?"

Once again, the old King laughed deeply and profoundly. "I have designed in my mind what you, Siddles, shall construct for me."

"What is it?"

"It is a special bow and arrow whose course runs straight to King Vanamir's heart! Only I can use it! You will see to that, my friend. When I am making my landfall in the balloon, the King will come outside to see what is happening. Then I shall take my shot!"

"But how shall you make your escape once you have accomplished this murder?"

"You shall come by instantaneously, and bring me in front of the people. I shall declare myself King!"

"But surely his Knights will be firing volley upon volley at us! We shall never accomplish such a feat."

Zivat-Or looked at Siddles and then at Gamedon, and said, "Maybe I don't care to be King after all. Maybe I will have done my final act and shall be free from this cursed existence!" Zivat-Or buried his head in the crook of his arm and began to sob like a child.

The Phemtas upon which he sat recoiled from this behavior, and leapt back as if under attack. Siddles got up and went over to him, and said softly, "It's alright, my Lord. We shall find another way to bring you peace."

Zivat-Or lifted up his head and laughed again, this time the loudest of all. "Fool! I am not crying from weakness! I am crying from strength! It is almost too much for me to bear to imagine the glory of this attack! Can you not see it? Our enormous balloon shall be marvelous, with ribbons and stripes and bright patches of all colors of the rainbow!"

"My Lord," said Siddles, "have you carefully considered the outcome of such an act? You shall be swept away into the heavens!"

"You, Siddles, have the magic power to make it happen perfectly! We shall begin here in the Black Mountains, from this very special spot. As I traverse the lands, it shall attract all the people in the countryside, and they shall follow me as best they can across the landscape up to the Gold Mountains.

"In the Castle itself, everyone shall wonder at the marvel of my passage across the sky … as I make my way to the King's quarters!

"There, the King himself will be drawn to the spectacle of my being, floating on my Phemtas throne, in the delightful balloon, as I head his way. Then, when he is within my sight, I take up the bow and draw back the arrow and let it fly! Hit my mark! The King goes down and you, Siddles, come and rescue me. By then, all the people will have assembled in front of me and I shall be their new King. That is it!"

"I thought you were above such thoughts, Sire," retorted Siddles. "I cannot be a part of such a plot. It is murder!"

Gamedon said, "Zivat-Or, my friend, you cannot put yourself in such a terrible situation. You shall surely never succeed!"

"As I said, Gamedon, I think it might be my last gesture. I am at peace with that."

Siddles stood up abruptly and said the magic words that made him regain his normal twelve-foot height. Whoosh! There he was in all his regal glory, shining his iridescent wings in the globe lights that surrounded them all continually.

"Zivat-Or!" He thundered down at the two of them, "Man of Rock! What you ask of me is within my powers and you know it! Right down to the colorful ribbons on the balloon. Yet how you can ask it of me tells me that we are not friends after all."

"Yes, we are great friends," came back the reply, "which is why you will do this for me."

"I will be the accomplice to a murder, and of a King!"

"You cannot live with that?"

"I can, but it will weigh heavily upon me."

"Wouldn't failing to help me resolve my 'bad luck,' as we might call it, weigh equally heavily upon you?"

"Yes."

"Then do what will make me happiest, Siddles. Let me have my way."

"I must ponder this, Zivat-Or. You must give me time. And now, if you will allow me, I shall take my leave for the evening." After farewell salutes, he took off into the night, flapping his mighty wings until he could soar away with the nocturnal winds, leaving Gamedon and Zivat-Or to turn and stare at each other. Their faces were lit by the globe lights which also shone on the Phemtas weed that writhed fiercely and comprised his throne.

"War?" asked the old man.

"Aye," said the old King, grasping the gold nugget around his throat. "War."

CHAPTER 34

ANDALORAX BECOMES A WISE WOMAN

ANDALORAX WONDERED DAILY THROUGHOUT HER education about what it meant to be a Galinda-Hussadi. She went to classes in her district schoolhouse and studied with the specialists for each subject.

To study totemism, one of her favorite subjects – Nature and all its wonders being her first love – the students were taught by Mr. Jethro Tuttle, who knew all there was to know about how the Hussadis each worshipped their own totem, be it an animal or a natural force.

As the professor explained on the first day of class: "When a child is born, the Wise Woman of that particular tribe endows it with a relationship to a certain animal or force of nature. That force must represent the true soul of that infant, for it to be his or her true totem."

All the students knew this, for all those in the schoolhouse – indeed, all the people on the island – had a totem.

"Yes," he continued, "everyone on this island has a totem, and these totems are meaningful to us because they signify who we are individually as we go through our lives until our deaths. A good Wise Woman takes her time to study the infant. She will move in with the family and spend days and nights with the baby. Only when she is confident in her choice, will she make her official announcement to the people of Budgerigar Island."

"Why," asked Andalorax, perplexed, "is it only a Wise Woman, and not also a Wise Man?"

Mr. Tuttle knitted his brows together and then laughed wryly and said, "There has only once been a Wise Man in the entire history of the Hussadis, Andie."

"And who was that?"

"A fellow who was most peculiar."

Professor Tuttle twirled his long mustache as he spoke. "He had a propensity for wandering about the island. It is even said that he once left the island and crossed the Sea of Iolanthe, traveling to both the west and the north. But of course that is a preposterous notion," went on Professor Tuttle, "because it would be impossible for anyone to brave the rough seas."

"Perhaps he had a boat," wondered Andalorax.

Tuttle laughed again, and leered at the class. "What boat could one single man build on this island without everyone knowing about it? It would have to be extremely large, big and wide, and made of many trees. Someone would have noticed such an object! No, no, my dear. He never traveled to foreign lands while he lived here." Tuttle leaned forward at his desk and stared at Andalorax. "But he did disappear!"

"Disappear?"

"Aye. One day he was gone, just like that!" Tuttle snapped his fingers together. "No one knew where he went. He lived alone."

"Who was this man? Did he live many centuries ago?"

"Nay, Andie. He lived … perhaps twenty years ago. I knew him. Well, I knew OF him, and saw him wandering about in the woods, by the edge of the sea, in the hills … just about everywhere!"

"What did he do?"

"He was an inventor."

"What did he invent?"

"Ooh, a great deal of things. They are all housed in the great Library, because they are so unique and must be protected from damage. But they weren't all quite functional, therefore there is only one of everything. None were worthy of copying or using."

"Why was he considered a Wise Man? It's hard to believe there is only one man in all your thousand-plus years of history who was a Wise Man."

Tuttle got up from his desk and looked out the window of the classroom and heaved a great sigh. "Ah, Andie," he said, his voice trailing off, "because he was a Wise Man. He could do all the things that Wise Women do."

"Then shall I receive a totem?" she asked.

"Hmm," responded the teacher. "It seems logical to me that you should." He rubbed his rotund belly. "But I doubt if the Wise Woman will take her time with you searching for your totem. You are already grown up, and assigning a totem is customarily done right after birth. As to why women only, it seems that Wise Women can sense things that men can't. Like, for instance, what your totem will be!"

"I wish I could meet the Wise Man," she said.

"He has disappeared; I told you that. No one has any idea of where he went, if he left the island, and, if he did, how he succeeded in doing so."

"Still … I wish …" whispered Andalorax.

"You wish what?"

"That he could give me my totem!" She slapped her hand upon the teacher's desk. "What was his name, Professor?"

"Frederick Janifur."

"That's a funny name."

"He was a different sort of fellow, I must say. Everyone on this island knew it. His father, too, was a strange man."

"Why strange?

"Marcus Janifur kept to himself, I hear. He, and his son Frederick after him, was fond of wandering around the island. Frederick was the Wise Man. But it was his father Marcus who built furniture and constructed wooden and metal objects. He also made many musical instruments. We still use them here at the school." Tuttle reached into a drawer at his desk and withdrew a small flute.

"It is said that he made this," he said, handing it to Andalorax.

She felt its lovely shape, and saw the inlays of various dark woods against the light wood of which it was constructed.

"And his mother?" She was still fingering the flute.

"Gerta Janifur? She still lives here, alone since her husband died," said Professor Tuttle, and he looked at the ceiling and counted on his fingers and added, "that was almost, oh, forty years ago, I'd guess. She is a reclusive old lady who is said to speak many languages." He coughed. "She has the Gift," he added.

"What languages? How could she know any other than what we speak here?"

"She spoke in tongues, I believe. That's what she told everyone anyway," he noted, retrieving the flute and tapping it in his palm. "But enough about the Janifur family." He slapped the flute on the tabletop and "Crack!" it broke into pieces.

Professor Tuttle was alarmed and emitted a small howl. "Oh no! What have I done?" he called out and he slipped the broken flute back into his desk drawer.

"Let us resume our previous lesson, everyone. Um, what were we talking about?"

"Totems," replied Andalorax. "And Wise Women. And Wise Men."

"Ah, yes. It is your totem in particular we were discussing. Although I don't see how you can be given a totem, as you are already grown up."

This of course raised a ruckus in the classroom, for all the children wanted to appoint a totem that would be most appropriate for "Andie," their new classmate.

"I say she's a Lion, because of all that hair!"

"Silly! Lions have red hair! She would be a Unicorn because of her long silvery-white hair and the feeling of magic that she emanates!"

"She's not a grounded animal; she's a bird! She's a Snowy Egret or a Great Blue Heron."

All this while, Professor Tuttle attempted to silence the classroom, until he finally evoked the spirit of his own totem and stopped all the discussion.

"Hissss!!" he spat out, as he employed the act of the cobra, his personal totem. He brought all the vibrations and energy of the venomous animal into the room. It stopped them mid-speech, for Tuttle certainly did not look like a serpent, but rather an old horse or donkey. Then, dropping his guise, he turned to Andalorax and said with a smile, "See, Andie? It works to have the proper totem!"

Turning to the class, he added, "We shall have to see a Wise Woman and have her discover the totem for Andalorax!"

The very next afternoon, all the students had done as their professor had instructed: they brought their lunches in cloth picnic bags and drinking water in glass bottles, and also a blanket for each of them to sit on. They set off on their class adventure as soon as the cuckoo clock on the wall struck twelve.

Two by two, they followed Professor Tuttle along a stone road that led to one made solely of earth and clay, then finally they reached a grassy area that they could see was the front lawn of someone's house. It was difficult to make out the details of the house as it was of dark wood covered with vines and branches from large, overhanging trees, and was surrounded by a thick, wispy mist. It was only one story high, but had two tall chimneys reaching out of what seemed to be one main central room. There was a wraparound screened-in porch, and sitting there on a chair was a woman, rocking slowly back and forth.

"Greetings, Lady Tallbanks," called out the Professor, waving his hands up in the air as the group approached her, crossing the grassy lawn. Once they reached the old, wide-spread branches of what the Professor noted to the class was, "a miniature forest of the mighty Portopuff trees, which we shall discuss later," they were engulfed in shadows.

It seemed to Andalorax that the clouds had suddenly blocked out the sun, for it was terribly dark in the miniature Portopuff forest.

"Maybe," thought Andalorax, "he means the forest itself is a miniature," for those trees weren't miniature; they were the tallest trees she had ever seen, and bore apple-sized powder puffs of bright red flowers all along their branches. Everything was dense; even the air seemed thick. She kept on going forward, following the rest of the class.

Then Professor Tuttle turned around, grabbed Andalorax by the hand, and brought her up to his side. The rest of the class stopped in their tracks.

Together, they approached the woman in the rocking chair. They stopped when they got to the landing of the porch railing, and he said once again, "Greetings, Lady Tallbanks!" He doffed his felt cap and bowed low in a humble greeting, and continued to speak.

"May I have the honor of presenting to you a person newly arrived and in need of a totem?"

"You may, Professor Tuttle."

"Here is Andalorax."

She bowed low, imitating her teacher.

"They call me Andie," she said in a low voice, and then looked up. There before her was a slender female figure dressed in a glittering cape encircled with real, living and sparkling faeries. They lit up the air all around her.

Lady Tallbanks wore several layers of mesh skirts that were of a lovely lilac color mixed with an avocado green. They all rustled when she moved, which she did as she rose from her chair. Her maroon cape glistened in the half-light of the tall, shadowy Portopuff trees. The sun's rays streamed down from high above them, and the entire area was flooded with the striped shafts of sunlight.

"Greetings, Andalorax," she said, in a voice with an accent that was quite thick, although Andalorax recognized it not. It was light and gleeful, and pleasant to the ear.

"It is many years since I have seen you, Professor. Good to know you are still in the schooling business!" She laughed, a gentle sound that soothed Andalorax's ears. She immediately liked Lady Tallbanks.

"Now, who is this you bring to me, who needs a totem?"

"Andalorax was delivered here several months ago, from the north across the Sea of Iolanthe, coming from the Kingdom of Pellah and the Black Mountains, Lady Tallbanks."

The slender woman looked Andalorax up and down slowly, then walked completely around her.

"I have heard of her, of course, in great detail. She has seen much in her short lifetime, Tuttle," noted Lady Tallbanks. "I must learn all I can about you, young Andie," she said, turning to Andalorax. "But you are already an adult so all rules about assignation of a totem go out the window!" She leaned forward, being quite tall, and a mist began to surround her, and cause her skirts to flutter. The straw hat she wore was blown away by a sudden gust of wind, but the faeries continued to buzz and hum around her like tiny hummingbirds. Andalorax squinted her eyes and took a closer look at these miniature creatures. They were dressed in fluffy outfits with puffy blouses and gossamer gowns.

"Apparently, judging by their outfits," she thought, "these faeries are all female."

Lady Tallbanks raised her voice and loudly said, "Tell me, Andalorax, right here and now, tell me, what animal or force of nature you align with in your heart? Speak NOW!" she said, and her voice thundered deep and growly, and the shafts of sunlight disappeared and all was in darkness.

Then Andalorax said, without thinking, "The moon, Lady Tallbanks. The moon!"

"Then the moon it shall be," decried the tall, slender Wise Woman. "I can see that you are at one with this natural elemental force, our beautiful moon which changes ever in its nightly travels."

Andalorax asked timidly, "That is it? It is all over? My totem is the moon?"

"Aye, Andie."

"But what does it mean, that you have discovered my totem? And why is it not an animal?"

"It can be an animal, it can be a force of nature, and in your case, it can be and is a celestial being. What does it mean? Ha! It means," and here the thin woman in her illusionary garb stepped down to the ground where Andalorax stood next to her Professor, and she took her hand, "It means that you are forever linked to the moon, that your personality is similar to that of the moon's, that you share its characteristics."

"Such as?"

"Such as being the beacon for night wanderers and animals that live in the moonlight. Such as orbiting our planet by force of gravity."

Now, this was something Andalorax could not understand: anyone wanting to be in the moonlight instead of shunning it! How was she like the moon? Being a beacon for those who wander by moonlight? And what was the "force of gravity?"

Lady Tallbanks seemed to be reading Andalorax's mind, for she immediately answered her question.

"Gravity is the magnetic pull of the earth that keeps everything solid on the ground. It's why we don't all fly off the surface of the globe."

"What are you talking about?" asked Andalorax. She had never been taught of totems and astronomy. "At least," she mused mindfully, "not yet!"

"At the core of our round planet Earth is a great big magnet that pulls everything towards the center, including the moon, your totem."

"And the stars?"

"They are fixed in the sky and do not adhere to the laws of gravity we have here on planet Earth."

"And the sun?"

"We circle the sun, Andalorax."

"All of this is quite new to me, Lady Tallbanks," she responded quietly. "It is quite fascinating to learn about the planet I live on. I knew it was called a planet, by the way, because my grandfather studied the stars. He charted them on paper, and drew images of clusters of stars that linked up together and took on the outlines of animals and people."

"So your grandfather studied what we call astrology," said Lady Tallbanks. "It claims to locate information about human affairs and terrestrial events by studying the movements and relative positions of celestial objects."

"But what then is astronomy?"

"Astronomy is by contrast a scientific study of celestial objects, not simply a claim to understanding life according to the relativity of the celestial objects such as stars and planets."

Andalorax was silent. She wasn't sure she truly understood.

"What your grandfather studied was astrology, and it is a valid study indeed. We practice it here on Budgie Island."

"You do?"

"Yes, we do. And you will too."

"When?"

"Very shortly. We have found an excellent instructor who will take you — metaphorically, mind you! — by the hand and walk you through the specialties of astrology and astronomy both. He knows the scientific as well as the mythological aspects of the celestial beings. One of the tools you will use will be a board game we have invented by a Wise Man, called Astroflash. It has been in use by the Galinda-Hussadi since that recent time."

"Please don't be insulted, Lady Tallbanks," said Andalorax, "but who was the Wise Man?"

"Frederick Janifur? He once figured largely in our appointing of totems. He had a special knack for doing it. No other man seems to have been able to do it!"

"Did you ever meet him? What was he like?"

"But of course I met him! He was unique in our history, you know. But he isn't around anymore."

"Disappeared?" asked Andalorax.

"Disappeared," said Lady Tallbanks. "Just like that," she said, snapping her fingers together. "While he was at one of our Wise Women conferences, about twenty years ago, he went up in a puff of smoke and disappeared."

"A puff of smoke?"

"Aye, Andie." She leaned forward and touched her cheek. "A puff of smoke."

Time marched on and three more months passed and Andalorax continued to go to school just as the Hussadis did. Yet her training sessions were significantly different from those of everyone else, because she almost always had Elvira with her, serving as the Guide she was meant to be. No one else had a Guide, because they already knew all about the Hussadis. No one else needed a Guide, after all! So Elvira translated life as a Hussadi for Andalorax and taught her all the ways of the Hussadis, from the way they set the dinner table to the elaborate rituals they went through to be at one with their totems.

The Library of the Hussadis was one large stone building, to keep the damaging sun's rays away from what they considered to be one of their finest treasures. It was there that Andalorax spent all her free time, when she wasn't in school or on a field trip with her classmates or teachers. She read about everything she could get her hands on, but mostly she read about Nature, which was her greatest love, along with her totem, the moon.

In the dark Library, made of stone blocks and without windows to keep out the dirt, the sun, and the rain, Andalorax discovered the inventions of Marcus Janifur under large white sheets, "to protect them from dust, I suppose," she thought.

She carefully lifted one sheet, and saw an array of bizarre mechanisms. Andalorax put her hands on one of them, and she had no idea what it was: there was a tubular shaped carriage with a set of rotary blades on top, and on the desk was a small sign that read: "Heli-copter." It was very small and fit in her palm, and had a tiny human doll seated inside the tube.

Next, Andalorax picked up a simple object labeled an "Egg Beater," which looked like two forks placed face-to-face that were bound together at their handles. That was normal-sized so she could hold it in her hand. Then there was a clock which was tall and had a pendulum handing from its face. It was encased in a large vertical crate and was dubbed the "Swinging Clock."

She was amazed at the quantity of items on the table; there must have been thirty or more.

"Marcus Janifur was certainly an uncommon man," she said to herself. "I wonder what his son Frederick was really like, being a Wise Man and then disappearing in a puff of smoke."

She continued to study the books and manuscripts in the Library. She read about the Galinda-Hussadi first stepping off their boat over one thousand and fifty years before and putting their feet on the soil, and she became absorbed in that literature, and forgot all about Marcus Janifur and his son Frederick.

All this time, every morning when she awakened, Andalorax thought of Siddles. Where was he and what was he doing? And then her mind would hurry over to Gamedon, and she worried about him, and then to Zivat-Or, the sad disgraced King she pitied so much.

Then she would force herself to turn her mind to other things, such as what would be happening in school that day, and afterwards, would she be able to go for a refreshing walk in the high and mighty Portopuff Forest?

But this day would bring something different to Andalorax. For as she walked along the edge of the Portopuff Forest this morning, her skin was abruptly covered with goose pimples.

She knew he was there.

Siddles!

Andalorax looked up and quickly caught the movement in the sky of her mighty friend circling over the wheat field, then slowing down and coming to a soft landing. He seemed to let something fall from one claw, but what it was she could not discern.

Siddles stood up, all twelve feet of him, and uttered the magic incantation that reduced his size, and thus became just under six feet tall.

"Siddles!" called out Andalorax, running in the wheat field as fast as she could. She finally caught up to him and stroked his shimmering black feathers with their bright red zig-zag stripes. The mighty bird leaned his head down and tapped his beak on the ground in his customary way of greeting. Then he said:

"I have no time for a civil greeting, Andalorax. This is an emergency! I have come here to inform you of dreadful news and to ask your help in its resolution!"

"What is it, dear Siddles?" she implored. "Come," she said, "let us walk towards my home." They followed the path across the wheat field.

"Zivat-Or has reached the final stage of his madness, I truly believe," said Siddles. "He is convinced that the current King of Pellah – our King Vanamir – must pay for what was done to him: making Zivat-Or an outcast in the Black Mountains, where he became a victim to that plant, Phemtas."

"Vanamir," whispered Andalorax. "I haven't heard that name in a long time, not since living in the Calicab Forest, not since before I met you, dearest Siddles."

"You know of this King?"

"Yes," she answered. "Surely I do. I know him personally." She remembered in a clear instant the last time she'd seen the King: She was with Gamedon, in the King's own private quarters in the Castle Pellah, and they knew he was conspiring in his mind to hold her prisoner for the rest of her life. He believed her destined to be the cause of his ultimate downfall one horrible day.

That was the night she and Gamedon fled the Castle.

"King Vanamir came to our town of Milorin regularly every year," said Andalorax, beginning the short tale as they walked along, heading for her home. "He was addicted to an herb which grew in abundance in our little valley." She stopped short.

"Siddles!" she cried out. "Little did we know then that the Phemtas of Zivat-Or and the herb of Vanamir were one and the same! At that time, we knew nothing about the Black Mountains and how Phemtas took root there. We only knew how it afflicted the Kings of Pellah, getting worse and stronger with each succeeding King.

"Then Vanamir learned as years went by that he could never succeed in having a male heir," she went on, stroking the fluffy tops of the wheat as they continued walking briskly, and also stroking Siddles' magnificent plumage as the sun was high in the sky and cast its strong rays across the wheat field. Oh how she missed her friend! Now he was here beside her ... speaking of an "emergency" ... so she went on with her story.

"His first wife had a daughter and could have no more children. He took a second wife, whose fate was the exact same: one daughter then no children. It meant no son! And so it has continued for over fifteen years.

"All these wives of his – there are many! – live in a large, high turret at the northern end of the Castle Pellah."

"How do you know all this information, when you were kept so isolated?" asked Siddles.

"Remember, Gamedon is my grandfather and I never spent one day in my life without him, that is, until you flew me away to this island. Gamedon taught me many things. Besides," she held up her chin and said, "My mother Mandir is one of those wives."

Siddles stopped. He turned to her. "But Andalorax! If your mother is his wife, then you are the daughter of the King?"

"No. I was born before Vanamir took my mother away. I do not know who my father is. Yet, once a woman marries Vanamir, she can give birth to but one daughter yet after that she becomes infertile. Every single year he hopes to escape this same fate, for he needs a male heir, not a daughter!"

Andalorax suddenly realized that she was brought up in a dynasty of male kings while now she knew of another world, the ways of the Galinda-Hussadi, of government and the will of the people.

"This sounds like magic to me," continued Siddles.

They walked along in silence, then Siddles said, "Thank you, Andalorax, for explaining all this to me. I did not understand about this King but that is crucial to understanding why I am here."

"It is magic," she answered. "Gamedon made that very clear to me. There is much magic in this world, including the magic that made you, Siddles!"

Siddles stopped, and looked into her dark eyes.

"You have gone through much," he told her, "but now I see that you have passed through it all and come into womanhood. You have become your own authentic self, Andalorax!"

She bowed her head. Then she looked back into his one red eye with its ovoid pupil, and they shared a moment of silent joy at this realization.

"Yes," she answered. "It is true, Siddles. I have become a woman since you last saw me. But come, let us hurry to my abode and you can tell me why you are here!"

As they walked there, Siddles told her more.

"Andalorax, Zivat-Or blames King Vanamir – the very King you just told me about, the only one living, the one who cannot have a male heir – for having been thrown out of the Kingdom in disgrace. Just because Zivat-Or objected to the Kingdom's stance about night and day, about black and white. But during those couple of centuries ago, that was high treason!"

"Is it not treason today as well?"

"I know not, but that has no significance in this instance. What is significant is that Zivat-Or has decided to kill King Vanamir to manifest his revenge."

"How will he kill him?"

"With a bow and arrow that I will craft for him and for him alone."

"Is that not against the law you live by: not to destroy?"

Siddles closed his one red eye, then opened it and looked up at the blue sky. He was weary from his long flight, and now weary of this woeful tale he was bringing to Andalorax. Nonetheless, they traipsed along through the field towards the edge of the Portopuff Forest in which her little yellow house was nestled. Andalorax was once again admiring his extraordinary plumage, whose mostly black feathers were shiny and iridescent like mother-of-pearl. His zig-zag red-and-white stripes were patterned like lightning bolts. His bony red beak and strong equally bright yellow feet stood out in the summer sunlight.

They reached her house and went up to the porch, where Andalorax sat down in her rocking chair and Siddles perched upon the banister.

"The entire plan is elaborate, and requires my magic, yes," he said, "that is true. Yet making a bow with an arrow that seeks and finds its target is the very essence of being an arrow. An arrow is not a killing machine. Oh yes!" he cried out. "This plan is rich in design and requires my participation completely. Perhaps Zivat-Or shall not be the one who fires the fatal blow. All I can say is, I shall craft such an arrow capable of causing death." Siddles sighed.

"But there is another item, my dear, which it requires."

"What is that?"

"Don't you see it yet, dear girl?" he asked, cocking his head in quizzical disbelief.

"Alright!" she cried out, and got up and stood beside his six-foot frame. "It requires me! I understand! This is part of my destiny. I've known the time would come when I would be called to action …."

"What is today's truth," added Siddles, "is that Zivat-Or plans to attack and kill King Vanamir!"

"What?" she cried out. "How can he even consider such an idea?" She could hardly believe her ears. Why, he was an old man, and kept plastered together by the evil Phemtas weed, plus he was attached, or so she assumed from what she saw, to the plant itself. It was his living throne.

"Siddles! How can Zivat-Or imagine getting close enough to King Vanamir to touch his little finger, let alone kill him?

The mighty buzzard stopped walking and turned to face this amazing woman who stood before him. "How she has changed," he sighed and looked up towards the heavens.

"He plans to use my magic powers," said the bird, and his raised beak opened up and issued forth such a terrible sound! It seemed to Andalorax that the Portopuff trees suddenly were whipped up into a frenzy, as the wind blew in swiftly from the north and rustled the enormous dark-green leaves and caused many red flower-puffs to fall to the ground.

"Why, his cry is the profound song of a humpback whale," thought the black and white girl, for now she had read about such creatures while in the land of the Galinda-Hussadi on Budgerigar Island. And she said to Siddles, "Your song is the song of disaster; it is the cry of a dying star!"

"Yes, I know the cry of the dying star and the song of the humpback whale, and I even know the sound of disaster," he answered.

They stood at the forest's edge and listened to the wailing of the wind. "Odd," thought Andalorax. "We are in the middle of summer, yet the chilling wind feels like winter is upon us." They were both silent for some time. Then Siddles continued his tale.

"He ordered me to create a special balloon that will obey my commands, for I shall be the magician who crafts it into being and hence be its true master. That balloon will carry him north from the Black Mountains all the way to the Castle Pellah, straight before the King, where Zivat-Or shall take his life."

"A special balloon? Can you do this?'

"Yes, I can."

"And will it carry him to the King where he can kill him?"

"Zivat-Or's idea is that it will carry him, but there is another detail about the basket that I have yet to tell. First, I must say that I am to fly overhead because after he has killed King Vanamir, he wants me to catch his balloon with him still in the basket, when he will descend before the people of Pellah Kingdom. Then and there they shall all make him King as is his rightful ending!"

"His rightful ending?"

"Because Zivat-Or was truly once a King, albeit long ago, who was ousted by his Ministers for his beliefs about the day and the night, it is his birthright, his lineage. And – because Vanamir will now be dead – Zivat-Or shall technically be the rightful heir to the throne of Pellah."

"I see," said Andalorax. She, too, looked up at the bright blue sky, where the sun was at its zenith while the wind still blew in strong.

She and Siddles were now staring into each other's eyes.

"And how shall he kill him? He will, as you said before, still be entrapped in the Phemtas plant that is his built-in throne. How can he achieve the use of a bow and arrow?"

"Zivat-Or may be ancient and hobbled by the plant, which – in the form of his throne – shall also hold him up. Aye, Andalorax," he said, "he can indeed do the deed."

"This is dreadful news. What thinks Gamedon of such a plan?"

"Gamedon is the one who sent me to you. He says you are part of all our destinies, Andalorax. All of ours."

"Yes, I know," she said softly, "including my own."

"Gamedon says that you will have to be included in what happens with Zivat-Or and Vanamir 'and the entire Kingdom,' he cried out to me when telling me to prepare for what to say to you now that we are together, Andalorax."

Andalorax leaned down and picked up a Portopuff leaf that had fallen from a nearby tree at the edge of the wheat field. It was soft and newly green. Why had a new leaf fallen? It was summertime.

"What a silly thing to ponder at a time like this," she thought.

She turned to Siddles. "How can he even consider the idea?" she asked, looking deep into the black pupil of his red eye. "It is insane! Did he send you here to actually consider such a performance? It would be an act of war, dearest Siddles! Does he want my blessing?"

"He does."

"Well, he doesn't get it."

"He needs more than that, however."

"What else does he need of me?" she asked. "Wouldn't my blessing be enough?"

"He needs you to fight the war with him, against King Vanamir."

"Me? To fight the war with him?" Andalorax spoke these words one by one, in disbelief of what she was saying.

Suddenly, old but sprightly Gamedon emerged from the woods and walked until he stood in front of his granddaughter. He was wearing the same clothes as six months ago, his old tattered cloak and scuffed, laced-up leather shoes.

"Aye, Andalorax!" Gamedon said in a strong voice. "Zivat-Or needs you to accomplish his goal."

"Oh, where did you come from, grandfather?" she cried out, throwing her arms about him.

"Siddles brought me here, just as he brought you, in his large claw. We decided I would run unseen by you – remember, I am a small man, Andalorax, and could easily be shorter that the wheat blowing in this field – to keep me hidden here amidst the Portopuff trees until Siddles told you of Zivat-Or's plan."

"Zivat-Or needs me to accomplish his goal? What goal, grandfather?" She was feeling confused. "Killing Vanamir isn't a goal – it's the way to a goal."

"No, no, Andalorax. It is not only to kill King Vanamir! This is a double-edged sword, granddaughter! It is to – for once and for all – put an end to the myth of night being bad and day being good. That was, after all, a myth carried on through the ages with the Kings of Pellah, to keep their people under control, to keep them indoors in the nighttime and avoid crime! To maintain a kind of peace."

Andalorax remembered very clearly at this point in the conversation what she had grown up believing: that she was to play a role in the end of King Vanamir's reign. And perhaps the reign of the entire Kingdom of Pellah.

Gamedon interrupted. "Let me be clear on this, Andalorax. The Kings banished me as well for my beliefs, so Zivat-Or and I have something very much in common!"

"Your banishment? You share that?"

"I speak of sharing our belief in the truth of night and day! There is no evil solely in the night and no glory solely in the day. That is what I want to hear from Vanamir: That I was cruelly and shamefully and illegally banished!!"

"Grandfather!" cried Andalorax in alarm. "You, too, feel you must be exonerated for your beliefs?"

"Aye, I do, dearest granddaughter. I truly do." He leaned forward and stroked her hair. Her tresses were white and long and thick, and filled with the colorful ribbons that were braided in it by her friendly roommates. They adored her hair! Ribbons, crystals, flowers – these were woven into her plaits. Now they were blowing in the wind.

"But Grandfather," she began, feeling the weakness of her youth return as she stood here before a man who once seemed like a king himself, but was truly just a little old man living in a dream now. "You cannot go against the King. How shall you accomplish this?"

Once again, Gamedon said, "We shall accomplish this with the magical aid and powers of the one and only Siddles."

"What role are you destined to play, then?"

"I, too, shall be in the balloon. I shall assist Zivat-Or in shooting his arrow into Vanamir's heart."

The big black bird, who had stood quietly all this time, now coughed. Andalorax turned around and looked at him.

"Are you in on this, Siddles?"

He halted for a few minutes, then looked her straight in the eyes with his one red one. "Aye, I am, but I am also strung out on a line against it. For you see, without my assistance, these two men shall never realize their dream on any level. I must give them that chance. I cannot desert them!"

Andalorax went over to him and put her hand on his shiny black and red feathers. The strong wind seemed to be calming down. She could feel the sun's heat on her face.

"I understand, dearest Siddles. But please give me time to consider what role I shall play in your war against Vanamir, the King of Pellah!"

"I do not have the gift of time to give you," he answered. "I took my time to ponder this plan but in the end, I made up my mind. You must follow me."

"I must? Follow you? To where?"

"Yes," said the buzzard. "You must come back with Gamedon and me to the Black Mountains. It is your destiny to participate in this saga of woe."

Gamedon looked into her coal-black eyes and said, "I am part of this tale as well, granddaughter. I am with Siddles and Zivat-Or." He stared into her eyes. "And you know that you must be, as well."

"If I must," she replied, lifting up her head, "then I shall. I fear that my time to act has come."

"We commence immediately. Meet us here in the wheat field when the sun rises tomorrow morning," said Siddles. "From there, I shall take off, in my normal twelve-foot-tall size, with both of you cradled in my large claw. We shall have the fullness of one whole day to fly across the Sea of Iolanthe and eventually reach Zivat-Or by nightfall."

"Take me to Zivat-Or and the Black Mountains," Andalorax announced. "I am ready to do what I must."

CHAPTER 35

THE MANY-COLORED GIRL RETURNS

AFTER THIS DRASTIC MEETING, ANDALORAX went home with her head reeling about what she had just learned. First of all, there was the return of Siddles and Gamedon! Then there was the war plan of Zivat-Or!

"I have also learned that the moon is my totem," she thought, as she walked home. She stumbled a little, feeling dizzy at this imploding news. "I know little – nay, I know nothing! – of what this could mean, especially to be happening at this time in my life. All my life I've known an exceptional future was in store for me ... but is this the time? Is this 'it?'"

She thought back to the days of the beginning of the Kingdom of Pellah, and wondered how – and why – the first King and the following succession of Kings came up with the idea that the moon was bad, and should be shunned ... That wicked, nasty beings which hid during the day, came out at sunset and perpetrated all sorts of foul deeds and nasty mischief, frolicking in their own way in the moonlight that they did not fear but was for them a precious object.

"Is this the connection I've been waiting for all my life? The long-awaited mysterious link between the fate of Vanamir and myself is the moon?" she wondered, as she leapt up the porch stairs and entered her house. "Can it be as simple as that?"

She swung open the door and standing there in front of her kitchen window looking out was the Many-Colored Girl! Andalorax shuddered. It had to be her! Already as she stood there, her silken garment changed from lavender to grass green.

The Many-Colored Girl turned away from the window and her purple eyes looked into Andalorax's black ones. As before, her eyes, her hair, and her garments were continually changing color. Her sweeping, layered gossamer dress flowed and rustled as she moved across the floor to come closer to Andalorax. As she moved, the dress glittered saffron orange, then became lemon yellow, and then turned burnt umber with each step she took. Her cloak became periwinkle blue, then turned light green, and yellow-brown. She walked towards Andalorax, and laughed as she did so. Her eyes flashed sapphire blue and then she stopped her giggling and settled into a lovely, wide smile and said sweetly and softly, "What do you think of our meeting once again, my pretty friend with the silken white tresses?"

Andalorax was so stunned at the unexpected appearance of this marvelous creature that she found herself speechless, her mouth agape. After a few seconds, she regained her composure and said: "You came back!"

"Aye, Andalorax," she said, as her purple eyes turned a pretty pink. "I've come back. Actually, I've come home, in a sense."

"Home? This is your home?"

"Wherever you are, that's my home," answered the colorful girl, taking a seat in the kitchen. "Don't you understand yet?" Then she started to whisper to herself: "This white-haired young lady has her head in the clouds! Why doesn't she understand who I am? Oh, well, I'll just keep trying!"

"What was that you said, beautiful colorful girl?" asked Andalorax.

"I'm not a beautiful colorful girl!" she retorted. "I do have a name, a real name. Why don't you understand yet what is my name?"

Andalorax walked over to the chair in her small kitchen and sat down. There they were, face to face, and Andalorax said, "Why don't you continue asking me riddles? Maybe then I can guess your name!"

The Many-Colored Girl shook her head nay. "We've already tried that. Hmmm … Oh! I know! I'll give you words that are hints! For example, what do you think of when I say, 'mirror'?"

Andalorax sat there for about one minute. Then she lifted her head and called out, "My image! I see myself when I look in the mirror."

The Many-Colored Girl clapped her hands in delight and said, "That's it, Andalorax. Do you get it now?"

"No. I don't."

"When you look in the mirror you see yourself, of course," said the Many-Colored Girl. "But who else do you see when you look?" Then she sighed greatly, and called out, "Come now, Andalorax. Let me show you for once and for all!"

With that, she lifted her arms and seemed to grow about seven feet tall, her dressing gown blowing wildly in the sudden booming gusts of wind, when she sang out this song:

> *Andalorax! Andalorax!*
> *It seems you cannot see the facts.*
> *Upon my word, I cannot see*
> *Why you cannot fathom me.*
>
> *I am not here without your will*
> *That brings me closer to you still.*
> *Yes, my dear, it cannot be*
> *That you just cannot figure me!*

With that song, the Many-Colored Girl smiled across the kitchen table at the confused face of Andalorax.

"I don't know who you are!" Andalorax cried out. "Can't you just tell me your name?"

The Many-Colored Girl leaned back in her chair. "Let me try another method," she said, then sang out these words:

> *Within your soul, there lives a girl*
> *Who is not black and white at all.*
> *Instead of being that, you see,*
> *She wears the cloak of tints – like me!*
> *For deep inside your heart, I find,*
> *There lives a rainbow of your mind.*

The Many-Colored Girl stopped her chanting and once again asked Andalorax, "Do you see now who I am and what my name is?"

Andalorax wrinkled her brow deeply, and opened her eyes wide, staring into the cerulean blue of the eyes of the Many-Colored Girl. Something seemed to click inside of her, and she took in a deep breath.

"You are somehow a part of me?" she asked. "I wear a cloak of many colors, such as you? How can that be?"

The Many-Colored Girl jumped up from her chair and clapped her hands in joy. And suddenly, something magical happened: Her cloak turned opalescent white and her eyes turned black, and her hair turned snow white.

In this mighty moment, both were transfixed by the explosive reality of the Many-Colored Girl's new appearance.

She looked just like Andalorax! All black and white and no other color. Then, she pulled out of her cloak a tiny mirror and held it up for Andalorax to look into it.

Lo and behold, Andalorax now took on the exact appearance of the Many-Colored Girl. She was now a Many-Colored Girl! Her own cloak shone a dazzling violet, and her long, waist-length hair fell down upon her shoulders, but it was now bright red, and bore within it many crystalline fragments of orange.

"You are me," Andalorax cried out, "and I am you! We mirror each other!"

The Many-Colored Girl laughed heartily, and grasped Andalorax's hands in hers.

"Yes!" she answered. "Now you know who I am and what is my name!"

Andalorax shook her head. "I don't understand," she said. "What is your name?"

"I'll sing another song for you, then," said the Many-Colored Girl, and she uttered these awesome words:

> *What you see when you see me,*
> *Is a girl of magic arts, you see.*
> *You are not just a simple girl*
> *With blackened eyes and whitened curl.*
> *Your secret nature lives within*
> *And makes us sisters, makes us kin!*

She took a step back from Andalorax and stared deeply into her now many-colored eyes with her now-black ones. "I am the natural part of you that has never come to the light of day. You are a receptacle for all the colors of the rainbow, Andalorax, and that is who you see when you see me."

"You mean to say, you are a part of me?"

"Yes," she replied, tossing her now-white mane. "I live in your imagination. If you did not have the capacity to experience all my many colors, all my thoughts and dreams, I would not exist."

The cloak Andalorax wore turned sunshine yellow, and she replied, "You mean, you are not real and only live in my mind?"

The Many-Colored girl laughed and answered, "Well, I am real, as long as you can see me."

"Can anyone else see you?"

"No. But those who truly know you, and love you, know that you are a woman of many colors, and not simply black and white. You are complex and smart and wise and kind."

Andalorax walked over to the kitchen sink and poured herself a glass of water. "I have another person living inside me?"

"No. You and I are one, dear lady."

"Why do you call me a woman, and a lady?"

"Because you are those things."

"I'm not a girl anymore?"

"No, you're not."

"What, then, is your name?"

"Xaroladna"

"What kind of a name is that?"

The Many-Colored Girl laughed again, and walked over to Andalorax, and took her by the arm. It was the first time they ever touched, and Andalorax felt the warmth of her hand.

"You are silly!" she cried out. "Don't you understand fully yet?

"No."

"Why, Xaroladna is Andalorax spelled backwards! You are looking in the mirror and in your reflection you see yourself as you are inside, and looking in a mirror always turns things around."

"Xaroladna," whispered Andalorax. "Xaroladna ... hmmm. I shall have to get used to that, I suppose. If we are one, I mean, truly one." She scratched her head, upon which her hair shone pink. "This is a new idea for me," she continued. "I have to get accustomed to it."

"Yes, you can do that. All you have to do is believe in yourself and you shall find me there within you. You have many sensibilities, many feelings, and the capacity to understand that we are one. All you have to do is …."

"Believe in myself?" interrupted Andalorax.

"Yes."

"And you are always with and within me?"

"Yes."

"Then let us get on with my mission," said Andalorax, who now continued to change colors, while Xaroladna stayed black and white.

"And these colors shall always be mine? From now until forever? And you shall always be as you look now?"

"Yes. And you shall have inside you all of my gifts and my magic." "Your magic?"

The Many-Colored Girl, who still was now simply black and white, answered, "Yes, my gifts and my magic which are rightly your inheritance, Andalorax."

"My inheritance?"

"I speak of your birthright, your growing up time, the Kingdom of Pellah, King Vanamir, and Siddles."

"You know of them?" Andalorax was astonished.

"I know all that you know! Every single moment since your birth in the Calicab Forest! That is now sixteen years ago, Andalorax. As for my magic, which is now your magic as well, you shall learn of it and your powers."

"My powers?"

"Yes. Your powers. Do not be afraid! I am with you. I don't live apart from you. Never forget: 'You are me, and I am you, but only one can change her hue.' Remember that, when you see me disappear, fine lady."

And with that, a sweeping gust of wind blew into the kitchen and enveloped the now black-and-white girl like a tiny tornado, and in an instant, she was gone.

And left standing there was Andalorax, now in all her colorful raiment. She shook her head of rainbow hair, peered into the space where her friend had been, and popped open her amber eyes.

"You are inside me now, correct?" asked Andalorax.

And she heard, without a sound, one single word.

"Yes."

BOOK FIVE

CHAPTER 36

PROPHESIES COME TO LIGHT

"MY ROBE! GET ME MY ROBE!" King Vanamir, awakened from a disturbing dream, called out in his deep baritone voice.

"Dreams! Dreams! Yet again, I am plagued …" he mumbled as his head rose from his pile of down pillows, all embroidered with a large "V." Again he heard the knocking sound that had torn him from his sleep. He sat up and shook his head, slowly opening his eyes.

"Enter!" he cried out.

The door to his bedchamber opened and his personal attendant entered swiftly, bearing in his outstretched hands a soft, silken pillow upon which was a pair of embroidered green velvet slippers. Perigore closed the thick wooden door behind him, locking it by pressing the eagle carved upon the large knob, and passed through the narrow foyer into the main room of the King's vaulted stone and wood chambers.

Three separate rooms jutted off this central, largest one: A dressing room with two sets of drawers, an armoire, and sufficient space for bathing in a large golden tub; his Library filled from floor to ceiling with ancient tomes and atlases plus the King's personal scribblings; and a workplace for conferences with his Knights and other men of business, replete with a long table and surrounded by a dozen high-backed chairs with padded green jacquard seat cushions.

Perigore made his way into the dressing room, past a standing wooden frame into which was deposited a deep ceramic bowl, which held a pitcher filled with clean water for the King's personal face- and hand-washing. Hand-woven towels were hung from pegs inserted into the frame.

Meanwhile, Vanamir looked out the closed window at the snow that lay upon the sill and at the icy crystalline patterns on the glass.

"Winter!" he mumbled. "I detest the cold." With that, he shivered and clasped his arms together for warmth.

Perigore set the pillow down upon the pitcher stand, removed the slippers, and walked softly over to the wide armoire, which reached almost to the high, domed ceiling. It was heavily carved and painted with the design of two men in the hunt. The figures wore breastplates and helmets, and were on horseback, holding raised bows and arrows with which to kill boars, which were depicted in defensive action, some of them already wounded or dead.

Opening wide the cabinet, Perigore procured a bright green velvet robe encrusted with embroidery sewn of purest gold threads. The dark green tassels on its hem scraped the ground as Perigore brought it over to the King, but Vanamir seemed not to notice. He was still under his bed covers, busily rubbing his forehead, as his long hair – not in braids at this frosty time of year – draped down his bulky back.

"Here is your bed robe, sire," said the tall man, as he crossed the red-and-yellow patterned rug that lay atop the cold stone floor. He lay the robe across the large wood-framed bed, reached out his arms, and helped to lift the King, who swung his naked feet to the tapestry on the floor. Then Perigore draped the robe across the King's broad but bent shoulders.

"And here are your slippers, my King," he said, kneeling down to put them on his ruler's smooth, clean feet.

"Shall I prepare your toilette, sire?"

"Aye, Perigore," replied the King. He didn't wish to escape from his soft, warm bed. But he knew he must because of his kingly duties. He was weary even after a long night's sleep. He sighed deeply.

"Those dreams," he interjected. "Those dreadful dreams that I must endure ...." He continued to rub his forehead, then lifted his face to see Perigore move over to the marble-topped counter in the dressing room. There, the King's personal necessities were spread out: several hairbrushes, a round hand-held mirror in a golden frame, some wooden combs, a pile of green silk handkerchiefs, a chunky marble mortar and pestle, and many jars and bottles filled with colored liquids and oils and powders. Most of these objects bore carved handles and bottle-tops, cut from precious woods, bearing the images of heads of horses, wild animals, and birds. Also atop the counter was positioned a very large ancient oval mirror, stained with black splotches at the edges along its wooden frame.

"Shall I attend to your Majesty's bath?" asked Perigore.

"Nay, I must pause and unravel my dreams," answered Vanamir, waving his hand in the air. "Be gone!"

Once Perigore was out the door, Vanamir rose and sat in his padded velvet chair opposite the mirror, and stared at himself in the glass. What he saw displeased him: he was haggard, lacking color, and his bedclothes were in disarray and wrinkled. He picked up one of his brushes and began to run it through his waist-length auburn hair.

The brush was hand-carved of Calicab wood especially for the Kings of Pellah; well he knew this particular one was used by Pellah's first Kings. The handle had ebony inlays that ran in stripes from its tip to the end of its bristles. The tip itself flanged out five or six inches and was shaped like a horse's head, with two eyes made of emeralds, and was fashioned in an ebony checkerboard pattern. It was a marvel of a brush!

As Vanamir stroked his thick tresses, staring at his mirror image, the handle of the brush became longer, and longer still, but the King seemed not to notice. Soon, when it was as long as his forearm, it ceased to grow.

The carved horse-head suddenly came to life, and whinnied. Vanamir was startled, looked at the brush, and realized what had happened.

"It's sorcery!" he cried out, thrusting his body backwards in his chair and dropping the brush on the countertop. "A bedeviled brush, here in my own chambers, after so many years of use," he said to himself. The two green emerald eyes shone brightly and moved in their inlaid sockets, to look directly into the eyes of the king.

The horse-head handle whinnied once more, this time quite loudly. Vanamir leapt from his seat, backing away.

"What's this awful magic?" he called out. "Whose voice is that?"

In a flash, a whirlwind of mist began to gather on the tabletop, increasing in size and strength, and within seconds, the tornado of mist reached clear up to the ceiling. 'Round and 'round the mist blew, in a rainbow of colors, propelling everything off the table and onto the floor. Vanamir's robe and hair, too, blew wildly in the thickening mist.

In an instant, the whirlwind leapt off the table and onto the red-and-yellow rug upon which the king was now standing. The colors swirling in the wind were blinding him, causing him to become dizzy. He fumbled and took some steps backwards and landed upon his bed, falling onto his silk, tasseled pillows. The enormity of his quarters left plenty of room for this huge horse and its rider.

"Who – who or what – what are you?" he stuttered.

A loud raging voice spoke back to him from within the misty tornado. Vanamir peered at it and it seemed to him he could see the horse head twirling inside.

"I am your Destiny, King Vanamir!" it roared.

As it spoke, hundreds of tiny sparks flew from inside it and soared into the air, creating minuscule fires throughout all the rooms. Some landed upon the bedsheets and the bedspread; others landed upon the rug; others soared into the Library; and still others flew into Vanamir's red hair.

All these flames quickly sputtered out and left tiny black holes throughout the bedchamber. Smoke hissed and rose from those black holes. Vanamir swatted the fires out of his hair and beard and watched in horror as the whirlwind continued its mad vortex.

"What do you want of me?" he called out, as he saw strands of his singed hair fall out and land upon his velvet robe.

"What do I want?" said the thundering voice, and then it burst into a terrible laughter that rattled all the furniture in the chambers. "Ha ha! I want to show you what lies ahead, Vanamir," it said. Then the whirlwind grew thick and its rainbow colors turned black as coal, as from within it erupted forth a vision that made the King's eyes burst open in terror.

Out of the black tornado exploded a large white horse – one that Vanamir could see through as if it were a ghost. The horse wore armor made of gold, including a protective shaffron upon its forehead and a crupper on its flank. Upon its back, in a leather saddle with strong leather reins studded with gold medallions at the bit, sat a young woman with white hair and black eyes, wearing a black cape. He could see through her as well.

She was carrying a sword made of purest gold and embedded with precious stones of many colors. This, she lunged out towards the king, landing its shining point upon his breast. He reached out his trembling hand, and it went right through the horse's head.

"They are not skeletons, but seem to be made of flesh and bone," he thought. "Yet I can feel the point of the rapier …."

"Vanamir!" called out the woman, in a strong, commanding voice. "Raise up your head and listen to what I say! You must look up into the sky and see what comes for you upon the wind … for it is flying in the clouds right now, heading your way most directly."

"What is it, oh mighty specter?" he mumbled in fear.

"Dare not question me!" she called out loudly, in a deep voice.

"Oh, no," he called out. "I do not question you. I am so frightened, that is all."

"Of course you are. You think you are in a dream. A bad dream. But this is no dream, King Vanamir of the Lands of Pellah!"

"I understand you to be my … Destiny?"

"Aye," she said, putting down her sword and replacing it in its scabbard. "That I am and nothing more. And you must listen to my words most carefully and obey me in every way."

"Oh, I shall, I shall!"

"First, when the time is right, you leave your chambers and ascend to the highest Tower of this Castle." She remained atop her white steed, who was chomping at the golden bit, its saliva spitting out of its mouth, and flailing its raised front hooves in the air right before Vanamir's face.

"Aye, my lady!"

"And you must do this alone!"

"Alone?" He was devastated. "I … I never go anywhere alone."

"You must!"

"Then I shall obey." He lowered his head.

"Look up, Vanamir! For here is my second command: You must be wearing your finest raiment. Your gold-embroidered velvet outfit. Your golden cloak. And above all, your heavy, jewel-encrusted crown. All these possessions must be with you. But you must be without your sword or any other weapon! Do you understand?"

"Aye, my lady. I understand. My finest clothing. My crown. No weapon."

"Third, once upon the highest turret, you must unclasp your gilded mantle and doublet and silk shirt and bear your naked chest to the sky."

The King, who was flung back by the violent whirlwind and lay spread out upon his comfortable bed with its silk sheets and fine velvet bedspread, thought, "Stop, Vanamir! Think! You cannot allow this apparition to sway you from your proper role as ruler of the Kingdom of Pellah and all its neighboring lands." So he summoned all his fortitude and sat up, facing the ghost horse and the woman seated upon it.

"No!" he cried out. "I shall never obey these orders! Who are you – or what are you – to order me about? I am King Vanamir!"

The horse came closer, reared its front legs, and flailed its hooves in the air, coming right up to Vanamir's face. This ghostly vision was still encased by the enormous black tornado. The woman seated upon the horse raised her sword yet again.

"What are you to me? Nothing!" she laughed terribly. "I have no fears of anything, least of all a puny king! You have no power over me; I have all the power! Remember, I am your Destiny! Stand up, Vanamir! Rise from your comfortable bed and stand before me!"

He did so, utterly confounded by this apparition. His burst of power fluttered away and he stood there, helpless before these ghostly images that were larger than life.

"Fear me and obey!" called the lady. "You shall be on the Tower, bare-chested as ordered. Your Destiny shall come to you on the wind, Vanamir."

"What will happen to me?"

"This, I cannot tell you. You will learn your fate when it strikes you."

"Am I going to my death?"

"This, too, I cannot tell you!"

"Perhaps, once upon the high turret," he stuttered, "I shall be cleansed of my sins ...."

The lady smiled wisely, showing a row of whitest teeth, and interrupted him, saying, "What are your sins, Vanamir? Pray, tell me! Do you know what they are?"

"Spectacle of Darkness, I swear to you that I have no sins, and there is nothing of which I need to be purged! But if I do as you say, I shall meet my death, surely, and so I tell you once again that I shall not obey!"

She laughed fiendishly. "You shall obey, Vanamir! When the time is right, you shall obey!"

"How will I know when the time is right?"

"You shall know the time beyond a doubt, weak and infinitesimally tiny king!"

Vanamir, still shaking, put his face into his cupped hands.

"What more do you want of me, oh Destiny?"

"That is all you need to know for the present," said the lady rider.

And just as quickly as the apparition arrived, so, too, did it immediately dissolve and disappear. It was as if nothing had ever happened. But Vanamir knew that was not the truth, for left in its wake were his personal objects that had fallen on the floor, the tiny black holes that were made by the sparks, and he himself, standing in disbelief and terror of what he had just witnessed.

"My Destiny!" he whispered. "So, it has come to me at last, as foretold by the prophesies."

It seemed to him as if an entire day had passed, when he finally summoned his strength as best he could, spoke more loudly still, and declared, "I shall never surrender to this apparition, this magic, this evil! I shall never climb to the highest battlement in the Castle Pellah! And least of all," he began to laugh, "never shall I bear my naked breast to the heavens. Ha! My Destiny indeed!"

He walked swiftly to his full suit of gold armor that hung on a mannequin in the corner of his dressing room, and moved the gauntlet away from its position, holding the sword. He retrieved the heavy sword from its sheath.

"This I swear," he cried out, raising the rapier, "by all that is sacred in my Kingdom! Never shall I obey!"

CHAPTER 37

RETURNING TO THE CASTLE

CHESTER AND GOSHEN WERE WEARY of their travels. The two young scouts sent by Vanamir and Malthor were still searching for the old man – they had long ago forgotten his odd name – and his granddaughter – whose name they never really could pronounce from when they first heard it spoken by their King, Vanamir.

In the early summertime, when they had set out on their mission, they traveled the long road that spiraled its way along the Golden River. They had gone all the way from the Castle in the north to the southernmost point in the Kingdom of Pellah. There, they ceased their travels at the town of Milorin, at the edge of the Calicab Forest. They had searched in every village and outpost along the way, taking the side roads that branched off the Golden Road to each destination.

They had looked into every house and barn, peered under every wagon and barrow, and climbed every sturdy tree to look out upon the landscape, yet they found no sign of their quarry. They were quite diligent in their search, having been given the duty by the King himself. From the send-off they had received, also being given this task by the King and being escorted across the bridge and over the moat by Malthor and the Twenty Men of the Eyes, they knew it was a significant assignment.

But now the summer and autumn were over and it was coming upon winter, and they were cold and wet from the abundant snow. When the autumn leaves had begun to fall, the duo had lingered in Milorin for several weeks, and had even ventured into the Calicab Forest. Then came the snow.

"Whatever shall we do now?" asked Goshen of his tall companion. "Wherever shall we go?"

Chester, leaning against a Calicab tree with the low sun casting long shadows across the forest, had to think carefully before he replied. He wasn't sure himself, but because he felt himself to be the leader, he knew he had to determine what to do next.

"We shall return home," he responded at last, pushing himself away from the splendid tree and standing up straight so that Goshen could see his height and therefore sense his superiority. "We have done all that we were sent to do, and we have done an excellent job of it, my little man," he continued as he walked toward his companion. Putting his arm across Goshen's shoulders, he announced: "First, however, we must sleep here in the forest once again, in the outdoors in the blackest and coldest of nights." Goshen automatically agreed with this decision with a big nod of his small head, and looked up to Chester and said: "Aye, captain. Time to go home." He didn't say a word about fear of sleeping outdoors.

Walking over to their ramshackle tent made of their two extra cloaks and tied to several Calicabs that were close to one another, they crawled underneath it and crouched at the perimeter of the abode. They started a small fire by aggressively rubbing a pointed stick into a hole in the rock which they saved for this daily cold-weather ritual. They had been doing this for several weeks, for winter was truly upon them now, and they were getting bored with the effort. Soon, however, sparks were flying and then tiny flames began to rise, when smoke blew in their faces with one big gust of wind.

The two young men began to cough from the smoke. Quickly, Chester fanned the flames using his checkered cap and the fire sprouted up and was soon bright orange and red with a blue center.

"When shall we leave here, Chester?"

"On the morrow, my boy. Bright and early, too! I'm fed up with this forest; there isn't anyone foolish enough to be camped out in this here woods in this here thigh-high snow."

Goshen laughed out loud.

"Yes, there is someone! It's us!

Chester turned beet red from being bested by this shorter man, upon whom he looked as a mere boy, really.

They both began to pound upon the roof of their tent so that the still-falling snow would drop off of it and not cause undue weight to have it come crashing down upon their heads. Doing so also had the effect of fanning the flames even more, and ushering out any further accumulation of smoke.

Getting out from under the tent, they put grasses into the feedbags of their two horses, and filled two collapsible containers made from waxed cloth with snow that would melt and give the horses water. Then, noticing that the sun had just set and darkness would soon be upon them, they prayed for protection from night-wights and curled up in their cloaks and fell asleep.

"What was that sound?" Chester asked Goshen in a barely audible whisper.

"Huh? What sound?" answered Goshen, clearly half-awake.

"Ssshh! Don't talk so loudly! There's something outside of our tent." Chester slowly and silently removed his cloak and stood up. His head hit the ceiling of their tent and knocked some snow off outside, which fell to the ground with a thud.

"Goshen, be quiet!" said Chester.

"Me? I didn't say a word! It was you …."

Goshen's voice was cut off by the sound of footsteps outside.

"How can whatever it is make any noise when it's walking on snow?" asked Goshen. "I don't understand how …."

"Quiet!" hushed Chester. "It is very noisy. Must be some dumb animal investigating our backpacks."

"Yes, that must be it. Let's go back to sleep!" Goshen rolled over on his side and covered his head with his cape.

"No, no, no! We must investigate!" said Chester.

With that, Chester slowly peeled back the makeshift doorway to their tent, and stuck his head outside.

"Now the noises have stopped," he said. Then they heard them again. Footsteps of a two-footed animal – or of a human.

"Who goes there?" cried Chester. "Make yourself known or I shall be forced to attack you, whoever you are!"

Silence. The footsteps ceased.

"Who goes there, I said!"

"'Tis I," came back a voice. "I mean no harm. Do not attack me, please."

Emboldened by the humility in the person's voice, Chester stepped outside of the tent and felt the heavy snowflakes falling down from the night sky.

"Make yourself known. Show me your face," he said.

"Alright," said the voice, "I will come to you." Out of the snowy fog there suddenly appeared a man, rather tall and gaunt, and wearing a cape, trousers, and laced-up leather boots.

"He could be a simple man from Pellah," thought Chester. "He looks just like we all do."

The stranger suddenly held up a lantern, which he proceeded to light with a match. Chester and Goshen were amazed at how the match made fire, without the rubbing together of sticks.

"What … what is that?" asked Chester. "That stick which made fire?"

The stranger smiled, and his face was now clearly visible in the lantern light. The two scouts looked the man up and down, and asked, "Where are you from? How comes it that you are out here in the nighttime when to do so is dangerous?"

The man laughed and said, "So you are from the Kingdom then. Well, I understand why you are surprised to see me here, but I have no fear of the nighttime. No, not I! Indeed, it's a belief that I never shared."

"Aren't you from the Kingdom?" asked Chester.

"Nay," answered the stranger. "I come from across the sea. But I have lived in this Calicab Forest for years now, and this is my home, here in these beautiful woods." He smiled.

"What is your name?" asked Chester.

"Frederick Janifur, at your service."

"Well, well, Mr. Janifur," said Chester, holding out his right hand, "pleased to meet you." He and Goshen both shook Frederick Janifur's hand. It was a strong hand that was accustomed to manual labor, they both noticed.

"What are you doing here in the woods at night?"

"I live here in the Calicab Forest. I was curious about you two and thought I could get a closer look at your belongings, and your horses, and your raiment. I figured you wouldn't be so accommodating during the daylight and perhaps overcome or even kill me.

"You see, I come from far away, and have little to no communication with other people. Haven't had any for years."

"Years?" asked Chester. "Wait. You say you live here in this forest? We have been through this woods for months now and have been searching for an old man and his granddaughter. We are on a mission for our King Vanamir. Why haven't we met before?"

Frederick Janifur smiled and said, "I stay far away from any kind of contact with people. I am what I suppose you would call a 'recluse.' But wait! You say you are searching for an old man and his granddaughter ... I know whom you mean! The pair lived here for a time, staying away from the rest of the Kingdom. Then they disappeared. I wonder what happened to them ...."

And he thought, "Gamedon and Andalorax! So they're after them ...."

"But why have you lived so many years here in this forest?"

"I have a great attachment to this forest. You see, I once lived in Milorin, the adjacent town – the southernmost town of the Kingdom, I believe."

Frederick Janifur smiled once more, and thought back in time ... to the days he lived in Milorin, and met a young woman, and they fell in love ... and then he heard she had a baby ... and she and her father and the babe were taken by the King to live in his Castle ....

"Aye, 'tis true. The southernmost town."

"It became too crowded for me and I moved into these woods. Besides, I didn't fancy the people of Milorin that much and sought out my own privacy. That's how I came to the forest. I have learned to live without a great many luxuries here."

Yet he thought, "After all these years watching and waiting for them to return to these woods ... hiding out away from them ... glad that when they returned just last year, I kept up my secret vigil."

Goshen laughed. "A luxury such as a roof to have over your head."

"I have always had a roof over my head. I have a small cabin I built almost twenty years ago." And he thought, "Those years I watched over her and her father here in the Calicab Forest, until they were taken away. And I waited for them to return ...."

Chester and Goshen looked at each other in amazement. "How could you have a cabin here," asked Chester, "when we have never come across it in all these months of traveling throughout these woods? And we have been searching with our eyes wide open, mind you!"

Frederick Janifur smiled once more and said, "I built it with my own magic, gentlemen. You see, I have learned a great many tricks and feats of magic as my life goes on. I worked mostly at night and slept during the daytime."

"Aren't you afraid of the dangerous evils of the nighttime?" asked Goshen in a trembling voice.

Frederick Janifur laughed and said, "Ah, that old fairy tale. It is not true, I say. It was made up and everyone goes on believing it." He laughed again. "I don't know why it was devised, this silly plot to frighten people of the night."

"It's true!" interrupted Goshen. "The night is bad and the day is good. That's all there is to it!"

"You can go on believing that," answered the stranger. "I, however, am living proof that it is not true. Else why would I be alive or not stark staring mad from living in this forest for nineteen years. No, wait, it may be twenty years. I lose count of time."

And again he looked back at the years that had passed since he guarded Gamedon and his daughter, Mandir, sixteen long years ago, and then their little daughter, Andalorax ... and once again when Gamedon and the little girl returned but without his beloved Mandir. Where was she, his beloved Mandir? All those years gone past ....

"You have been here in this forest for that amount of time? I'm without words! And you said you came from far, far away, across the sea. Do you mean the Sea of Iolanthe?" asked Chester.

"Aye, that I do."

"What land lies beyond that sea?"

"Budgerigar Island," answered Frederick Janifur. "I was born and raised there. My father was a magician of sorts, an inventor of many interesting unique objects that sprang out of his brilliant mind and came to fruition with his very special hands."

"How did you cross the sea? It is so rough! Did you come in a large boat with many others?"

"No," said Frederick Janifur. "I came in a small craft which I outfitted simply for me. Of course, I built it myself, a single-masted ship with a broad spreading sail. Made of Portopuff wood."

"Portopuff? What's that?"

"A wood unique to Budgerigar Island," he answered. "Very lightweight but hard and seaworthy."

"How did you manage to cross the sea yourself?"

"I called out to the deepest part of my magic and sorcery, and conjured up an enormous wind on a cloudless day …."

Chester and Goshen jumped back in alarm. "Sorcery? Are you a demon of the night?"

Frederick Janifur laughed.

"You might say I am! Yes, indeed, you might say that. For compared to everyone else, it is true."

He rubbed his hands together in a gleeful manner. While doing so, his felt hat fell off. Chester reached down to pick it up and hand it over to the stranger. But the stranger didn't seem to notice.

Chester and Goshen looked at each other, looked back at Frederick Janifur, and turned and ran back to their little tent, now covered in a thick layer of snow.

"That was close," huffed Chester, now out of breath from running.

"We actually met up with a night-wight!"

"It's a wonder the roof hasn't caved in," muttered Chester. "That's true."

"I never imagined we'd run across such a person here in these woods."

"Was he real?" asked Goshen. "Or was he just a bad dream in the night?"

Chester held onto the stranger's felt hat.

"You and I didn't have the same dream, you fool! He was real, alright," he said, holding out the felt cap. "See this? He was definitely real." They both huddled under their capes but stayed awake the entire rest of the night.

In the morning, they got up to saddle their horses, first poking their faces outdoors through the tent flap.

"Hey, look," said Chester, pointing to the snow all around them. "There are the footsteps of only two people here. We met the stranger right here at the entrance to our tent. Goshen, where are those of Frederick Janifur?"

They searched everywhere but came up with only two sets of footsteps.

"You must be right," Chester told Goshen as they mounted their steeds. "He must have been a demon of the night."

Meanwhile, a tall, slender man hunched high up in a Calicab tree watched them pass directly under him. He blended in with the leaves and branches, even though he wasn't dressed in green.

It was Frederick Janifur.

CHAPTER 38

VANAMIR MEETS HIS DESTINY

IT TOOK VANAMIR QUITE A while to get over the phantom horse and rider's appearance in his quarters, and also their sudden disappearance into thin air. When he had caught his breath at last, he went into his office and sat at the head of the long desk in his royal padded velvet chair with padded arms that curved at the ends with carved-out lions. Vanamir rested his palms upon the heads of those lions, which were chunky and massive. The bodies of the lions made up the arms of the chair, and Vanamir rested his forearms upon those. He put his head back upon the central carving of the powerful chair, into which was fashioned a lion's head, staring straight out ahead.

Vanamir knew this chair would assuage his current torment, as it was made for Pellah's first King many, many centuries ago and carried with it an enormous amount of magic. It was constructed at the same time by the same craftsmen as his bed, which had robust prophetic powers having been blessed by sorcerers and magicians.

Both were elaborately carved and had precious gems embedded in the eyes of the animals which were depicted throughout their frameworks. All along the sides of the wooden bed was a panoply of running horses being chased by wolves, their teeth showing and their long talons reaching out to snatch the flesh of the terrified horses. At the bed's backboard was a forest scene, with a glen, and stamped with trees and flowers – the only peaceful design in the room.

But Vanamir knew what he had to do now, here in his private chambers. He rose, went over to a far corner in the office, and pressed upon a certain stone interred within the wall with his thick open palm.

Lo and behold! A piece of the stone floor slid slowly open, a large slab of rock that was previously unrecognized as being separate from all the rest of the slate flooring. It exposed a very large, dark hole in the earth beneath it, from which emanated a fetid stink of mold and mildew. A mist of heavy vapors rose up from within the ground. King Vanamir crouched down and stuck his head into the hole and inhaled deeply.

"Aahh!" he sighed, as he exhaled the fumes. He repeated his inhalation several times, each intake of breath seeming to please him more than the last, for now Vanamir was smiling. He exposed his white teeth that were twinkling with the pieces of gold which were embedded within several teeth. Quickly, he lifted his head and darted around, to make certain no one was in the chamber with him.

"Of course, I am alone!" he said aloud, and laughed raucously in his deep baritone voice. He thought, "I have been doing this for all of my lifetime; why should I be afraid of anyone's presence?" Again, he laughed, more loudly this time, and thought, "No one would dare to enter the King's private rooms."

Then he had a sudden vision of his past: he saw the old man, the one who called himself Gamedon, in his mind. The little underling in his worn-out cloak seemed to be there, at his side. Vanamir could see his green eyes twinkling, surrounded by many wrinkles. Yet, Vanamir knew this could not be real – it had to be his memory coming to haunt him, for if anyone could be there in his chambers, it would be that one man. The King didn't remember whether or not Gamedon knew the secret to entering his private rooms.

"My once-trusted confidante!" muttered the King. Again, he laughed, this time at the thought of having put his faith in that doddering old fool. Then he remembered Gamedon's granddaughter, Andalorax. A cold chill went through his entire body as he envisioned her presence as well. She, tall and slender, with her white waist-length curls and intense coal-black eyes, the only one in his Kingdom to appear so hideously.

"Witch!" he said aloud. "A dream … I seem to recall a dream … wherein she played a part of my destiny … "as he turned his head around and saw the portentous bed carved by the wise men of the ages. He recalled a muscular phantom stallion, breathing steam in the night air, clambering up the sides of a slippery slope and fighting with foamy waves from the sea below it, attempting to reach him ….

"Too much!" he cried out, covering his eyes with his hands. "Too much for me to bear!"

But the vapors which continued to rise from beneath the secret stone in the floor continued to envelop him. They wafted around him and crawled into the air in the office. He inhaled deeply yet again.

"My magic staircase!" he spoke. "I must pay attention to my needs!"

Then, sitting on the ground and placing his feet in the hole, he began to descend, step by step on the magic staircase that wound its way into the cold stones that served as support. It was an ancient stairway, created during the years of construction of the mighty Castle. All of this was overseen by the first King of Pellah more than a millenium before, and was sanctified by the ancient wizardry of wise men who had crossed the southern waters long ago with the first of whom would become the Pellah citizenry.

Vanamir reached the bottom of the staircase, his feet now firmly planted on a slate floor. The scent and mist wound around him like a cloak. His inhalations increased. He turned towards the sole contents of this small chamber: a row of fat barrels crafted of Calicab wood, bound with iron hoops. In the corner stood several empty barrels, and the rest – but for one – were sealed tightly with black tar.

This one cask stood unsealed, and it was to this that the King turned his attention. Its lid was lying somewhat askew atop the barrel. It was from this vat that the thick, dense vapors emanated and filled the storage room – empty save for the barrels.

Vanamir had to crouch somewhat to keep his head from banging on the ceiling. "Those old Kings were short indeed," he thought, remarking in his mind how tall and statuesque he was himself. He took but five steps and found himself standing directly at the unsealed cask. Removing its lid, he placed it gently on the ground, and reached his right hand down into the barrel.

His arm went all the way in, down to his elbow.

"Aha!" he called out. "My pretty flowers!" He smiled. "Show yourselves to me, your King of Kings!"

Pulling out his hand, which was now tightly clutching a gathering of dried leaves and slender stems with brown buds, he watched as the desiccated herbs began to make their magic.

At first, what seemed to be musty and dried out, the plants began to flesh out and become supple. Vapors continued to rise from them, seemingly from nowhere as the air in the cavern was dry and infertile. These vapors wound themselves around King Vanamir, and he inhaled deeply, again and again, until he fell atop the vat into a swoon.

"Phemtas!" he whispered. "Thou art my mind and heart, nay, my very soul! Work thy magic upon me! I am in great need of thy powers to restore my weakening strength! Swirl and twirl about me, and fill me with potency as only thou canst do and have done for all the Kings throughout all of Pellah time! I await thy vigorous and vital charms!"

As Vanamir lay there, half falling into the wide cask, half teetering on the brink of it, he began to feel the sublime gifts of Phemtas, Herb of Kings.

"Thou restoreth my senses and my will, dearest of all herbs, plants and flowers upon this wretched soil! Enter the prison which is called my heart, fill the cauldron which is called my brain, with thy enormous, vast magical forces!"

And the plant, which once traveled with the magicians and wizards of the past who sowed their seeds in more ways than one upon the Kingdom of Pellah and its Kings – this same plant which now covered the once-blooming green lands of the Black Mountains – did indeed wind its spell upon King Vanamir.

Just as now on this very same day, it wound its spell upon the rusty, dusty forgotten King Zivat-Or and held him up upon his vigorous throne. Siddles and Andalorax were ready, too, in the resounding airs that were, at that very moment, bringing the four of them – including Gamedon and Zivat-Or – all in haste to the Castle and to the destiny that would forever alter the landscape of every person in this Kingdom known as Pellah.

CHAPTER 39

LIFE IN THE CASTLE

VANAMIR DRESSED HIMSELF AFTER THE phantom horse and its wraithlike rider had disappeared, and he had imbued his lungs and body with Phemtas in his secret cellar.

Now he had his strength back.

He put on his silk, tightly-woven undershirt with the long sleeves, then over that his loose-fitting silk blouse with the long flouncy cuffs interlaced with ribbons throughout. Then came his leather pants, studded down the side-seams with gold rivets. As he was pulling on his heavy leather boots, he turned towards the set of body armor and wondered if he should put it on today.

"Just because of the see-through girl on the magic horse and her admonishment to go to the top of my highest Tower, perhaps I should wear my armor," he thought. But, so saying, he vigorously shook his head left and right.

No!" he declared. "I shall not let her determine my movements! Besides, they probably were only an invention of my imagination in my weakened state, needing Phemtas. No!" he repeated, now lacing up his boots. "Today shall bring me nothing but the usual business and pleasures."

Yet the Phemtas also brought him intuition and wisdom, which he could feel coursing throughout his blood and controlling his mind – even if it did not control his heart and innermost desires. He knew that he must follow through with what the vision showed him and listen well to what it said – even if he wanted business as usual.

Following his heart was not within his power no matter how much he wished it to be so.

"I shall reach the top of the Pinnacle Tower," he suddenly decided, "and I shall do so to face my fate. We will then discover which is greater—Destiny or the King of Pellah!"

Vanamir stood in the center of his bed chamber. His eyes wandered over to his bed, made over one thousand years ago by sorcerers long dead yet whose powers lived on. He felt strengthened by this knowledge, that all the centuries of Pellah Kings were here living in his breast, in his body, in his mind!

"Yes," he thought, "I shall look my so-called fate in its face and conquer it after all! I am the strongest, not this phantom!" So spoke the Phemtas as well, coursing through his veins, as surely as his own blood.

So he continued dressing, without his valet, for he did not enjoy being disturbed after inhaling his share of the dried plant. Perigore had, indeed, knocked upon his door earlier, but Vanamir called out, "Go away, nuisance!" which his servant had done promptly and most willingly.

"I don't wish to see the King this morning," murmured Perigore, as he turned around and began to walk down the series of steps that wound around the Castle's interior. "There is much aflutter in the kitchen," he continued speaking quietly, "and I mean to learn what it is. Besides," he added, reaching a lower landing and pushing open the doorway to the cook's quarters, "I am in need of food myself."

The outsized kitchen was filled with staff, all bustling about with their specific duties. Every corner of the large space held groups of chefs, sous-chefs and pantry maids. Central to the room was one long wooden table surrounded by workers busily chopping venison, wild boar and pheasants, while others styled the meat and fowl atop attractive platters twisted and twirled into fabulous shapes and embellished with winter cherries, dried herbs soaked in liqueurs, small potatoes and red onions. All the dishes were pierced with abundant tiny wooden sticks that bore the Pellah flag in miniature at their protruding tips.

Scattered throughout the room were ten or twelve servants dressed in dapper, olive green velvet attire, braided down the seams and with lace cuffs; they were carrying trays – all prepared with green folded napkins and golden forks, spoons and knives – ready to bring the serving platters into the dining room where the King's Knights and Ministers sat, eagerly awaiting breakfast.

Perigore made his way over to a large porcelain sink, where a hefty woman stood washing what seemed like a mountain of turnips.

"Elisabetta," he said to her, "it certainly is busy in here this morning!"

"Aye, Perigore," said the woman, turning to him. "Everyone is in a tizzy, too."

"And why should that be, Elisabetta?"

"There is a wind-storm brewing in the far southlands," she answered, "and I fear it is headed in this direction."

"Why should you think any of this to be true?"

"I have heard it from the chief cook, just an hour ago."

"How can you believe it?"

"He knows many people," said Elisabetta. "He also listens to what the wait staff tells him, when they return from serving the King's squadron of soldiers. They are waiting right now for their meal in the dining hall. Ha! I shall jolly well enjoy hearing the gossip they'll come back with!" Then she pinched Perigore's nose (which made him sneeze) and added, "Besides, it was the big news last night when the two scouts sent by the King returned from their travels."

"Do you mean Chester and Goshen?"

"Aye, that I do," said Elisabetta, nodding her head. "But how is it that you know their names? They have been gone a long time, more than two seasons!"

"Remember for whom I am the private valet, Elisabetta!" Perigore pulled himself up straight in his boots and added, "This shall be great news for the King! I must tell him at once that they have returned from their travels. But how is it that they have returned without the knowledge of King Vanamir?"

"They blew in, so to speak," said the woman as she finished washing her turnips and began to toss them in an enormous wooden bowl, "on the night winds and are only just now dressing and heading for the King's quarters to give him news of their travels."

With a quick farewell, Perigore immediately turned on his heels and left the kitchen. "And me still without breakfast," he muttered, as he went back into the stairway that encircled the outer ring of the Castle Pellah.

"Chester, why can't we get a few more hours of sleep?"

"You know as well as I do, Goshen, that if we delay in bringing news of our long voyage to our King, we shall pay dearly in one manner or the other. It is dawn now and he will surely be awake."

So saying, both men pulled on their leather boots, threw their capes across their young muscular shoulders, clasped them at the throat with their special envoy medallions, and went out the chamber door.

They quickly wound their way up the winding staircase, practically running, and suddenly came crashing into Perigore, whose advancing steps down were slower than theirs.

"What's this?" cried out the King's valet, reaching for the dagger hidden in his waist belt. "Who rushes up this private stairwell that approaches the King's private quarters?"

"Hold on now," cried out Chester, the taller of the two, while searching for his own weapon, lost somewhere in the folds of his cloak. "We are the King's envoys just returned from the south."

"Chester and Goshen? Why, 'tis too good to be true that we meet thus, both on the way to the King."

"We come with news for the King," added Goshen.

"Well, I certainly hope you have news, having been gone for so many months," said Perigore, slipping his dagger back in its sheath and groaning. "I am his private valet and servant, Perigore. Let me announce you to him."

Chester, figuring that they must be at the King's doorway, reached out for some kind of doorknob when Perigore held up his right hand.

"Stop!" he whispered. "We must approach his chamber door gently. Be quiet now! This door has magic charms and must be dealt with gracefully. I know how to do this. You two just stand there and wait."

Perigore came up to the door, and put his hand on the carved wooden tablet that was attached just above the gold knocker. He pressed it with his palm, and a voice called out, "Who goes there?"

The sound of the voice was deep and resonant. Yet from where did it come, wondered the two scouts, looking askance at each other.

"I don't know about such things," whispered Goshen to his comrade. "I never heard of a speaking door!"

"Be quiet!" ordered Chester.

"Aye, will do."

As the two scouts huddled nervously in the corridor, Perigore spoke up:

"'Tis I, Perigore!"

At this, the door spoke once more.

"Perigore! At the door!" it announced.

The King's voice came from behind it. "Just you wait, as I am coming to give you entrance." Then they all heard the heavy booted footsteps of the King as he approached the door, and then heard him say, "Open, Door! For Perigore!"

At that vocal command, the heavy wooden door creaked upon its hinges, slowly opening inwards. When it was fully open, it stopped.

"Perigore," asked Vanamir, looking past his valet's silhouette, "who are those two men behind you?"

"My King," he answered, "'tis your own true scouts, freshly returned from their travels throughout the Kingdom."

"My scouts?"

"Aye, my King. Chester and Goshen. You sent them many months ago on a journey to find the old grandfather and his granddaughter, that young girl with the white hair."

The King pulled on his long red beard, and reflected for a moment. "Aha! Yes! Well, let them in, Perigore! They bring me news, surely, or would not dare to venture so close to me!"

Quietly, though, the King thought perhaps he could glean some information from them as to what he had to face this afternoon.

Chester and Goshen, their mouths dry and their hands shaking, timidly approached their King. They couldn't help but notice he was not yet fully clothed, without his vest and jacket, and most certainly without his crown. Evidently, he had just woken. But, they wondered, what was that scent rising from the far corner of his chambers?

Perigore, accustomed to the smell of Phemtas but knowing nothing of what it was, did not even notice the odor of the herb. He did notice, however, that his King was somewhat changed and now in superb condition, considering how confused and weakened he appeared earlier in the morning. This brought him glee, for when his King was pleased, he was treated well. So he ventured to speak:

"My King, these two men have recently arrived, in the middle of the night in fact. I know you shall be wanting to hear of their travels and if they did indeed find their quarry. So I shall leave you!"

"You shall leave when I dismiss you!" ordered Vanamir.

"Aye, my King," said Perigore, humbly curtsying.

"You are dismissed!" laughed Vanamir. "Be gone!" Vanamir swatted his hand at him like a fly.

Then, after Perigore left them, Vanamir looked his two scouts up and down, from their weathered feathered caps right down to their worn-out leather boots.

"Well, now, lads," he said cheerfully. "Come and sit down here in my private office. Tell me what news you have of your mission."

"Sire," said Chester, "we bring news that will bring you both joy and dismay."

"How can it be both?"

"Well," gulped Chester, "the good news is that we found nothing to be worried about. Not one person has seen or heard of them anywhere throughout the lands. We ventured as far as the Calicab Forest, and went into it, even in the nighttime, Sire. There were no reports of their whereabouts."

"And the dismay?"

"There is no news in the entire Kingdom about these two escapees."

"That is the dismay?"

"Aye, for you wanted us to capture them, the old man and the young girl. Yet we did not do so."

"You failed in your mission?"

Chester looked down at this feet. "I guess you could say that, my King." Then his face brightened and he added, "We decided that, well, no news is the best news!"

King Vanamir stood staring at them both, thinking, "These poor fools," and he, standing one full head higher than them, could see the beginnings of baldness upon the taller one's pate.

Then he exploded in an uproar of laughter that sent both Chester and Goshen reeling back against the stone wall of the room. "Why, you were sent to find Gamedon and Andalorax! And throughout the entire Kingdom, MY entire Kingdom, you heard no news, saw no evidence of their presence, and learned nothing from anyone that they even existed?" Again, he laughed. "This, I find delightful! They do not exist, according to you! Why, I have lived with them for fifteen years and I can assure you, they do exist, my fine fellows. It is indeed a shame that you came home with such a failure in your bonnets!"

"Well, Sire," retorted Chester, "We did find one thing."

"And that thing was?"

"We met a man who lives in the Calicab Forest, and he had not encountered anyone either."

"Lives in the forest, you say? Hmmm. Tell me about this man."

"He says he is from an island off the southern coast, across the Sea of Iolanthe."

"Impossible!" roared the King. "No one can cross that rough sea. How did he say he arrived in the Kingdom?"

Chester started shaking, wondering how he could answer this question. He decided just to tell the truth, as he heard it.

"He sailed across."

"What? Must have been a big ship. How many people were with him on this voyage?"

"No one," said Chester, "except himself."

"Impossible!"

"Yes, Sire. He … he told us he crafted his small boat himself using his magic powers!"

King Vanamir laughed and said, "This is preposterous! His own magic? Ha! He must have been a sorcerer."

"That's why we ran away from him quick as the silver fox."

Chester said nothing about the absence of his footsteps in the snow, but he did hand the stranger's felt hat to his King.

"We managed to escape with this," said Chester, "which is proof of his existence."

The King took the cap and, bemused by this tale, began to chuckle.

"Seems he was real, alright," he said, twirling the old cap on his index finger.

"How long ago did this man come to the Calicab Forest?"

"Nineteen or twenty years ago, he told us."

"What? So long a time? What was he doing there all those years?"

"We don't know," Chester said, casting a glance at Goshen. "He said he just loved the forest. He said he used to live in the town of Milorin but moved into the forest."

"Ah! That forsaken little town at our southernmost borders. I have been there many a time to collect my royal dues. Never heard of this stranger. What was his name, if he had one?"

"Frederick. Frederick Janifur."

"Well, this Frederick, whoever he was, has nothing to do with me. I regret that you two failed to produce Gamedon and his granddaughter," said the King as he fingered the felt cap.

"What other news do you have for me, you two fools?"

"There is a powerful wind-storm that's been brewing in the south, and it has followed us up clear along the Golden River all the way to the Castle."

"'Tis true that the season for wind-storms is upon us," responded the King, his eyes glancing out his window upon the fallen snow that lay on the ledge, while twirling his thick beard which hung down upon his chest. "But why should anyone be in an uproar about that?"

"This storm is not a natural storm, if you don't mind me saying so, my Lord," said Chester, while Goshen nodded at his side. "Those clouds are boiling black and round and are full of mischief! They are like big fat balls of fire, black fire, rolling in upon the winds. I tell you, it isn't a natural storm. And it's coming in fast behind us! Who knows when it will be here?"

King Vanamir was in shock when he heard this statement. He froze, motionless. A simple storm, and yet he found himself wandering into the far recesses of his mind, remembering the past.

"Not a 'natural storm' he says … A wind-storm from the southlands is what was foretold years ago, many long years ago, by the Sibyl of Milorin!" King Vanamir was talking to himself in a low whisper.

"That year," he continued mumbling, "when I brought old Gamedon and his black-and-white granddaughter Andalorax back to the Castle with me. And her mother, what was her name? Merry? Marry? Mandy? Mandir! That's it!" He slapped his hand upon his thigh. "Living over in the Wives' Turret in the Castle with my other wives."

While he was meandering in the past, the two scouts stared at him, dumbfounded.

"What's he mumbling about, Chester?" whispered Goshen.

"Fixed if I know."

"Something about an old man … Say! Do you think he means the old man we were sent to find?"

"Could be."

"And his black-and-white granddaughter? Do you suppose …."

"Yes, Goshen. I suppose. Must be. The girl we were sent to find."

Meanwhile, Vanamir, his eyes glazed over, kept on talking to himself. "And my dreams, on my bed built by the first King of Pellah with his sorcerers … my bed whereon enchanted dreams are made, dreams which cannot lie and are meant to reveal the future. My prophetic bed! Let me remember more ...."

He gazed up at the vaulted ceiling and put his forefinger to his lips. "Whatever was that extraordinary dream ... ah, yes! The one with the big white horse scrambling up the cliff, coming for me, trying to smell me out ... Why, it's the same as the see-through white horse that just visited me, bearing that white-haired enchantress right here in my chamber, this selfsame chamber!"

The room fell silent as Vanamir suddenly stopped talking. He turned his head towards his assembly room, and to the far corner where his secret staircase lay hidden, covered over by the big stone.

He knew what he had to do.

"You two must away instantly," he commanded the two scouts. "Away! On the instant! Door! Open!" At these words, the thick wooden door to the King's chambers creaked open.

"Aye, Your Majesty!" yelped Chester, touching his royal scout medallion and bending low.

"We will be gone now, my King!" added Goshen, and they backed out as fast as their legs could carry them. Once past the portal, they ran for the spiral stone staircase and disappeared around a corner.

Vanamir commanded the door to close, then went over to his hidden entrance to the secret chamber which contained the barrels of Phemtas. Down the stairs he went once more, where he proceeded to repeat his morning's performance of inhaling the magic dried herb. Upon so doing, he then reached into the casket and removed a bunch of the leaves, stuffing them into his silk shirt pocket.

"You are what I need!" he proclaimed, as he put the lid back on the open cask. "Yes, you are what I need!"

Chester and Goshen burst into the dining room, where all the King's Knights and Ministers were seated, eating their breakfast. Platters were filled with omelets with sautéed onions, green peppers and tomatoes; braised pig and game sausages; and various cheeses made from goat's and cow's milk. There were also pies stuffed with apples and cherries, and muffins with bananas and nuts. Coffee and frothy cream and various teas were also served. It was a raucous get-together in that Great Hall.

The vaulted ceiling reached almost thirty feet high, and had a central dome that contained a round stained-glass window. Through it, the bright early morning sunlight filtered in and shot shafts of light down upon the hearty feast and all the red-haired men talking and laughing below. The wooden portion of the ceiling itself was painted with frescoes detailing the exploits of the Kings and their Ministers and Knights.

There were also some illustrations depicting women and children in gardens and playing in the more gentle wooded areas of the lands of Pellah. The walls were almost entirely made of shutters that opened wide to display the great outdoors and the pastoral scenes of the Castle's environs, for the Great Hall was high up in Castle Pellah and overlooked the entire countryside.

Indeed, the Great Hall was, in itself, in one of the highest turrets of the Castle and on the southern side. Yet it was not the highest turret; that was farther to the north, near the Gold Mountains themselves. From the north, they could even see the highest peak of those mountains, at whose beginnings lay the Castle.

Chester wandered over to the head chef's corner where she was busily giving orders to the sous chefs and other kitchen staff as to details of the evening's upcoming feast.

"Now, as to serving the veal chops, we must not forget," Hermione Sugarbush rattled off to some of her staff, "that they are to be cooked very crispy on the outside but bloody rare on the inside. The King's men also will be feasting on roasted pig slathered with winter cherries, sides of venison with baked potatoes and sweet green onions, a hearty pheasant soup with earth roots including parsnips, turnips, carrots and rutabaga …."

She felt a tug at her sleeve and looked askance at whoever was interrupting this important diatribe. Then she spotted him.

"Chester!" she exclaimed. "Why, whatever are you doing here, my dear nephew, in my own kitchen, when you're supposed to be down south scouring the woods for those escapees?"

"I returned only last night, Hermoine."

"That's Miss Aunt Hermoine, Chester," she admonished him, large cleaver in hand.

"Very well. Miss Aunt Hermoine. I returned last night and have already seen the King!"

"What?" She turned away from him and shouted, "Dismissed!" to all the sous-chefs and cooks who were listening to her orders and left immediately. Then, turning back to the tall, gaunt scout who was her sister's son, she looked him up and down, staring at his worn-out raiment, and she asked, "You must be hungry, Nephew!" Laying down her blade, she immediately took a large empty plate and began to prepare him a meal from the food spread out before her.

"How was your trip, Chester? Did you find the runaways? And how is it with our Lordship? Is he coming to the Great Hall for breakfast? Oh me oh my, I must make certain that all his Knights know of this and are prepared for his arrival! Jessie! Beth! Marlene! Come here immediately and …."

"Aunt – er, I mean, Miss Aunt Hermoine," interrupted Chester, "the King was not yet fully dressed when I came upon him in his quarters, so I doubt that you need to rush."

"Tsk! Tsk! Of course I must rush. 'Tis our King!"

Chester shrugged his shoulders, took the plate loaded with food, and walked away, while Hermoine continued to give orders to set up the King's proper eating station, on his high throne-like chair, amply padded with green velvet and woven golden rope tassels, and carved from the precious woods of the faraway Calicab Forest.

Chester found his partner Goshen in the Great Hall, eating from his own plate with great relish. He sat down next to him and they both began to eat voraciously.

Suddenly, every voice went silent, for in marched King Vanamir, who walked over to his dais and stood before his chair. Two Knights jumped up and stood at attention to his left and right, holding high their staffs. Vanamir raised his hands, palms outstretched.

"All my men!" he said loudly, "listen carefully to what your King has to say."

No man moved a muscle, their green eyes all on their ruler.

"Today is a day of huge uncertainty for our Kingdom. I have been informed of a great Apocalypse that is headed our way, coming from the southlands. Its intent is to seal our doom!"

Now the men began to rustle about and breathe deeply, each one wanting to speak but none daring to do so – except for Malthor, the Chief Knight of the Men of the Eyes and close man-at-arms to Vanamir.

"Apocalypse?" he said straight out. "How comes your Lordship to hear of this when no one here has any clue of such a thing?" King Vanamir turned to Malthor and said, "It came to me in the form of a phantom horse and rider, in my chambers, just this morning. I was told: 'Your Destiny shall come to you on the wind.' You all know, of course," he said, turning 'round to see the faces of his men, "that my chambers were built by sorcerers at the beginning of time! My chambers are magical!"

Now everyone began to mumble and whisper to one another.

"An Apocalypse?"

"A phantom horse and rider?"

"Magical? How can this be so?"

"Quiet!" roared Vanamir, and his two attendants pounded their staffs upon the ground beside him. "Yes, we are all to meet this day with our faces turned to the south, and we must also look up in the air, beyond the clouds. We must look to the wind!"

King Vanamir sat himself down upon his royal chair, and summoned Malthor closer to his side, beckoning him with his thick index finger to lean down.

He whispered something in Malthor's ear. Malthor, upon hearing this soft speech, raised his eyelids and turned to face the King.

"This is true, my lord?"

"Aye, Malthor."

"Then we must make haste. Let me assemble my Twenty Men of the Eyes ere the sun is high in the sky. We shall face this southern storm immediately."

"Aye, Malthor. Gather your Twenty Men of the Eyes and also the Twenty Men of the Teeth. Let the Ten Men of the Coffers bring their stockpile of Phemtas to the secret hideout. Have the Eyes and the Teeth meet me at the main gateway to the Pinnacle Tower within the hour." He paused then added, "Let them flank the entranceway to left and right of me, for I shall be standing at the very door itself, ready to give the command for the mighty Golden Gates to open."

Malthor looked into the emerald green eyes of his King, and for a moment he thought he saw a kind of madness shining within them. Yet he said, "It shall be as you say, King Vanamir."

Looking sideways at the men in the Great Hall, Malthor perceived their abrupt stillness upon observing the private banter between him and their King. He knew all too well that they were on edge, wanting to know what was happening.

"Vanamir," he whispered in his King's ear, "your men are chafing at the bit for knowledge of our parlance. We must, I think, offer them some tidbit of our thinking."

"Very well, Malthor."

The King stood upright and raised his right hand and spoke out, "Ye men of Pellah! We are about to face a storm the likes of which we have never known. I myself know only that it shall be filled with wind, hail and thunderbolts! These things I have envisioned in my chambers!

"Hence, you are all to hasten immediately to the stables and the Rooms of War. Prepare yourselves in your armor and battle dress. I know not what truly comes, but it shall be forceful and we must be ready to meet whatever form it takes.

"Go now, and get to your stations, and follow the orders of Malthor as if he were your Imperial Lord and Master, for I shall already be busy with other, greater matters at the Pinnacle Tower. Now, make haste!" cried out the King.

His sentiments were echoed by Malthor, who pulled his mighty sword from its sheath and held it high in the air, crying out, "Movement! Precise and calculated! Energy and rapid-fire movement! These things the King our great Lord and Master and I do beckon each one of you to follow and obey. Be off, now! To the Pinnacle Tower at noon!"

At that pronouncement, all the men immediately rose and noisily left the Great Hall, leaving platters of food half-eaten upon the wooden tables, and napkins freshly soiled upon the stone floor.

The sun, rising from the horizon, cast brightening rays upon them all as it entered through the central stained glass window on the ceiling.

CHAPTER 40

FORCES ON THE MOVE

DURING THE LONG DARK HOUR before dawn, Andalorax arose and dressed in the new outfit Siddles had created for her since her meeting with the Many-Colored Girl. She told him all about it, from the beginning – when she first met the girl by the lake near the Castle Pellah until her recent meeting on Budgerigar Island just before Siddles flew away with her and Gamedon in his enormous claw and deposited them back here, in the Black Mountains.

She wore long slim trousers tied at the waist with a cotton sash and a buttoned-up, close-knit body shirt over which was a silk blouse with long lace cuffs; atop this was a felt cape that went down to the floor, and had velvet lapels and cuffs and large pockets. On her hands were sturdy leather gloves with whip-stitching, and on her head was a felt beret with feathers stuck into it. Her soft suede ankle boots were laced up with leather straps.

And, of course, now that she and the Many-Colored Girl had switched identities, Andalorax's raiment changed colors continually, as did her irises and her hair. Once only dressed in simple black and white, she now sparkled with the ever-changing hues that once were among the powers of the Many-Colored Girl.

"Xaroladna!" she said, pronouncing each syllable. "Xa-ro-lad-na."

Yes, that was the girl's name, Andalorax remembered. Everything was in a spin now, almost as if in a dream. But the reality was here! She couldn't ignore or deny it. She saw her long tresses turn purple then orange upon her cloak, which in turn changed from green to pink.

"Yet," she wondered, "what are her other powers? Powers which now are mine, or so she told me." She sighed. "I hope I shall discover them along the way. I shall need all the powers I can get."

As her outfit continually changed colors, Andalorax brushed aside the draped netting that served as the door at the entrance to her home and looked out. Siddles had indeed created the house to resemble her home when she lived in the Calicab Forest with her grandfather last spring. It was basically just a small tent made of strong waxed cotton to keep out any rain – although it never rained here in the Black Mountains. The sides were of the soft boughs of the Calicab trees, draped downwards to the floor, which was made of soil. The greenish, mossy-colored soil resembled the forest floor, for it was soft and warm from the fallen Calicab leaves being pressed underfoot.

Andalorax was living inside the creation of her mind, made manifest through Siddles' powers. But nothing had changed outside of that tiny world. Looking out the doorway of the tent, she saw the same landscape of the Black Mountains. That had never changed. It was the world of Zivat-Or and Phemtas. It made her heart plummet in her chest. How, at this very moment, she yearned for the life of the Galinda-Hussadi – yes, and even the Calicab Forest of her infancy, or even the Castle Pellah where she spent the first fifteen years of her life with Gamedon and her mother in the nearby Wives' Turret.

Here, there was nothing but desolation and the crawling span of death brought on by the Phemtas plant.

And now, today, they were to attempt to leave these wretched peaks that held mere patches of the verdant, vibrant earth that once covered all the lands. But that was before Phemtas took control, she thought, her mind wandering away from her serious mission.

It was a mission founded in a new reality, for there – a bit farther away from her, where she could see the archway that was the lintel of Zivat-Or's cave – was the multi-colored, hot-air balloon.

It stood out like a blast of cold air in a hot dungeon. It was fabricated from the mind of Siddles, he having seen one once during his aerial voyages as a young bird. Thus, it was a jolly-looking object: vertical stripes of red and orange and white ran down its sides, with stars plastered about it, and from the straw basket that dangled at its bottom were ribbons of every color in the rainbow – especially purple. Siddles liked the color purple so he threw that into his fascinations. The balloon and basket were tied to the black stones with thick leather straps, attached to clips hammered into the stone – all by the seemingly never-ending magic of Siddles.

"Andalorax!"

She heard Siddles call her name. "Aye, Siddles," she answered softly.

"Come here, dear girl."

She stepped out of her small tent and walked towards the great bird. He was standing on the black pedestal where he often stood, or sat, and beckoned her with a nod of his large, bony red beak.

"Are you prepared?"

"Aye, Siddles. Today is the day. I am prepared." She hesitated. "What about you and Zivat-Or?"

"Our condition is that we are completely ready. Zivat-Or has settled himself within his Phemtas throne, having gleefully ascertained that at last he could indeed separate himself from the rest of his hermitage here in the mountains."

"In other words," she responded, standing beside him and putting her hand upon his iridescent black wing, "his plant throne is no longer rooted to the rest of the Phemtas from which it sprang."

"That is correct. He is free."

"You can hardly say he is free, Siddles."

"That is true, Andalorax. He is still a part of that sprig of Phemtas upon which – and within which – he resides."

"Let me see."

They walked over past the globes of light which guided them in the darkness of the pre-dawn morning air.

There before them sat the ancient Zivat-Or, one of the true Kings of Pellah, the only man still alive from those two and a half centuries of time. He sat upon the white writhing tubular roots and stems of the Phemtas plant that formed his throne. It was not attached to anything; it was, indeed "free." But Zivat-Or himself was not free, being most definitely attached to this sprig. It was still holding him together and he was still feeding off of it.

He turned towards them and watched as they made their way towards his stony, black lair. He smiled widely when they stood finally before him.

"Here you are, my friends!" declared the wrinkled old man, rubbing his two hands together, intertwining them in an oblivious mimicry of the plant upon and within which he sat.

Zivat-Or and Phemtas were, indeed, one.

"Well, off we shall go!"

"Wait!" called out Siddles. "We must make some sort of ceremonial declaration before we ascend and depart these Black Mountains, for we may never return."

"Aye," answered Zivat-Or. "As we all know, I myself do not plan upon returning, for I shall be crowned the new King of Pellah once Vanamir is dead. I shall rule from the Castle Pellah, which I know inside and out, thanks to Gamedon."

So saying, he reached into the neck of his shirt and extracted the chain therein, holding the chunk of gold, next to which now hung another object.

It was the gold key that Gamedon had copied from King Vanamir's Library, where he met with King Mundarak.

He had given it to Zivat-Or.

"I shall use this key to find the prophesies of King Mundarak, which declare that this is meant to be! That a new Ruler shall appear in the Kingdom at this time of the year. Those prophesies will convince the people of Pellah that this person is I!"

Gamedon suddenly and swiftly appeared from behind a large rock within the cave. Once more, he had used his ability to melt into his surroundings.

"Zivat-Or," he said, "You must return that key to me."

"Why, pray tell?"

"I will most probably be the one to have use of it. I alone know how to enter the Library – indeed, I alone know of its whereabouts."

"Can you not tell me where it is?"

"No," answered Gamedon. "You shall not be able to penetrate that area of the King's domain." So saying, he held out his hand. Zivat-Or unfastened his gold chain, removed the key, and handed it over to Gamedon, who added: "Aye, 'tis true that I have navigated you, Zivat-Or, through the Castle's innards. But I doubt that you shall be able to live there in peace."

"We have gone over this a thousand times these past few months, Gamedon," scowled the ancient King. "The people must declare me their rightful King, for I shall be the only living man of that true lineage. And King Mundarak confirms this in his prophesies."

"That matters not," said Gamedon, fastening the little key to the chain about his own neck, "for even if Vanamir is vanquished, you are a part of these mountains now and forever, and a part of Phemtas as well."

"And," added Siddles, "the people do not know you and you do not know them.

They will never accede their throne to an unknown, wizened old man whose throne is a floating plant!"

"We shall see about that," retorted Zivat-Or. "I am mighty and powerful, and Phemtas has maintained these qualities in my being. Besides," he added, "I am beyond a doubt the rightful king."

"Might and power do not always make the winner, just as good does not always triumph over evil."

"Are you saying that I am evil?" sneered Zivat-Or.

"No. You are not evil," noted Gamedon. "But King Vanamir might consider you to be so – especially if you attempt to kill him. Things do not always work out in favor of the right, or, in this case, the rightful King."

Siddles interjected with a graceful nod of his head, perched upon his long neck, and said, "He's right, you know. What one thinks should happen does not always happen. Life isn't always black and white."

"We shall see, we shall see," said Zivat-Or, once more interlacing his fingers together. He gave one last great laugh as they all headed over to the aerial transport. The laugh made Andalorax's skin crawl, for it had a sinister tone. Then Zivat-Or began coughing vigorously, causing the plant to back away from him while he did so.

Siddles himself spread and flapped his wide-spanned wings, displaying their red-and-white zig-zag stripes. While doing this, the great bird stomped his enormous yellow feet upon the black stone of the mountain abode. He was preparing his resilient body for the flight alongside the aerial vessel while it floated along the cold winter air currents that he had summoned up precisely for this occasion.

"Come here!" called out Malthor. "You, all my Knights, must make ready for departure at once!" The Twenty Men of the Eyes stood at attention, while standing in their vast quarters. Off of this great meeting room were their sleeping areas. The Knights lived and slept apart from their wives and children, with whom they all had little family time.

They were all dressed in their leisure attire, having come from the Great Hall with all the other King's men and not having been prepared for the King's speech and his sudden volley of news, especially that he, their King, had received a vision that same morning.

"A vision indeed!" thought Pontick, one of the Knights, as he used his fine-tuned eyesight to watch his chief, Malthor, explaining what was about to happen.

"We shall all dress in our warrior clothing," he informed his men, "including some elements of your body armor – specifically, your padded leather uniforms underneath your chain mail jackets, your hauberks. You shall also wear your gorgets."

There was a great moan from some of the Knights, which irritated Malthor, who called out, "Silence! This is no joke. Our King has solemn revelations that call for the complete performance of our actions on his behalf and on the behalf of our entire Kingdom. He relies upon us to make his desires real. Therefore, listen to what I say.

"Your hauberks will offer protection from what our King perceives as enemies coming from the skies. They are your basic body armor. Your gorgets will protect your throats should anything swoop down from the skies and attack your necks and eyes, and reach your vital blood vessels."

These commands were met with resounding silence from his Knights. They understood that Malthor was deadly serious and respected him greatly, so they responded accordingly. However, they did jab each other with their elbows every now and then, especially when he told them what body armor they were to wear. Their armor was kept gleaming, but also kept in cupboards; some of the younger Knights had never even worn them, for there was no need.

Life had been peaceful in the Kingdom of Pellah.

"What happens if there is a storm but it does not come from the skies?" asked Benniman, one of the Knights.

"Don't be ridiculous. All storms come from the skies," answered Malthor.

"I mean … in the Great Hall, King Vanamir spoke of a vision, a dream, that told him of some kind of danger – perhaps a war – coming from the south and that we were to look to the skies. But suppose there is also an enemy on the ground?"

"Afoot?"

"Yes, afoot."

"But surely, the King refers to a battle, not merely a storm, an elemental storm? Perhaps there shall be soldiers and men ready for battle?"

"Hmmm … This is true." Malthor stroked his long red beard in contemplation, thinking: "Well now … The King said that the vision told him: 'Your Destiny shall come to you on the wind.' I wonder if Benniman has some sense in his head after all." Then he brushed his hand in a broad stroke as if to wipe away the thought and said, "It comes from the skies, I tell you!"

King Vanamir headed towards the two Towers of the Castle that rose high into the air by passing through several tunnels known only to him and his men. The tunnels had been secretly installed when the Castle was constructed one thousand two-hundred and fifty years earlier by the wizards who came to Pellah with their first King. No one else knew of their existence; the secret was passed along from King to King, who in turn showed the tunnels to their Knights and men-at-arms. Each tunnel opened onto a Tower, meant for use in battle. It was through use of a Tower that the lookout warrior in the Castle Keep could see for miles in all directions, and be forewarned of any approaching enemy.

But no battle had ever been fought in the Kingdom of Pellah. The first King and his people along with his Knights and wizards had sailed here. They knew not what unforeseen dangers or hostile people they might come upon when they stepped off their well-crafted ships and first touched the soil which they declared to be the Kingdom of Pellah.

But that was long ago.

First, holding a sturdy oil lamp, King Vanamir headed up the circular stone staircase that wound its way along the entire interior circumference of the Castle's main building. Then he felt his way along the wall at a certain point where he knew the entrance to the first tunnel should be. It took him some time to find it and he began to lose patience but eventually his thick fingers discovered the hiding place: a round stone that, when pressed, slid open a rectangular rock in the wall. It revealed an entrance that was wide enough for two large men or even a horse to pass through.

Making their way through this, and eventually through three more tunnels each of which opened to one of the two smaller Towers, Vanamir reached the final secret doorway. Pressing upon the largest circular stone of them all, this one bearing the carved image of a wild magical beast, and going through this opening, he found himself turning a winding curve in the staircase that revealed a shred of light which became brighter with each step he took.

Then, there before him, stood a great gate.

It was made of solid gold.

The King knew then that he had reached his ultimate goal, that which they named Pinnacle Tower. He had to pass through the Golden Gates to reach it. He knew that would be no easy feat, for the gate had magic charms woven through its metal when built by craftsmen and sorcerers. But when he became King, he had been told the secret of how to enter and worried not.

The Pinnacle, which was round, was built of huge stones carved by masons and also many of the hearty townspeople of the newly dedicated Pellah soil. The Tower was ten stories high and had lookout openings through which soldiers had great visibility of the surroundings and could aim their arrows and other missiles at any attacking enemy. It also had decorative but useful turrets reaching out along its sides and at the topmost point for added visibility; weapons of war were stored in the turrets as well.

This turret, Vanamir's goal, stood before him in simple yet majestic glory. "I have arrived at last," said the King in a firm voice. Then, approaching the Golden Gates, he performed the ritual that would open them to his advantage and further use.

Vanamir stood before the enormous gates and stood tall, raising his arms up into the air, and said:

Confis gutmano dink!

The gates swung open wide and the King crossed their threshold with one big step. Then there he was, standing before the Pinnacle Tower, in the fresh outdoors on this glorious morning.

"So much has happened since the sun has risen today," he thought. Then, as he remembered the phantom horse and rider, his anxiety grew into the tremblings of real fear. It was at this point that he remembered as well what he had brought in his shirt pocket: Phemtas, the Plant of Kings! With a quick gesture, he reached in and extracted the weed. Holding it up to his face, he received the strong scent of its dried buds and flowers with a great intensity of purpose.

"Now I shall find the power – nay, not just one but all the powers that I need – to defy and fight this thing called my Destiny!"

Discarding some of the used-up Phemtas leaves upon the stone floor, he strode quickly into the main wooden door to the Tower, and saw the interior rows of steps that wound along the curved, rising walls. He began to climb them. As he rose, he passed lookout openings and could see nothing outside save the blue skies and the green earth, and, farther away, the homes of Pellah citizens.

He also saw the Wives' Turret, where all his many wives lived in secrecy and isolation from the entire Pellah world. They had each given him a daughter, then become fallow and could bear no more, not one giving him a son.

There was one exception: Mandir lived there as well, although she had not born him even a daughter. Vanamir looked upon that Tower with a great shudder, for he recalled that Mandir had brought Andalorax with him.

"That wicked wench, Mandir!" he thought, "And her ugly daughter who lives in a colorless bodily form, being all black and white. Aye, Mandir resides there, too."

King Vanamir paused and looked out at the Wives' Turret, created by masons just for him twenty years ago for this specific purpose. The first five years it served to house his first nine wives – "the infertile womenfolk," he thought. The last fifteen years, it continued to serve him, although he never abandoned the hope of finding a suitable wife to bear him a son. Those fifteen years were when Andalorax, "and her faltering, doddering old grandfather, Gamedon, lived there!" thought the King. It came to his mind that he should reinvigorate his desire for a son, and begin afresh his search for a suitable wife.

"Aye, this shall I commence when this Destiny business is done with," he thought, and laughed aloud heartily, which brought him some relief from ponderous imaginings. Then the King continued on his winding way, heading up to the top of the Pinnacle.

At last he found himself at the topmost point, and viewed the entirety of his realm in a circular fashion, steering his eyes along the glorious horizon and seeing nothing of any importance that could bring him his Destiny.

To the east, the King saw meadows covered in snow, for that expanse of land was as yet undiscovered. To the west, plowed acres lay before him, and there were farmhouses in the distance with smoke coming from their chimneys, and horses standing in their fields, licking salt and eating fresh hay from their stalls. To the north, he saw the Gold Mountains, which gleamed as the midday sun reflected off their majestic peaks.

"But wait," he said aloud. "What is that to the south?"

Surely it could not be, that he saw the rising clouds of a tumultuous storm blowing in upon great gusts of wind and rain and hail, with clouds billowing one upon the other like waves from the sea, coming towards the Castle Pellah and the Pinnacle Tower and all that was grand in his life therein.

CHAPTER 41

WAR!

ANDALORAX, ZIVAT-OR AND GAMEDON WERE in the woven straw basket of the airborne balloon created by Siddles. He himself, the great bird, flew alongside the colorful gondola.

"'Tis a rickety craft," thought Siddles, as he soared on the winds high above the clouds and the wild weather. Down below, he could see the tops of those clouds, and he knew what they brought: ferocious wind squalls, freezing rain, chunks of snow, pelting hail, and lightning and thunderbolts.

He knew what was below for he had himself created it all. Just as Zivat-Or had imagined and commanded.

They had left the Black Mountains early that morning, just when the dawn light was about to appear along the ragged horizon's peaks. They calculated their journey would bring them to their destination in the early afternoon. That suited their plan perfectly. So they sailed on with the help of the strong winds, heading north, as the sun rose to their right in the east.

But it wasn't a warm sun, for Siddles had taken care that wintertime would be cold and sharp this year. He also had autumn arrive early, to prepare them all for the cold winter that was about to come. This affected not only the Black Mountains, but all the domains about them including the entire Kingdom of Pellah and all its little villages, the vast Calicab Forest, the lands of the faeries, the Golden Mountains in the north, and even Budgerigar Island far to the south.

In the cramped basket, the three of them did not speak. There was nothing to say; it had all been said earlier during the summer and fall and even last night. Gamedon sat now on the floor of the hamper, looking up at the sky, which was unreasonably blue despite the wintery weather down below. When the balloon had lifted off about an hour earlier, he was looking at the remnants of the stars. "I'm glad the sky is blue," he thought. "It is one last vestige of peace before the violence that will soon befall us."

Zivat-Or was shrouded by his Phemtas throne, which floated within the basket. He, too, said not a word, but his mind was racing along at a reckless pace.

"I shall be King at last, I shall be King once again!" he thought. "I shall find that King Vanamir at the Castle as arranged; I know it inside and out from Gamedon's many stories after living there for fifteen years … Where are we now, I wonder? Passing over the southern border of the Kingdom of Pellah? Too bad we can't see through the clouds … I want to see what will soon be all mine … mine again as it once was when I was King, before they banished me … I wish Siddles had made this basket bigger, my throne is squeezing me …."

Andalorax stood quietly, looking north, the wind blowing her hair and cape away from her face and body. The many colors of her hair and cape and irises continued to vary, just as they had on land. Yet she didn't see these things. She saw only the blue sky and felt the wind blowing against her.

"I wonder where Xaroladna is right now," she thought. "Should I be able to know where she is? Does she know where I am? Does she know I still wonder what my powers are, my powers given to me by her?" Andalorax stared straight ahead while the balloon rose up in the Black Mountains, while it sailed across Milorin and the Calicab Forest, while it continued on its way across the midlands of the Pellah Kingdom, heading north.

She had asked Siddles to create a bow and a quiver full of arrows, which she herself had designed, having learned the craft of archery from the Galinda-Hussadi. She herself had designed the set, right down to the metal tips of the arrows, and she had arranged for the types of feathers. She felt the hefty weight of it all where it now rested, slung across her left shoulder.

"Granddaughter," said Gamedon, looking up from the floor, "what is on your mind?"

"I am wondering where Xaroladna is and what powers she has given me. I am wondering how soon we shall make our destination."

"We should not have very far to go, dear child," he said.

She laughed and said with a smile, "Grandfather, you still refer to me as a child! I am a young woman now."

"In my eyes, in my heart, you shall always be a child," Gamedon replied. "Yet I know that you have seen many things in this world, granddaughter." He watched as her eyes turned blue as the sky, her hair turned lilac, and her cape turned pear green. He smiled back at her.

"You have the wondrous traits of your many-colored friend, and they continue to astonish me every time I look at you. Those ever-changing hues are a sight to behold. I, too, wonder what powers she has bequeathed to you upon transitioning into your body. But nothing else has altered in you, dear child. Or shall I simply call you Andalorax from now on?"

"Aye," she answered. "Call me by my name, Grandfather. That will make everything simple and straightforward, and I shall truly feel my age after all my years with and without you! Just remembering where we are now qualifies me for being a truly grown-up woman, don't you think?"

"Aye, Andalorax." He smiled up at her from where he was sitting, and she, smiling back at him, reached over and took his hands in hers. Her hair blazed fire red, her eyes were blood orange, and her cape became canary yellow. They continued to look at each other, and Andalorax said, "Stand up, Grandfather! Stand here beside me so we can experience this together."

The old man rose up, aided by Andalorax's strong arms. "She has indeed become a young woman," he thought, "strengthened in mind and body by her life's experiences."

He stood side by side with her, facing north, heading towards their destination, and the destiny of many. All the while, Siddles soared alongside the gondola, and thought many significant things, including the visions of what probably lay before them and would soon come into view.

Precisely at noon, Malthor stood before his Twenty Men of the Eyes and the Twenty Men of the Teeth. His second lieutenant, Dithmore, had been put in command of the latter group years earlier but remained under Malthor's supervision. A big burly man whose thick, braided beard came down to his waist belt, Dithmore also had the gold teeth of his group implanted upon his own teeth at that time. He greatly admired his gold teeth because they gave him a definite prominence among the other Knights who were not on his level of power, or so he believed.

"Dithmore," said Malthor, as they stood before their two companies of Knights, "we have achieved our goal of being exactly where we are supposed to be – here at the Golden Gates, at the entrance to the Pinnacle Tower."

"Aye, Malthor. So it appears. But where is the King?"

"I, too, wonder. He said he had important business to attend to and would meet us here."

"Perhaps he is already inside?"

"Aye, either that or on his way," said Malthor, twirling the tip of his immaculate braided beard. "I am fortunate to have been shown the secret tunnels and how to enter them, else we would not have been able to achieve our ultimate goal. At least, we are standing here, at the ready."

"It would be pleasing were the King to have us gather at the front entrance to the Castle, by the drawbridge over the moat," mentioned Dithmore. "Then we could have our steeds with us, and much more ammunition when we face the enemy – whoever that shall be."

"Remember, Dithmore, the King said that our enemy will be coming from the southern skies. I told you this as we were preparing our armor and attire."

Dithmore was silent for a moment, then responded, "What can come from the skies? All I see is weather most foul and possibly disastrous, for our only battle equipment is kept in the turrets and that is only bows and arrows."

"Aye. At least at the drawbridge on the ground we would have access to cannon and slingshots."

Both men stood still of a sudden, for there came a clattering noise from within the Pinnacle. They could not see beyond the Golden Gates, for entrance was not given them to that particular area.

"Did you hear that?" asked Dithmore.

"Aye. Quiet now!"

Malthor held his index finger to his lips and looked Dithmore in the eye. The two stood still, as did their forty Knights. Then another clattering sound came from beyond the Golden Gates, and within the Pinnacle.

Malthor continued to press his finger to his lips. Not a sound could be heard. Suddenly a rumbling boomed into the air, and the two men gasped as they saw a large rectangular stone in the wall of the Pinnacle slide to the left.

"Never have I seen such magic!" whispered Dithmore.

"Silence!" retorted Malthor.

Revealed behind the stone was a tall robust man, dressed in a suit of armor beneath which was the finest golden mail: The Knights all saw his breastplate, helmet, a pair of gauntlets, and a gorget at his throat. All were decorated with scrollwork and patterning that indicated the armor was, most likely – or so thought Malthor – made under some magic charm by wizards long dead.

"Behold your King!" called a voice from behind the closed helmet, as King Vanamir raised the eye cover to reveal his emerald irises.

"'Tis truly you, my King?" asked Malthor.

"Aye! 'Tis I, Vanamir, verily. Stand at attention, my Knights, for we are soon to reckon with a storm."

So saying, King Vanamir walked through the stone portal and stood before them at the other side of the Golden Gates. With his thunderous voice, he pronounced these words:

Gates of the Pinnacle, Gates of Gold
Open up to what you hold!
Upon your roof
I bring the King
To show the world his naked soul!

Without a sound, the Golden Gates unfolded and opened themselves without a single human touch. When they stopped, the King said in his baritone voice, "Come hither, Malthor and Dithmore! Come speedily now!"

The two Knights stepped across the threshold and found themselves face-to-face with their King.

"It seems that we have entered another land," thought Malthor, for there appeared to be a mist enveloping his King – indeed, quickly enveloping all three of them – a violet mist that held many tiny yellow sparkling lights. A shudder ran through his body. Dithmore experienced the same thing and responded similarly, yet both soldiers moved not a muscle. They, too, were in body armor same as the King, but theirs had not the same decorative etchings and embossed medallions.

Yet the King wore his crown and no helmet. Jewel-encrusted, made of purest gold, and etched with symbols and ancient words of magic, the crown had passed from King to King throughout the centuries.

He wore his crown because that was what the woman on the phantom horse had told him he must do, just that morning.

"Your men shall enter the Pinnacle Tower upon my signal," said King Vanamir, "and quickly scatter throughout the interior. Do you hear me, my Knights?" He turned and faced them all. "You shall station yourselves two by two at each gap and arrowslit along the walls, having first outfitted yourselves with bow and arrow stored within the turrets. You are an army of forty men including Malthor and Dithmore here before me, and that should be sufficient; however, you two shall follow me."

He turned to look at Malthor and Dithmore. "When the remaining Knights reach the top of the Tower, they are to stand at the battlements, ready to shoot arrows from the arrowslits."

"Aye, my Lord," said both Knights.

"And every man shall look towards the skies for possible attack," said the King. At this, Vanamir looked again past the two men and saw the rows of soldiers and smiled widely. "I am protected mightily and I am secure," he thought. "No harm shall come to me this day, despite being foretold by the phantom woman upon the horse!"

At this remembrance of what occurred in his bed chamber only a few hours before, Vanamir felt a shudder go through his body, but he could not help himself and burst out in one loud guffaw. The Knights turned their faces and looked upon each other, wondering what was driving this King.

"Surely it must be madness," thought one.

"What is it that is coming from these windswept skies?" pondered another.

Every man was in confusion and bewilderment, but they all stood firm and ready to do their King's bidding.

Vanamir, Malthor and Dithmore all raised their heads and gazed southward. They saw dark gray clouds rolling in, tumbling over one another like waves in the sea. A sheet of purplish rain came pouring out of the clouds, followed by the pelting of hailstones the size of apples. Then suddenly there was a tremendous bolt of lightning followed by a thunderclap that caused every Knight to jump to attention. This continued several more times, until they thought it would never cease. But then the cloudburst became almost black and spread over the land like an expansive sheet, causing a dark shadow to fall upon the snow-covered lands below.

"Now!" called King Vanamir, unsheathing his large sword and raising it in the air with his right hand. "Enter and take your stations, men! The danger is coming! I feel it in my body and spirit!"

At this gesture and command, all the Knights took to their feet and hurried past the Golden Gates and entered the Pinnacle Tower. Two by two, they grabbed bow and arrow from a large turret and climbed the interior staircase, stationing themselves at each battlement. As they climbed, they took position and fitted their bows with arrows, waiting for what would appear from the skies.

King Vanamir, Malthor and Dithmore all rushed up the stairs, past the busy men, and reached the top of the Tower. They stood at the topmost point of the Castle Pellah, staring at the spectacle taking place in the firmament.

Another series of lightning bolts and thunderclaps burst into the air, and the sky was still almost as dark as night. Suddenly, an opening in the cloud cover let in a pinhole of blue sky, and this pinhole expanded, and became wider and wider, allowing rays of sunlight to shoot down upon the lands below. The Pinnacle was bathed in the light, and the arc of a gigantic rainbow appeared in the skies.

King Vanamir stared at the blue spot which revealed the sky, and clasped his sword, raising it high in the air. It glistened gold in the amazing beams of sunlight, which also caused Vanamir's green eyes to glisten brightly and illuminated his carrot-red beard. It seemed that everything about them here atop the Pinnacle was bathed in abundant light.

Then Vanamir cried out, "Look! Here it comes!" and he pointed with his left hand towards the blue opening in the clouds which was encircled by the rainbow.

All the heads of the forty Knights raised up to see what was happening, including those of Malthor and Dithmore. Their jaws dropped, and so did some of their arrows, when from out of the blue hole in the boiling black clouds appeared when they saw some sort of round object with a big basket dangling from it. Colorful streamers blew alongside in the wind. As the round object came closer, penetrating the clouds and heading north towards them, they realized it was a flamboyant hot-air balloon.

"It's being carried by the wind," said a Knight.

"I've never seen anything like it," said another.

"I've seen it in picture books in school," said yet a third.

"What is it?" cried out a fourth.

"It's a hot-air balloon, with a hanging basket carrying its occupants," answered Malthor, whose sword remained unsheathed as he stood alongside his King.

Vanamir was standing motionless, his outstretched left arm still pointing – now somewhat uselessly, for his object was very evident – into the blue opening in the clouds.

The hot-air balloon was being carried along by the great winds of the storm, which still rumbled all around it. Vanamir strained his eyes to see it more clearly. He soon made out the red, orange and white vertical stripes of the balloon itself, then he saw the bright blue stars that were emblazoned upon it. He saw ribbons streaming from the large basket, garlands of varietal colors. He couldn't make out who or what was in the basket itself. Wait! He saw three objects inside it … two people standing facing north, facing him … and another being seemingly floating behind them. He couldn't make out what that being was, as it was encased in something waxy-white.

"Malthor! Dithmore!" he said, without turning away from the object in the air, "Tell me what you see coming out from the blue hole in the clouds."

"I see a balloon," answered Malthor, "a gigantic balloon of many colors, with a basket hanging from it."

"Aye, my Lord," agreed Dithmore. "'Tis exactly what I see as well."

"And within that basket?"

Malthor, First Eyeman of the Twenty Knights of the Eyes, squinted and said, "I see two individuals … no, wait, I see three … but the third doesn't appear to be actually within the basket …."

As all three of them stared, as did all the Knights, their arrows at the ready, a dark object came into view. It followed behind the basket and balloon, sweeping into sight suddenly out of the blue hole in the clouds. Malthor alone could make it out.

"My King," he cried out, "it is a giant bird!"

As Malthor moved his finger and pointed just above the gondola, Siddles swooped down, negotiating the same aerial path as the balloon. The flash of his black body patterned by his bright, red-striped wings, his yellow feet and powerful crimson beak, was an astonishing sight for everyone in Pinnacle Tower.

But the Pellah citizens on the ground also did not miss out on this terrifying spectacle. All eyes of the people throughout the Kingdom were on the stormy skies as the clouds blew in from the south. People as far south as Milorin near the Calicab

316

Forest were experiencing the terrible storm, and saw the clouds part and open up to the patch of blue. They too saw the arrival of the balloon and now Siddles. Eventually they saw, as well, Andalorax and Gamedon standing in front of the basket, and Zivat-Or – wrapped in something waxy-white floating along with the two others.

They gasped, they screamed, they were breathless. They ran outdoors and pointed in the air, grabbed their children and then ran back in their houses, hiding in fear. Never in their wildest imaginations did these simple people conceive of a frightening storm of such magnitude, let alone see the skies parting to reveal the descent of a striped balloon and a basket filled with two people and a third being, such a strange character!

And descend it did. Siddles, now flying in front of the balloon, led the way, aiming directly towards the Castle Pellah.

Malthor, with his keen vision, could actually see Siddles' one eye as the great vulture-like bird zoomed northward, coming closer and closer to earth.

"My King, they are descending and they are coming towards us," he said, as he stood frozen on the spot.

Vanamir suddenly wondered what to do. His Phemtas strength was leaving his body; he wanted another bath in its opulent, smoky fumes. He recalled the phantom horse and rider.

"They are not coming for me," he reflected quickly. "They are not challenging me, not threatening me! I must be safe then … but who are these three beings in the peculiar basket? And who is making such magic as to dazzle with that extraordinary balloon?"

Then he remembered what he had done when he had left his chambers: He had put some Phemtas leaves in his silk shirt breast pocket! He pressed his left hand against it; he could feel the shape of it in his imagination, even though it was beneath layers of chain mail and his gold breastplate.

"How can I get to it?" he wondered. "Dare I do such a thing, here in front of my Knights?" He imagined removing his armor but realized he could not do this; time was not on his side. "By the time they get to me, I will only have time to remove my breastplate … I have to give up the idea of my blessed Phemtas empowering me once again before I face my Destiny!"

Then he realized what he was facing, coming down in the clouds directly towards him.

"It is my Destiny!" he cried out. "The phantom woman with the white hair on that white horse was correct! I must do as they said. I must bare my breast to it as I was warned to do."

And he thought, "That way, I can get to my precious Phemtas!"

With those thoughts in his racing mind, he said, "Malthor, you must help me now. This is what I was told to do by the vision in my bed chamber. You must remove my body armor, my breastplate and mail and gorget. I must bare my naked chest to this oncoming Destiny!"

"But, Sire, you cannot expose yourself to this danger …."

"Do as I say! At once!"

"Aye, my King," responded Malthor, who commenced to unhook the body armor.

"Quickly now! All speed!"

With his eyes still on the enormous bird and the balloon and the basket, Malthor, First Eyeman, called his Knights to help him to do as his King commanded.

"Make haste!" cried out Vanamir, whose eyes, too, were upon what he felt to be his descending Destiny.

And descending it was. Sailing through the dark clouds and the rain and lightning that continued, that never stopped, the company slowly made its way towards the Pinnacle Tower. The blue hole in the clouds had closed and disappeared. The rainbow was gone. All the sky was dark again.

Andalorax reached behind her with her right hand and felt her quiver full of arrows, and the bow which was slung across her left shoulder. She had strung the bow just prior to entering the basket, to ascertain that it was tight and resilient.

She sighed, and her hair turned lavender and her eyes turned orange, and her fluttering cape became bright blue. Gamedon watched this continual change in her appearance but still had difficulty getting accustomed to it.

With the wind blowing in their faces, Gamedon had to yell to be heard. "Andalorax," he said, "can you choose the colors?"

She laughed but he could hardly hear it. "No, Grandfather. It just happens. And I have attempted to select a color – for example, Siddles loves the color purple so I thought I'd amuse him by turning my hair, my eyes and my cape different shades of purple – but I couldn't do a thing!"

They both looked at each other and smiled.

After a while, as they descended towards the Castle Pellah – which looked like a stony blot on the snowy landscape below – he asked her, "What will happen when we reach the King?"

"I do not know."

"Surely you have some idea?"

"No, Grandfather. I do not know. I will do whatever I am supposed to do, whatever that may be."

"How will you know what you are supposed to do?"

"I do not know. I only know this: I shall do something. I am meant to do something. You know that, Grandfather. I was brought up believing that a special moment would come and I have a feeling that now is the time for that moment to arrive."

Gamedon had nothing to say, for over the years he had said everything he wanted to say, so he just nodded his head in agreement. "Aye," he thought. "My little girl is right and ready."

They could not see the hustling and bustling of the Knights as they undressed King Vanamir on the snowy roof of the Pinnacle Tower. While the air crackled with the cold and the clouds rumbled with lightning strikes, Andalorax and Gamedon began to see from their perch high up in the sky that people were scrambling on the rooftop of the highest Tower of the Castle Pellah. They looked like little dots rolling around on a tilting surface, for the balloon rollicked to and fro in the high winds. They were focused on a central figure, who they silently decided to be the King.

The King was finally relieved of his battle dress and wearing only his undergarments. He was shivering in the cold but no matter, he managed to find his pocketful of Phemtas.

"I don't care who sees me," he said to himself. "I need my power, which wanes with every breath." Reaching into his silk undershirt pocket he pulled out the dried brownish green weed, held it to his face, and breathed deeply. He performed this ritual three or four times, to the shock of his Knights. They knew not what their King was doing, and stared in silence.

With every gust that Siddles produced in the skies, the balloon came closer and closer to its mark: King Vanamir. Zivat-Or sat on and within his throne of living Phemtas, straining his eyes to see the King.

"My life is becoming complete," he said aloud to himself – not knowing that Gamedon and Andalorax were listening – "for my dream of returning to my Kingly station is coming true."

By and by, the passengers in the balloon could see more clearly that the King was atop the highest Tower in the Castle Pellah, and he was also divested of his armor and stood there in his underclothes. They also saw that he was surrounded by men at arms, and they were in full armor dress, carrying bows and arrows, and almost all of them were facing upwards, towards the extraordinary, striped balloon.

But it wasn't the balloon they were looking at – it was the giant black bird that flew alongside it. Its enormous wingspan made it seem almost as large as the gondola itself.

Then the bird let out a piercing cry that seemed to fill the darkened skies with fear and danger.

"*Raaak-aah-whoo,*" it called out.

The sound was long and menacing and deep-throated. It repeated its cry three times:

"*Raaak-aah-whoo!*" it screamed, then it swooped down toward the Pinnacle Tower itself. It seemed to the Knights to be the straightest, strongest arrow they had in their arsenal, yet it was most definitely not an arrow but a living creature heading right for them where they stood awkwardly, scattered around their King and his discarded raiment.

"Never have I seen such a frightening bird!" called out Malthor. "Men! Circle 'round our King, for surely this beast is headed towards him. Be at the ready with your arrows! Make haste now!" The men scrambled to create a circular barrier around Vanamir, who was still deeply inhaling his Phemtas. He looked to be in a trance, his eyes half-lidded, and his pupils full and dark.

Then he looked up and saw that his Knights had encircled him, and seemed to be protecting him from something.

"What is it?" Vanamir wondered. Then he looked beyond the Tower and saw the snow-covered lands and the blackened sky, rumbling and thundering as huge clouds poured upon the earth like the crashing waves of a great sea.

"My dream!" he remembered. "It is almost twenty years ago, in my bedchamber, when I saw the white horse that was washed up on the shores by gigantic white waves, and was scrambling to make it to the top of a cliff … When it was seeking me out … When I killed Haldown ….” And then he recalled the white phantom horse of just last night, and the transparent woman who commanded his presence at the top of the highest Tower in the realm.

“And here I am!” he cried out. “Meeting my Destiny. Ah, but this Phemtas has just renewed my strength and power, and I shall meet it head on, and defy and overcome it!” So saying, he once again retrieved his golden sword and began to wave it in the air, striking at some presence only he could see … the white horse … the ghostly woman … his Destiny!

Siddles, with his mighty scarlet beak, had grabbed a hold of a clutch of streamers from the balloon, and began to navigate it and the basket towards the Pinnacle Tower. Andalorax stood silently at the prow of the gondola, alongside Gamedon. She stared at the landscape before her; their destination was now within two hundred yards. She saw the King himself, who stood there, holding his bright shining golden sword in his right hand, with his left hand clutching at his breast. She saw his body; then, as they closed in, she saw his face.

It was filled with a raging scowl, but she also noticed that his whole physique was trembling. Many Knights encircled him, but two men stood faithfully at his side. They were all holding their bows and arrows at the ready. And then, when the balloon was one hundred yards away, she heard one of the two men shout, “Now! Commence shooting!” The group of men shot many arrows in the air towards her, Gamedon and Zivat-Or.

Still, Siddles dove down into the group, pulling the balloon behind him, dragging it along as it was being aided by the rigorous air currents.

Gamedon stood still, facing the Castle and its many Knights atop the high Tower. He said nothing and moved not a muscle.

“I shall let everything take its natural course,” he thought.

Zivat-Or, floating within his living Phemtas plant, started to yell. “We are coming for you! We shall get you, King Vanamir! I shall be King once again! You shall all rue the day when you cast me out into the Black Mountains to live for decades in suffering and despair! We are coming for you! We shall get you!”

At that same moment, Andalorax, easily and unnoticed, reached behind her with her right hand, and withdrew an arrow from her large leather quiver. Then she tightened her grip on her bow – so taut, so resilient. She placed the arrow horizontally against the bow, holding it in her firm grip. Her cape, now bright red, was blowing rearward in the ferocious wind as it brought her even closer to her quarry. Her hair became bright purple; her eyes, a cool lavender.

When there were fifty yards between her and the top of the Tower, she stood up tall and leaned forward over the bow of the gondola, her crossbow strung. She pulled back with all her pliant energy, took aim, and let the arrow fly.

It went straight to King Vanamir's naked chest, straight into his heart.

And he clutched at the arrow in his breast, he fell down on his knees, and cried out, "My Destiny!" He fell forward, pushing the arrow straight through his body so that it pierced clear through to the other side, and he was dead.

Zivat-Or could not believe what had just happened, and let out with a robust, "You got him!" He is on the ground! He must be dead! Surely he is dead!"

Gamedon turned around to him and looked into his ancient, emerald green eyes and said, "Aye, my Lord. King Vanamir is dead. Long live King Zivat-Or!"

CHAPTER 42

DEATHS OF KINGS

MALTHOR AND DITHMORE AND THE other thirty-eight Knights, who now they saw had encircled King Vanamir in vain, speedily withdrew more arrows from their quivers and were about to let them fly at Andalorax, Gamedon and Zivat-Or. But Siddles, upon watching them pull back upon their bowstrings, suddenly spread out his wings and made them become an enormous shield. They completely hid the balloon and its occupants.

Siddles' wings were now immense in size due to his powers and magic, and their terrible red zig-zag stripes stood out like lightning bolts against the dark stormy sky still raging on. So seconds later when the Knights did let fly their arrows, they bounced off Siddles' wings like raindrops on a tin roof.

"Men," cried out Malthor, "your arrows are useless against these assassins! Retreat into the Keep of the Tower and avoid being killed yourselves!" All the Knights immediately followed his command and rushed inside the Tower – but for Malthor and Dithmore, who stood, swords in hand, at either side of their fallen King.

"Siddles!" cried out Zivat-Or, "set us down! Set us down among my people and my servants!"

The balloon, having been carried along in the strong air currents by Siddles so as to maneuver it into the precise position for Andalorax's arrow, then came slowly floating down to the top of the Pinnacle Tower.

There it finally rested.

The Knights were aghast when they saw, from their arrow slits and battlements, who was in the basket: Andalorax, a young woman in all her ever-changing hues, who had just killed their King; Gamedon, an old man in a tattered cloak and cockeyed felt hat with gray hair and green eyes; and the phenomenon of Zivat-Or, a presence they could not understand, for he was a man of whom they could only see the top half as the rest of him was covered by a white writhing vine.

"Place me in front of my people, Siddles," commanded Zivat-Or. "You there," he said in a commanding voice, indicating Malthor, "stand up and bow to me, for I am your new King."

"You are not my King," declared Malthor, rising to his full six-foot height and looming large over Zivat-Or, who still sat within his Phemtas throne.

"My King lies dead! You and your people have killed him!"

"Yes, yes!" cried Zivat-Or with glee, clapping his hands. "King Vanamir is indeed dead! But I didn't do it," he declared. Pointing to Andalorax, he said, "She did it, with her arrow flying straight into his heart! Look! See her bow? She did it!"

All eyes turned towards Andalorax.

"Kill her!" called out Zivat-Or. "I am your King! Do as I say!"

Malthor stood in confusion for a moment, not knowing what made sense. He did see the woman in the multi-colored cape and long rainbow-like hair shoot her arrow and kill his King as the balloon approached. Perhaps he should take revenge for his fallen Master? But who was this man – if he could call him a man – to command his actions?

But he dared not move, for Siddles was still enormous and shielding them, although they had lifted themselves from the straw basket and now stood firmly atop the Pinnacle Tower.

Somehow, by some magical force, it seemed, the enormous bird had changed his size – not as he usually did, but now he was a true giant – and was as wide as the Pinnacle Tower itself. Siddles was a colossal opalescent, black, one-eyed, buzzard-like bird with an enormous red, horn-billed beak and gigantic craggy yellow feet with talons that could rip out their eyes should he want to do so. Who was this creature who had pulled the balloon along in the strong stormy clouds, and brought it down to safety on their Tower? Never had they seen such a sight as he.

But Zivat-Or! Now here was a thing they truly could not understand, for he was, to all appearances, a being half-man, half-plant. And his two accomplices had hailed him as King upon the murder of King Vanamir – who were they, they wondered, and from where do they come, and why do they come? This creature who declared himself King was the greatest riddle of all.

When all were assembled upon the rooftop, standing before the Knights – who had returned from hiding in their battlements and now stood all dressed in their full armor, and the King lay prone on the floor, the arrow having pierced clear through his body, Malthor asked:

"Who are you all? Why have you killed our King?"

CHAPTER 43

REBIRTH

MALTHOR COULD NOT BELIEVE HIS EYES when he saw how magnificent and magical was this young woman with her many-colored hair, eyes and cloak. And he was not alone in this wonderment: every Knight, including Dithmore, was staring at her in tremendous disbelief. They were dumbfounded.

"Who is this creature?" Malthor asked himself. Then he managed to speak.

"Who are you and why have you killed our King?"

"We are travelers from the Black Mountains and faraway lands," answered Andalorax, as she hefted her bow and replaced it in the quiver upon her left shoulder. "We come on a quest to fulfill the Destiny of a former Pellah King to the throne. Here he is," she added, pointing to Zivat-Or.

Malthor's eyes opened wide when he saw Zivat-Or.

"Are you referring to this 'thing' in the balloon basket? This is a Pellah King? It cannot be so!"

"He is of the lineage of your true Kings and has been living a life of banishment for over two hundred and fifty years." Malthor's jaw dropped and he started to speak but Andalorax stopped him by holding up her right hand.

"How can he be so old, you wonder? He exists under the spell of the plant called Phemtas." Andalorax reached down and picked up what she had noticed on the turret floor next to the dead King Vanamir. It was the bit of Phemtas plant from Vanamir's breast pocket. Holding it out for Malthor to see, she asked "Are you not familiar with it?"

"No and I have no interest in this plant. What has it to do with the murder of my King? Why have you killed Vanamir?"

Andalorax turned towards Zivat-Or and said, "You must speak now; it is up to you."

Zivat-Or was at a loss for how to do this, but knew he must act quickly. He sought out his Phemtas plant, writhing and hissing about him, holding him up, embracing him and giving him his power.

"You see this plant upon which I sit? It is the herb of Kings, and always has been! Did your King Vanamir not share this knowledge with his people?"

Malthor summoned his speech and said, "Nay, this never came to pass. And yet she," he said, pointing to Andalorax, "says you are my new King. This is monstrous! Prove this to me."

"What is your name?" asked Zivat-Or.

"Malthor. And once again I ask, why have you killed our King? Why are you our new King?"

"To explain why would take many days of conversation, Malthor." He lifted himself with his plant and drifted away from the balloon, then placed himself – floating on his Phemtas throne – before the First Eyeman.

"Can you not see that I am sitting upon a magical herb? It is called Phemtas. It gave all your past Kings their strength and power. Same as for me, Zivat-Or. It has served me well these two hundred and fifty years since I was your King."

"You have lived that long? But how?"

"I told you, it is due to the power of this plant. But come now, Malthor. Let us not trouble ourselves about this item. What is of a more poignant reality is that your King Vanamir is dead, and I am his rightful heir."

"How can I believe this nonsense?"

Gamedon came forward and said, "I have the proof. About sixteen years ago, I read this same prophesy – that has now become fact – in the King's Library. The prophesy was written in the words of a former Pellah King, Mundarak. If you allow us to take you there, you shall learn it for yourself." So saying, he reached his hand beneath his shirt, and withdrew a golden chain. Dangling from that chain were several keys, one of which shone more brightly than all the rest.

"The key to the King's Library," said Gamedon, fingering it delicately. And he remembered when he had taken it back from Zivat-Or in the volcano, thinking, "How wise I was to do that."

Malthor laughed loudly.

"Two hundred and fifty years old, provided by a magical herb?" He removed his feathered helmet and placed it on the ground beside him. "A secret kept by the

Pellah Kings for one thousand two-hundred and fifty years? Read prophesies in the King's Library foretelling of this event? What are you talking about?"

Malthor stepped forward and stared into the ancient, wrinkled green eyes of Zivat-Or.

"We stand here on the topmost turret of the Castle Pellah," he solemnly said to Zivat-Or, "while a storm rages about us, and you have just killed our King. Yet you matter-of-factly maintain that you are his successor and we are to bow down to you." Again, he laughed. "This is ridiculous!"

"Please note," intervened Siddles, standing still the great size he became when shielding the basket and its inhabitants, "that the storm is no longer raging."

Everyone looked around them, and this talking bird was, indeed, correct, for the dark skies had all blown away and the sky was now blue and clear. The snow was still on the ground, however. Little did they know that it was Siddles the One-Eyed who both created the storm and then ended it. Indeed, little did they suspect that he also was the one who created the balloon, and arranged for its descent to the top of the Tower.

"Now we have a talking bird of enormous height," announced Malthor. "This is some kind of witchery, being perpetrated upon us despite the fullness of the sun and the absence of the moon."

Zivat-Or and Gamedon glanced at each other, sharing the fact that they both were banished from the Kingdom for disbelieving what they called a myth. This glance was not lost upon Siddles.

"We do not share in that belief about the night being bad and the day being good," Siddles said, turning his one red eye upon Malthor. Then, pausing to turn fully around and regard the Knights, their hands full with arrows and bows, standing there speechless and not moving, Siddles went on to say, "Ye Knights of the Kingdom, be not afraid of us. We are different from what you are familiar with, that is true. But we are real, make no mistake about that. And we are here to fulfill a mission."

"That being what?" asked Dithmore, who now found his tongue.

"To remove your King Vanamir and install King Zivat-Or in his place," answered Siddles. He turned towards the ancient King, who was surrounded on his Phemtas throne being adored and hissed upon by the vines and leaves of the plant.

Siddles continued as he called out in his deep scratchy voice, still hissing his "esses."

"Ye Knights of the Kingdom of Pellah! Let me explain!"

All became hushed in a moment.

"This man is Zivat-Or; he was a true Pellah King about two hundred and fifty years ago, and was banished to the Black Mountains. This herb Phemtas has given him long life and strength. And he is here to alter the course of all your people, to abolish the fake decree about the characteristics of the night and the day."

"And I am part of that plan," interrupted Gamedon. "I, too, was banished from the Kingdom for not believing the false story about night and day."

"Why would it be false?" asked Malthor. "That is as ridiculous an idea as believing in this … this old 'man's' age. And a magical plant?" Again Malthor roared with laughter, then controlled himself.

"This is a grave moment," he said, lowering his voice. "Remember, our King Vanamir lies dead upon the snow, staining it red with his blood! You think this old man – if you can call it a man – should take Vanamir's place? Preposterous! In any case," he went on, turning towards the Knights circled around the turret's perimeter.

"Men!" he cried out. "Knights of the Kingdom of Pellah! You are to care for the body of our King, and bring him indoors and tend to him."

He continued, now beginning to lose his confusion and wonderment about this strange group of beings and taking control of himself. He continued: "There is no further use of our bows and arrows, and other forms of weaponry, as we have been assailed by this group of – people, plus a talking Wood Stork."

"I am not a Wood Stork," intervened Siddles. He was still as large as when he swelled his body up and let all the arrows glance off his body to protect those in the balloon. Andalorax had never experienced him as such; he was enormous! Practically as tall as a Portopuff tree!

"What are you then? I shall make something up: a Red-Beaked, Yellow-Footed Hornbill!" Malthor erupted once again in laughter. "No matter. You have the temerity to arrive in a balloon and kill our King with one fatal arrow. And," he turned to Andalorax, asking, "you are the one who shot it? You are the culpable party?"

"Aye, that is true."

Malthor noticed finally that her cloak wasn't the same color as it once was. As he stared further, he saw that her eyes and hair, too, were changing color as he watched.

"Are you a witch?" he asked. "Why are you so many different colors?"

"That's part of who I am," she replied. "I am the Many-Colored Girl. My name is Andalorax." She held out her hand to Malthor, who hesitated.

"I don't understand what is going on here," he said, "but I feel that somehow this is King Vanamir's fabled Destiny come to life. He warned us all that this was about to happen."

He took her hand.

"I do not understand, it is true, but in a strange way, I accept what has happened. Our good King Vanamir knew this would be his final hour. It was meant to be. Come, let us leave this bleak turret and go inside. I would learn more of what will come next."

Inside the Great Hall, now empty of the dishes and food of that morning's breakfast, Andalorax and Gamedon and Zivat-Or sat opposite Malthor and Dithmore. The Knights sat around the enormous dining table, all of Vanamir's Men of the Eyes, the Men of the Teeth, and also the Ten Men of the Coffers. Zivat-Or floated just a few inches above his chair, still ensconced by Phemtas.

But Siddles stood opposite Malthor, and said:

"You want to know why we killed your King?" His voice was like thunder. "I alone can answer that," he said, and he instantly pronounced his enchantment and reduced himself to his six-foot-high size. The Knights all gasped at this wizardly bird who must be dangerous or, at worse, evil.

"For generations now, since your people first set foot on this land and formed the Kingdom of Pellah, you have been controlled by a plant. A magical plant that has put a spell on every King since the very first one who was crowned one thousand two-hundred and fifty years ago.

"This plant, known as Phemtas, has wreaked havoc upon every succeeding King until it became necessary for it to be imbibed, or smoked, or eaten, or inhaled, in order for your Kings to maintain their power.

"This man you see here," he said, indicating Zivat-Or, as he sat upon his throne of Phemtas – which was writhing madly now as if it knew it was the center of attention – "has been most seriously afflicted. More so than any other of your Kings."

"Does this include Vanamir, who lies now within the dead man's vault, covered with a blanket made for the dead?" asked Malthor.

"Aye, it does. Vanamir was taken and consumed by Phemtas just as all his ancestral fathers were. But it is Zivat-Or, the man upon the Phemtas throne, who is most devoured and brought to ruin.

"And now that the lineage of the Kings of Pellah is finished, so, too is the power of Phemtas!"

Everyone was silent. They were all staring at Siddles. After a while, Andalorax spoke.

"You mean, the plant has no more strength over the will of the Kingdom of Pellah?" she asked.

"Exactly," answered Siddles. "There is no more King to devour, it is satiated, and it can do no more harm for there is no one alive who can be touched by it."

"Not so!" cried out Zivat-Or. "I alone wear the Phemtas mantle! I am one with the plant! It is my power and strength!"

"Alas, no more," sighed Siddles. His one red eye stared directly into the green ones of the ancient King. "Phemtas cannot live anymore, except for you. And you, Zivat-Or, cannot live anymore as well. Without it, you should have died many, many years ago. And now it is your fate, your Destiny if you will, to pass into that realm we know of as death."

Zivat-Or wrestled in his mind with an answer to this speech, but he was without words. Then he spoke:

"I do not want to die!" he cried out. "You did not tell me this when we made our plans! And why wasn't it I who shot the arrow that gave the King his mortal wound?"

"Our plans have changed," answered Siddles. "Andalorax was meant to destroy Vanamir, and this she did."

Zivat-Or cried out, "I don't want to die! I am the true King of Pellah!"

But at that very moment, the plant upon which he sat, which all this time had writhed and curled around him, instantly dissolved and dissipated, and turned to dust and fell in an ash-like substance upon the floor of the Pinnacle Tower. A breeze came and blew that dust away.

All that stood there was a very old man, a man over two hundred and fifty years old, a man who had no more energy and power to live.

"Alas, no more," repeated Siddles. "Your power is gone, King Zivat-Or, and you shall join your ancestors."

"What shall happen to the lands of the Black Mountains, my homeland?" he asked, his voice becoming feeble.

"Phemtas has seen its death, as did Vanamir, and as shall you. You will dissolve and turn to ash just as the Phemtas plant did here right now. The lands shall spring anew with greenery and life as they once were, and the Black Mountains shall be black no more."

Andalorax spoke up and said, "You mean, when you took me across the landscape and showed me the white plant that had taken life from everything and left only bare black rock … that shall be no more?"

"Aye, Andalorax," answered Siddles, ruffling his feathers and straightening out his posture. "And while I am speaking to you now, it is happening in the Black Mountains. Come now! Do not be confused! This is reality in the world of magic. Indeed, there is nothing so real as magic! We shall rename them the Rainbow Mountains for there will be color everywhere."

He turned to Zivat-Or.

"You, my King, shall move on as was intended by your natural life."

"I can feel myself withering away," he answered, his voice weakening to a whisper. Without his Phemtas throne, he was a skinny wrinkled old man in a baggy suit of brown fabric. "I somehow am in agreement. I understand. I go willingly."

And then the magic spell was reality and he turned to ashes and dust and another breeze came and blew it all away.

CHAPTER 44

THE RIGHTFUL RULER

WHILE ALL THIS HUBBUB WAS still happening in the Great Hall, Gamedon slid from his chair and disappeared from the crowd, silently gliding through an open doorway.

It was dark for quite a while and he had to light his bit of candle, but he finally came into the illuminating light coming through the cracks in doorways as he passed them by.

Using his remarkable powers of hiding in plain sight, he slipped past courtiers and their wives chatting away. The people of Pellah Castle knew not yet what had happened atop the Pinnacle Tower and that their King was dead, so they chatted easily. He passed children playing and skipping down the stairs that wound their way around the perimeter of the stairway. But he made his way up, up and higher up still. He was heading for a secret doorway, the one leading to the King's Library.

Gamedon suddenly sensed that he was in an area with which he was familiar, and right enough, he passed the carved Calicab door to his old chamber and Laboratory. "Beautiful door!" he said, rubbing his hand across its polished surface, "You still hold magic, yet I shall not need you, nor what memories you protect, on this day."

He then passed the small simple wooden door to Andalorax's old rooms, and eventually reached the massive doorway to the King's chambers. He felt along the stone wall. Finally, he touched a dark patch of stone and he knew he had found it: the hidden door to the King's Library. He reached his hand under his shirt, and felt the small golden key in his hand.

"Aha!" he said aloud. "My sweet little piece of gold! Come and do what you were meant to do." He felt along the wall for the small keyhole, found it, and then inserted the little replicated key inside of it. "Now comes the moment of truth," he said, and gently turned the key in the lock.

It rotated easily and the stone doorway slid open.

"I am relieved," he spoke aloud, "to learn that you – my tiny key that I forged so long ago the night we fled the Castle – actually works!" He laughingly clapped his hands together and did a little dance in the darkened staircase. "You have made me happy, you infinitesimally small, golden wonder! Now," he continued, pushing the door open, "let us enter."

Immediately the scent of old leather and paper and cold stone assailed his nostrils, and he recognized the familiarity of that odor from well over a year ago. It brought a sense of nostalgia to his heart, as he remembered what had driven him mad inside of this haunting set of rooms on the eve of their secret departure.

"Mundarak," he whispered, and a chill ran down his spine. "I shall find you again, old King of Pellah, for I have need of you yet once more."

So saying, the old man went to the shelves way to his left, in a far corner of the room. He found the rows of manuscripts just as they had been when he was searching for the prophesies of which King Vanamir had foretold him over a year ago.

They were chronologically arranged. In that far corner, the beginnings of the Kingdom were inscribed in ancient diaries of the first Kings. He saw once again the five books of Mundarak, neatly bound and tooled. He pulled down the fifth and last one that bore the inscription "Mundarak." It was easily found, as he remembered clearly holding the book in his hands before.

The leather binding, dark and smooth, bore gold letters stamped upon its surface. They read:

King Mundarak: Prophysyes
Pellah Years 275-321

He opened the book. The pages were yellow and fairly crumbling at his touch. Gently, Gamedon ran his fingers across the first pages that bore words of those early days some thousand years ago. He recalled opening this book before – the main part of it, at least.

"Now," he thought, "I can read it through to the end."

Holding his thick piece of candle aloft, he stopped and looked up at the ceiling, vaulted and made of stone and Calicab wood.

"Where are you, King Mundarak?" he said aloud. "Let me find you once again!"

A cold wind passed through the Library chambers, and Gamedon actually felt a draft wash across his fingers. The breeze flipped open the pages of the diary. When the pages stopped turning, towards the end of the book, Gamedon looked down and read what he saw: that the dates of these prophesies were later than when he had read Mundarak's words last year, just prior to escaping with Andalorax.

"Mundarak, I call you to come to me!" he cried out loudly. "What am I to read on these pages that you lead me to?"

He heard a moaning sound which grew louder and louder. Then he heard these words of the voice, which was deep and yet seemed to fill the room:

> *Whosoever followeth myn Eye*
> *Wyth hys lyfe's Bloode*
> *Shalle sygnyfye.*

He had heard these words before and knew just what to do. Without hesitation, Gamedon unclasped his cloak and pricked the index finger of his left hand with the pin and let the blood drop onto the page to which the wind had brought him. The thick red blood sizzled and dried instantly.

"Aye, King Mundarak! Lead me on to wherever you want me to go. I shall follow!"

The wind began again, and a howling came seemingly from nowhere, but reverberated throughout the room.

> *Aiee! Aiee! He calles me back*
> *And speakes the nayme of Mundarak!*
> *Gamedon, come to me once more*
>
> *Tap! Tap! His foote ypon this floore*
> *Hold high the lyghte, open the doore*
> *And I will show you so much more!*

Gamedon turned his head around to see where there might be a door. He saw none. He got up and felt along the walls where there were no shelves. Still no door.

"*Tap! Tap! His foote ypon this floore* ..." he repeated Mundarak's words, in the ancient accent. Then he knew once more what he must do: he must tap his foot upon the floor! Raising the candle high above his head, he tapped upon the floor.

Then he heard a loud crunching sound, as if glass were being ground into sand. Right before his eyes, Gamedon saw a stone doorway slide open, then stop.

"Mundarak! I call you back! What more shall you show me?"

Gamedon heard the voice say:

> *Beyond the doore, beyond the staire,*
> *You will find a lady fayre,*
> *Her eyes be black, her hair be long,*
> *Her hands be white, she synges a song.*
> *This fayre damselle will then show*
> *You what you want to know!*

Gamedon went to the doorway and stuck his head in the opening. Cold air wafted up from a dark cellar down below. A narrow stone staircase stood before him, and he knew he must descend. But he turned his head back to the table whereon the diary of Mundarak rested. Its yellowed pages moved not, for the breeze had stopped. He knew he must first read on and so returned to the table.

"Mundarak," he called out. "What lies beyond the door? What more is there to read before I descend the stairway?"

The voice answered:

> *Start at the page whereon you see*
> *A tiny reference to me.*
> *For I shall guide your steps along*
> *When the fayre damsylle sings her song.*

> *He who reads my words must turn*
> *This page, if he shalle want to learn*
> *Wherein the damsylle does abide*
> *And from the reader will not hide*
> *The future of the world unseen,*
> *Wherein resides a newfound Queen.*

Gamedon turned the page, which crackled and crumbled a bit as he did so. The next page bore a drawing of a horse with a rider astride, a rider with long flowing locks and wearing a dress.

"A newfound Queen!" he called out, and recited what came into his head:

Make your Highness known to me,
As I wait here for your prophesy!

Silence fell into the chambers of the Library. Gamedon moved not. Mundarak spoke not. And neither damsel nor Queen made herself visible. Gamedon waited patiently … then he heard these words:

Gamedon, man of words and wytte,
Behold the chayre whereon you sit.
For it shall brynge you to the place,
Wherein you'll find your new Queen's face.

Suddenly, the arms of Gamedon's chair grew longer and wider, and the legs lifted it and took him away from the table and the diary of King Mundarak. It rose from the stone floor and floated over to the wall. Gamedon sat patiently, for he suspected and hoped there was some secret, unseen opening through this wall that would reveal Mundarak's "damsel" and "newfound Queen." He leaned forward and touched the cold stone, pressing his hand against it and moving his fingers inch by inch along its seams and fissures. Finally, he found a small wooden button, which he pushed. A doorway revealed itself.

"What lies beyond?" wondered Gamedon.

The large chair drifted loosely into the opening carrying Gamedon with it. Then it sat itself down and resumed its normal size. A blaze of many candles unexpectedly lit themselves up inside this small room filled with spider webs and dust and nothing else.

"Mundarak!" he called out. "Show me what I am meant to see!" The same resounding gravelly voice that echoed in the Library was now inside this little room.

You have no further need of me
So I now seek eternity.
Begone from me, old Gamedon man
I have shown you all I can.
Farewell, my final prophysye
Is you shalle set the new Queen free.

Gamedon lifted his head from the manuscript, and spoke into the cool, moist air of the Library.

"Mundarak!" he said. "Not so fast, I beg of you! Where shall I find the damsel and the Queen?"

"Aiee! Aiee!" called out the resounding voice. "Gamedon, thou knowest thou must read further in my diary! I shall open to the page!" With that, the diary fanned its pages open a little further, then stopped and lay still.

The voice moaned some more.

"Aiee! Aiee! Go hither, Master Gamedon. Read to the end of the manuscript!"

At the same time, a great whirlwind rose up from the center of the room, and Gamedon saw the remnants of a vaporized crowned King disappearing into the whirling mist.

"Read on to the end!" the voice called out one final time.

Then the flash of a vision of Mundarak inside the whirlwind became a breeze that wafted over to Mundarak's diary. The breeze was sucked into the pages, and the book's leather cover slammed shut and it echoed in the stone and wood rooms therein. Magically, the cord re-wrapped itself around it and tied itself into a knot.

"Mundarak! I call you back!"

Nothing.

The room was calm and silent. Gamedon knew then what had happened. The ancient King Mundarak was gone forever.

Gamedon sighed, arose from the chair – somehow now its normal size – and lifted it, moving it back into the main room of the Library, where it had been just before, in front of the diary on the desk. Gamedon sat down and stared at the manuscript now tied up. Stamped atop the leather binding were these words:

King Mundarak: Prophysyes
Pellah Years 275-321

He untied it and opened it yet again, and turned to the page where he had just been reading. He found the site. It was towards the last pages of the diary.

He read on.

> *Your King is dead this afternoon,*
> *The King, who makes us fear the Moon!*
> *No longer now shall our Kingdom fight*
> *The black beliefs about the Night.*
>
> *But now upon the scene shall enter*
> *The Queen, who brings us to the center.*
> *The Queen! Who shall replace the King;*
> *You'll know her by her sacred ring.*

Gamedon stopped and reread these words, Mundarak's final prophesies. "A Queen?" he said, then called out, "Show yourself!"

Then he saw a mist come creeping out of the open doorway from the empty room wherein he had encountered King Mundarak for this second time. The mist formed into a small tornado-shaped whirlwind, which caused a great commotion in the room by summoning up much wind.

"Now what is this?" asked Gamedon.

"'Tis I, but the Wind, Master Gamedon!" came a booming voice that echoed in the small room and made Gamedon's ears hurt.

"Oh, Wind!" he cried, "Why am I summoned to meet with you? Are you in King Mundarak's prophesies?"

"Aye, 'tis that I am. In the prophesies, I appear everywhere throughout all time and space. King Mundarak traveled in time and space, seeing into the future for centuries to come. You yourself have witnessed such a thing, Master Gamedon! Here, in this same chamber!

"Aye, 'tis true," said the old man. "But tell me, Master Wind, why am I sent to you? What can you show me about the time yet to come? If anything, please, I beg of you, let me know!"

"I have a message for you, Master Gamedon."

Gamedon stood still as he repeated those words in his head. "A message? What can it be, coming from the Wind?"

The Wind blew in cold and chilly, with drafts skirting off the stones in the wall and making quite a ruckus. Then the Wind started to swirl in the middle of the room – surrounded by those dusty manuscripts and books – and turn and become a wind cone of swirling bright lights, like a carousel. The lights appeared like twinkling stars in the skies, not solid but ephemeral and impossible to focus upon.

Then it sang out these words in a soft and gentle tone:

> *They chose the Wind*
> *For it best can sing*
> *The legend of*
> *The murdered King.*
>
> *What shall follow?*
> *And be seen?*
> *A vision of*
> *A mighty Queen.*
>
> *There comes a man*
> *Who has guided her along*
> *Yet he must let her go*
> *And sing her song.*

The Wind calmed down after it had sung these words to Gamedon, yet it stayed in the room, causing perpetual breezes.

"Master Wind," he said, "you certainly can sing a marvelous song. I think you have a most powerful voice and you have tremendous range from octave to octave."

"Well, I thank you kindly."

"Tell me, in your poem, is that man who guides the Queen along supposed to

340

be me, Master Wind?"

"That I do not know. I can merely sing for you what has been recited in my ears – so to speak. Have you guided someone along?"

"Aye," answered Gamedon with a spark in his eye. "My granddaughter Andalorax."

'Well, then, you must let her go, in my humble opinion," said the Wind, in loud terms that echoed off the shelves of books. "That was in my message, remember?"

"Must I?"

"Aye."

"Then who is the Queen?" asked Gamedon.

"Surely you must know, for I don't!"

"Once again, I must answer: 'Andalorax.'"

"A funny name," laughed the Wind. It kept up its laughter until it – in the form of great gusts – appeared to be rushing back and forth, as if it were drunk, like a twirling top leaning back and forth, side-to-side.

Then the Wind suddenly swirled around yet again, and then began to reduce itself into a tiny tornado, twirling atop the Library desk.

"My message is not finished," it said. "Do you wish to hear the rest of it?"

"Aye, I surely do."

"Very well," announced the Wind. "Here I go!"

He raised her up to be a Queen –
But Queen of Where is to be seen!

"What does that mean?" queried Gamedon to the still-twirling tornado.

"I know not," answered the Wind. "But now I must be going. There are other messages that will go to people, delivered by me, the Wind! Fare thee well!" sang out a voice that sounded far, far away, for it was coming from deep within the tornado.

"'Queen of Where?'" repeated Gamedon, once the Wind volcano had disappeared and the Library became still yet again. The candles stopped flickering.

"Does the message refer to Andalorax?" he pondered. "Surely it must! Whom else could it be?"

He looked down at the table where the Wind had been in the form of a human-sized tornado, and there, sparkling in the candlelight, was a gold ring.

Gamedon picked it up and looked at it, turning it all around. It was made of purest gold; Gamedon easily knew the sight of gold from that one year with Zivat-Or. He knew the old King's shirt of solid gold mail – without which Gamedon had never seen him – and the long, serpentine gold chain he wore around his neck with its many gold keys. And he also knew gold after his fifteen years at the Castle Pellah living just at the foot of the Gold Mountains.

He looked inside the ring for an inscription, but there was none. Yet, atop the ring, there was one oval-shaped single stone, about as large as his thumbnail, shining and sparkling, of a deep wine-red color. It was surrounded by diamonds.

He held the ring up to a candle and examined the stone.

"A ruby," he said. "And quite a rare and beautiful one at that." Holding it up to the candlelight, he then went on:

"I can look deeply into this stone and become hypnotized. This ring must be the ring that I am to give to the new Queen." He slapped his palm upon the wooden table. "Yes, of course! The prophesy is coming true as I sit here. Right now, at this very moment!" Gamedon became excited and he jumped a little jig as was his wont when he was lucky. "For here is the ring that was spoken of in the book from which I only just now read!"

But who was the Queen?

Andalorax.

None other.

It had to be!

And yet, what did the Wind say, its final message … "Let me think oh yes!" the old man said, touching his forehead. He closed his eyes and repeated the final words that were Messages on the Wind:

He raised her up to be a Queen –
But Queen of Where is to be seen!

Nothing happened.

Gamedon was glad. He read on, turning to the last page.

Page one hundred and fifty-five.

Gamedon stood up and stretched his arms and wondered what this question meant, "Queen of Where."

Yes, Queen of Where indeed?

The Kingdom of Pellah! That became his instant yet logical answer.

"It must therefore now follow that Andalorax will become Queen of the Kingdom. For now there is no male heir and the Pellah line of Kings is finished forever." He laughed and did his jig.

"Yes," he then decided, calming down. "She will be Queen of the Kingdom, from the Calicab Forest down south to the Gold Mountains up north!"

Gamedon pulled out the magic chair and sat down, touching once again the lion's paws curved into the arm rests. He pulled himself forward towards the table. He untied the portfolio's slender but supple braided-leather binding straps and opened yet again King Mundarak's *Prophysyes* He turned to the page where he had just been reading. He found the site. It was on page one hundred and fifty-six, which he saw was the next to last page of the diary.

"Yes! There remains only one page!" he whispered.

So there, on page one-hundred and fifty-six, he had read about the Queen, "'who wears a sacred ring,' according to King Mundarak," thought Gamedon. But then another thought came to his mind:

"And also, I must ask, shall this new Kingdom now and forever forfeit the ancient Pellah Belief System wherein the day is good and the night is evil? Wherein the day brings us happy faeries and the night, malevolent witches?"

Gamedon rubbed his eyes and looked up. The room was still. He thought, "This would mean a tremendous thing is about to happen: both I and King Zivat-Or are exonerated by the Kingdom! We are now innocent, we who had been banished for not agreeing with the Kingdom's beliefs, we whose lives had been uprooted and, in the case of Zivat-Or, demolished." Gamedon quickly remembered the old King, who only that day, had still been alive.

He turned to the last page, anticipating King Mundarak's final prophesies. Gamedon was astonished at what he saw. There, the four sides of the margins were adorned with beautiful gold scrollwork, clearly framing what writings and markings were inside.

"Presumably, Mundarak could draw," thought Gamedon, "Unless some loyal scribe of his created these designs at Mundarak's orders."

But what made Gamedon gasp was what was on the book's last page: At the top, a heading read, "Visits." Underneath that, there were about twenty different signatures and dried drops of blood next to each one. Some were scribbled; others were neat and trim; still others were unrecognizable and illegible. Gamedon scrutinized each one.

Suddenly, what he was looking for appeared on that page one hundred and fifty-seven: It was the signature which read these telling words.

"King Vanamir, 1240."

The handwriting was large but legible and in blue ink.

"So Vanamir has been here," said Gamedon aloud, "to this very last page. This means he knew about what was to happen to him! He had read the portents of issues of a greatly personal matter to him – such as, the 'murdered King,' and the 'mighty Queen.' Surely he knew that there was no escaping his Destiny."

Gamedon began to read some of the other names signed to that page, but suddenly the book slammed shut, and the ribbon rewrapped itself yet again. When he returned the diary to its proper spot in the Library, he said, "Farewell, little room. You have given me much."

A chill blast of breeze swept into the room and Gamedon heard, "Old man! Listen!" It was the Wind, returned.

"Forget not my messages to you," it cried out, moaning low, "and forget not all the words therein! Forget not the murdered King, nor the mighty Queen! And most of all, forget not that the Guide must let go of his apprentice, his pupil, his granddaughter!"

Gamedon was aghast at what the Wind just said.

"Then there is no doubt, Master Wind," he asked, as the Wind swirled around him, "that Andalorax is the mighty Queen who shall replace the murdered King?"

"No doubt," cried out the Wind, in a woeful tone.

"Why do you moan?" asked Gamedon.

"Because you do not yet know the answer to the key question!"

"And what is that?"

"The question is: 'The Queen of Where?'" called back the Wind.

"The Queen of the Kingdom of Pellah, of course!" answered Gamedon. "Just as Vanamir was King of the Kingdom."

"That does not have to be."

The Wind began to laugh heartily, sending brisk little breezes right there in the calm, stone Library.

"Where else is there?"

"Don't you remember, old man? Ha! Ha!" The Wind laughed raucously.

"No! I don't know. Where?"

"Why," laughed the Wind, "she could choose to be Queen of the place that has been instantly cleansed and purged of the Phemtas plant! That is the magic of Siddles! She could choose to be part of curing the damage done over the years. After all, that is what Siddles shall choose. The place flourishes anew thanks to the magic of Siddles who can heal the countryside by providing abundant natural resources."

The Wind ceased its talking and whipped up a small storm that whooshed around Gamedon's head.

"Yes," it said, "Andalorax could choose to be Queen of that magical place instead of the Kingdom of Pellah and all its people who will want her to be their Queen."

"And where is that, Master Wind?"

"Where, you ask? Ha ha! You ask me still?" it laughed loudly, causing the ground beneath them to fly up in a dusty flurry.

"Queen of The Rainbow Mountains, of course," said the Wind, "you silly old man!" And with that, the Wind swirled up into a dark gray tornado that reached the ceiling, then spun like a top, and exploded into the air and disappeared, just as Gamedon caught Mundarak's diary and kept it from blowing off the table.

The next day found Andalorax, Siddles, Gamedon and Malthor once more atop the Pinnacle Tower. They were flanked by the other nineteen Men of the Eyes, the Twenty Men of the Teeth, and the Ten Men of the Coffers. Up so high, they could view far, far away, and see the ribbon of the Golden River winding its course southwards.

Siddles – now six feet tall instead of his normal twelve feet – raised his heavy head to the fresh breezes that blew hard up there.

"I shall be making my departure," he said. "My work here is finished."

"When shall that be, dearest Siddles?" asked Andalorax.

"Any day now, my Queen!"

"I am not your Queen!"

"Oh yes, you are my Queen. You are THE Queen. But Queen of Where remains to be decided."

"I am not Queen of the Kingdom of Pellah!" she announced. "I choose to be Queen of the Rainbow Mountains!"

The entire assembly cheered, "Hurrah! Hurrah for the Queen of the Rainbow Mountains!"

Gamedon lifted his head to the wind and stared at her. Tears sprang from his eyes as he said, "I knew you would decide that, Andalorax. And it is just and fit. But who shall rule the Kingdom?"

"Why, Gamedon, it shall be you!" answered Siddles, stretching and spreading his wide wings and then settling them against his enormous chest.

Gamedon turned to him. "Me? Oh no! I cannot accept such a position."

"It must be you."

"I am too old!"

"No, Gamedon, dear Grandfather," exclaimed Andalorax, "you are not too old. You are perfect for the role of King. You are wise from your many years of life, including especially those fifteen years here in the Castle with the King."

Gamedon asked, "But will the people accept me?"

Malthor interjected: "Aye, they shall accept you."

He raised his staff and the flag of Pellah at its top blew in the breeze up at the Pinnacle Tower.

"Being the First Eyeman, riding always just behind King Vanamir, I am officially the temporary ruler of the Kingdom, now that he has died. The people know this. But you shall not be King! We no longer shall have a King. I shall decree your newly created position to Supreme Ruler of the Kingdom."

"No longer a King?" He looked at his granddaughter, tall and multi-colored.

"No," said the former Chief Knight of Vanamir. "Now you shall be the Supreme Ruler. The old days are gone. The fears of night have been revealed for what they were: a ruse developed by the Kings to keep our people indoors at sunset – thus ensuring peace in the land."

Siddles laughed in his now-familiar way, with his gruff and deep voice.

"Well spoken, Malthor. I am proud of you to have accepted this premise as fact and reality." He turned to Andalorax and said, "This is excellent, Granddaughter!"

Then to Gamedon he said, "I know you do not feel yourself fit for this role, Gamedon. But it shall come to you as time passes. Yet I shall instill in you a power to rule, a power of which you have never known."

So saying, Siddles bent his head down and whispered in Gamedon's ear, and said:

"And I shall endow you with gifts that will help you make this transition. You shall see what I have in store for you!"

With that, Siddles turned towards Andalorax and bowed low, tapping his hard red beak on the floor of the Pinnacle Tower, in his manner of supplication and respect for the newly named Queen.

Andalorax nodded in acceptance of his humility, and added, "In fact, as of today, I shall declare Gamedon's high position to be my final wish here in the Kingdom."

"And you, Andalorax," Gamedon turned to her and asked, "shall you abandon the hopes of the people of the Kingdom and return to the Black Mountains?"

She turned towards Gamedon and laughed. "They are now the Rainbow Mountains, as you know," she said. "The control that Phemtas had over those mountains and valleys is gone, with the magic of Siddles." She turned to the great bird and smiled widely.

"Aye, that is true," echoed Siddles. "Yet we shall be accompanied by many of the people here who wish to begin life anew in that prosperous place which is now filled with young greenery, sprouting trees and flowers and grasses, and of course hope and love."

"You shall be going there, as well?"

"Aye," said Siddles. "To the Rainbow Mountains."

"So we must begin preparations for our journey," stated Andalorax. "We shall commence our departure once Gamedon has been accepted by the people as Supreme Ruler and has accustomed himself to that position. And I shall not fly in Siddles' claw this time!" At this, she laughed loudly and everyone cheered.

"How shall you travel then, Andalorax?" asked Malthor, his red beard shining in the sunlight, braided down his chest.

"We shall ride on horseback," she answered, "in a caravan of citizens of Pellah who will be relocating to the Rainbow Mountains with their families and friends. Malthor, please arrange with your Knights to announce this to the citizenry so that they may make plans. They will need their horses for travel, but they shall also be bringing their farm animals as well as their belongings and furniture and tools and other equipment."

"Quite the caravan!" said Malthor, still holding high his staff with the Pellah flag atop. "Of course, my Queen, I shall do this immediately. And I shall also retain a written record which notes every single person – from babes to elders – who is leaving for the southern flanks of our borders."

With Malthor's proclamation, Andalorax raised high her arms and her multi-colored cape flared out in the wind. She seemed larger than life to those watching, and everyone bowed down to her.

"Long live the Queen of the Rainbow Mountains!" they cheered, and added, "Long live the Supreme Ruler of the Kingdom of Pellah!"

"Let us leave this place," Andalorax declared loudly to those present. "Let us all begin anew our occupations and our actions that shall move us all forward into the future."

"Whether that future be good or bad," stated Gamedon.

Andalorax shook her head and replied, "No, Gamedon. It shall all be grand and good for all the people of all these great lands. I hereby decree that this is how we are to view our tomorrows!"

With that, her cape turned blood red, her hair became bright yellow, and her eyes flashed purple.

"Ah!" said Siddles. "Purple eyes, my Queen. Purple is my favorite color."

"Well do I know that, my dear Siddles," she said with a smile. "Although it's not within my power to select the colors that change upon my body, purple shall be the main color of our new flag in the Rainbow Mountains."

Siddles smiled in his fashion, with his beak closed but the muscles on either side of it curled back towards his cheeks.

"In fact," continued Andalorax, "I shall design the new flag of the Rainbow Mountains right now! I shall make it a lovely warm shade of purple, with a white full moon and a golden sun within its center, and the flag shall be surrounded all along its four borders with stars. Let the stars be all the colors of the rainbow: violet, blue, green, yellow, orange and red. So, let this be my first ruling as Queen of the Rainbow Mountains!"

Andalorax turned towards Siddles and asked, "Can you fabricate such a flag here and now for us?"

Siddles called out:

Krimskee Satchom flibbet!

There, in front of the crowd, next to Malthor, a flag appeared, flying from a wooden flagpole stuck in the ground.

The Knights all tossed their caps in the air as they admired the beautiful flag.

She turned to the Knights and said, "That is enough decision-making today! Let us all disperse and go about our business!"

"Long live Andalorax, Queen of the Rainbow Mountains!" they all shouted.

Siddles nudged her in the shoulder with a wingtip and whispered, "Aye, my Queen! Long shall you reign!"

CHAPTER 45

ANDALORAX & MANDIR MEET

"MOTHER," CRIED OUT ANDALORAX, "'TIS I, your Andalorax, come to see you and set you free from your confinement in this Tower."

Upon hearing her daughter's voice – which she knew from meeting her annually upon Andalorax's birthday – Mandir stood up from her rocking chair and rushed over to open the door to her apartment. They embraced, holding each other tightly for a long silent moment, and kissed one another. Mandir burst into tears.

Then she stood back, as the pair held hands, and she immediately noticed the many colors her daughter sported, and that also changed constantly – her cape and dress, her hair, and her eyes. Right now, Andalorax had azure blue eyes, flaming orange hair, and wore a purple cape with lilac dress.

"How comes it that you are able to change colors, my daughter?" She was genuinely perplexed.

"Magic, plain and simple, Mother dear," said her daughter. "I have been given this gift by a friend who conferred it upon me. Oh, 'tis a long tale, and will take much time to tell. But from now on, we will have all the time we want, for I have come to liberate you from this room in the Wives' Turret."

"What has happened?"

"King Vanamir is dead. I am the one who did the deed by shooting him in his heart with a fateful arrow."

"You? You killed the King?"

"Aye," said Andalorax, "and that, too, is a long tale to tell. Let us sit down and talk about what is happening here in the Kingdom of Pellah – which is now called the Nation of Pellah!"

Mandir led her daughter to a plush sofa, fit for two, and they sat themselves down.

"Mother," began Andalorax, "I am here not only to free you but also all the King's wives."

"When did this happen?"

"Three days ago, and I have been busy with the Knights, and the King's Ministers and counsellors, making arrangements for the new Nation and all its people. We have announced this news to the people of the Castle, and surely this news will spread all over the lands quite quickly. You and the other wives, shielded as you all are from the news of Pellah, are among the last to hear of it."

Mandir, slowly becoming accustomed somewhat to her daughter's changing hues, smiled brightly at this news of her liberation.

"I and all the other wives are to be set free?"

"Aye, Mother. Immediately!"

Mandir turned her head and looked out the sparkling stained-glass windows that afforded her a view of the rest of the Castle and the Gold Mountains to the north, very far away but shining in the sunlight. She pressed her hand into her daughter's, and began to cry once more.

"These are tears of joy, my dearest daughter," she said, when Andalorax looked perturbed at seeing the tears flow down her mother's cheeks. "What is to happen to me now?"

Andalorax had never been here before, in her mother's rooms. Now, as she looked about her, she was instantly surprised at the pleasant accommodations, from the lush raised bed and down comforter covered in a velvet spread to the carved wooden writing desk and chair, and the comfortable seating arrangement upon which she now found herself.

"Now, let me tell you the tale of my many colors, dearest Mother," she said, and proceeded at the beginning when she first met the Many-Colored Girl in the woods outside the Castle, and at the Silent Lake, and also on Budgerigar Island in the land of the Galinda-Hussadi. Then she told her of the meeting when the Many-Colored Girl identified herself as Xaroladna, and the two of them switched their appearances.

After that, catching her breath, she went on to tell her about King Zivat-Or and Siddles, which, upon hearing these tales, made Mandir open wide her eyes with the visualization of it all.

"A talking bird who can create but not destroy!" said Mandir, at the end of this long history. "A two-hundred and fifty-year-old King! A plant which had overtaken the Kings of Pellah and the Black Mountains – which are now the Rainbow Mountains! The island of the Galinda-Hussadi! It is almost too much to take in, daughter dear."

Andalorax then finished her story with the final flight in the hot-air balloon, and the assassination of King Vanamir, shot in the heart by her own hand. Mandir was truly surprised at this final episode.

"Well do I remember that morning when I bared you as a babe to the King. I had no idea you would grow up to become such a fierce young woman."

Then Andalorax asked her mother the question she had always had locked up in her heart.

"Mother," she whispered, taking her hand in hers, "who is my father?"

Mandir and Andalorax looked deeply into each other's eyes – Mandir's being a deep forest green and her daughter's, at that particular moment, were tangerine. Mandir had by now become accustomed to the changing of colors in her daughter. As she stared into Andalorax's tangerine irises, they transformed into sky blue, and her costume became bright pink.

A few seconds passed until she replied, "I cannot tell you this, my daughter."

"Cannot or will not?"

"Both."

"Why?"

"I have never revealed his identity, as he came from a world that I knew nothing about, although I can tell you, at the time you were born, he was living in Milorin."

"Yet you knew him well?"

"Aye, daughter. We knew each other very well. But I can tell you this: he was not from the Kingdom of Pellah."

"From where was he?"

"This I never learned. Only that he was a foreigner to our Kingdom and lived in Milorin by choice."

Andalorax began to fidget but held onto her mother's hand.

"Did you love him?"

"Aye, we loved each other greatly."

"Can you tell me something about him?"

"Well, he was extremely intelligent and handsome and quite tall. At least, he seemed to be that way to me! But he did not share the red hair and green eyes of the people of the Kingdom."

"What did he look like?"

Mandir hesitated, letting go of her daughter's hand and arising and going over to the stained-glass windows. She stared out and then said, "Come here, Andalorax. I wish to show you something."

Andalorax got up and went over to her mother, and realized she once more had tears in her eyes.

"Mother, you are crying!"

"Aye, my daughter. The memory of your father brings back much sentiment and even sadness, for, as you know, I had to leave Milorin – and your father – when King Vanamir took us away to his Castle. I suffered greatly when that happened, and I still do."

"He could not follow you?"

"Absolutely not. I was to become a wife of the King, after all. It would have been highly inappropriate. The King would never have approved and danger might result. Besides, dearest daughter, Milorin was his home, even though he was neither born nor raised there."

"Where, then, did he come from?"

"As I told you, I do not know. And if I did, I would not tell you. He made me promise this secrecy when you and I were taken away."

Both mother and daughter stared outside the window, looking down at the ground below. There was a park with a gold-tiled pathway, and many topiaries and statues and small fountains. Women and young girls sat or walked on benches along that path.

"Pay attention down below, daughter." Mandir tapped the glass and pointed. "Do you see the other wives of the King with their daughters? They used to be obliged to wear scarves over their faces. That has changed now that Vanamir is dead and your grandfather – my father – is in his place as Supreme Ruler. You can see their countenances now, take note!

"Each of those wives represented Vanamir's hopes for a son to carry on in his stead," continued Mandir. "None was able to give him one; they all had one daughter then became infertile. The King continued his search almost yearly for one wife after the other to fulfill his hopes for a boy.

"Andalorax, my daughter, as you know, those girls are all the King's daughters.

Also as you know, a daughter was never allowed to become a ruler of the Kingdom, only sons. They are reuniting. This I know now that he is dead, and surely they are all learning of his death, and life in the Kingdom has completely altered and we are free at last."

"What has this to do with my father?"

"I am told by way of travelers throughout the Kingdom that after your birth and after King Vanamir took us away, your father disappeared from Milorin and was never seen again."

"Not even by you?"

"Not even by me." Mandir wiped her eyes and went on with her story.

"I am the only one of the King's wives who never even gave him a daughter. Upon arrival here at the Castle, I apparently became infertile almost immediately. I could not give him even a daughter." She stared out the window.

Then Mandir turned around and looked once more into her daughter's eyes, which were now purple, and said in a firm voice, "You see, I am different from all those wives. I had no daughter with Vanamir. And you are different not only from the King's daughters – because he is not your father – but from everyone! You have a father who is known to no one but me, and I know very little of him, at that." After a quiet moment, Mandir added, "but nonetheless, we were very much in love."

Andalorax held her mother close and kissed her on both cheeks. Mandir's tears had ceased by then. Then she told her daughter, "I understand from your long tale just now that you are going to the Rainbow Mountains to be Queen there. I also understand that quite a few people of this Kingdom will be accompanying you on your journey there – and who knows how many individuals and families will join you as you pass them by on the Golden River Road."

"Yes, Mother. That is what I have heard and plan for. We shall be at the Rainbow Mountains when a new beginning comes to be."

Mandir smiled.

"I will be part of that new society, my daughter, if you shall allow me my fondest wish to be part of your life for the first time in these sixteen years."

Andalorax's eyes turned bright yellow, her cloak and gossamer-like dress became violet, and her hair was now cerulean blue as she answered her mother by throwing her arms around her and saying, "Mother, dear! I was hoping for this moment to come true! Of course, you are most welcome and shall travel by my side on the entire route. Siddles shall create a real home for us – not a Castle! And we shall be together from that time forward."

"Then I had best start packing, for I know you will want to leave very soon."

"Aye, mother. We shall be on the road within a week. But do not bring these dreary clothes that remind us of your troubles here as a wife of the King. Siddles shall generate your wardrobe – he can do these things, you know!

"So bring only yourself, and all your dreams of the future we shall have together."

After visiting her mother, Andalorax went back to her rooms, which were the supremely and personally plush and embroidered chambers of King Vanamir. She had been here three days and nights now, ever since the day when she shot the arrow that killed him. All the Kingdom, now including at last the King's Wives and their daughters, had heard the news of the death of their King, and of the powers of Andalorax – who now was inhabiting the King's intimate rooms, in his magic bed.

The King's chambers were all carefully planned and designed when the Castle was being built, about one thousand two-hundred and fifty years earlier. They bore vaulted ceilings with carved timbers that had been, all those many centuries ago, hauled from their recent lumber discovery, the Calicab Forest. The new settlers had found it to be the perfect wood for almost every use: home building, walls and floors, furniture and cabinets, even boats. The Calicab also had a delicious, ruby red fruit.

The magnificent arts of the sorcerers were used not only in the building of the entire Castle Pellah, but those arts were used especially throughout the King's chambers and furniture. The carved Calicab wood bed and its mattress, the armoire, the washing cabinet, the table with the mirrored glass, the long meeting desk with the King's throne-like chair – it was all made using some form of magic at the beginning of the Kingdom. Every object was flourishing with portentous powers.

Yet when Andalorax lived in the Castle Pellah before, from her infancy to when she was fifteen, her living abode was one small room with one slender bed. In there, neither the walls nor the furniture seemed to have any magic powers.

Right now, though, everything had changed. On the first evening of the assassination of King Vanamir – just three days ago! – it was Andalorax who finally, after much discussion into the night with the King's Men and especially his right-hand man, Malthor, yes, it was she who strode into the King's bedroom and threw herself backwards upon the huge, comfortable bedIt was Andalorax who felt the many feathers in her stuffed pillow, and breathed in the fresh scent of linens and comforters still hand-embroidered with the "V" of the dead King. But now, there was no longer a King of Pellah. The King was dead and left no male heir.

Andalorax remembered the arrangement for government that the Galinda-Hussadi had made: a place where everyone's voice was heard – where they all made the laws together. She wondered, why can't there be a Queen instead of a King? Why not a female heir, one who was not even a descendant of Vanamir.

Such as herself.

She had thought of it before. But right now, all she could do was close her eyes and fall asleep.

BOOK SIX

CHAPTER 46

THE RAINBOW MOUNTAINS

SIDDLES SWOOPED ACROSS THE RAINBOW Mountains until he came to the volcano in which Zivat-Or had made his abode. Plunging downwards into it, he settled down on the ground and uttered the words that transformed his normal twelve-foot size down to six feet.

Haspir madji-bay Siddles Mitsbee Zandorfska!

The giant bird ruffled his iridescent black and red feathers, stomped his big yellow feet in the volcanic dust and settled down on the ground.

In his traditional way of greeting, he nodded his head and tapped the ground beneath his yellow feet.

"Greetings, My Queen! I am back," he declared to Andalorax, who stood before him. She had watched him as he descended from the azure blue sky.

"What have you found?" she asked.

"The central valley's Silver Lake is bursting with fresh water and greets the shoreline, My Queen. Tributaries are many and long and winding. There are, of course, other lakes but Silver Lake is the largest of them all by far." Siddles looked around him and saw the wide arch of black stone that once held Zivat-Or's hideaway. There was no one there except the two of them.

"My work here cleansing Zivat-Or's lair is finished," she told him. "I have eliminated the detritus of the entire passageway and cave where the globes once fluttered, illuminating the old King and his world." She smiled. "I want to thank you for bringing me down here."

She shivered. "It is cold down here! Please, Siddles," she said, "take me up and away from here, and bring me to my home on the outside."

"Your wish ...."

"Is my command, I know, Siddles! I simply am not accustomed to being called a Queen. Especially not by you, who has become my dearest friend." She smiled at him and he smiled back, his awkward smile wherein he kept his beak closed but pulled back the muscles on the sides of his cheeks.

They both laughed out loud.

Then Siddles enlarged himself, took her in his claw, and flew back up and out of the volcano. Once free of the deep crevasse that comprised the volcano, she took in the astounding, wide view and breathed deeply as she surveyed the lands beneath and before her.

From up there, with the wind causing her long, multi-colored hair to rush behind her, Andalorax saw the vast amount of greenery that was flourishing everywhere, blanketing the Rainbow Mountains and its numerous hills and valleys with vegetation. She spotted sprouting forests, fields of yellow spring daffodils and white daisies and pink asters, and the large central Silver Lake with its streams and rivers branching out into what would, she hoped, one day be central to newly created towns and villages. The mountain peaks, covered in snow for the first time in over two centuries, shone brightly in the sunlight, glazed with ice that would melt into the rivers and lakes below.

"Siddles," she noted, "Phemtas has certainly disappeared! It seems there are endless plots of land for our company of inhabitants and citizens."

Then she pointed to a wide valley. "What about that area over there, next to the budding Calicab Forest?" asked Andalorax, calling out from her position within his canary yellow claw.

"Looks unspoiled to me," he called back to her as they flew high over a valley in the Rainbow Mountains. "It has plenty of new growth and flatlands wherein people can build their farms and ranches."

"Then let us inform them that this is yet another region in which they can live. I shall make a note in my mind of this particular place."

Siddles laughed as the wind blew in his face and pierced his wide nostrils. Today, they were flying in the southern area of the Rainbow Mountains, way above the highlands and dells, scouting for prime locations such as this one. It was a very overcast morning and there was a mist over the valleys, but they could see plainly enough that the lands were fertile and growing.

Eventually they came to a field where Siddles could easily land, and he did so quite gently, letting Andalorax spill out of his claw. He reduced his size back to six feet, noting, "I'm getting accustomed to doing this several times a day!" They both laughed.

There was a throng of people waiting for them despite the chilly cloudy air, about one thousand who had come to the Rainbow Mountains in search of a new or different life. They traveled via carts led by teams of horses, although some were free spirits such as cowboys and mountain men, wanderers and Mayors. People were dressed in clothing that represented their professions, from farmers and ranchers to ballerinas and actors. They had all spotted the big bird soaring above, and gathered for his imminent approach.

"Queen Andalorax!" they all called out and bowed low as she stood facing the crowd. Cries of "Cheers!" and "Welcome!" and "Hurray!" followed as she made her way through the throng, and reached a makeshift platform that Siddles had created for her.

"Greetings and welcome to the Rainbow Mountains!" she called out, her cape and dress, now violet, blowing in the wind along with her magenta hair and yellow eyes. "First of all, I want to tell you: Do not be concerned with my changing appearance, which is caused by magic forces in the universe and is not under my control. It does not alter the steady rhythm of my heart and mind about being your Queen and of wanting to begin anew the lands here which were once under the power of the weed known as Phemtas."

At these words, some of the crowd exchanged glances indicating that this was new knowledge to them – although many who had traveled southward with her from the Castle already knew of these things.

"We do not understand, but we are with you, Queen Andalorax!" cried out some of them. But many cheers of "We are happy to be here!" and "Yay!" followed. Andalorax was enjoying the excitement and communication of her subjects, who numbered over one thousand former citizens of the Kingdom of Pellah.

She looked out at the multitude of individuals and noted their dress: farmers and ranchers in jeans and checkered shirts; farriers with their horses in tow; musicians with their various instruments (one family had even carried a small piano in their cart); and there were men and women of science, carrying their notebooks and pencil cases. Many, though, were indistinguishable from one another, being there in their simple wardrobes or with families.

"My fellow citizens of the Rainbow Mountains," she called out, "we are all here with one strong purpose in mind: to rebuild the territories with new homes and farms and schoolhouses and all those many things that are needed in a society which will flourish.

"Those of you who left the Castle Pellah were signed up by Malthor, attendant to Gamedon, the newly established Supreme Ruler. Yet, many of you have joined our caravan as we passed by your towns and dwellings. Therefore, I wish to make a complete roster of your names and professions, be they from mathematicians to stonemasons."

She pointed to a wooden table near her side, which Siddles had also created, and had upon its surface a thick book bound in leather. The wind blew up and flipped open the pages of the book, as more clouds appeared above. Andalorax shut it and kept her hand upon its cover.

"In this journal, you shall each sign and fill out the personal information requested in the opening page. This way, I can assure you that we will be able to construct the records in our own Library of the historic beginnings of the Rainbow Mountains.

"That Library has yet to be built! In fact, all of our dwellings are also not yet constructed, from simple huts to larger ranches and farms spread out across the vast territories of these Rainbow Mountains.

"Therefore, Siddles – please stand up here beside me, my dear friend!" she announced, "shall be in charge of helping each and every one of you to create the dreams and visions you all carry, each and every one of you, for your futures."

Siddles, suddenly quite shy, did as she asked and stood on the dais beside Andalorax. She asked him, "Siddles, can you help these people?"

"Aye, My Queen!" he replied.

"Louder, please, Siddles!" she cried out. "This, my friends, is the One-Eyed bird who has been a major part in this episodic adventure we have accomplished. We have destroyed the monarchy and will install a state where the people make the rules. We'll make a commonwealth."

One tradesman called out, "What is a commonwealth, My Queen?"

"This, as you shall all discover with the passing of time, means we all, each and every one of us, will have a say in the governing of our society. The rule of law, not my rule as Queen, shall prevail. And we shall all participate in the creation of those laws."

Once again, the throng turned to one another with quizzical faces, not knowing any "rules of law" other than those imposed by a King.

Andalorax smiled widely.

"As I stated, you shall find out what a commonwealth is as the days and months and years pass. But it means we are each individuals who have a say in what is good and what is bad in our new world. Be pleased, my people! For this is excellent for us!"

Everyone faithfully raised their voices in happiness and joy at the words of their new Queen.

"We shall each have a voice in making the laws?" asked one woman to her husband. "That is surely terrific!"

Andalorax turned to Siddles and again smiled broadly.

"Siddles," she said to him in a voice loud enough for all to hear, "are you willing to be available to every one of these people with your gift for creation?"

"Aye, My Queen," he said. And in his customary style of acquiescence and humility, he bowed low, tapping his bright red beak on the platform.

"Then I shall dub you the Wizard of Creation!"

"My Queen, I am proud to receive such a title. I hope to be worthy of it!"

"Siddles, oh mighty Wizard of Creation, I have a special request of you," said Andalorax. "Please perform one of your miracles and show everyone what you can do. Please make the wind subside, and make the sky bright blue and cloudless."

The giant bird – still only six feet – raised his wings to the sky and faced the sun, barely visible behind the many puffy clouds.

"Ach mad garib day-oft" he cried out.

Immediately, the clouds disappeared and the wind grew still, and the sun warmed the faces of all in the crowd, who were looking up.

Everyone cheered, still not fully knowing that Siddles had the power to not only alter the weather but also to build homes and furnish them, create forests and lakes, and fashion almost anything they could desire. He had decided to assist everyone in their tasks and dreams, but to allow them to create their lives in their own way, in their own time. He would simply assist. But he said nothing, not a word, and simply lowered his big bony head and tapped the dais with his beak.

"Just so you know," said Queen Andalorax, "Siddles can produce in many ways, not merely change the weather! "Then she raised her arms as her cloak became lime green and her hair flowed pale pink and her eyes turned orange, and said, "Come, my people! Here is the book and pen. Line up and write in your names and the information requested on its first page."

It was a long line they made, and it would take them hours – days even – but with the sun shining brightly now and the weather clear, no one complained. They were all smiling.

"Andalorax," whispered Siddles, "was that a good enough trick I played to show off my skills?"

She laughed and said, "Surely, my friend, you could not have done anything better! Everyone loves to see the sunshine!"

CHAPTER 47

THE STRANGER TRAVELS

FREDERICK JANIFUR LISTENED TO THE birds who, he noticed, were busily talking amongst themselves in the Calicab Forest of late. There were wrens, bobolinks, black-throated blue warblers, chickadees, finches, orioles, budgerigars, blue- and gray-jays and other songbirds. It was a veritable chorus.

"Did you hear about Andalorax?" they were repeating in their sing-song voices. In particular, a white-crowned sparrow was having a busy conversation with a vermillion flycatcher about this.

"What about her grandfather, the little man named Gamedon?" wondered a cluster of indigo buntings chatting amongst themselves.

"They both went to the Black Mountains!" Some robins, roosting in a Calicab just above Frederick's head, were sure this was the fact.

"No, we all believe they went to the Castle of the Pellah Kingdom!" agreed summer tanagers and vesper sparrows.

"Not so! Not so!" called out a pair of cardinals. "Andalorax is going to the Rainbow Mountains and leaving everything and everyone else behind her!"

Frederick wondered about this news, and he knew they were singing and chirping the truth. Some far-flying birds sailed across the Sea of Iolanthe often, especially the swifts and kites and geese who traveled far during migration periods. They brought back news of the Kingdom of Pellah and its northern border, the Gold Mountains.

He could understand all their talk because he had the Gift, which his father Marcus and his mother Gerta also had. He could speak with all the animals, but here in the forest the birds were actively involved in the movements of the black-and-white girl, Andalorax, and her grandfather, Gamedon, so it got his enthusiastic attention.

Tall and lean with black hair and brown eyes, broad shoulders and very large hands and feet, Frederick knew they were all speaking truths about the pair whom he watched over in the Calicab Forest just eight months ago when they were hiding out from the King's Knights.

He, too, wondered where they had gone. One day, they had simply disappeared, when the giant bird came and took them away.

"I worry about them … and I also miss them," he said to the congregation of birds. "Where are they now?"

A veritable chorus of birds of all variety began to speak to Frederick Janifur. They repeated what he had been hearing for days, and what he was listening to right now. But one bird, an old astute owl, said, "I've been listening to the kites. They were in the Kingdom of Pellah amidst terrible dangers. The Kingdom has tumbled down and Andalorax has been named a Queen."

"A Queen? Of where?"

The owl turned his head and pecked at his feathers, and said, "She is Queen of the Black Mountains."

"Not of the Kingdom?"

"No. She chose to leave the Kingdom. Her grandfather has been put in place as the King."

"No! No! No!" protested a blue jay. "She is now Queen of the Rainbow Mountains and Gamedon is the Supreme Ruler of Pellah, you silly old bird!"

Frederick Janifur was confused. "The Rainbow Mountains? Where are they?"

The blue jay screeched and responded, "The Black Mountains are now called the Rainbow Mountains! Squawk! Squawk!"

"How did this happen?" asked Frederick.

A sooty tern intervened, saying, "I was there when it happened. The change in names, I mean. Yes sir, indeedy! I was flying north, ahead of a great storm heading for the Castle Pellah, when I saw Andalorax and Gamedon and another, third person sailing the skies in an aerial gondola. A hot-air balloon, to be specific. This contraption with a hanging basket, with streamers flowing behind it, was being pulled by the giant bird, known as Siddles. They landed atop the Castle amidst a great brouhaha. The King was killed!"

"Killed?" Frederick was astounded.

"Yes. By an arrow shot by Andalorax. Chirp! Chirp!" went the tern.

"Hmmm ... She became a warrior, then, by all means," thought Frederick. Then he said, "I always knew she had a forceful power incubating within her. Now she is Queen of the Rainbow Mountains? My, my, that is something to think about."

"What is there to think about?" asked a robin. "Those are the facts." The robin continued chirping.

"There are more than facts in life, my friend," noted Frederick. "There must be quite a story in the details of that voyage in the gondola and the killing of the King ... and in the crowning of Andalorax as Queen. Also, how did the Black Mountains get such a sudden name change? We all know it is an infertile landscape there. 'Rainbow' is quite a different appellation that hardly seems to befit such a landscape!"

A red-tailed hawk replied, "I've been to the Black Mountains, a few years ago. I swooped over the hills and dales. Yes, sir! It was the oddest thing: The entire landscape was covered in a waxy-white plant. Nothing else was growing there. Now that I contemplate it, I think nothing could grow there in that wasteland."

Suddenly, a goose interrupted with a loud "Honk!" and said, "I was there just a few days ago, with my flock. We are migrating these days, you know. We all saw that the white plant was gone, just gone! In its place were green grasses and tree shoots. There was also a big lake in the middle of one of the valleys, a lake with tributaries spewing out and spreading across the countryside."

"Why, I'm awestruck, Mr. Goose!" said Frederick, scratching his head. "How can such a thing happen overnight?"

The wise old owl opened wide his big eyes and answered, "Magic, pure and simple."

Frederick put his hands in his pockets and paused. All the birds were paused as well and busy watching him as they preened their feathers. He began to think hard about what the birds were telling him.

"Magic?" he pondered. Then, snapping his fingers, he called out, "Of course! The sorcery of Siddles, the great bird. I knew it! I just knew it! Why, months ago, I saw that majestic bird change size right before my eyes, and sweep Andalorax away. Both she and Gamedon were snapped up in one of his claws and taken away. Probably to the Black Mountains, where I think he lives."

"Squawk! You mean the Rainbow Mountains!"

The sun began to set as this conversation was going on, and it was time for the birds to disperse and fly to their various nests. They all sang out "Good night!" and "Farewell!" and "Sleep well!" and flew away quite quickly, leaving Frederick standing there in the Calicab Forest.

He sat down and tried to make a timetable in his mind about these tales of Andalorax and Gamedon, while he watched the sunset in a beautiful display of colors: reds, pinks, yellows … "The Rainbow Mountains … I must go there at once," he thought, "and find Andalorax! Every time she has been in the Calicab Forest, from her birth sixteen years ago until her hiding out last year, I've been watching over her; I cannot stop now!"

So saying, he returned to his secret cabin, which was a treehouse he had built high up in an enormous Calicab at the edge of the woods near Milorin. Once he had climbed up there, he stood upon the small platform at the front door, from which he could see almost the entire forest.

"Nothing out of the ordinary," he said to himself as he looked out across the treetops, using the binoculars that had been designed and built by his father, Marcus. "Now, at last, the time has come for me to begin my quest."

Then he went inside the little aerial cabin up in the sky, which he had built many years ago. There, he put together in his rucksack a few bits of clothing and various implements – including his trusty compass, his powerful, magic walking stick, and his pocket knife – which he thought might be handy on the road. Then Frederick Janifur lay down upon his soft feather bed for the night.

But sleep never came to Frederick Janifur. His mind was too active. He thought back to his disappearance from Budgerigar Island almost twenty years earlier, and smiled when he recalled how surprised and frightened all his comrades were. He remembered the voyage across the Sea of Iolanthe in his small one-person boat, and how, using his magic powers inherited from his father Marcus, he generated the winds to carry him across to the Ravenal Forest.

"Little did the inhabitants of the island know of my personal powerful magic!" he thought, and chuckled out loud.

So when the dawn was showing signs of coming up in the east, he put on his walking boots made of thick leather and wrapped himself in several layers of clothing. Then he took his small traveling package and hefted it upon his shoulders, and climbed down the handmade ladder.

He knew exactly in which direction he must go: north by northwest.

"Farewell, little home," he declared. "If I have any luck, I shall never see you again."

Musing on his voyage as he walked, he whispered to the trees, "I must find Andalorax." He began to whistle.

The birds, now awake and listening to his gentle song, shadowed him as he made his way along the forest trail. Eventually, he was at the edge of the woods, and a mockingbird called out to him, "Where are you going?"

"To the Black Mountains."

"Hey there!" screeched the old owl as he turned his head around and blinked his yellow eyes. "You mean the Rainbow Mountains, yes, sir!"

CHAPTER 48

XAROLADNA AWAKENS

GAMEDON AWOKE AND STARED AT the ceiling in the King's quarters. He saw the plaster festoons and wooden carvings high above him, designed and constructed by the sorcerers of old, one thousand two hundred and fifty years ago. He looked at the frescoes painted there as well, with scenes of the hunting of boars and other wild animals, and the central design of women with little children washing themselves by a stream.

He propped his head upon the silken feather pillows and smoothed the soft surface of the embroidered green velvet bedspread covering the feather comforter beneath it. Straight ahead was the armoire and washstand, sitting there quietly. Gamedon thought that perhaps these objects – like all the other ones in the chambers – could tell stories of all the Kings who had slept and lived there, the last one being King Vanamir.

Now it was Gamedon's turn to inhabit these quarters. Not as a King, though, but as Supreme Ruler of Pellah.

"The very idea makes me quake," he thought. "Can I handle this?" He inhaled deeply and said aloud, "Of course I can!" He smiled and added, "because I must!"

He knew Andalorax was counting on him to do his best, which he figured was all he could truly accomplish. And then there was the entire Kingdom that was looking to him to rule over them all. "I must become very wise," he thought, then laughed and said, "I already am wise, says Andalorax. I must uphold her faith in me."

So he tossed aside his feather comforter and velvet bedspread, slipped his feet into Vanamir's large velvet slippers with their embroidered "V" upon them, and went over to the dressing table and sat down in front of it, staring at himself in the grand mirror opposite him.

"I am an old man," he said. "Old men can be tired and helpless, but they can also be clever with years of knowledge about life." He smiled at his wrinkled face, and added, "I choose to be wise!"

The brushes and combs were laid out before him. He picked up a particularly strange-looking brush with a long handle in the shape of a horse. He began to brush his bushy red-and-gray hair and braided beard, when he heard a knocking at the door.

"Who goes there?"

"'Tis I, Perigore, Sire. I have come to assist you in your dressing."

"Come in, Perigore."

Perigore pressed upon the wooden button in the center of the magic carved door.

"Perigore, at the door," Gamedon heard him say. And the door swung open.

"What shall I do for His Majesty this morning?" he asked Gamedon.

"Why, Perigore," Gamedon answered, "how pleasant to meet you! Are you the King's valet?"

"Aye, Sire. That is who I am – or, rather, was. I am now your valet, Sire. At your service."

"Please do not call me 'Sire,' as I am not a King."

"Aye, My Lord. What shall I call you then?"

"Why, call me by my name, which is Gamedon, in case you haven't heard!"

He smiled at Perigore, which made Perigore feel strange.

"Vanamir never smiled at me," he thought. "Hmmm...."

So Perigore hesitated a moment and then replied, "Aye, Sir Gamedon. What is it that I may do for you this early morning? Shall I prepare your dressing gown, or shall you choose to wear your breeches and silken shirts and velvet jacket?"

"I do not know, Perigore. What would the King have done this day?"

"He would choose to dress fully, as he would be doing what is expected of you to do: Meet the people! They await you in the Great Hall … Gamedon."

"Then that is what I shall do. Thank you for your assistance, Perigore. You may select from the garments in the armoire and help me dress accordingly." And so Perigore opened the clothes cabinet and selected Vanamir's best raiment, and helped Gamedon to put on the silken undershirt, the silken blouse with the lace cuffs, the velvet vest, and the velvet jacket – all various and lovely shades of green.

Placing his feet in Vanamir's slippers proved almost comical to him, for they were way too large for his smaller feet. All the clothing hung upon him like loose drapery from a small window.

"Perigore," he asked, as the valet laced up the large boots, "what other duties did you perform for your King?"

"I bathed him, dressed him, and waited upon him for all his requests regarding his costume. I also assisted him with his meetings with his Ministers and Knights, by way of bringing in food, and taking orders for any of their special needs."

"Well, you may assist me in those things, Perigore, but I first must ask that you arrange for clothing which fits me!" So saying, he splayed out the excess fabric of Vanamir's clothing and laughingly said, "This simply will not do!"

"I shall have the seamstresses come immediately, Master Gamedon."

"Perigore, you are wonderful and doubtlessly capable. I suspect you are a treasure!" Gamedon smacked his thigh and began to laugh. Perigore didn't know what to make of that. "And now, away with you, for I shall have no more need of you this day. Perhaps tomorrow! And have a set of clothing made for me by tomorrow, if you please!"

After Perigore backed out of the dressing room and closed the heavy wooden door behind him, Gamedon removed Vanamir's clothing and put on his own old pants, shirt and worn-out cloak and suede shoes.

"Aha, I am more comfortable now," he spoke to his face in the mirror.

"Are you, Gamedon?" asked a soft voice.

He saw in the mirror that, standing behind him was the figure of a woman!

He knew in an instant it was Andalorax's Many-Colored Girl. She looked identical to his granddaughter except for the coloring. Now it was Andalorax whose cloak and dress, hair and eyes changed color continually. It was the Many-Colored Girl who was black and white.

Dressed now in a hooded white cape, white skirt, and a white flowing shirt with billowing sleeves that were wide at the wrists and draped down to her legs, she stood behind him and said, "I can read your mind, Grandfather! Yes, you think rightly: 'Tis me, the Many-Colored Girl, Xaroladna! Fear me not, for I am here to help you in your station as Supreme Ruler."

"But the white seems iridescent," thought Gamedon, "for it reflects light from its surface that appears as if a prism." Her hair, too, was white. "And she is barefoot!" he noticed. He bowed down to her, saying, "Hello, my Queen."

"Ha ha! 'Tis funny to be listening to your inner thoughts, Gamedon. But no, I am not your Queen. Andalorax, my twin, is your Queen. I am still the Many-

Colored Girl, Xaroladna. I have merely transferred my power to alter my appearance over to her, and I have become what she looked like."

"It's that simple?"

"Aye, Gamedon. That it is." She smiled and said, "I know you are wondering why I am here."

"Yes, why have you come to me?"

"I have come to accompany you on your voyage to becoming a Supreme Ruler. It's a rather new road for you, wouldn't you say?"

"Absolutely. Brand new. I am grateful for any help you can give me. How does one go about becoming a Supreme Ruler? I haven't the faintest idea."

"First and foremost, you must be yourself, for it is you who is the chosen one – because of who you are."

Gamedon thought about this and answered, "But I have no experience in this role."

"You do not require experience, my friend. You require the gifts that you were born with and the wisdom you have earned throughout your lifetime up until today."

"I don't know that my 'gifts' and 'wisdom' qualify me for the position. I don't have that many gifts and my wisdom is slim and marginal."

"Gamedon, my Grandfather, you have many gifts and much wisdom. Do not doubt!"

"If you say so, Xaroladna. By the way, you call me 'Grandfather.' Am I your grandfather, as I am grandfather to Andalorax?"

"Aye, Gamedon. Andalorax and I are twins, cut from the same cloth, so to speak."

"Very well. You can be my other granddaughter then. Now, what else must I know to become a true Supreme Ruler?"

"You must give yourself completely to the job at hand." She reached out and held up her right hand.

"See this gold ring on my finger? It is a Ring of Power, Grandfather. I shall give it to you!"

On the pointer finger of that hand was a golden ring embedded with one large ruby surrounded by diamonds. Xaroladna reached out her and took Gamedon's right hand.

"This ring shall give you powers that are boundless. Not even I know its limits!" She removed the ring and put it on Gamedon's right pinkie finger.

Gamedon looked down at the Ring of Power, which had many facets and gave the ring a tremendous amount of reflected light. It was prismatic! It was sacred! He suddenly recalled the words of Mundarak the second time he saw him in the King's Library:

But now upon the scene shall enter
The Queen, who brings us to the center.
The Queen! Who shall replace the King;
You'll know her by her sacred ring.

Gamedon knew at once that Mundarak's prophesy had this very moment come to be. He held out his right hand and looked upon the luminous Ring of Power on his right pinkie finger. It sat there quietly, a ruby with diamonds embedded in purest gold, not revealing its secrets. He wondered what powers it had; Xaroladna had said she herself did not know them all. Perhaps he would find out ....

Xaroladna then reached out her arms, her white robe's long sleeves hanging down at her side, and she cupped her hands, and blew into them as if starting a fire. A bright light began to sparkle in her palms. Even though the two of them were ensconced in the King's chambers with the windows closed, a gust of wind swept up and made her white cloak begin to blow and flap. Its hood blew back from her face. Her white hair, loose now, whipped up in the wind. Her dark eyes shone like black coals.

The light within her palms shimmered and began to grow until it filled her cupped hands. 'Round and 'round the whirling wind began to swirl and expand until there appeared a gold crown studded with finely chiseled diamonds, emeralds and rubies. The light coming in through the stained glass windows made them spill prisms around the dull rock walls, making Gamedon feel as if he was inside those brilliant precious stones.

Xaroladna took a firm hold of the crown and told Gamedon: "I place this crown upon your head to denote your new station in life." As Xaroladna was about six inches taller than Gamedon, who was a rather little man, she easily leant forward and put the crown upon his head. Then she stood back and looked at him and smiled.

"It suits you to perfection!"

Gamedon reached his hands up and touched the crown. It was heavy. He moved his head around left and right, up and down, and said, smiling, and with a twinkle in his eyes said, "It does fit!"

"With this crown and the Ring of Power, you are officially the Supreme Ruler of the Kingdom of Pellah," announced Xaroladna. "But, we must not call it a Kingdom anymore." Xaroladna, whose hands still held magic dust and brilliant sparkling air, was busy thinking.

After a few minutes, she said: "The Nation of Pellah! That's it! After all, as Andalorax was taught in the land of the Galinda-Hussadi, this is now a free state." She threw her hands above Gamedon's head and let the whirling wind sprinkle its magic dust upon him and his new crown. That dust tumbled down and spread over his entire body, down to his old laced-up suede boots.

"You are going to help me, Xaroladna?" He was still fingering his crown, running his hand along the undulating shape created by the curved rows of gold, shapes which held a large stone at the top of each ripple.

"Aye, Gamedon, that I am. I will show you how to command, how to negotiate, how to win over your people! It shall be easy because I shall be alongside of you every step of the way."

"Shall the people be able to see you?"

"No. None shall see me, not even you," Xaroladna replied.

"How will I know you are there?"

At that moment, the Many-Colored Girl, dressed in white with coal-black eyes, was sucked up into the air and disappeared. Gamedon felt a thump in his chest, right where his heart was.

"You shall not see me, Grandfather. But you shall always know that I am here inside you."

Gamedon placed his hand upon his chest and asked, "Are you going with me now, as I exit these chambers which I knew so well when King Vanamir was alive, and go outside to meet the people in the Nation of Pellah?"

"Aye, Grandfather Gamedon. That I shall. Don't you feel it, don't you know it?"

Gamedon grinned. "Aye, Xaroladna. I feel it. I know it. You are my faithful friend."

"Friend, yes; faithful, yes. Forever. Just as my twin, the true Queen, Andalorax. Now, let us greet the throng which awaits you."

CHAPTER 49

FREDERICK JANIFUR

ANDLORAX TOOK THE TRAIL THROUGH the Portopuff Forest that Siddles had created between her mother's home and hers. She walked slowly, enjoying the fresh scent of the breeze ruffling the flowers of the mighty Portopuff boughs.

Suddenly she heard a cockatiel in a tree above her say, "My Queen, you tarry way too long here in the woods. Siddles awaits!"

"Thank you for the notice," she chirped back in bird language, and picked up her speed. Ahead, she could see the yellow painted building she called home, and as she approached the porch that encircled it, she saw Siddles standing there. He was in his six-foot frame this time, and looking somewhat anxious.

"There you are, Andalorax," he said as she approached him. "Where have you been?"

"Just talking with some of my ministers," she replied, as her eyes flashed bright pink. "What's happening?"

"I have been waiting for a long time," he replied. "We have a visitor."

"And who might that be?"

"Come inside and have a look," he answered.

She opened her front door and stepped into the central living area. Sure enough, seated there on her favorite armchair was a man in old, battered clothing. Next to him was a backpack and long walking stick. His leather boots were laced up to the knees, and his black hair, flecked with gray, was in a long braid down his back.

He stood up, removed his hat, and bowed low. "I salute you, Queen Andalorax," he said, lifting his head and looking straight into her bright pink eyes.

"Greetings to you, sir," she replied, thinking, "His garb is worn out and dusty from probable long travels. His eyes bespeak that he is on a mission, for they stare into mine without hesitation yet with great compassion. Certainly, this mission concerns me."

"And whom do I have the honor of addressing?" she asked.

Sweeping to his side his wide-brimmed felt hat that bore a few brightly-colored feathers, he answered, "My name is Frederick Janifur, My Queen."

Andalorax immediately recognized the name. Marcus Janifur was the "magician," the man whose inventions were in the Library on Budgerigar Island. Frederick was his son.

She decided to continue a lighthearted conversation.

"And where do you come from? It is clear from your appearance that you have been traveling far and wide."

"I come from the Calicab Forest."

Andalorax sucked in her breath. Never before in her lifetime had she met anyone who uttered those words, or had, even silently, indicated that he even knew about those remote woodlands.

"The Calicab Forest?" she repeated. Silence entered the space between them, with Siddles standing by their side. "How can this be? Please tell me more about yourself and your long journey here, Frederick Janifur. First, shall we be seated?"

They all three arranged themselves comfortably in Andalorax's living room. Then, the tall man took his walking stick in hand and leaned forward and answered, "My Queen, this has been a long journey indeed, one that goes back many years."

"Years? How many?"

"Eighteen or so, if I have counted correctly."

"But how long have you been on the road to the Rainbow Mountains? Surely that has not taken you eighteen years!"

Frederick Janifur smiled pleasantly, pulling back his full lips and showing a row of white teeth. He had neither beard nor mustache. He looked at her with his brown eyes and sighed.

"Queen Andalorax," he said softly, "I come originally from an island south of the Sea of Iolanthe. Budgerigar Island is its name. I believe you are familiar with it, are you not?"

Andalorax stood wide-eyed, staring at this most strange fellow. Realizing she may have been making him uncomfortable, she turned her eyes away and looked towards Siddles.

"Budgerigar Island, he says, dear Siddles. What think you of this?"

"It is most interesting, to say the least, my Queen."

"That is all you can say?"

"Let this man speak for himself about this point, of an island south of the Sea of Iolanthe and the Calicab Forest." He looked at her with his one red eye, and, if she was not mistaken, he batted his eyelashes with a big wink!

Andalorax turned back to the man, saying, "Frederick Janifur. A most intriguing, unique name."

Then at that instant, she remembered being in the Library of the Galinda-Hussadi.

"Of course!" she cried out. "You are the son of Marcus and Gerta Janifur! The inventor whose designs I have seen in the Hussadi Library." She pulled herself up straight and sighed. She exchanged glances with him.

"You are also a magician, for you can make yourself disappear and come across the Sea of Iolanthe all alone in a tiny boat!"

"Aye, My Queen," he replied, "a magician who was born and grew up on Budgerigar Island, Your Majesty."

"And why said you that you hailed from the Calicab Forest?"

"That was my most recent place of habitation … for almost twenty years." He smiled. "And well do I know that you have been there."

"And how comes it to be that you know this?" Andalorax asked.

"The birds have told me, with their chirps and songs."

"Do you mean to tell me that you have the Gift?" She was astonished and that was becoming apparent, as her cheeks blushed pink.

"Aye, that I have. As do you."

"You seem to know much about me," she retorted, feeling somewhat visible by this stranger and not particularly enjoying it.

"No one knows about my life on the island," she thought, "so how can he? Does he know about my life in the Calicab Forest while hiding out from King Vanamir?"

"What else have the birds told you, Frederick?" she asked.

"They have told me about your birth in the Calicab Forest, and of your transport to the Castle Pellah, where you lived for fifteen years. They have told me of your journey to the Black Mountains – now called the Rainbow Mountains – and of the great bird Siddles."

He turned toward the giant bird, and said to him, "Siddles, shall I go on? Please give me your advice."

Andalorax simultaneously turned towards Siddles and asked, "What do you know about this man, my friend? It appears to me that you are hiding something of great importance and perhaps significance to me about his journeys and his life."

"Aye, Andalorax," agreed the great bird. "There is much to learn about Frederick Janifur."

Looking at the traveler, and facing him, he bent low and, in his customary way, tapped his strong red beak of the floor, saying, "It is time for you to speak, Frederick."

"Very well, Siddles, I shall do so." He pulled himself up straight and tall, and inhaled deeply.

"My Queen, I have followed your life personally since your birth. I know of all your travels and travails."

"Why is this?" she asked.

"I am your father."

Andalorax opened her eyes wide and gazed upon this strange man. They exchanged a deep look into each other's' eyes, she into his brown irises and he into her now deep blue ones. At that very moment, her eyes turned golden yellow, her cloak and dress became an iridescent lavender, and her hair changed into hot pink.

Frederick Janifur seemed not to notice the change, but to accept it as normal.

"My father?"

"Aye, Andalorax. I am your father, the lover and devotee of your mother Mandir and a friend to Gamedon, Mandir's father and your grandfather. This was when we all lived in Milorin, near the Calicab Forest. Gamedon had no idea that Mandir and I were a couple as we kept it secret even from him.

"I remember well when you were born, and when King Vanamir absconded with you and Mandir, removing both of you from my life and taking you to Castle Pellah. I remember that, as once again the birds told me over the years, you lived in the Castle throughout your childhood into adolescence. I know that Mandir became one of King Vanamir's wives and was subsequently held a virtual captive in the Turret of the Wives. I remember that you escaped his clutches because he was going to forever imprison you."

He stopped speaking. She and he were still eye-to-eye. A moment of deep silence ensued, then Andalorax asked him, "Why did you not come for me and my mother?"

Frederick Janifur leaned on his walking stick, and sighed. "I have certain powers, my daughter," he said, "but certainly not powers that are strong enough to battle the King's Knights and the Castle stronghold itself. I was resigned, therefore, to rely upon the animals – mostly the birds – to keep me apprised of your life and movements as the years passed.

"However," he continued, "I knew you were safe, under the protection of Gamedon's watch. So, one year after your departure to the Castle, I left the town of Milorin behind, and moved into the deepest part of the Calicab Forest. I sought isolation and freedom to roam about the woods. I had no friends in Milorin, in any case. There, in the forest, I have lived all these years, in my treehouse which I fashioned with my own hands."

"And yet," asked Andalorax, "you say that you are from Budgerigar Island and the lands of the Galinda-Hussadi. How came it to be that you lived in Milorin?"

"When I was a very young man," he responded, "I longed for adventure. I tired of the life on the island. As well, my father – who always guided me with his brilliant ways – was disrespected. When he died, I decided to leave.

"I do have certain powers," he went on, still looking into Andalorax's eyes, which had turned a vivid purple, "and among them is the ability to control the weather and, to some extent, the geography around me.

"So I built a small wooden boat and kept the Sea of Iolanthe calm and free from cresting waves, all the while summoning up the wind and clear skies." He laughed. "That part was quite the adventure! But it was easy for me to accomplish. Upon landing at the Cliffs of Iolanthe, I roamed freely and easily through the woods and fields, over hills and across valleys, living in the wilderness, talking with all the animals, simply wandering – that is, until I found Milorin, at the southernmost area of the Kingdom of Pellah.

"It seemed a kind of outpost town, at the end of somewhere and the beginning of nowhere. In Milorin, therefore, I entrenched myself among the inhabitants; no one questioned me, thinking I was just another nomad from somewhere in the Kingdom. I took up a living as a wood-cutter and led a simple life in a small house with a small garden.

"When I met your mother Mandir, one sunny day in the woods, I fell instantly in love – as did she. We met secretly in the darkness of night, keeping to ourselves, especially as Mandir lived in concealment with her father. Gamedon had long before been banished from Milorin for his so-called heretical philosophy about the goodness of only of the daytime and the wickedness of the night."

Siddles interrupted the traveler, interjecting, "And you did not believe such a thing to be true?"

"No. On Budgerigar Island, that is not a belief. The day and the night are both filled with joy and delights, with sadness and pain. Such is life."

He turned towards Andalorax and said, "You know this, my daughter, from your time there but also from the teachings of Gamedon."

She was awestruck by his tale of adventure and romance. "Is this man telling the truth?" she asked herself. Yet in her heart, she believed his every word and could not deny herself this reality.

"Frederick Janifur," she said, "how comes it that you find yourself here in the Rainbow Mountains?"

The traveler laughed and pointed at Siddles. "Ask your giant bird!"

Siddles puffed out his broad chest and declared, "My Queen, I was flying over the countryside to the south, and with my keen sight, focused upon a man walking near the edge of the mountains.

"Swooping lower, I could see the details of his comportment and dress, and saw as well that he carried no weapon. Not even a bow and arrow.

"Upon landing in front of him, I asked him who he was and what he was doing there. His reply was basically a synopsis of what he has told us here. He said he was your father; he said he was in search of you and had heard from the animals that you were located here in these Rainbow Mountains.

"So once that was all settled, time was of the essence as this was a great situation. One doesn't leave the father of the Queen to wander alone along the mountains and cliffs. Therefore, I swept him up in my claw, and brought him here, to your home."

Siddles looked somewhat downfallen as he added, "I entrust that I have done the right thing, My Queen."

"Certainly, yes," she answered. "You have thoroughly taken his tale to be the truth – and I, myself, have no doubt that it is so." Upon saying these words, she turned towards Frederick Janifur and said, "I am pleased to meet you, Father." She extended her arm and they clasped right hands, both placing their left hands upon them in the manner of the Hussadis, signifying the strength of their encounter.

"Father, do you understand why my raiment, and my hair and my eyes change color?"

"Aye, I am aware of Xaroladna, the Many-Colored Girl," he answered. "Again, I heard this from the birds, chiefly the budgerigars, who have been so very close to my heart from the day I was born. I know, too, that you were not born this way, but exchanged identities with Xaroladna, your supernatural twin."

"Know you where she is today? I would welcome contact with her happily."

"Nay, Andalorax," he replied. "Presumably, she inhabits a land of magic and sorcery. I know not where it is – in the heavens or here upon our planet. These domains are kept undisclosed from us by the great powers that be."

"Father," she continued, "you are welcome here in my home. But I must tell you that you have a surprise coming to you."

"What may that be?"

"My mother Mandir is here in the Rainbow Mountains."

"Yes. I am aware of this, my daughter."

"You heard of it by way of the animals?"

"Aye, Andalorax," he replied. "Most specifically, through the sooty terns who have flown with me from Budgerigar Island as they migrate towards the Golden Mountains to the north of the Kingdom of Pellah."

"We call it the Pellah Nation now, Father."

"Oh! Of course! That makes sense!" They both laughed, an act which seemed to clear the air of some of the formality of this meeting.

"In a way," he continued, "it also shows how well you learned the ways of the Hussadis."

Andalorax pointed towards the living room. "Let us sit down upon the sofa and chairs, while Siddles rests his bulk upon the stoop of the fireplace."

Frederick Janifur smiled broadly and said, "You don't know how significant it is to me to finally be face to face with you, my dearest daughter Andalorax."

"Oh," she replied, "but I do, I do. I feel the same way, dear Father. Come, let us chat more and you may lie down and rest in a little while. Tomorrow morning," she went on, "I believe we shall go and see Mandir."

"I do have one request of you, Andalorax. It has been my dream lo these many years."

"What might that be?"

"Please call me 'Papa.'"

CHAPTER 50

ANDALORAX & XAROLADNA

GAMEDON WAS NOW BEGINNING TO feel accustomed to his position as Supreme Ruler. Several weeks had gone by, and, with the help of Xaroladna and his many Knights and Ministers – all eager to bring to life the new Nation of Pellah – he was succeeding.

"I am thunderstruck," he said to Xaroladna late one evening while they were in the business room of the King's old chambers, which Gamedon now called his own, "that the people so readily believe the new dictum about the night not being evil."

"Aye, Gamedon. But the people are not as easily fooled as the Kings all believed. They knew the truth, over all these many centuries. After all," she said, sitting down in a leather and velvet chair, "nothing has ever happened to anyone even though many, over the years, have tried it or experienced it through necessity.

"Think of Chester and Goshen, who spent many nights in the outdoors while searching for you and Andalorax in the Calicab Forest. Think, too, of Malthor and his Knights doing the same thing. Nothing bad ever happened to any of them."

Gamedon nodded his head in agreement.

"This seems to be logical," he said. "I suppose they were just waiting for the right time!"

"It took centuries, my friend! I should think the time is ripe today, finally!"

Xaroladna leaned forward and put her soft white hand upon his old, wrinkled and sun-blotched one. "Come now, Gamedon. Let us put the past behind us and look to tomorrow."

"I continue to muse upon Andalorax, wondering what is happening to her in the Rainbow Mountains."

"She is surely safe and strong," answered Xaroladna, "else we would have heard otherwise from Siddles, who promised to keep us apprised of any dangers which might befall her or the citizens of their new Nation."

Suddenly, Gamedon felt himself extremely sleepy and yawned. Xaroladna laughed upon seeing this, got up, and made her gentle leave-takings, easily disappearing into a mist as was her daily wont.

Gamedon lay back upon the green velvet coverlet and put his weary head upon the pillows. He quickly fell asleep.

But something awakened him, as he lay there still dressed in his newly-made costume that befitted his station: A silken shirt with lace cuffs, a bright green vest with gold buttons with matching doublet, leather pants and sturdy suede boots laced up to his knees. It seemed the people of the newly-formed Nation of Pellah still admired green, in all shades.

"What is that sound?" he asked himself, quickly opening his eyes and lifting his head. "It seemed to come from the area of the looking glass just opposite this bedroom." He heaved his tired body up and went over to the mirror, and seated himself upon the King's royal chair, carved in Calicab wood with lion's heads on the arms and a lion's head upon the backrest.

Upon the dressing table was King Vanamir's array of combs and brushes and hand mirrors. One comb in particular – a large one with a long handle that was carved in the shape of a horse – drew him closer. The horse had an emerald eye. He picked it up.

All of a sudden, the comb grew and grew, longer and thicker, until Gamedon could no longer hold it and had to let it fall to the floor. Out of the comb sprang a white horse ridden by a woman all in white.

They were transparent.

"Who are you?" he cried out.

"I am the vision that came to King Vanamir the morning of his death," she replied, her white dress fluid in the air behind her, blowing as if there were a wind when there was none. "I cautioned him of his upcoming meeting with his Destiny, and I come to you bearing a similar greeting."

"I am to die?" asked Gamedon.

"Nay, old man. I come with a spectacle of hope and praise."

"Have mercy upon me! I am humbled by your magnificence!"

The lady in white smiled. Gamedon could see right through her and her enormous white horse, who suddenly raised his forelegs high in the air in a menacing way.

"Calm, calm," said the phantom woman to her stallion. "This is Gamedon we have come to meet, not the malevolent King as before."

The horse whinnied and then settled down, but it had its wide eyes with their wide pupils still upon him.

Together, the vision of horse and rider filled the room.

"You have seen apparitions in the past, old man," said the beautiful lady. "Not all of them bear fearful messages."

"Why have you come to me?"

"To give you this message: Fear not, Gamedon. 'Tis true, your Destiny is come and I am the form it takes! You may be an old man but you have many years before you, years in which you shall rule this new nation with wisdom and grace. Already, your people admire you and are willing to follow your lead, for they have whispered amongst themselves, sharing the tales of your years with Andalorax and King Vanamir. They know you are strong and capable of equality and justice!"

Gamedon was taken aback, yet he rose from his chair and reached out to touch the vision. His hand went clear through it. He shook his head in disbelief, trying to awaken from what he thought might be a dream.

"I am no dream, Gamedon," retorted the lady upon the horse. "I am come from a supernatural area of upper space and air, wherein live many other spirits. Yet fear me not! My reason for coming is to give you hope for the future.

"Do not think yourself too old or feeble," she went on. "You have powers, powers acquired over the long years of your life. You have lived in darkness and banishment; you have lived as a Minister to King Vanamir; you have always protected Andalorax and helped her come to the mighty stage whereon she now rests. You have learned the art of becoming somewhat invisible by melting into your background, with inner camouflage. You have helped Zivat-Or – who shared the bane of banishment for his beliefs – in his quest for retribution, even though his Destiny was imminent death."

With this, the lady commanded her horse to kneel down, and she alighted, standing before Gamedon on the floor of the dressing room.

"Come," she said, beckoning him with her hand. "Let me tell you of your Destiny."

A whirlwind whipped up before them, seemingly out of nowhere. It grew quickly high up to the ceiling, swarming like a tornado, thick and gray. The lady stepped before it, and the horse followed.

"Gamedon," she announced with a deep and fearful voice, "your future is bright and long, and those who follow you shall praise your goodness throughout all time! That is your Destiny!"

So saying, she stepped into the midst of the tornado, holding the horse's reins so that it, too, was swept up into it. In an instant, they disappeared. At that very moment, the tornado exhausted itself and became thinner and thinner until it, too, vanished completely.

"My Destiny, fair lady!" called out Gamedon, who now truly felt his inner strength. "It beckons me and I shall follow it to the end of my days!"

"Aye!" came the lady's voice, seemingly bouncing from every wall in the room, echoing with resilience and power. "Be strong, Gamedon, Supreme Ruler of the Nation of Pellah. Long shall you reign!"

Frederick Janifur and Andalorax walked through the Portopuff Forest, heading for Mandir. They had been following the narrow trail that Siddles had made for her under the shade of the high trees. The sun was just rising in the east, and the skies were cloudless.

"Papa," she asked, "Did you make this weather just for us this lovely day?"

He laughed and took her hand. "Nay, darling daughter. Nature has done that of her own accord. We are blessed!"

They finally approached Mandir's home, and stepped along the walking stones towards her front door.

"Mother," called out Andalorax. "'Tis I, your daughter. I bring with me a surprise guest."

Father and daughter heard the gentle footsteps of one in soft slippers, and at that moment Andalorax's hair turned soft lilac and her eyes became a sky blue; her raiment was buttery yellow and fanned out in the gentle breeze.

There was a quiet "click" as the door handle turned, and lo, there was Mandir. She wore her purple dress, banded at the waist with a red belt sewn with golden threads. In her hands was the purple sweater she was knitting for Andalorax.

"Who is this surprise guest?" she asked, looking at her daughter. And suddenly, there before her, she saw Frederick.

Silently, they looked into each other's eyes. Then he reached out his right hand and she took it in hers. Together, in silence, they put their left hands above the right, in the manner of the Galinda-Hussadi that Andalorax had taught her. Frederick was already familiar with it, having been born on Budgerigar Island and therefore being a "Hussadi" himself.

There they stood, speechless. Then Mandir said, "Come in, Frederick."

He and Andalorax stepped over the threshold and entered her small but ample and colorful abode. The morning sunlight shone in through its many windows, causing a crisscross pattern to flood across the walls. Flowers were in several vases and jars throughout the living room, with a lovely tapestry rug across the floor — it, too, catching the bright beams of early afternoon light. There was the scent of peppermint in the air, caused by the tea made from fresh leaves in Mandir's garden.

"Come, Frederick and Andalorax, and sit down" said Mandir, indicating with a sweep of her arms the wooden chairs which surrounded the circular table in the middle of the room. At one seat was a steamy cup of peppermint tea, a slice of lemon, and buttered toast with a swish of raspberry jam on top.

"You haven't changed at all, my dear one," he finally said to Mandir.

"Neither have you," said she, and blushed.

Andalorax laughed out loud.

"It has been eighteen years and you both think you haven't changed? That is a novel idea indeed!"

"When love is in your heart, your vision of your loved one remains eternally the same, no matter the span of time," he said. Looking at Mandir, he asked, "Isn't that true, my dear?"

"Aye, Frederick," she said, then pronounced, "I never thought I would be saying that name again in my lifetime. How comes it that you are here, in my house in the Rainbow Mountains?"

"'Tis a long story, but one worth the telling. Yet we have all the time in the world now to do so, don't we?"

"That, too, is something I never thought I would hear from your own lips, my love."

And then Mandir smiled widely and said, "You realize, Frederick, we are here standing before our daughter!"

He looked towards the multi-colored vision that was Andalorax, and answered, "Aye, Mandir. That thought didn't enter my head until just now, and I thank you for bringing that lovely word into our midst – that of 'family.'"

And so they sat there, the three of them, when Mandir reached out her arms across the table and took both her lover's and her daughter's hands in hers. Andalorax and Frederick held hands as well, forming a completed circle. They all automatically bowed their heads, and Frederick broke the spell by turning his head upwards towards the wood-beamed ceiling.

"Let us commence saying words we never thought to speak, into faces we never thought we would see again."

Andalorax stood up, breaking the chain.

"I shall be leaving you two to tell your stories to each other. I must go and see Siddles on an urgent errand."

"Until later, then," said Mandir, beaming now with a broad smile across her face.

"Aye, Mother. Until later."

Andalorax made her way back home through the Portopuff Forest, and found Siddles squatting on her front steps. She walked up to him, tapping him on his iridescent black wing with the red-and-white zig-zag pattern, and went over to her rocking chair. There, she sat down with a loud sigh.

The great bird turned around to face her.

"Did they meet?" he asked.

"Aye, Siddles. They are together again, at last."

"You have brought your mother a visitor. Now I bring one to you. I, however," he said, "shall be off, before you go inside to greet your friend."

"Where are you going?"

"I must continue my vigil across the countryside in these Rainbow Mountains, finding more excellent sites for our citizens to build upon. You may not see me for a few days, perhaps a week even, as I shall be traveling far and wide."

With that, the huge buzzard arose and, stooping his great red beak down to the floor and pecking it with a soft thud, he said, "I shall see you soon, My Queen."

Siddles pronounced the incantation that enlarged him to his normal twelve-foot height, and away he flew.

Andalorax rocked in her chair, wondering who her guest could be. Then she sighed again, and opened her front door.

There, leaning on the kitchen countertop, was Xaroladna. This afternoon, she wore her ebony cloak and it was draped down to the ground, and her white hair tumbled down her back. Her eyes remained coal black.

"Xaroladna! Greetings!" said Andalorax.

"Greeting to you, My Queen!" returned Xaroladna.

"Am I your Queen as well?"

"Aye, you are Queen and therefore so am I. Remember, we are twins."

"What brings you to me?" Andalorax felt somewhat concerned to see her, thinking Xaroladna to be in the Pellah Nation at the Castle with Gamedon.

"Could something be amiss?" she wondered?

With a laugh, Xaroladna said, "You know, I can always read your mind, and therefore I say to you, nothing is wrong in the Nation of Pellah. All is well."

Andalorax smiled, feeling somewhat relieved. "After all," she thought, "I have just experienced the life-changing event of seeing my parents reunited. Now, of a sudden, Siddles is off on another journey here in our Rainbow Mountains. So why is my twin visiting me?"

"I am here on a great mission, one that concerns both of us, my Queen."

"What may that be?"

"We are to achieve what you may consider to be impossible, dearest twin sister. I am going to retrieve my original costume of being the Many-Colored Girl and you are to return to being Andalorax, the black-and-white one."

At these words, Andalorax's looked down upon herself and watched as her cloak turned purple, her hair became bright red, and her eyes flashed orange. "I am still changing color, Xaroladna! How are we achieve this transformation?"

"'Tis easy," she replied. "With my magic, I have the power to switch us back to our original states. Watch me now!"

Xaroladna raised her arms, her cloak draping down her sides. She uttered this incantation:

Whoom madjibay queritsme!

Suddenly, the Many-Colored Girl was back in her original body, and Andalorax became the person she was at birth. She looked down at herself and saw the immediate change. Her cloak was black, her dress was white, her hair was white, and, she suspected, her eyes were black.

Standing before her, the Many-Colored Girl was like a prism of hues, changing colors rapidly as if celebrating her original state of being. Her raiment alternated rapidly from pink to green to yellow; her hair went from red to orange to purple. And Xaroladna was laughing loudly with joy!

"See?" she called out. "I told you it was easy to do!"

"But why are we doing it?"

"You may as well ask why we originally transformed and traded each other's identities in respect to color."

"Aye, Xaroladna. I do wonder why. Can you explain it to me?" Andalorax reached down and ran her hands down her cape and dress, feeling a sense of being herself again.

"You had the colors of the rainbow within your soul, even when you were just black and white. No one could see it, but it was there! You needed to experience your inner beauty, your inner self, and your inner colors that all existed from your birth, although it wasn't visible to anyone or any animal in the world, including yourself."

"And you? Who are you?"

"I am your inner spirit, Andalorax," said her twin. "When the world gazes upon you from now on, they will see the black and white Queen. But you shall know that, deep in your heart and mind, you are a person containing all the colors there are to be seen. And I am the personification of that. Do you understand?"

Andalorax was, at first, quite confused. But when she looked down at herself, she remembered who she really was: a black-and-white woman filled with a rainbow of thoughts and dreams.

"Aye, Xaroladna. I understand."

But then she asked, "What will happen now?"

"You shall continue as you always were and are today: a newborn in the Calicab Forest, a young girl in the Castle Pellah, and a Queen of the Rainbow Mountains."

"But what about you?"

The Many-Colored Girl suddenly began to dissolve and become transparent.

Finally, as she disappeared, she said, "I am here inside you, forever and always."

Andalorax sensed a chill go up and down her spine. But she didn't really feel any different.

"I know you are inside me, Xaroladna. Forever and always."

And she went outside to her porch and sat down on her rocking chair. "Well, I shall always be me. Andalorax and Xaroladna."

A voice inside her head echoed her sentiments.

"Aye. Forever and always."

She was herself again, and, knowing that, she was a happy Queen.

Printed in the USA
CPSIA information can be obtained
at www.ICGtesting.com
LVHW081055140923
757948LV00011B/286